The Litigators

JOHN GRISHAM
The Litigators

HODDER &
STOUGHTON

First published in Great Britain in 2011 by Hodder & Stoughton
An Hachette UK company

2

Copyright © Belfry Holdings, Inc. 2011

The right of John Grisham to be identified as the Author of the Work has been
asserted by him in accordance with the Copyright, Designs and Patents Act 1988.

A CIP catalogue record for this title is available from the British Library

Hardback ISBN 978 1 444 72970 2
Trade Paperback ISBN 978 1 444 72971 9
eBook ISBN 978 1 444 72973 3

Printed and bound by Clays Ltd, St Ives plc

Hodder & Stoughton policy is to use papers that are natural, renewable
and recyclable products and made from wood grown in sustainable
forests. The logging and manufacturing processes are expected to
conform to the environmental regulations of the country of origin.

Hodder & Stoughton Ltd
338 Euston Road
London NW1 3BH

www.hodder.co.uk

THE LITIGATORS

CHAPTER 1

The law firm of Finley & Figg referred to itself as a "boutique firm." This misnomer was inserted as often as possible into routine conversations, and it even appeared in print in some of the various schemes hatched by the partners to solicit business. When used properly, it implied that Finley & Figg was something above your average two-bit operation. Boutique, as in small, gifted, and expert in one specialized area. Boutique, as in pretty cool and chic, right down to the Frenchness of the word itself. Boutique, as in thoroughly happy to be small, selective, and prosperous.

Except for its size, it was none of these things. Finley & Figg's scam was hustling injury cases, a daily grind that required little skill or creativity and would never be considered cool or sexy. Profits were as elusive as status. The firm was small because it couldn't afford to grow. It was selective only because no one wanted to work there, including the two men who owned it. Even its location suggested a monotonous life out in the bush leagues. With a Vietnamese massage parlor to its left and a lawn mower repair shop to its right, it was clear at a casual glance that Finley & Figg was not prospering. There was another boutique firm directly across the street—hated rivals—and more lawyers around the corner. In fact, the neighborhood was teeming with lawyers, some working alone, others in small firms, others still in versions of their own little boutiques.

F&F's address was on Preston Avenue, a busy street filled with old bungalows now converted and used for all manner of commercial activity. There was retail (liquor, cleaners, massages) and professional (legal, dental, lawn mower repair) and culinary (enchiladas, baklava, and pizza to go). Oscar Finley had won the building in a lawsuit twenty years earlier. What the address lacked in prestige it sort of made up for in location. Two doors away was the intersection of Preston, Beech, and Thirty-eighth, a chaotic convergence of asphalt and traffic that guaranteed at least one good car wreck a week, and often more. F&F's annual overhead was covered by collisions that happened less than one hundred yards away. Other law firms, boutique and otherwise, were often prowling the area in hopes of finding an available, cheap bungalow from which their hungry lawyers could hear the actual squeal of tires and crunching of metal.

With only two attorneys/partners, it was of course mandatory that one be declared the senior and the other the junior. The senior partner was Oscar Finley, age sixty-two, a thirty-year survivor of the bare-knuckle brand of law found on the tough streets of southwest Chicago. Oscar had once been a beat cop but got himself terminated for cracking skulls. He almost went to jail but instead had an awakening and went to college, then law school. When no firms would hire him, he hung out his own little shingle and started suing anyone who came near. Thirty-two years later, he found it hard to believe that for thirty-two years he'd wasted his career suing for past-due accounts receivable, fender benders, slip-and-falls, and quickie divorces. He was still married to his first wife, a terrifying woman he wanted to sue every day for his own divorce. But he couldn't afford it. After thirty-two years of lawyering, Oscar Finley couldn't afford much of anything.

His junior partner—and Oscar was prone to say things like, "I'll get my junior partner to handle it," when trying to impress judges and other lawyers and especially prospective clients—was Wally Figg, age forty-five. Wally fancied himself a hardball litigator, and his blustery ads promised all kinds of aggressive behavior. "We Fight for Your Rights!" and "Insurance Companies Fear Us!" and "We Mean Business!" Such ads could be seen on park benches, city transit buses, cabs, high school football programs, even telephone poles, though this violated several ordinances. The ads were not seen in two crucial markets—television and billboards. Wally and Oscar were still fighting over these. Oscar refused to spend the money—both types were horribly expensive—and Wally was still scheming. His dream was to see his smiling face and slick head on television saying dreadful things about insurance companies while promising huge settlements to injured folks wise enough to call his toll-free number.

But Oscar wouldn't even pay for a billboard. Wally had one picked out. Six blocks from the office, at the corner of Beech and Thirty-second, high above the swarming traffic, on top of a four-story tenement house, there was the most perfect billboard in all of metropolitan Chicago. Currently hawking cheap lingerie (with a comely ad, Wally had to admit), the billboard had his name and face written all over it. But Oscar still refused.

Wally's law degree came from the prestigious University of Chicago School of Law. Oscar picked his up at a now-defunct place that once offered courses at night. Both took the bar exam three times. Wally had four divorces under his belt; Oscar could only dream. Wally wanted the big case, the big score with millions of dollars in fees. Oscar wanted only two things—divorce and retirement.

How the two men came to be partners in a converted house on Preston Avenue was another story. How they survived without choking each other was a daily mystery.

Their referee was Rochelle Gibson, a robust black woman with attitude and savvy earned on the streets from which she came. Ms. Gibson handled the front—the phone, the reception, the prospective clients arriving with hope and the disgruntled ones leaving in anger, the occasional typing (though her bosses had learned if they needed something typed, it was far simpler to do it themselves), the firm dog, and, most important, the constant bickering between Oscar and Wally.

Years earlier, Ms. Gibson had been injured in a car wreck that was not her fault. She then compounded her troubles by hiring the law firm of Finley & Figg, though not by choice. Twenty-four hours after the crash, bombed on Percocet and laden with splints and plaster casts, Ms. Gibson had awakened to the grinning, fleshy face of Attorney Wallis Figg hovering over her hospital bed. He was wearing a set of aquamarine scrubs, had a stethoscope around his neck, and was doing a good job of impersonating a physician. Wally tricked her into signing a contract for legal representation, promised her the moon, sneaked out of the room as quietly as he'd sneaked in, then proceeded to butcher her case. She netted $40,000, which her husband drank and gambled away in a matter of weeks, which led to a divorce action filed by Oscar Finley. He also handled her bankruptcy. Ms. Gibson was not impressed with either lawyer and threatened to sue both for malpractice. This got their attention—they had been hit with similar lawsuits—and they worked hard to placate her. As her troubles multiplied, she became a fixture at the office, and with time the three became comfortable with one another.

Finley & Figg was a tough place for secretaries. The pay was low, the clients were generally unpleasant, the other lawyers on the phone were rude, the hours were long, but the worst part was dealing with the two partners. Oscar and Wally had tried the mature route, but the older gals couldn't handle the pressure. They had tried youth but got themselves sued for sexual harassment when Wally couldn't keep his paws off a busty young thing. (They settled out of court for $50,000 and got their names in the newspaper.) Rochelle Gibson happened to be at the office one morning when the then-current secretary quit and stormed out. With the phone ringing and partners yelling, Ms. Gibson moved over to the front desk and calmed things down. Then she made a pot of coffee. She was back the next day, and the next. Eight years later, she was still running the place.

Her two sons were in prison. Wally had been their lawyer, though in all fairness no one could have saved them. As teenagers, both boys kept Wally busy with their string of arrests on various drug charges. Their dealing got more involved, and Wally warned them repeatedly they were headed for prison, or death. He said the same to Ms. Gibson, who had little control over the boys and often prayed for prison. When their crack ring got busted, they were sent away for ten years. Wally got it reduced from twenty and received no gratitude from the boys. Ms. Gibson offered a tearful thanks. Through all their troubles, Wally never charged her a fee for his representation.

Over the years, there had been many tears in Ms. Gibson's life, and they had often been shed in Wally's office with the door locked. He gave advice and tried to help when possible, but his greatest role was that of a listener. And with Wally's sloppy life, the tables could be turned quickly. When his last two marriages blew up, Ms. Gibson heard it all and offered encouragement. When his drinking picked up, she saw it clearly and was not afraid to confront him. Though they fought daily, their quarrels were always temporary and often contrived as a means of protecting turf.

There were times at Finley & Figg when all three were snarling or sulking, and money was usually the cause. The market was simply overcrowded; there were too many lawyers loose on the streets.

The last thing the firm needed was another one.

CHAPTER 2

David Zinc made it off the L train at the Quincy Station in downtown Chicago, and he managed to shuffle down the steps that led to Wells Street, but something was going wrong with his feet. They were getting heavier and heavier, his steps slower and slower. He stopped at the corner of Wells and Adams and actually looked at his shoes for a clue. Nothing, just the same standard black leather lace-ups worn by every male lawyer in the firm, and a couple of the females as well. His breathing was labored, and in spite of the chill he felt moisture in his armpits. He was thirty-one years old, certainly too young for a heart attack, and though he'd been exhausted for the past five years, he had learned to live with his fatigue. Or so he thought. He turned a corner and looked at the Trust Tower, a glistening phallic monument jutting one thousand feet upward into the clouds and fog. As he paused and looked up, his heart rate quickened and he felt nauseous. Bodies touched him as they jostled by. He crossed Adams in a pack and plodded on.

The atrium of the Trust Tower was tall and open, with plenty of marble and glass and incomprehensible sculpture designed to inspire and provide warmth, when in reality it seemed cold and forbidding, at least to David. Six escalators crisscrossed each other and hauled hordes of weary warriors up to their cubicles and offices. David tried, but his feet would not carry him to an escalator. Instead, he sat on a leather bench beside a pile of large painted rocks and tried to understand what was happening to him. People rushed by, grim-faced, hollow-eyed, stressed-out already, and it was only 7:30 on this gloomy morning.

A "snap" is certainly not a medical term. Experts use fancier language to describe the instant when a troubled person steps over the edge. Nonetheless, a snap is a real moment. It can happen in a split second, the result of a terribly traumatic event. Or it can be the final straw, the sad culmination of pressure that builds and builds until the mind and body must find a release. David Zinc's snap was of the latter variety. After five years of savage labor with colleagues he loathed, something happened to David that morning as he sat by the painted rocks and watched the well-dressed zombies ride upward to yet another day of useless labor. He snapped.

"Hey Dave. You going up?" someone was saying. It was Al, from antitrust.

David managed to smile and nod and mumble, then he stood and followed Al for some reason. Al was a step ahead as they got onto an escalator, and he was talking about last night's Blackhawks game. David kept nodding as they rose through the atrium. Below him and following behind were dozens of lonely figures in dark overcoats, other young lawyers rising, quiet and somber, much like pallbearers at a winter funeral. David and Al joined a group at a wall of elevators on the first level. As they waited, David listened to the hockey talk, but his head was spinning and he was nauseous again. They rushed onto an elevator and stood shoulder to shoulder with too many others. Silence. Al was quiet. No one spoke; no one made eye contact.

David said to himself: "This is it—my last ride in this elevator. I swear."

The elevator rocked and hummed, then stopped at the eightieth floor, Rogan Rothberg territory. Three lawyers got off, three faces David had seen before but didn't know by name, which was not unusual because the firm had six hundred lawyers on floors seventy through one hundred. Two more dark suits got off at eighty-four. As they continued to rise, David began to sweat, then to hyperventilate. His tiny office was on the ninety-third floor, and the closer he got, the more violently his heart pumped. More somber exits on ninety and ninety-one, and with each stop David felt weaker and weaker.

Only three were left at ninety-three—David, Al, and a large woman who was called Lurch behind her back. The elevator stopped, a bell chimed pleasantly, the door opened silently, and Lurch stepped off. Al stepped off. David refused to move; in fact, he couldn't move. Seconds passed. Al looked over his shoulder and said, "Hey, David, this is us. Come on."

No response from David, just the blank, hollow gaze of someone in another world. The door began to close, and Al jammed his brief-case in the opening. "David, you okay?" Al asked.

"Sure," David mumbled as he managed to move forward. The door slid open, the bell chimed again. He was out of the elevator, looking around nervously as if he'd never before seen the place. In fact, he'd left it only ten hours earlier.

"You look pale," Al said.

David's head was spinning. He heard Al's voice but didn't compre-hend what he was saying. Lurch was a few feet away, staring, puzzled, as if watching a car wreck. The elevator pinged again, a different sound, and the door began to close. Al said something else, even reached out a hand as if to help. Suddenly David spun and his leaden feet came to life. He bolted for the elevator and made a diving reentry just as the door slammed shut. The last thing he heard from the outside was Al's panicked voice.

When the elevator began its descent, David Zinc started to laugh. The spinning and nausea were gone. The pressure on his chest vanished. He was doing it! He was leaving the sweatshop of Rogan Rothberg and saying farewell to a nightmare. He, David Zinc, of all the thou-sands of miserable associates and junior partners in the tall buildings of downtown Chicago, he and he alone had found the spine to walk away that gloomy morning. He sat on the floor in the empty elevator, watching with a wide grin as the floor numbers zipped downward in bright red digital numbers, and he fought to control his thoughts. The people: (1) his wife, a neglected woman who wanted to get pregnant but found it difficult because her husband was too tired for sex; (2) his father, a prominent judge who had basically forced him to go to law school, and not just anywhere but Harvard Law School because that's where the judge had gone; (3) his grandfather, the family tyrant who'd built a mega firm from scratch in Kansas City and still put in ten hours a day at the age of eighty-two; and (4) Roy Barton, his supervising partner, his boss, a prickish crank who yelled and cursed throughout the day and was perhaps the most miserable person David Zinc had ever met. When he thought of Roy Barton, he laughed again.

The elevator stopped at the eightieth floor, and two secretaries started to enter. They paused momentarily when confronted with David sitting in a corner, briefcase at his side. Carefully, they stepped over his legs and waited for the door to close. "Are you okay?" one asked. "Fine," David answered. "And you?"

There was no response. The secretaries stood rigid and quiet during the brief descent and hustled off at seventy-seven. When David was alone again, he was suddenly worried. What if they came after him? Al would no doubt go straight to Roy Barton and report that Zinc had cracked up. What would Barton do? There was a huge meeting at ten with an angry client, a big-shot CEO; in fact, as David would think about things later, the showdown was probably the tipping point that finally caused the Snap. Roy Barton was not only an abrasive prick but also a coward. He needed David Zinc and others to hide behind when the CEO marched in with a long list of valid complaints.

Roy might send Security after him. Security was the usual contingent of aging uniformed door guards, but it was also an in-house spy ring that changed locks, videoed everything, moved in the shadows, and engaged in all manner of covert activities designed to keep the lawyers in line. David jumped to his feet, picked up his briefcase, and stared impatiently at the digital numbers blinking by. The elevator rocked gently as it fell through the center of the Trust Tower. When it stopped, David got off and darted to the escalators, which were still packed with sad folks moving silently upward. The descending escalators were unclogged, and David ran down one. Someone called out,

"Hey, Dave, where are you going?" David smiled and waved in the general direction of the voice, as if everything was under control. He strode past the painted rocks and bizarre sculpture, and he eased his way through a glass door. He was outside, and the air that had seemed so wet and dreary moments earlier now held the promise of a new beginning.

He took a deep breath and looked around. Gotta keep moving. He began walking down LaSalle Street, quickly, afraid to look over his shoulder. Don't look suspicious. Be calm. This is now one of the most important days of your life, he told himself, so don't blow it. He couldn't go home because he was not ready for that confrontation. He couldn't walk the streets because he would bump into someone he knew. Where could he hide for a while, think about things, clear his head, make a plan? He checked his watch, 7:51, the perfect time for breakfast. Down an alley he saw the red-and-green flashing neon sign of Abner's, and as he grew closer, he couldn't tell if it was a café or a bar. At the door he glanced over his shoulder, made sure Security was nowhere in sight, and entered the warm, dark world of Abner's.

It was a bar. The booths along the right were empty. The chairs were sitting upside down on the tables, waiting for someone to clean the floor. Abner was behind the long, well-polished wooden counter with a smirk on his face, as if to ask, "What are you doing here?"

"Are you open?" David asked.

"Was the door locked?" Abner shot back. He wore a white apron and was drying a beer mug. He had thick, hairy forearms, and in spite of his gruff manner he had the trusting face of a veteran bartender who'd heard it all before.

"I guess not." David walked slowly to the bar, glanced to his right, and at the far end saw a man who'd apparently passed out, still holding a drink.

David removed his charcoal-gray overcoat and hung it on the back of a stool. He took a seat, looked at the rows of liquor bottles aligned in front of him, took in the mirrors and beer taps and dozens of glasses

Abner had arranged perfectly, and when he was settled, he said, "What do you recommend before eight o'clock?"

Abner looked at the man with his head on the counter and said, "How about coffee?"

"I've already had that. Do you serve breakfast?"

"Yep, it's called a Bloody Mary."

"I'll take one."

Rochelle Gibson lived in a subsidized apartment with her mother, one of her daughters, two of her grandchildren, varying combinations of nieces and nephews, and even an occasional cousin in need of shelter. To escape the chaos, she often fled to her workplace, though at times it was worse than home. She arrived at the office each day around 7:30, unlocked the place, fetched both newspapers from the porch, turned on the lights, adjusted the thermostat, made the coffee, and checked on AC, the firm dog. She hummed and sometimes sang softly as she went about her routine. Though she would never admit it to either of her bosses, she was quite proud to be a legal secretary, even in a place like Finley & Figg. When asked her job or profession, she was always quick to state "legal secretary." Never just a garden-variety secretary, but a legal one. What she lacked in formal training she made up for in experience. Eight years in the middle of a busy street practice had taught her a lot of law and even more about lawyers.

AC was a mutt who lived at the office because no one there was willing to take him home. He belonged to the three—Rochelle, Oscar, and Wally—in equal shares, though virtually all of the responsibilities of his care fell upon Rochelle. He was a runaway who'd chosen F&F as his home several years earlier. Throughout the day he slept on a small bed near Rochelle, and throughout the night he roamed the office, guarding the place. He was a passable watchdog whose bark had chased away burglars, vandals, and even several disgruntled clients.

Rochelle fed him and filled his water bowl. From the small fridge in the kitchen, she removed a container of strawberry yogurt. When the coffee was ready, she poured herself a cup and arranged things just so on her desk, which she kept in immaculate order. It was glass and chrome, sturdy and impressive, the first thing clients saw when they walked through the front door. Oscar's office was somewhat tidy. Wally's was a landfill. They could hide their business behind closed doors, but Rochelle's was in plain view.

She opened the *Sun-Times* and started with the front page. She read slowly, sipping her coffee, eating her yogurt, humming softly while AC snored behind her. Rochelle treasured these few quiet moments of the early morning. Before long, the phone would start, the lawyers would appear, and then, if they were lucky, clients would arrive, some with appointments, others without.

To get away from his wife, Oscar Finley left home each morning at seven, but he seldom got to the office before nine. For two hours he moved around the city, stopping by a police station where a cousin handled accident reports, dropping in to say hello to tow truck drivers and catch the latest gossip on the most recent car wrecks, drinking coffee with a man who owned two low-end funeral parlors, taking doughnuts to a fire station and chatting with the ambulance drivers, and occasionally making his rounds at his favorite hospitals, where he walked the busy halls casting a trained eye for those injured by the negligence of others.

Oscar arrived at nine. With Wally, whose life was far less organized, one never knew. He could blow in at 7:30, fueled by caffeine and Red Bull and ready to sue anyone who crossed him, or he could drag in at 11:00, puffy eyed, hungover, and soon hiding in his office.

On this momentous day, however, Wally arrived a few minutes before eight with a big smile and clear eyes. "Good morning, Ms. Gibson," he said with conviction.

"Good morning, Mr. Figg," she responded in similar fashion. At Finley & Figg, the atmosphere was always tense, with a fight just one comment away. Words were chosen carefully and received with scrutiny. The mundane early morning salutes were cautiously handled because they could be a setup for an attack. Even the use of "Mr." and "Ms." was contrived and loaded with history. Back when Rochelle had been only a client, Wally had made the mistake of referring to her as a "girl." It had been something like, "Look, girl, I'm doing the best I can here." He certainly meant no harm by it, and her overreaction was uncalled for, but from that moment on she insisted on being addressed as "Ms. Gibson."

She was slightly irritated because her solitude was interrupted. Wally spoke to AC and rubbed his head, and as he headed for the coffee, he asked, "Anything in the paper?"

"No," she said, not wanting to discuss the news.

"No surprise there," he said, the first shot of the day. She read the *Sun-Times*. He read the *Tribune*. Each considered the other's taste in news to be rather low.

The second shot came moments later when Wally reappeared. "Who made the coffee?" he asked.

She ignored this.

"It's a bit weak, don't you think?"

She slowly turned a page, then had some yogurt.

Wally sipped loudly, smacked his lips, frowned as though swallowing vinegar, then picked up his newspaper and took a seat at the table. Before Oscar won the building in a lawsuit, someone had knocked out several of the walls downstairs near the front and created an open lobby area. Rochelle had her space on one side, near the door, and a few feet away there were chairs for waiting clients and a long table that was once used somewhere for dining purposes. Over the years, the table had become the place where newspapers were read, coffee consumed, even depositions taken. Wally liked to kill time there because his office was such a pigsty.

He flung open his *Tribune* with as much noise as possible. Rochelle ignored him and hummed away.

A few minutes passed, and the phone rang. Ms. Gibson seemed not to hear it. It rang again. After the third ring, Wally lowered his newspaper and said, "You wanna get that, Ms. Gibson?"

"No," she answered shortly.

It rang a fourth time.

"And why not?" he demanded.

She ignored him. After the fifth ring, Wally threw down his newspaper, jumped to his feet, and headed for a phone on the wall near the copier. "I wouldn't get that if I were you," Ms. Gibson said.

He stopped. "And why not?"

"It's a bill collector."

"How do you know?" Wally stared at the phone. Caller ID revealed "NAME UNKNOWN."

"I just do. He calls this time every week."

The phone went silent, and Wally returned to the table and his newspaper. He hid behind it, wondering which bill had not been paid, which supplier was irritated enough to call a law office and put the squeeze on lawyers. Rochelle knew, of course, because she kept the books and knew almost everything, but he preferred not to ask her. If he did, then they would soon be bickering over the bills and unpaid fees and lack of money in general, and this could easily spiral down into a heated discussion about overall strategies of the firm, its future, and the shortcomings of its partners.

Neither wanted this.

Abner took great pride in his Bloody Marys. He used precise amounts of tomato juice, vodka, horseradish, lemon, lime, Worcestershire sauce, pepper, Tabasco, and salt. He always added two green olives, then finished it with a stalk of celery.

It had been a long time since David had enjoyed such a fine breakfast. After two of Abner's creations, consumed rapidly, he was grinning goofily and proud of his decision to chuck it all. The drunk at the end of the bar was snoring. There were no other customers. Abner was a man about his business, washing and drying cocktail glasses, taking inventory of his booze, and fiddling with the beer taps while offering commentary on a wide variety of subjects.

David's phone finally rang. It was his secretary, Lana. "Oh, boy," he said.

"Who is it?" Abner asked.

"The office."

"A man's entitled to breakfast, isn't he?"

David grinned again and said, "Hello."

Lana said, "David, where are you? It's eight thirty."

"I have a watch, dear. I'm having breakfast."

"Are you okay? Word's out that you were last seen diving back into an elevator."

"Just a rumor, dear, just a rumor."

"Good. What time will you be in? Roy Barton has already called."

"Let me finish breakfast, okay?"

"Sure. Just keep in touch."

David put down his phone, sucked hard on the straw, then announced, "I'll have another." Abner frowned and said, "You might want to pace yourself."

"I am pacing myself."

"Okay." Abner pulled down a clean glass and started mixing. "I take it you're not going to the office today."

"I am not. I quit. I'm walking away."

"What type of office?"

"Law. Rogan Rothberg. You know the outfit?"

"Heard of it. Big firm, right?"

"Six hundred lawyers here in the Chicago office. Couple of thousand around the world. Currently in third place when it comes to size, fifth place in hours billed per lawyer, fourth place when looking at net profits per partner, second place when comparing associates' salaries, and, without question, first place when counting assholes per square foot."

"Sorry I asked."

David picked up his phone and asked, "You see this phone?"

"You think I'm blind?"

"This thing has ruled my life for the past five years. Can't go anywhere without it. Firm policy. It stays with me at all times. It's interrupted nice dinners in restaurants. It's dragged me out of the shower. It's woken me up at all hours of the night. On one occasion it's interrupted sex with my poor neglected wife. I was at a Cubs game last summer, great seats, me and two buddies from college, top of the second inning, and this thing starts vibrating. It was Roy Barton. Have I told you about Roy Barton?"

"Not yet."

"My supervising partner, a pernicious little bastard. Forty years old, warped ego, God's gift to the legal profession. Makes a million bucks a year but he'll never make enough. Works fifteen hours a day, seven days a week, because at Rogan Rothberg all Big Men work nonstop. And Roy fancies himself a really Big Man."

"Nice guy, huh?"

"I hate him. I hope I never see his face again."

Abner slid the third Bloody Mary across the counter and said, "Looks like you're on the right track, pal. Cheers."

CHAPTER 3

The phone rang again, and Rochelle decided to answer it. "The law firm of Finley & Figg," she said professionally. Wally did not look up from his newspaper. She listened for a moment, then said, "I'm sorry, but we do not handle real estate transactions."

When Rochelle assumed her position eight years earlier, the firm did in fact handle real estate transactions. However, she soon realized this type of work paid little and relied heavily upon the secretary with almost no effort from the lawyers. A quick study, she decided she disliked real estate. Because she controlled the phone, she screened all calls, and the real estate section of Finley & Figg dried up. Oscar was outraged and threatened to fire her but backed down when she mentioned, again, that she might sue them for legal malpractice. Wally brokered a truce, but for weeks things were more tense than usual.

Other specialties had been cast aside under her diligent screening. Criminal work was history; Rochelle didn't like it, because she didn't like the clients. DUIs were okay because there were so many of them, they paid well, and they required almost no involvement on her part. Bankruptcy bit the dust for the same reason that real estate had—paltry fees and too much work for the secretary. Over the years Rochelle had managed to streamline the firm's practice, and this was still causing problems. Oscar's theory, one that had kept him broke for over thirty years, was the firm should take everything that walked in the door, cast a wide net, then pick through the debris in the hope of finding a good injury case. Wally disagreed. He wanted the big kill. Though he was forced by the overhead to perform all sorts of mundane legal tasks, he was always dreaming of ways to strike gold.

"Nice work," he said when she hung up. "I never liked real estate."

She ignored this and returned to her newspaper. AC began a low growl. When they looked at him, he was standing on his small bed, nose tilted upward, tail straight and pointing, eyes narrow with concentration. His growl grew louder, then, on cue, the distant sound of an ambulance entered their solemn morning. Sirens never failed to excite Wally, and for a second or two he froze as he skillfully analyzed it. Police, fire, or ambulance? That was always the first issue, and Wally could distinguish the three in a heartbeat. Sirens from fire trucks and police cars meant nothing and were quickly ignored, but a siren from an ambulance always quickened his pulse.

"Ambulance," he said, then placed his newspaper on the table, stood, and casually walked to the front door. Rochelle also stood and walked to a window where she opened the blinds for a quick look. AC was still growling, and when Wally opened the door and stepped onto the front porch, the dog followed. Across the street, Vince Gholston exited his own little boutique and cast a hopeful look at the intersection of Beech and Thirty-eighth. When he saw Wally, he flipped him the bird, and Wally quickly returned the greeting.

The ambulance came screaming down Beech, weaving and lurching its way through heavy traffic, honking angrily, causing more havoc and danger than whatever awaited it. Wally watched it until it was out of sight, then went inside.

The newspaper reading continued with no further interruptions— no sirens, no phone calls from prospective clients or bill collectors. At 9:00 a.m., the door opened, and the senior partner entered. As usual, Oscar wore a long dark overcoat and carried a bulky black leather briefcase, as if he'd been laboring away throughout the night. He also carried his umbrella, as always, regardless of the weather or forecast. Oscar toiled far away from the big leagues, but he could at least look the part of a distinguished lawyer. Dark coats, dark suits, white shirts, and silk ties. His wife did the shopping and insisted that he look the part. Wally, on the other hand, wore whatever he could pull from the pile.

"Morning," Oscar said gruffly at Ms. Gibson's desk.

"Good morning," she replied.

"Anything in the newspaper?" Oscar was not interested in scores or floods or market reports or the latest from the Middle East.

"A forklift operator got crushed in a plant out in Palos Heights," Ms. Gibson responded promptly. It was part of their morning ritual. If she did not find an accident of some variety to brighten his morning, then his sour mood would only get worse.

"I like it," he said. "Is he dead?"

"Not yet."

"Even better. Lots of pain and suffering. Make a note. I'll check it out later."

Ms. Gibson nodded as if the poor man were practically signed up as a new client. Of course, he was not. Nor would he be. Finley & Figg rarely got to the accident scene first. Chances were the forklift operator's wife was already being hounded by more aggressive lawyers, some of whom were known to offer cash and other goodies to get the family on board.

Buoyed by this good news, Oscar walked over to the table and said, "Good morning."

"Morning, Oscar," Wally said.

"Any of our clients make the obituaries?"

"I haven't got that far yet."

"You should start with the obituaries."

"Thank you, Oscar. Any more tips on how to read a newspaper?"

Oscar was already walking away. Over his shoulder he asked Ms. Gibson, "What's on my calendar for today?"

"The usual. Divorces and drunks."

"Divorces and drunks," Oscar mumbled to himself as he stepped into his office. "What I need is a good car wreck." He hung his overcoat on the back of the door, placed his umbrella in a rack by his desk, and began unpacking his briefcase. Wally was soon standing nearby, holding the newspaper. "Does the name Chester Marino ring a bell?" he asked. "Obit. Age fifty-seven, wife, kids, grandkids, no cause given."

Oscar scratched his close-cropped gray hair and said, "Maybe. Could've been a last will and testament."

"They got him down at Van Easel & Sons. Visitation tonight, service tomorrow. I'll snoop around and see what's up. If he's one of ours, you wanna send flowers?"

"Not until you know the size of his estate."

"Good point." Wally was still holding his newspaper. "This Taser thing is out of control, you know. Cops in Joliet are accused of Tasering a seventy-year-old man who went to Walmart to buy Sudafed for his sick grandchild. The pharmacist figured the old man was using the stuff for a meth lab, so the pharmacist, being a good citizen, called the cops. Turns out the cops all got themselves brand-new Tasers, so five of these clowns stop the old man in the parking lot and Taser his ass. Critical condition."

"So we're back doing Taser law, are we, Wally?"

"Damn right we are. These are good cases, Oscar. We gotta get a few."

Oscar sat down and sighed heavily. "So this week it's Taser guns. Last week it was diaper rashes—big plans to sue the makers of Pampers because a few thousand babies have diaper rashes. Last month it was Chinese drywall."

"They've paid four billion bucks already in the drywall class action."

"Yes, but we haven't seen any of it."

"That's my point, Oscar. We have got to get serious about these mass tort cases. This is where the money is. Millions in fees paid by companies that make billions in profits."

The door was open, and Rochelle was listening to every word, though this particular conversation was getting a bit stale.

Wally was talking louder. "We get us a few of these cases, then hook up with the mass tort specialists, give them a piece of the cake, then ride their coattails until they settle, and we walk away with a truckload. It's easy money, Oscar."

"Diaper rashes?"

"Okay, that didn't work. But this Taser thing is a gold mine."

"Another gold mine, Wally?"

"Yep, I'll prove it."

"You do that."

The drunk at the end of the bar had rallied somewhat. His head was up, his eyes were partially open, and Abner was serving him coffee and chatting away, all in an effort to convince the man it was time to leave. A teenager with a broom was sweeping the floor and arranging tables and chairs. The little pub was showing signs of life.

With his brain coated with vodka, David stared at himself in the mirror and tried in vain to put things into perspective. One moment he was filled with excitement and proud of his bold escape from the death march at Rogan Rothberg. The next moment he was fearful for his wife, his family, his future. The booze gave him courage, though, and he decided to keep drinking.

His phone vibrated again. It was Lana at the office. "Hello," he said quietly.

"David, where are you?"

"Just finishing breakfast, you know."

"David, you don't sound so good. Are you all right?"

"I'm fine. I'm fine."

A pause, then, "Are you drinking?"

"Of course not. It's only nine thirty."

"Okay, whatever. Look, Roy Barton just left here, and he's in a rage. I've never heard such language. All kinds of threats."

"Tell Roy to kiss my ass."

"I beg your pardon."

"You heard me. Tell Roy to kiss my ass."

"You're losing it, David. It's true. You're cracking up. I'm not sur-prised. I saw this coming. I knew it."

"I'm fine."

"You're not fine. You're drunk and you're cracking up."

"Okay, I may be drunk but—"

"I think I hear Roy Barton again. What should I tell him?"

"To kiss my ass."

"Why don't you tell him, David? You have a phone. Give Mr. Bar-ton a call." With that, she hung up.

Abner was easing over, curious to get the scoop on this latest phone call. He was rubbing the wooden counter again, for the third or fourth time since David had planted himself at the bar.

"The office," David said, and Abner frowned as if this were bad news for everyone. "The aforementioned Roy Barton is looking for me, throwing things. Wish I could be a fly on the wall. Hope he has a stroke."

Abner moved closer. "Say, I never caught your name."

"David Zinc."

"A pleasure. Look, David, the cook just got here. You want some-thing to eat? Maybe something loaded with grease? French fries, onion rings, a big thick burger?"

"I want a double order of onion rings and a large bottle of ketchup."

"Attaboy." Abner disappeared. David drained his latest Bloody Mary and went to look for the restroom. When he returned, he assumed his seat, checked the time—9:28—and waited for the onion rings. He could smell them back there somewhere sizzling in hot oil. The drunk to his far right was gulping coffee and struggling to keep his eyes open. The teenager was still sweeping floors and arranging furniture.

The phone vibrated on the counter. It was his wife. David made no move to answer it. When the vibrating was over, he waited, then checked the voice mail. Helen's message was about what he expected: "David, your office has called twice. Where are you? What are you doing? Everyone is very worried. Are you all right? Call me as soon as possible."

She was a doctoral student at Northwestern, and when he had kissed her good-bye that morning at 6:45, she was still under the covers. When he arrived home the night before at 10:05, they had dined on leftover lasagna in front of the television before he fell asleep on the sofa. Helen was two years older and wanted to get pregnant, something that was looking more and more unlikely given her husband's perpetual exhaustion. In the meantime, she was pursuing a Ph.D. in art history, and doing so at a leisurely pace.

A soft beep, then a text message from her: "Where are you? Are you okay? Please."

He preferred not to speak to her for several hours. He would be forced to admit he was cracking up, and she would insist he get professional help. Her father was a shrink and her mother was a marriage counselor, and the entire family believed that all of life's problems and mysteries could be solved with a few hours in therapy. At the same time, though, he couldn't stand the thought that she was frantically worrying about his safety.

He sent a text: "I'm fine. I had to leave the office for a while. I'll be okay. Please don't worry."

She replied: "Where are you?"

The onion rings arrived, a huge pile of golden-brown circles covered in thick batter and grease, hot from the fryer. Abner placed them in front of David and said, "These are the best. How about a glass of water?"

"I was thinking about a pint of beer."

"You got it." Abner found a mug and stepped to the tap.

"My wife's looking for me now," David said. "You got a wife?"

"Don't ask."

"Sorry. She's a great girl, wants a family and all, but we can't seem to get things started. I worked four thousand hours last year, can you believe it? Four thousand hours. I usually punch in at seven in the morning and leave around ten at night. That's a typical day, but it's not unusual to work past midnight. So when I get home, I crash. I think we had sex once last month. Hard to believe. I'm thirty-one. She's thirty-three. Both in our prime and wanting to get pregnant, and big boy here can't stay awake." He opened the bottle of ketchup and unloaded a third of it. Abner placed a frosty pint of lager in front of him.

"At least you're making plenty of dough," Abner said.

David peeled off an onion ring, dipped it in ketchup, and stuffed it in his mouth. "Oh, sure, they pay me. Why would I subject myself to such abuse if I weren't getting paid?" David glanced around to make sure no one was listening. No one was there. He lowered his voice as he ground away on the onion ring, and said, "I'm a senior associate, five years in, my gross last year was three hundred K. That's a lot of money, and since I don't have time to spend it, it's just piling up in the bank. But look at the math. I worked four thousand hours but billed only three thousand. Three thousand hours, tops in the firm. The rest of it got lost in firm activities and pro bono work. Are you with me, Abner? You look bored."

"I'm listening. I've served lawyers before. I know how dull they are."

David took a long swig of lager and smacked his lips. "I appreciate your bluntness."

"Just doing my job."

"The firm bills my time at five hundred bucks an hour. Times three thousand. That's one point five mill for dear old Rogan Rothberg, and they pay me a measly three hundred K. Multiply that by five hundred associates all doing pretty much the same thing, and you understand why law schools are packed with bright young students who think they want to join a big law firm and make it to partner and get rich. Are you bored, Abner?"

"Fascinating."

"You want an onion ring?"

"No thanks."

David stuffed another large one into his parched mouth, then washed it down with half a pint. There was a loud thud at the end of the bar. The drunk down there succumbed once again. His head was on the counter.

"Who's the guy?" David asked.

"His name's Eddie. His brother owns half of the place, so he runs a tab that never gets paid. I'm sick of the guy." Abner eased away and spoke to Eddie, who didn't respond. Abner removed the coffee cup and wiped the counter around Eddie, then slowly made his way back to David.

"So you're walking away from three hundred grand," Abner said. "What's the plan?"

David laughed, much too loud. "A plan? Haven't got that far. Two hours ago I reported for work as always; now I'm cracking up." Another swig. "My plan, Abner, is to sit here for a long time and try to analyze my crack-up. Will you help me?"

"It's my job."

"I'll pay my tab."

"Sounds like a deal."

"Another pint, please."

CHAPTER 4

After an hour or so of reading the newspaper, eating her yogurt, and enjoying her coffee, Rochelle Gibson reluctantly went to work. Her first task was to check the client register for one Chester Marino, now resting quietly in a modestly priced bronze casket at Van Easel & Sons Funeral Home. Oscar was right. The firm had prepared a last will and testament for Mr. Marino six years earlier. She found the thin file in the storage room next to the kitchen and took it to Wally, who was hard at work amid the debris on his desk.

The office of Wallis T. Figg, Attorney and Counselor-at-Law, had been a bedroom in the original scheme of things, but over the years, as walls and doors were reconfigured, the square footage had been expanded somewhat. It certainly gave no hint of once being a bedroom, but then it didn't much resemble an office either. It began at the door with walls no more than twelve feet apart, then doglegged to the right, to a larger space where Wally worked behind a 1950s-style faux-modern desk he'd snapped up at a fire sale. The desk was covered with stacks of manila files and used legal pads and hundreds of phone message slips, and to anyone who didn't know better, including prospective clients, the desk gave the impression that the man behind it was extremely busy, maybe even important.

As always, Ms. Gibson walked slowly toward the desk, careful not to upset the piles of thick law books and old files stacked along the route. She handed him the file and said, "We did a will for Mr. Marino."

"Thanks. Any assets?"

"I didn't look," she said, already backtracking. She left without another word.

Wally opened the file. Six years earlier, Mr. Marino was working as an auditor for the State of Illinois, earning $70,000 a year, living with his second wife and her two teenagers, and enjoying a quiet life in the suburbs. He had just paid off the mortgage on their home, which was their only significant asset. They had joint bank accounts, retirement funds, and few debts. The only interesting wrinkle was a collection of three hundred baseball cards that Mr. Marino valued at $90,000. On page 4 of the file, there was a Xerox copy of a 1916 card of Shoeless Joe Jackson in a White Sox uniform, and under it Oscar had written: $75,000. Oscar cared nothing for sports, and he had never mentioned this little oddity to Wally. Mr. Marino signed a simple will he could have prepared himself for free, but instead paid Finley & Figg $250 for the honors. As Wally read the will, he realized its only real purpose, since all other assets were jointly owned, was to make sure his two stepchildren didn't get their hands on his baseball card collection. Mr. Marino left it to his son, Lyle. On page 5, Oscar had scribbled: "Wife doesn't know about cards."

Wally estimated the value of the estate at somewhere in the $500,000 range, and under the probate scheme currently in place the lawyer handling Mr. Marino's final affairs would earn about $5,000. Unless there was a fight over the baseball cards, and Wally certainly hoped there would be, the probate would be painfully routine and take about eighteen months. But if the heirs fought, then Wally could drag it out for three years and triple his fee. He did not like probate work, but it was far better than divorce and child custody. Probate paid the bills, and occasionally it led to additional fees.

The fact that Finley & Figg prepared the will meant nothing when it was time to probate it. Any lawyer could do so, and Wally knew from his vast experience in the murky world of client solicitation that there were scores of hungry lawyers poring over obituaries and calculating fees. It was worth his time to check on Chester and lay claim to the legal work necessary in tidying up his affairs. It was certainly worth a drive-by at Van Easel & Sons, one of many funeral homes on his circuit.

Three months remained on the suspension of Wally's driver's license for drunken driving, but he drove nonetheless. He was careful, though, keeping to the streets near his home and office where he knew the cops. When he went to court downtown, he took the bus or the train.

Van Easel & Sons was a few blocks outside his comfort zone, but he decided to roll the dice. If he got caught, he could probably talk his way out of trouble. If the police didn't budge, then he knew the judges. He used the backstreets as much as possible and stayed away from the traffic.

Mr. Van Easel and his three sons had been dead for many years, and as their funeral parlor passed from one owner to another, the business had declined, as had the "loving and thoughtful service" that was still advertised. Wally parked in the rear, in an empty lot, and walked through the front door as if he were there to pay his respects. It was almost 10:00 a.m., on a Wednesday morning, and for a few seconds he saw no one else. He paused in the lobby and looked at the visiting schedule. Chester was two doors down on the right, in the second of three visiting rooms. To the left was a small chapel. A man with pasty skin, brown teeth, and a black suit approached and said, "Good morning. May I help you?"

"Good morning, Mr. Grayber," Wally said.

"Oh, it's you again."

"Always a pleasure." Though Wally had once shaken hands with Mr. Grayber, he made no effort to do so again. He wasn't sure, but he suspected him to be one of the morticians. He had always remembered the soft, chilly touch of his palm. And Mr. Grayber kept his palms to himself as well. Each man disliked the other's profession.

"Mr. Marino was a client," Wally said gravely.

"His visitation is not until this evening," Grayber said.

"Yes, I see that. But I'm leaving town this afternoon."

"Very well." He sort of waved in the direction of the viewing rooms.

"I don't suppose any other lawyers have stopped by," Wally said.

Grayber snorted and rolled his eyes. "Who knows? I can't keep up with you people. We had a service last week for an illegal Mexican, got himself pinned under a bulldozer, used the chapel there," he said, nodding at the chapel door. "We had more lawyers here than family members. Poor guy's never been so loved."

"How nice," Wally said. He had attended the service last week. Finley & Figg did not get the case. "Thanks," he said and walked away. He passed the first viewing room—closed casket, no mourners. He stepped into the second, a dimly lit room, twenty feet by twenty, with a casket along one wall and cheap chairs lining the others. Chester was sealed up, which pleased Wally. He put his hand on the casket as if fighting back tears. Just he and Chester, sharing one last moment together.

The routine here was to hang around for a few minutes and hope a family member or friend showed up. If not, then Wally would sign the register and leave his card with Grayber with specific instructions to tell the family that Mr. Marino's lawyer stopped by to pay his respects. The firm would send flowers to the service and a letter to the widow, and in a few days Wally would call the woman and act as though she were somehow obligated to hire Finley & Figg because they had prepared the will. This worked about half the time.

Wally was leaving when a young man entered the room. He was about thirty, nice looking, reasonably dressed with a jacket and tie. He looked at Wally with a great deal of skepticism, which was the way a lot of people initially viewed him, though this no longer bothered him. When two perfect strangers meet at a casket in an empty viewing room, the first words are always awkward. Wally finally managed to state his name, and the young man said, "Yes, well, uh, that's my father. I'm Lyle Marino."

Ah, soon-to-be owner of a nice collection of baseball cards. But Wally could not mention this. "Your father was a client of my law firm," Wally said. "We prepared his last will and testament. I'm very sorry."

"Thanks," Lyle said, and seemed relieved. "I can't believe this. We went to the Blackhawks game last Saturday. Had a great time. Now he's gone."

"I'm very sorry. So it was sudden?"

"A heart attack." Lyle snapped his fingers and said, "Just like that. He was at work Monday morning, at his desk, all of a sudden he started sweating and breathing hard, then he just fell on the floor. Dead."

"I'm very sorry, Lyle," Wally said as if he'd known the young man forever.

Lyle was patting the top of the casket and repeating, "I just can't believe this."

Wally needed to fill in some blanks. "Your parents divorced about ten years ago, right?"

"Something like that."

"Is your mother still in the city?"

"Yes." Lyle wiped his eyes with the back of his hand.

"And your stepmother. Are you close to her?"

"No. We don't speak. The divorce was ugly."

Wally suppressed a smile. A feuding family would run up his fees. "I'm sorry. Her name is . . ."

"Millie."

"Right. Look, Lyle, I gotta run. Here's my card." Wally deftly whipped out a business card and handed it over. "Chester was a great guy," Wally said. "Call us if we can help."

Lyle took the card and stuffed it into his pants pocket. He was staring blankly at the casket. "I'm sorry, what's your name?"

"Figg, Wally Figg."

"And you're a lawyer?"

"Yes. Finley & Figg, a small boutique firm with lots of business in all major courts."

"And you knew my father?"

"Oh yes, very well. He loved to collect baseball cards."

Lyle took his hand off the casket and looked square into the shifty eyes of Wally Figg. "You know what killed my father, Mr. Figg?"

"You said it was a heart attack."

"Right. You know what caused the heart attack?"

"Well, no."

Lyle glanced at the door to make sure they were still alone. He glanced around the room to make sure no one could possibly be listening. He took a step closer so that his shoes were almost touching those of Wally, who by now was expecting to hear that old Chester had been murdered in some clever fashion.

In a near whisper, Lyle asked, "Ever hear of a drug called Krayoxx?"

There was a McDonald's in the shopping center next to Van Easel's. Wally bought two cups of coffee, and they huddled in a booth, as far away from the counter as possible. Lyle had a stack of papers—articles pulled from the Internet—and it was obvious he needed someone to talk to. Since his father's death forty-eight hours earlier, he had become obsessed with Krayoxx.

The drug had been on the market for six years, and its sales had grown rapidly. In most cases, it lowered the cholesterol of obese people. Chester's weight had slowly climbed toward three hundred pounds, and this had caused other increases—blood pressure and cholesterol, to name the most obvious. Lyle had hounded his father about his weight, but Chester couldn't stay away from the midnight ice cream. His way of handling the stress of the ugly divorce was to sit in the dark and knock out one pint after another of Ben & Jerry's. Once the weight was on, he couldn't get it off. His doctor prescribed Krayoxx a year earlier, and his cholesterol dropped dramatically. At the same time, he began complaining of an irregular heart rate and shortness of breath. He reported these to his doctor, who assured him there was nothing wrong. The dramatic dip in his cholesterol far outweighed any of these minor side effects.

Krayoxx was made by Varrick Labs, a New Jersey firm currently number three on Big Pharma's list of the world's ten largest drug companies, annual sales of some $25 billion, and a long, ugly history of bruising battles with federal regulators and tort lawyers.

"Varrick makes six billion a year off Krayoxx," Lyle was saying as he sifted through research. "With an annual increase of 10 percent."

Wally ignored his coffee as he scanned a report. He listened silently, though the wheels were turning so fast he was almost dizzy.

"And here's the best part," Lyle said, picking up another sheet of paper. "Ever hear of a law firm called Zell & Potter?"

Wally had never heard of Krayoxx, though at 240 pounds and with a slightly elevated cholesterol he was mildly surprised his doctor had not mentioned the drug. Nor had he heard of Zell & Potter, but, sensing they were major players in something important, he wasn't about to admit his ignorance. "I think so," he said, frowning, searching.

"Big plaintiffs' firm in Fort Lauderdale."

"Yep."

"They filed suit in Florida last week against Varrick, a huge lawsuit for wrongful deaths caused by Krayoxx. Here's the story in the *Miami Herald*."

Wally scanned the story as his heart rate doubled.

"I'm sure you heard about this lawsuit," Lyle said.

Wally was constantly amazed at the naïveté of the average guy. Over two million lawsuits are filed in the United States each year, and poor Lyle here was thinking that Wally had noticed one filed in south Florida. "Yep, I've been watching this one," Wally said.

"Does your firm handle cases like this?" Lyle asked, so innocently.

"It's our specialty," Wally said. "We cut our teeth on injury and death cases. I'd love to go after Varrick Labs."

"You would? Have you ever sued them before?"

"No, but we've gone after most of the major drug companies."

"This is great. Then you're willing to take my dad's case?"

Damn right I'll take it, Wally thought, but through years of experience he knew not to rush in. Or at least not to seem overly optimistic. "Let's just say the case has real potential. I'll need to confer with my senior partner, do some research, chat with the boys down at Zell & Potter, do my homework. Mass tort work is very complicated."

And it could also be insanely lucrative, which was Wally's primary thought at the moment.

"Thank you, Mr. Figg."

At five minutes before eleven, Abner became somewhat animated. He began watching the door as he continued shining martini glasses with his white towel. Eddie was awake again, sipping coffee but still in another world. Finally, Abner said, "Say, David, could you do me a favor?"

"Anything."

"Could you move two stools over? The one you got now is reserved at eleven each morning."

David looked to his right—there were eight empty stools between him and Eddie. And to his left there were seven empty stools between him and the other end of the bar. "Are you kidding?" David asked.

"Come on." Abner grabbed his pint of beer, which was almost empty, replaced it with a full one, and situated everything two stools to the left. David slowly lifted himself up and followed his beer. "What's the deal?" he asked.

"You'll see," Abner said, nodding at the door. There was no one else in the pub, other than, of course, Eddie.

Minutes later, the door opened, and an elderly Asian man appeared. He wore a dapper uniform, a bow tie, and a little driver's cap. He was helping a lady much older than himself. She walked with a cane, unassisted but with the driver hovering, and the two of them shuffled across the floor toward the bar. David watched with fascination—was he finally seeing things, or was this for real? Abner was mixing a drink and watching too. Eddie was mumbling to himself.

"Good morning, Miss Spence," Abner said politely, almost with a bow.

"Good morning, Abner," she said as she slowly lifted herself up and delicately mounted the stool. Her driver followed her movements with both hands but didn't touch her. Once she was properly seated, she said, "I'll have the usual."

The driver nodded at Abner, then backed away and quietly left the bar.

Miss Spence was wearing a full-length mink coat, thick pearls around her tiny neck, and layers of thick rouge and mascara that did little to hide the fact that she was at least ninety years old. David admired her immediately. His own grandmother was ninety-two and strapped to a bed in a nursing home, absent from this world, and here was this grand old dame boozing it up before lunch.

She ignored him. Abner finished mixing her drink, a baffling combination of ingredients. "One Pearl Harbor," he said as he presented it to her. She slowly lifted it to her mouth, took a small sip with her eyes closed, swirled the booze around her mouth, then offered Abner the slightest of heavily wrinkled grins. He seemed to breathe again.

David, not quite plastered but well on his way, leaned over and said, "Come here often?"

Abner gulped and showed both palms to David. "Miss Spence is a regular, and she prefers to drink in silence," he said, panicky. Miss Spence was taking another sip, again with her eyes closed.

"She wants to drink in silence in a bar?" David asked in disbelief.

"Yes!" Abner snapped.

"Well, I guess she picked the right bar," David said, flopping an arm around and taking in the emptiness of the pub. "This place is deserted. Do you ever have a crowd around here?"

"Quiet," Abner urged. His face said, "Just be cool for a while."

But David kept on. "I mean, you've had just two customers all morning, me and old Eddie down there, and we all know that he doesn't pay his tab."

At the moment, Eddie was lifting his coffee cup in the general direction of his face but was having trouble finding his mouth. Evidently, he did not hear David's comment.

"Knock it off," Abner growled. "Or I'll ask you to leave."

"Sorry," David said and went silent. He had no desire to leave because he had no idea where to go.

The third sip did the trick and loosened things up a little. Miss Spence opened her eyes and looked around. Slowly, and with an ancient voice, she said, "Yes, I come here often. Monday through Saturday. And you?"

"My first visit," David said, "but I doubt it's my last. After today, I'll probably have more time to drink and more reasons for doing so. Cheers." He leaned across with his pint of lager and ever so carefully touched her glass.

"Cheers," she said. "And why are you here, young man?"

"It's a long story, and getting longer. Why are you here?"

"Oh, I don't know. Habit, I guess. Six days a week for how long, Abner?"

"At least twenty years."

She apparently did not want to hear David's long story. She took another sip and looked as though she wanted to nod off. David was suddenly sleepy too.

CHAPTER 5

Helen Zinc arrived at the Trust Tower a few minutes after noon. Driving downtown, she had tried to call and text her husband for the umpteenth time, with no recent success. At 9:33 he had sent her a text message instructing her not to worry, and at 10:42 he'd sent his second and final text, in which he had said: "No swaet. Am ok. Don't wory."

Helen parked in a garage, hurried down the street, and entered the atrium of the building. Minutes later she stepped off the elevator on the ninety-third floor. A receptionist led her to a small conference room where she waited alone. Though it was lunchtime, the Rogan Rothberg culture frowned on anyone leaving the building to eat. Good food and fresh air were almost taboo. Occasionally, one of the big partners would take a client out for a splashy marathon, an expensive lunch that the client would ultimately pay for through the time-honored tricks of file padding and fee gouging, but as a general rule—though unwritten—the associates and lesser partners grabbed a quick sandwich from a machine. On a typical day, David had both breakfast and lunch at his desk, and it was not unusual to have dinner there as well. He once bragged to Helen he had billed three different clients an hour each as he shoved down a smoked tuna with chips and a diet soda. She hoped he was only joking.

Though she wasn't sure of the exact number, he had put on at least thirty pounds since their wedding day. He ran marathons back then, and the extra weight was not a problem yet. But the steady diet of bad food along with a near-complete absence of exercise worried both of them. At Rogan Rothberg, the hour between 12:00 and 1:00 was no different from any other hour of the day or night.

It was Helen's second visit to the office in five years. Spouses were not excluded, but they were not invited either. There was no reason for her to be there, and, given the avalanche of horror stories he brought home, she had no desire to see the place or spend time with the people. Twice a year she and David dragged themselves to some dreadful Rogan Rothberg social gathering, some miserable outing designed to foster camaraderie among the battered lawyers and their neglected spouses. Invariably, these turned into sloppy drinking parties with behavior that was embarrassing and impossible to forget. Take a bunch of exhausted lawyers, ply them with booze, and things get ugly.

A year earlier, on a party boat a mile out on Lake Michigan, Roy Barton had tried to grope her. If he hadn't been so drunk, he may have succeeded, and that would have caused serious problems. For a week she and David argued about what to do. David wanted to confront him, then complain to the firm's Standards Committee. Helen said no, it would only harm David's career. There were no witnesses, and the truth was that Barton probably didn't remember what he'd done. With time, they stopped talking about the incident. After five years she had heard so many Roy Barton stories that David refused to mention his boss's name at home.

Suddenly there he was. Roy walked into the small conference room with a snarl on his face and demanded, "Helen, what's going on here?"

"Funny, I have the same question," she shot back. Mr. Barton, as he preferred to be called, ran over people by barking first and trying to embarrass. She would have none of it.

"Where is he?" he barked.

"You tell me, Roy," she said.

Lana, the secretary, and Al and Lurch appeared together, as if they'd been subpoenaed by the same marshal. Quick introductions were made as Roy closed the door. Helen had spoken to Lana many times on the phone but had never met her.

Roy looked at Al and Lurch and said, "You two, tell us exactly what happened." They tag-teamed through their version of David Zinc's last elevator ride and without the slightest bit of embellishment presented a fairly clear picture of a troubled man who'd simply snapped. He was sweating, breathing hard, pale, and he actually dived headfirst back into the elevator, landing on its floor, and, just as the door closed, they heard him laughing.

"He was fine when he left home this morning," Helen assured them, as if to emphasize the point that the crack-up was the firm's fault and not hers.

"You," Roy barked in the direction of Lana. "You've talked to him."

Lana had her notes. She had spoken to him twice, then he stopped answering the phone. "In the second conversation," she said, "I got the clear impression that he was drinking. His tongue was a bit thick; his syllables were not as sharp."

Roy glared at Helen as if she were to blame.

"Where would he go?" Roy demanded.

"Oh, the usual place, Roy," Helen said. "The same place he always goes when he cracks up at 7:30 in the morning and gets plastered."

There was a heavy pause in the room. Evidently, Helen Zinc felt free to sass Mr. Barton, but the others certainly did not.

In a lower tone, Mr. Barton asked her, "Is he drinking too much?"

"He doesn't have time to drink, Roy. He comes home at ten or eleven, sometimes has a glass of wine, then he's out on the sofa."

"Is he seeing a shrink?"

"For what? Working a hundred hours a week? I thought that was the norm around here. I think all of you people need to see a shrink."

Another pause. Roy was getting his ass handed to him, and this was very unusual. Al and Lurch stared at the table and worked hard to conceal grins. Lana was a deer in headlights, ready to be fired on the spot.

"So you have no information that might help us here?" Roy said.

"No, and evidently you have no information to help me either, right, Roy?"

Roy had had enough. His eyes narrowed, his jaws clenched, his face turned red. He looked at Helen and said, "He'll show up, okay, sooner or later. He'll get in a cab and find his way home. He'll crawl back to you, and then he'll crawl back to us. He gets one more chance, you understand? I want him in my office tomorrow morning at 8:00 sharp. Sober, and sorry."

Helen's eyes were suddenly wet. She touched both cheeks and, in a cracking voice, said, "I just want to find him. I want to know he's safe. Can you help me?"

"Start looking," Roy said. "There are a thousand bars in downtown Chicago. You'll find him sooner or later." And with that Roy Barton made a dramatic exit from the room, slamming the door behind him. As soon as he was gone, Al stepped forward, touched Helen on the shoulder, and said softly, "Look, Roy's an asshole, but he's right about one thing. David's in a bar getting drunk. He'll eventually get in a cab and go home."

Lurch stepped closer too and said, "Helen, this has happened before around here. In fact, it's not that unusual. He'll be fine tomorrow."

"And the firm has a counselor on the payroll, a real pro who deals with casualties," Al added.

"A casualty?" Helen asked. "Is that what my husband is at this point?"

Lurch shrugged and said, "Yes, but he'll be okay."

Al shrugged and said, "He's in a bar. I'd love to be with him."

At Abner's, the lunch crowd had finally arrived. The booths and tables were full, and the bar was packed with office workers washing down burgers with pints of beer. David had moved one stool to his right so that he was now next to Miss Spence. She was on her third and last Pearl Harbor. David was on his second. When she offered him his first, he had initially declined, claiming he had no taste for fussy mixed drinks. She insisted, and Abner whipped one up and slid it in front of David. Though it looked as harmless as cough syrup, the drink was a lethal combination of vodka, melon liqueur, and pineapple juice.

They found common ground at Wrigley Field. Miss Spence's father had taken her there as a small girl, and she had followed her beloved Cubs her entire life. She had held season tickets for sixty-two years, a record, she was certain, and she had seen the great ones—Rogers Hornsby, Ernie Banks, Ron Santo, Billy Williams, Fergie Jenkins, and Ryne Sandberg. And she had suffered greatly, along with all Cubs fans. Her eyes danced as she told the well-known story of the Curse of the Billy Goat. Her eyes moistened when she remembered, in detail, the Great Fall of 1969. She took a long sip after recounting the infamous June Swoon of 1977. She let it slip that her late husband had once tried to buy the team but was somehow outmaneuvered.

After two Pearl Harbors, she was fairly smashed. The third was putting her away. She had no curiosity about David's situation; rather, she preferred to do most of the talking, and David, who was in slow motion, was content to just sit and listen. Abner ventured by occasionally, making sure she was happy.

At precisely 12:15, just as Abner's lunch business hit full stride, her Asian driver arrived to collect her. She drained her glass, said good-bye to Abner, made no effort to pay a tab, thanked David for the company, and left the bar, her left hand tucked inside her driver's elbow and her right hand working the cane. Her walk was slow, but erect, proud. She'd be back.

"Who was that?" David asked Abner when he got close enough.

"I'll tell you later. You having lunch?"

"Sure. Those burgers look good. Double cheese, with fries."

"You got it."

The cabdriver's name was Bowie, and he was a talker. As they left the third funeral home, his curiosity could no longer be restrained.

"Say, pal, I gotta ask," he chirped over his shoulder. "What's with all these funeral homes?"

Wally had covered the rear seat in obituary pages, city maps, and legal pads. "Let's head over to Wood & Ferguson on 103rd Street near Beverly Park," he said, temporarily ignoring Bowie's question. They had been together for almost two hours, and the meter was approaching $180, a nice chunk in terms of cab fare but chump change in the context of Krayoxx litigation. According to some of the news articles Lyle Marino had given him, the lawyers were speculating that a wrongful death case involving the drug could potentially be worth $2 to $4 million. The lawyers would take 40 percent, and Finley & Figg would, of course, have to share their fee with Zell & Potter or another tort firm spearheading the litigation. Still, after all the fee splitting, the drug was a gold mine. The urgent issue was finding the cases. As they rushed around Chicago, Wally was confident he was the only lawyer out of a million in the city who was, at that moment, shrewd enough to be combing the streets in search of Krayoxx victims.

According to another article, the drug's dangers had just been discovered. And another one, quoting a trial lawyer, said that the medical community and the public in general were not yet aware of the "Krayoxx fiasco." But Wally was now aware, and he didn't care how much he spent on cab fare.

"I was asking about all these funeral homes," Bowie chirped again. He was not going away, and he would not be ignored.

"It's one o'clock," Wally announced. "You had lunch?"

"Lunch? I've been with you for the past two hours. You seen me eat lunch?"

"I'm hungry. There's a Taco Bell up there on the right. Let's use the drive-thru."

"You're paying, right?"

"Right."

"I love Taco Bell."

Bowie ordered soft tacos for himself and a burrito supreme for his passenger. As they waited in line, Bowie said, "So I keep thinking,

'What's this guy doing at all these funeral homes?' you know? None of my business, but I've been driving for eighteen years, and I've never had a ride who popped in on funeral homes all over town. Never had a ride who had that many friends, know what I mean?"

"You're right about one thing," Wally said, looking up from even more of Lyle's research. "It's none of your business."

"Wow. Zinged me on that one, didn't you? Pegged you for a nice guy."

"I'm a lawyer."

"From bad to worse. Just kidding, you know, my uncle's a lawyer. Jerk."

Wally handed him a $20 bill. Bowie took the sack of food and distributed it. Back on the street, he crammed a taco into his mouth and stopped talking.

CHAPTER 6

Rochelle was secretly reading a romance novel when she heard footsteps on the front porch. She deftly stuffed the paperback into a drawer and moved her fingertips to the keyboard so she seemed to be hard at work when the door opened. A man and a woman entered timidly, their eyes darting around, almost in fear. This was not unusual. Rochelle had seen a thousand come and go, and they almost always entered with grim and suspecting faces. And why not? They wouldn't be there if they were not in trouble, and for most it was their first visit to a law office.

"Good afternoon," she said professionally.

"We're looking for a lawyer," the man said.

"Divorce lawyer," the woman corrected. It was immediately obvious to Rochelle that she had been correcting him for some time, and he was probably fed up. They were in their sixties, though, a bit too old for a divorce.

Rochelle managed a smile and said, "Please have a seat." She pointed to two nearby chairs. "I'll need to take down some basic information."

"Can we see a lawyer without an appointment?" the man asked.

"I think so," Rochelle said. They backed into the chairs and sat down, then both managed to scoot the chairs farther away from each other. This could get ugly, Rochelle thought. She pulled out a questionnaire and found a pen. "Your names, please. Full names."

"Calvin A. Flander," he said, beating her to the punch.

"Barbara Marie Scarbro Flander," she said. "Scarbro's the maiden name, and I might take it up again, haven't decided yet, but everything else has been worked out, and we've even signed a property settlement agreement, one I found online, and it's all right here." She was holding a large sealed envelope.

"She just asked for your name," Mr. Flander said.

"I got that."

"Can she take her old name back? I mean, you know, it's been forty-two years since she's used it, and I keep telling her that no one will know who she is if she starts going by Scarbro again."

"It's a helluva lot better than Flander," Barbara shot back. "Flander sounds like someplace in Europe or somebody who sleeps around—fi-lander or fi-lander-er. Don't you think so?"

Both were staring at Rochelle, who calmly asked, "Any minor children under the age of eighteen?"

Both shook their heads. "Two grown," Mrs. Flander said. "Six grandkids."

"She didn't ask about grandkids," Mr. Flander said.

"Well, I damn sure told her, didn't I?"

Rochelle managed to guide them through birth dates, address, Social Security numbers, and employment histories without serious conflict. "And you say you've been married for forty-two years?"

Both nodded defiantly.

She was tempted to ask why, and what went wrong, and couldn't this be salvaged? But she knew better than to start that conversation. Let the lawyers deal with it. "You mentioned a property settlement. I assume what you have in mind is a no-fault divorce, on the grounds of irreconcilable differences."

"That's right," Mr. Flander said. And the sooner the better.

"It's all right here," Mrs. Flander said, clutching the envelope.

"House, cars, bank accounts, retirement accounts, credit cards, debts, even furniture and appliances?" Rochelle asked.

"Everything," he said.

"It's all right here," Mrs. Flander said again.

"And you're both satisfied with the agreement?"

"Oh yes," he said. "We've done all the work, all we need is for a lawyer to draw up the papers and go to court with us. No hassle whatsoever."

"That's the only way to do it," Rochelle said, the voice of experience. "I'll get one of our lawyers to meet with you and go into more detail. Our firm charges $750 for a no-fault divorce, and we require half of that to be paid at the initial conference. The other half is due on the day you go to court."

The Flanders reacted differently. Her jaw dropped in disbelief, as if Rochelle had demanded $10,000 in cash. His eyes narrowed and his forehead wrinkled, as if this was exactly what he expected—a first-class shaft job by a bunch of slimy lawyers. Not a word, until Rochelle asked, "Is something wrong?"

Mr. Flander growled, "What is this, the old bait and switch? This firm advertises no-fault divorces for $399, then you get us in the door and double the price."

Rochelle's immediate reaction was to ask herself, What has Wally done now? He advertised so much, in so many ways, and in so many odd places that it was impossible to keep up with him.

Mr. Flander stood abruptly, yanked something from his pocket, and tossed it on Rochelle's desk. "Look at this," he said. It was a bingo card from VFW Post 178, McKinley Park. Across the bottom was a bright yellow ad announcing: "Finley & Figg, Attorneys, No-Fault Divorces as Easy as Pie, $399. Call 773-718-JUSTICE."

Rochelle had been surprised so many times that she should have been immune. But bingo cards? She had watched as prospective clients rifled through purses, and bags, and pockets to pull out church bulletins, football programs, Rotary Club raffles, coupons, and a hundred other little pieces of propaganda that Attorney Figg littered around Greater Chicago in his ceaseless quest to drum up business. And now he'd done it again. She had to admit that she was indeed surprised.

The firm's fee schedule was always a moving target, with the costs of representation subject to change on the fly depending on the client and the situation. A nicely dressed couple driving a late-model car might get a quote of $1,000 for a no-fault from one lawyer, and an hour later a working stiff and his haggard wife could negotiate half that much from the other lawyer. Part of Rochelle's daily grind was ironing out fee disputes and discrepancies.

Bingo cards? Easy as pie for $399? Oscar would blow a gasket.

"Okay," she said calmly, as if bingo card advertising were a long tradition at their firm. "I need to see your property settlement."

Mrs. Flander handed it over. Rochelle scanned it quickly, then gave it back.

"Let me see if Mr. Finley is in," she said. She took the bingo card with her.

Oscar's door was closed, as always. The firm had a rigid closed-door policy that kept the lawyers shielded from each other and from the street traffic and riffraff that ventured in. From Rochelle's perch near the front, she could see every door—Oscar's, Wally's, the kitchen, the downstairs restroom, the copy room, and a small junk room used for storage. She also knew the lawyers had a tendency to listen quietly through their closed doors when she was grilling a prospective client. Wally had a side door he often used to escape from a client who promised trouble, but Oscar did not. She knew he was at his desk, and since Wally was hitting the funeral homes, she had no choice.

She closed his door behind her and placed the bingo card in front of Mr. Finley. "You're not going to believe this," she said.

"What's he done now?" Oscar asked as he scanned the card. "Three hundred and ninety-nine dollars?"

"Yep."

"I thought we agreed that $500 was the minimum for a no-fault?"

"No, we agreed on $750, then $600, then $1,000, then $500. Next week I'm sure we'll agree on something else."

"I will not do a divorce for $400. I've been a lawyer for thirty-two years, and I will not prostitute myself for such a meager fee. Do you hear me, Ms. Gibson?"

"I've heard this before."

"Let Figg do it. It's his case. His bingo card. I'm too busy."

"Right, but Figg's not here, and you're not really that busy."

"Where is he?"

"He's visiting the dead, one of his funeral laps around town."

"What's his scheme this time?"

"Don't know yet."

"This morning it was Taser guns."

Oscar laid the bingo card on his desk and stared at it. He shook his head, mumbled to himself, and asked, "What kind of tormented mind could even conceive of the notion of advertising on bingo cards in a VFW?"

"Figg," she said without hesitation.

"I might have to strangle him."

"I'll hold him down."

"Dump this riffraff on his desk. Make an appointment. They can come back later. It's an outrage that people think they can just walk in off the street and see a lawyer, even Figg, without an appointment. Give me a little dignity, okay?"

"Okay, you have dignity. Look, they have some assets and almost no debt. They're in their sixties, kids are gone. I say you split 'em up, keep her, start the meter."

By 3:00 p.m., Abner's was quiet again. Eddie had somehow disappeared with the lunch crowd, and David Zinc was alone at the bar. Four middle-aged men were getting drunk in a booth as they made big plans for a bonefishing trip to Mexico.

Abner was washing glasses in a small sink near the beer taps. He was talking about Miss Spence. "Her last husband was Angus Spence. Ring a bell?"

David shook his head. At that moment, nothing rang a bell. The lights were on, but no one was home.

"Angus was the billionaire no one knew. Owned a bunch of potash deposits in Canada and Australia. Died ten years ago, left her with a bundle. She would be on the Forbes list, but they can't find all the assets. The old man was too smart. She lives in a penthouse on the lake, comes in every day at eleven, has three Pearl Harbors for lunch, leaves at 12:15 when the crowd comes in, and I guess she goes home and sleeps it off."

"I think she's cute."

"She's ninety-four."

"She didn't pay her tab."

"She doesn't get a tab. She sends me a thousand bucks every month. She wants that stool and three drinks and her privacy. I've never seen her talk to anyone before. You should consider yourself lucky."

"She wants my body."

"Well, you know where to find her."

David took a small sip of a Guinness stout. Rogan Rothberg was a distant memory. He wasn't so sure about Helen, and he really didn't care. He had decided to get wonderfully drunk and enjoy the moment. Tomorrow would be brutal, and he would deal with it then. Nothing, absolutely nothing, could interfere with this delightful slide into oblivion.

Abner slid a cup of coffee in front of him and said, "Just brewed it."

David ignored it. He said, "So you work on retainer, huh? Just like a law firm. What could I get for a thousand bucks a month?"

"At the rate you're going, a thousand won't touch it. Have you called your wife, David?"

"Look, Abner, you're a bartender, not a marriage counselor. This is a big day for me, a day that will change my life forever. I'm in the middle of a major crack-up, or meltdown, or whatever it is. My life will never be the same, so let me enjoy this moment."

"I'll call you a cab whenever you want."

"I'm not going anywhere."

For initial client conferences, Oscar always put on his dark jacket and straightened his tie. It was important to set the tone, and a lawyer in a black suit meant power, knowledge, and authority. Oscar firmly believed the image also conveyed the message that he did not work cheap, though he usually did.

He pored over the proposed property settlement, frowning as if it had been drafted by a couple of idiots. The Flanders were on the other side of his desk. They occasionally glanced around to take in the Ego Wall, a potpourri of framed photos showing Mr. Finley grinning and shaking hands with unknown celebrities, and framed certificates purporting to show that Mr. Finley was highly trained and skilled, and a few plaques that were clear proof he had been justly recognized over the years. The other walls were lined with shelves packed with thick, somber law books and treatises, more proof still that Mr. Finley knew his stuff.

"What's the value of the house?" he asked without taking his eyes off the agreement.

"Around two-fifty," Mr. Flander replied.

"I think it's more," Mrs. Flander added.

"This is not a good time to be selling a house," Oscar said wisely, though every homeowner in America knew the market was weak. More silence as the wise man studied their work.

He lowered the papers and peered over his drugstore reading glasses into the expectant eyes of Mrs. Flander. "You're getting the washer and dryer, along with the microwave, treadmill, and flat-screen television?"

"Well, yes."

"In fact, you're getting probably 80 percent of the household furnishings, right?"

"I suppose. What's wrong with that?"

"Nothing, except he's getting most of the cash."

"I think it's fair," said Mr. Flander.

"I'm sure you do."

"Do you think it's fair?" she asked.

Oscar shrugged as if it weren't his business. "Pretty typical, I'd say. But cash is more important than a trainload of used furniture. You'll probably move into an apartment, something much smaller, and you won't have enough room for all your old stuff. He, on the other hand, has money in the bank."

She shot a hard look at her soon-to-be-ex-husband. Oscar hammered away. "And your car is three years older, so you're getting the old car and the old furniture."

"It was his idea," she said.

"It was not. We agreed."

"You wanted the IRA account and the newer car."

"That's because it's always been my car."

"And that's because you've always had the nicer car."

"That's not true, Barbara. Don't start exaggerating like you always do, okay?"

Louder, Barbara responded, "And don't you start lying in front of the lawyer, Cal. We agreed we would come here, tell the truth, and not fight in front of the lawyer. Didn't we?"

"Oh, sure, but how can you sit there and say I've always had the nicer car? Have you forgotten the Toyota Camry?"

"Good God, Cal, that was twenty years ago."

"Still counts."

"Well, yes, I remember it, and I remember the day you wrecked it."

Rochelle heard the voices and smiled to herself. She turned a page of her paperback. AC, asleep beside her, suddenly rose to his feet and began a low growl. Rochelle looked at him, then slowly got up and walked to a window. She adjusted the blinds to give herself a view, then she heard it—the distant wail of a siren. As it grew louder, AC's growl also picked up the volume.

Oscar was also at a window, casually looking at the intersection in the distance, hoping for a glimpse of the ambulance. It was a habit too hard to break, not that he really wanted to stop. He, along with Wally and now Rochelle and perhaps thousands of lawyers in the city, couldn't suppress a rush of adrenaline at the sound of an approaching ambulance. And the sight of one flying down the street always made him smile.

The Flanders, though, were not smiling. They had gone silent, both glaring at him, each hating the other. When the siren faded away, Oscar returned to his chair and said, "Look, folks, if you're going to fight, I can't represent both of you."

Both were tempted to bolt. Once on the street, they could go their separate ways and find more reputable lawyers, but for a second or two they were not sure what to do. Then Mr. Flander blinked. He jumped to his feet and headed for the door. "Don't worry about it, Finley. I'll go find me a real lawyer." He opened the door, slammed it behind him, then stomped past Rochelle and the dog as they were settling into their places. He yanked open the front door, slammed it too, and happily left Finley & Figg forever.

CHAPTER 7

Happy hour ran from five to seven, and Abner decided his new best friend should leave before it started. He called a cab, soaked a clean towel with cold water, then walked to the other side of the bar and gently punched him. "David, wake up, pal, it's almost five o'clock." David had been out for an hour. Abner, like all good bartenders, did not want his after-work crowd to see a drunk facedown on the bar, comatose, snoring. Abner touched his face with the towel and said, "Come on, big guy. Party's over."

David suddenly came around. His eyes and mouth flew open as he gawked at Abner. "What, what, what?" he stammered.

"It's almost five. Time to go home, David. There's a cab outside."

"Five o'clock!" David shouted, stunned at the news. There were half a dozen other drinkers in the bar, all watching with sympathy. Tomorrow it could be them. David got to his feet and with Abner's help managed to pull on his overcoat and find his briefcase. "How long have I been here?" he asked, looking around wildly as if he'd just discovered the place.

"A long time," Abner replied. He stuffed a business card into a coat pocket and said, "Call me tomorrow and we'll settle the tab." Arm in arm they staggered to the front door and through it. The cab was at the curb. Abner opened the rear door, wrestled David into the seat, said "He's all yours" to the driver, and closed the door.

David watched him disappear into the bar. He looked at the driver and said, "What's your name?"

The driver said something unintelligible, and David barked, "Can you speak English?"

"Where to, sir?" the driver asked.

"Now, that's a really good question. You know any good bars around here?"

The driver shook his head.

"I'm not ready to go home, because she's there and, well, oh, boy." The inside of the cab had started to spin. There was a loud honk from behind. The driver eased into traffic. "Not so fast," David said with his eyes closed. They were going ten miles an hour. "Go north," David said.

"I need a destination, sir," the driver said as he turned onto South Dearborn. Rush-hour traffic was already heavy and slow.

"I might be sick," David said, swallowing hard and afraid to open his eyes.

"Please, not in my car."

They stopped and started for two blocks. David managed to calm himself. "A destination, sir?" the driver repeated.

David opened his left eye and looked out the window. Next to the cab was a city transit bus waiting in traffic, packed with weary workers, its exhaust spewing fumes. Along its side was an ad, three feet by one, proclaiming the services of Finley & Figg, Attorneys. "Drunk Driving? Call the Experts. 773-718-JUSTICE." Address in smaller print. David opened his right eye and for an instant saw the smiling face of Wally Figg. He focused on the word "drunk" and wondered if they could help in some way. Had he seen such ads before? Had he heard of these guys? He wasn't sure. Nothing was clear; nothing made sense. The cab was suddenly spinning again, and faster now.

"Four eighteen Preston Avenue," he said to the driver, then passed out.

Rochelle was never in a hurry to leave, because she never wanted to go home. As tense as things could get around the office, they were far tamer than her cramped and chaotic apartment.

The Flanders' divorce got off to a rocky start, but with Oscar's skillful manipulation it was now on track. Mrs. Flander had hired the firm and paid a retainer of $750. It would eventually be worked out and settled on no-fault grounds, but not before Oscar clipped her for a couple of grand. Still, Oscar was fuming over the bingo card and lying in wait for his junior partner.

Wally rolled in at 5:30, after an exhausting day looking for Krayoxx victims. The search had turned up no one but Chester Marino, but Wally was undaunted. He was onto something big. The clients were out there, and he would find them.

"Oscar's on the phone," Rochelle said. "And he's upset."

"What's up?" Wally asked.

"A bingo card showed up: $399."

"Pretty clever, huh? My uncle plays bingo at the VFW."

"Brilliant." She gave him the quick version of the Flander situation.

"See! It worked," Wally said proudly. "You gotta get 'em in here, Ms. Gibson, that's what I always say. The $399 is the bait, then you pull the switch. Oscar did it perfectly."

"What about false advertising?"

"Most of what we do is false advertising. Ever hear of Krayoxx? Cholesterol drug?"

"Maybe. Why?"

"It's killing people, okay, and it's gonna make us rich."

"I think I've heard this before. He's off the phone."

Wally went straight to Oscar's door, rapped it as he pushed it open, and said, "So you like my bingo card ads, I hear."

Oscar was standing at his desk, tie undone, tired, and in need of a drink. Two hours earlier he'd been ready for a fight. Now he just wanted to leave. "Come on, Wally, bingo cards?"

"Yep, we're the first law firm in Chicago to use bingo cards."

"We've been the first several times, and we're still broke."

"Those days are over, my friend," Wally said as he reached into his briefcase. "Ever hear of a cholesterol drug called Krayoxx?"

"Yeah, yeah, my wife's taking it."

"Well, Oscar, it's killing people."

Oscar actually smiled, then caught himself. "How do you know this?"

Wally dropped a stack of research onto Oscar's desk. "Here's your homework, all about Krayoxx. A big mass tort firm in Fort Lauderdale sued Varrick Labs last week over Krayoxx, a class action. They claim the drug vastly increases the risk of heart attack and stroke, and they have experts to prove it. Varrick has put more crap on the market than any of the Big Pharmas, and it's also paid more in damages. Billions. Looks like Krayoxx is its latest boondoggle. The mass tort boys are just now waking up. This is happening now, Oscar, and if we can pick up a dozen or so Krayoxx cases, then we're rich."

"I've heard this all before, Wally."

When the cab stopped, David was awake again, though semiconscious. With some effort, he managed to toss two $20 bills over the front seat and with even more effort managed to extricate himself from the cab. He watched it drive away, then vomited in the gutter.

Afterward, he felt much better.

Rochelle was tidying up her desk and listening to the partners bicker when she heard heavy footsteps on the porch. Something hit the door, then it swung open. The young man was wild-eyed, red-faced, unsteady on his feet, but well dressed.

"Can I help you?" she said with great suspicion.

David looked at her but didn't see her. He looked around the room, wobbled, squinted as he tried to focus.

"Sir?" she said.

"I love this place," he said to her. "I really, really love this place."

"How nice. Could I—"

"I'm looking for a job, and this is where I want to work."

AC smelled trouble and walked around the corner of Rochelle's desk. "How cute!" David said loudly, giggling. "A dog. What's his name?"

"AC."

"AC. All right. Help me out here. What does AC stand for?"

"Ambulance Chaser."

"I like it. I really, really like it. Does he bite?"

"Don't touch him."

The two partners had moved quietly into view. They were standing in the door of Oscar's office. Rochelle gave them a nervous look.

"This is where I want to work," David repeated. "I need a job."

"Are you a lawyer?" Wally asked.

"Are you Figg or Finley?"

"I'm Figg. He's Finley. Are you a lawyer?"

"I think so. As of eight o'clock this morning I was employed by Rogan Rothberg, one of six hundred. But I quit, snapped, cracked up, went to a bar. It's been a long day." David leaned against the wall to steady himself.

"What makes you think we're looking for an associate?" Oscar asked.

"Associate? I was thinking more in terms of coming straight in as a partner," David said, then doubled over in laughter. No one else cracked a smile. They were not sure what to do, but Wally would later confess he thought about calling the police.

When the laughing stopped, David steadied himself again and repeated, "I love this place."

"Why are you leaving the big firm?" Wally asked.

"Oh, lots of reasons. Let's just say I hate the work, hate the people I work with, and hate the clients."

"You'll fit in here," Rochelle said.

"We're not hiring," Oscar said.

"Oh, come on. I went to Harvard Law School. I'll work part-time—fifty hours a week, half of what I've been working. Get it? Part-time?" He laughed again, alone.

"Sorry, pal," Wally said dismissively.

Not too far away, a driver hit the horn, a long frantic sound that could only end badly. Another driver slammed his brakes violently. Another horn, more brakes, and for a long second the firm of Finley & Figg held its collective breath. The crash that followed was thunderous, more impressive than most, and it was obvious that several cars had just mangled themselves at the intersection of Preston, Beech, and Thirty-eighth. Oscar grabbed his overcoat. Rochelle grabbed her sweater. They followed Wally out the front door, leaving the drunk behind to take care of himself.

Along Preston, other offices emptied as lawyers and their clerks and paralegals raced to inspect the mayhem and offer solace to the injured.

The pileup involved at least four cars, all damaged and scattered. One was lying on its roof, tires still spinning. There were screams amid the panic and sirens in the distance. Wally ran to a badly crumpled Ford. The front passenger door had been torn off, and a teenage girl was trying to get out. She was dazed and covered in blood. He took her arm and led her away from the wreckage. Rochelle helped as they sat the girl on a nearby bus bench. Wally returned to the carnage in search of other clients. Oscar had already found an eyewitness, someone who could help place blame and thus attract clients. Finley & Figg knew how to work a wreck.

The teenager's mother had been in the rear seat, and Wally helped her too. He walked her to the bus bench and into the waiting arms of Rochelle. Vince Gholston, their rival from across the street, appeared, and Wally saw him. "Stay away, Gholston," he barked. "These are our clients now."

"No way, Figg. They're not signed up."

"Stay away, asshole."

A crowd grew quickly as onlookers rushed to the scene. Traffic was not moving, and many drivers got out of their cars to take a look. Someone yelled, "I smell gas!" which immediately increased the panic. A Toyota was upside down, and its occupants were trying desperately to get out. A large man with boots kicked at a window but could not break it. People were yelling, screaming. The sirens were getting closer. Wally was circling a Buick whose driver appeared to be unconscious. Oscar was handing out business cards to everyone.

In the midst of this mayhem, a young man's voice boomed through the air. "Stay away from our clients!" he yelled, and everyone followed the voice. It was an amazing sight. David Zinc was near the bus bench, holding a large, jagged piece of metal from the wreckage, waving it near the face of a frightened Vince Gholston, who was backing away.

"These are our clients!" David said angrily. He looked crazed, and there was no doubt he would use the weapon if necessary.

Oscar moved next to Wally and said, "That kid may have some potential after all."

Wally was watching with great admiration. "Let's sign him up."

CHAPTER 8

When Helen Zinc pulled in to the driveway at 418 Preston, the first thing she noticed was not the well-worn exterior of Finley & Figg, Attorneys-at-Law; rather, it was the flashing neon sign next door advertising massages. She turned off the lights and the engine and sat for a moment to gather her thoughts. Her husband was alive and safe; he'd just had "a few drinks," according to one Wally Figg, a somewhat pleasant man who'd phoned an hour earlier. Mr. Figg was "sitting with her husband," whatever that meant. The digital clock on the dash gave the time as 8:20, so for almost twelve hours now she had been worrying frantically over his whereabouts and safety. Now that she knew he was alive, she was thinking of ways to kill him.

She glanced around, taking in the neighborhood, disapproving of everything about it, then got out of her BMW and slowly headed for the door. She had asked Mr. Figg how, exactly, her husband made his way from the tall buildings of downtown Chicago to the blue-collar neighborhood around Preston Avenue. Mr. Figg had said he didn't have all the details, and it would be best if they talked about it later.

She opened the front door. A cheap bell rattled. A dog growled at her but made no effort to attack.

Rochelle Gibson and Oscar Finley were gone. Wally was sitting at the table, clipping obituaries from old newspapers, and dining on a bag of chips and a diet soda. He stood quickly, swiped his hands on his pants, and offered a big smile. "You must be Helen," he said.

"I am," she said, almost flinching as he thrust out a hand to shake.

"I'm Wally Figg," he said, already sizing her up. A very nice package. Short auburn hair, hazel eyes behind chic designer frames, five feet eight, slender, well dressed. Wally approved. He then turned and waved an arm in the direction of the cluttered table. Beyond it, against the wall, was an old leather sofa, and on the sofa was David Zinc, dead to the world, comatose again. His right pants leg was torn—a small wound from the car smashup and its aftermath—but other than that he looked quite undisturbed.

Helen took a few steps over and gave him a look. "Are you sure he's alive?" she asked.

"Oh yes, very much so. He got into a scuffle at the car wreck and tore his pants."

"A scuffle?"

"Yep, guy named Gholston, a slimeball across the street, was trying to steal one of our clients after the big wreck, and David here chased him off with a piece of metal. Somehow he tore his pants."

Helen, who had endured enough for one day, shook her head.

"Would you like something to drink? Coffee, water, Scotch?"

"I don't drink alcohol," she said.

Wally looked at her, looked at David, looked back at her. Must be a strange marriage, he thought.

"Neither do I," he said proudly. "There's fresh coffee. I made a pot for David, and he drank two cups before taking his little nap."

"Yes, thank you," she said.

They sipped coffee at the table and spoke softly. "The best I can tell," Wally said, "is that he snapped on the elevator this morning as he was going to work. Cracked up, left the building, and wound up in a bar where he pretty much spent the whole day drinking."

"That's what I gather," she said. "But how did he get here?"

"Haven't got that far yet, but I gotta tell you, Helen, he says he's not going back, says he wants to stay here and work."

She couldn't help herself as she glanced around the large, open, cluttered room. It would be difficult to imagine a place that appeared to be less prosperous. "Your dog?" she asked.

"That's AC, the firm dog. He lives here."

"How many lawyers are in your firm?"

"Just two. It's a boutique firm. I'm the junior partner. Oscar Finley's the senior partner."

"And what kind of work would David do here?"

"We specialize in injury and death cases."

"Like all those guys who advertise on television?"

"We don't do TV," Wally said smugly. If she only knew. He worked on his scripts all the time. He fought with Oscar about spending the money. He watched with envy as other injury lawyers flooded the airwaves with ads that, in his opinion, were almost always poorly done. And, most painfully, he imagined all the lost fees from all the lost cases scooped up by less talented lawyers willing to roll the dice on a TV budget.

David made a gurgling sound and followed it up with a quick nasal snort, and though he was at least making noises, there was no indication he was anywhere near consciousness.

"Do you think he'll remember any of this in the morning?" she asked as she frowned at her husband.

"Hard to say," Wally observed. His romance with alcohol was long and ugly, and he had spent many fogged-in mornings struggling to remember what had happened. Wally took a sip and said, "Look, really none of my business and all, but does he do this often? He says he wants to work here, and, well, we need to know if he might have a problem with the bottle."

"He doesn't drink much at all. Never has. He might occasionally at a party, but he works too hard to drink much. And since I rarely touch the stuff, we don't keep it around the house."

"Just curious. I've had my problems."

"I'm sorry."

"No, it's okay. I've been sober for sixty days now."

That didn't impress Helen as much as it worried her. Wally was still fighting the bottle, with victory far away. She was suddenly tired of the conversation and tired of the place. "I suppose I should take him home."

"Yes, I suppose. Or he could stay here with the dog."

"That's what he deserves, you know? He should wake up in the morning here on the sofa, still dressed, a splitting headache, upset stomach, parched tongue, and have no idea where he is. That would serve him right, don't you think?"

"It would, but I'd rather not clean up after him again."

"He's already—"

"Twice. Once on the porch, once in the restroom."

"I'm so sorry."

"It's okay. But he needs to go home."

"I know. Let's get him up."

Once awake, David chatted pleasantly with his wife as if nothing had happened. He walked unaided from the office, down the front steps, and to the car. He yelled a long good-bye and a hearty thanks to Wally and even offered to drive. Helen declined. They left Preston and headed north.

For five minutes nothing was said. Then Helen casually began, "Look, I think I have most of the major plot points, but just a few details might help. Where was the bar?"

"Abner's. A few blocks from the office." He was sitting low, with the collar of his overcoat turned up over his ears.

"Been there before?"

"No, great place, though. I'll take you there sometime."

"Sure. Why not tomorrow? And you walked into Abner's at what time this morning?"

"Between 7:30 and 8:00. I fled the office, ran a few blocks, found Abner's."

"And started drinking?"

"Oh yes."

"Recall what you consumed?"

"Well, let's see." He paused as he tried to remember. "For breakfast, I had four of Abner's special Bloody Marys. They're really good. Then I had a plate of onion rings and several pints of beer. Miss Spence showed up, and I had two of her Pearl Harbors, wouldn't want to do that again."

"Miss Spence?"

"Yep. She shows up every day, same stool, same drink, same everything."

"And you liked her?"

"I adored her. Very cute, hot."

"I see. She married?"

"No, a widow. She's ninety-four and worth a few billion."

"Any other women?"

"Oh no, just Miss Spence. She left sometime around noon, and, uh, let's see. I had a burger and fries for lunch, then back to the beer, and then at some point I took a nap."

"You blacked out?"

"Whatever."

A pause as she drove and he stared out the windshield.

"So how did you get from the bar to that law office back there?"

"A cab. Paid the guy forty bucks."

"Where did you get into the cab?"

A pause. "Don't remember that."

"Now we're making progress. And the big question: How did you find Finley & Figg?"

David began shaking his head as he pondered this. Finally, he said, "I have no idea."

There was so much to talk about. The drinking—could there be a problem, in spite of what she'd told Wally? Rogan Rothberg—was he going back? Should she bring up Roy Barton's ultimatum? Finley & Figg—was he serious? Helen had a lot on her mind, plenty to say, a long list of complaints, but at the same time she couldn't help but be slightly amused. She had never seen her husband so plastered, and the fact that he'd jumped from a tall building downtown and landed in the outback would soon become a family tale of legendary proportions. He was safe, and that was really all that mattered. And he probably wasn't crazy. The crack-up could be dealt with.

"I have a question," he said, his eyelids getting heavier.

"I have lots of questions," she replied.

"I'm sure you do, but I don't want to talk now. Save it for tomorrow when I'm sober, okay? It's not fair to hammer me now when I'm drunk."

"Fair enough. What's your question?"

"Are your parents, by chance, in our home at this moment?"

"Yes. They've been there for some time. They're very concerned."

"How nice. Look, I'm not walking into our home if your parents are there, got that? I don't want them to see me like this. Understand?"

"They love you, David. You scared all of us."

"Why is everyone so scared? I texted you twice and said I was okay. You knew I was alive. What's all the panic about?"

"Don't get me started."

"So I had a bad day, what's the big deal?"

"A bad day?"

"Actually, it was a pretty good day, come to think of it."

"Why don't we argue tomorrow, David? Isn't that what you asked?"

"Yes, but I'm not getting out of the car until they leave. Please."

They were on the Stevenson Expressway, and traffic was heavier. Nothing was said as they inched along. David struggled to stay awake. Helen finally picked up the cell phone and called her parents.

CHAPTER 9

About once a month Rochelle Gibson arrived for work expecting her usual quiet time, only to find the office already opened, the coffee brewed, the dog fed, and Mr. Figg bustling around with excitement over a new scheme to stalk injured people. This irritated her immensely. It not only ruined the few tranquil moments in her otherwise noisy day but also meant more work.

She was barely inside the door when Wally nailed her with a hearty "Well, good morning, Ms. Gibson," as if he were surprised to see her arrive at work at 7:30 on a Thursday.

"Good morning, Mr. Figg," she replied with far less enthusiasm. She almost added "And what brings you here so early?" but held her tongue. She would hear about his scheme soon enough.

With coffee, yogurt, and the newspaper, she settled at her desk and tried to ignore him.

"I met David's wife last night," Wally said from the table across the room. "Very cute and nice. Said he doesn't drink much, maybe blows it out from time to time. I think the pressure gets to him occasionally. I know that's my story. Always the pressure."

When Wally drank, he needed no excuse. He boozed it up after a hard day, and he had wine with lunch on an easy day. He drank when he was stressed, and he drank on the golf course. Rochelle had seen and heard it all before. She also kept up with the score—sixty-one days without a drink. That was the story of Wally's life—a count of some sort always in progress. Days on the wagon. Days until his driving suspension was over. Days until his current divorce was final. And sadly, days until he was released from rehab.

"What time did she get him?" she asked without looking up from the newspaper.

"After eight. He walked out of here, even asked if he could drive. She said no."

"Was she upset?"

"She was pretty cool. Relieved more than anything else. The big question is whether he'll remember anything. And if he does, then the question is whether he'll find us again. Will he really walk away from the big firm and the big bucks? I got my doubts."

Rochelle had her doubts too, but she was trying to minimize the conversation. Finley & Figg was not the place for a big-firm type with a Harvard degree, and, frankly, she didn't want another lawyer complicating her life. She had her hands full with these two.

"I could use him, though," Wally went on, and Rochelle knew the latest scheme was now on the way. "You ever hear of a cholesterol drug called Krayoxx?"

"You've already asked me this."

"It causes heart attacks and strokes, and the truth is just now coming out. The first wave of litigation is unfolding, could be tens of thousands of cases before it's over. The mass tort lawyers are all over it. I talked to a big firm in Fort Lauderdale yesterday. They've already filed a class action and are looking for more cases."

Rochelle turned a page as if she were hearing nothing.

"Anyway, I'm spending the next few days looking for Krayoxx cases, and I could sure use some help. Are you listening, Ms. Gibson?"

"Sure."

"How many names are in our client database, both active and retired?"

She took a bite of yogurt and seemed exasperated. "We have about two hundred active files," she said.

At Finley & Figg, though, a file deemed active was not necessarily one that received attention. More often than not, it was simply a neglected file that no one had bothered to retire. Wally usually had about thirty files he would touch in a week's time—divorces, wills, estates, injuries, drunk drivers, small contract disputes—and another fifty or so he diligently avoided. Oscar, who was more willing to take on a new client but was also slightly more organized than his junior partner, had about one hundred open files. Throw in a few that were lost, hidden, or unaccounted for, and the number was always around two hundred.

"And retired?" he asked.

A sip of coffee, another grunt. "Last time I checked, the computer showed three thousand files retired since 1991. I don't know what's upstairs."

Upstairs was the final resting place for everything—old law books, outdated computers and word processors, unused office supplies, and dozens of boxes of files Oscar had retired before he added Wally as a partner.

"Three thousand," Wally said with a satisfied grin, as if such a large number were clear evidence of a long and successful career. "Here's the plan, Ms. Gibson. I have drafted a letter that I want you to print on our stationery. It goes to every client, current and past, active and retired. Every name in our client database."

Rochelle thought of all the unhappy clients who had left Finley & Figg. The unpaid fees, the nasty letters, the threats of malpractice lawsuits. She even kept a file labeled "Threats." Over the years, half a dozen or so disgruntled ex-clients had been angry enough to put their feelings on paper. A couple promised ambushes and beatings. One mentioned a sniper's rifle.

Why not leave these poor people alone? They had suffered enough having passed through the office the first time.

Wally jumped to his feet and walked over with the letter. She had no choice but to take it and read it.

Dear _____:

Beware of Krayoxx! This cholesterol drug, made by Varrick Labs, has been proven to cause heart attacks and strokes. Though it has been on the market for six years, scientific evidence is just now revealing the deadly side effects of this drug. If you are using Krayoxx, stop immediately.

The law firm of Finley & Figg is at the forefront of Krayoxx litigation. We will soon be joining a national class action lawsuit in a highly complicated move to bring Varrick to justice.

We need your involvement! If you or anyone you know has a history with Krayoxx, you may have a case. More important, if you know of anyone who has taken Krayoxx and has suffered a heart attack or stroke, please call immediately. A lawyer from Finley & Figg will be at your home within hours.

Don't hesitate. Call now. We anticipate a huge settlement.

Sincerely,

Wallis T. Figg, Attorney and Counselor-at-Law

"Has Oscar seen this?" she asked.

"Not yet. Pretty good, huh?"

"This for real?"

"Oh, it's so real, Ms. Gibson. This is our biggest moment."

"Another gold mine?"

"Bigger than a gold mine."

"And you want to send three thousand letters?"

"Yep, you print 'em, I'll sign 'em, we'll stuff 'em, and they go out in today's mail."

"That's over a thousand bucks in postage."

"Ms. Gibson, the average Krayoxx case will generate something like $200,000 in attorneys' fees, and that's on the low side. Could be as high as $400,000 per case. If we can find ten cases, the math gets real easy."

Rochelle did the math, and her reluctance began to fade. Her mind began to drift. With all the bar journals and newsletters that crossed her desk, she had seen a thousand stories about big verdicts and big settlements. Lawyers making millions in fees.

Surely, they would give her a fine bonus.

"All right," she said, shoving her newspaper aside.

Oscar and Wally had their second Krayoxx fight not long afterward. When Oscar arrived at 9:00 a.m., he could not help but notice the flurry of activity around the front desk. Rochelle was working the computer. The printer was in high gear. Wally was signing his name to letters. Even AC was awake and watching.

"What's all this?" Oscar demanded.

"The sounds of capitalism at work," Wally answered cheerfully.

"What the hell does that mean?"

"Protecting the rights of the injured. Serving our clients. Purging the market of dangerous products. Bringing corporate wrongdoers to justice."

"Chasing ambulances," Rochelle said.

Oscar looked disgusted and continued to his office, where he slammed the door. Before he could remove his coat and park his umbrella, Wally was at his desk, nibbling on a muffin and waving one of the letters. "You gotta read this, Oscar," he said. "This is brilliant."

Oscar read it, the wrinkles in his forehead getting deeper and deeper with each paragraph. When he finished, he said, "Come on, Wally, not again. How many of these are you sending out?"

"Three thousand. Our entire client list."

"What? Think of the postage. Think of the wasted time. Here we go again. You'll spend the next month running around chirping about Krayoxx this and Krayoxx that, and you'll waste a hundred hours looking for worthless cases, and on and on. We've been here before, Wally, come on. Do something productive."

"Like what?"

"Like go hang out in an emergency room somewhere, wait for a real case to come in. I don't have to tell you how to find good cases."

"I'm tired of that crap, Oscar. I wanna make some money. Let's hit it big for a change."

"My wife's been taking the drug for two years. Loves it."

"Did you tell her to stop, that it's killing people?"

"Of course not."

As their voices grew louder, Rochelle eased over and quietly closed the door to Oscar's office. She was returning to her desk when the front door suddenly opened. It was David Zinc, bright and sober with a big smile, sharp suit, cashmere overcoat, and two thick briefcases loaded to the max.

"Well, well, if it ain't Mr. Harvard," Rochelle said.

"I'm back."

"I'm surprised you could find us."

"It wasn't easy. Where's my office?"

"Well, uh, let's see. I'm not sure we have one. Perhaps we should ask the two bosses about this." She nodded to Oscar's door, beyond which voices could be heard.

"So they're here?" David asked.

"Yes, they usually start the day with a round of bickering."

"I see."

"Look, Harvard, are you sure you know what you're doing? This is another world. You're taking a plunge here, leaving the fancy life of corporate law for the bush leagues. You might get hurt out here, and you sure won't make any money."

"I've done the big-firm thing, Ms. Gibson, and I'll jump off a bridge before I go back. Just give me a little room somewhere to park myself, and I'll figure it out."

The door opened, and Wally and Oscar emerged. They froze when they saw David standing in front of Rochelle's desk. Wally smiled and said, "Well, good morning, David. You look surprisingly healthy."

"Thank you, and I'd like to apologize for my appearance yesterday." He nodded at all three as he spoke. "You caught me at the tail end of a rather unusual episode, but it was nonetheless a very important day in my life. I quit the big firm, and here I am, ready to go to work."

"What type of work do you have in mind?" Oscar asked.

David gave a slight shrug as if he didn't have a clue. "For the past five years, I've labored in the dungeon of bond underwriting, with emphasis on second- and third-tier aftermarket spreads, primarily for foreign multinational corporations that prefer to avoid paying taxes anywhere in the world. If you have no idea what that is, then don't worry. No one else does either. What it means is that a small team of us idiots labored fifteen hours a day in a room with no windows creating paperwork, and more paperwork. I've never seen the inside of a courtroom, or a courthouse for that matter, never met a judge when he was wearing a robe, never offered a hand to help a person who needed a real lawyer. To answer your question, Mr. Finley, I'm here to do anything. Think of me as a rookie fresh out of law school who doesn't know his ass from a hole in the ground. But I'm a quick study."

Compensation should have been the next issue, but the partners were reluctant to talk money in front of Rochelle. She, of course, would take the position that anyone they hired, lawyer or otherwise, should be paid less than she was.

"There is some space upstairs," Wally said.

"I'll take it."

"It's a junk room," Oscar said.

"I'll take it," David said, lifting his two briefcases, ready to move in.

"I haven't been up there in years," Rochelle said, rolling her eyes, obviously unhappy with the firm's sudden expansion.

A narrow door next to the kitchen led to a stairway. David followed Wally, with Oscar bringing up the rear. Wally was excited about having someone to help hustle Krayoxx cases. Oscar was thinking only of how much this might cost in salary, withholding taxes, unemployment deductions, and, heaven forbid, health insurance. Finley & Figg offered little in the way of benefits—no 401(k), no IRA, no retirement of any kind, and certainly no health or dental plan. Rochelle had been griping for years because she was forced to buy her own private policy, as did the two partners. What if young David here expected health insurance?

As Oscar climbed the stairs, he felt the burden of a heavier overhead. More spent at the office meant less to take home. His retirement seemed even more elusive.

The junk room was exactly that, a dark, dusty landfill with spiderwebs and pieces of old furniture and boxes of files. "I like it," David said when Wally switched on the light.

He must be crazy, Oscar thought.

But there was a small desk and a couple of chairs. David saw only the potential. And there were two windows. Sunlight would be a nice addition to his life. When it was dark outside, he would be at home with Helen, procreating.

Oscar swiped away a large spiderweb and said, "Look, David, we can offer a small salary, but you're gonna have to generate your own fees. And this won't be easy, at least initially."

Initially? Oscar had been struggling to generate meager fees for over thirty years.

"What's the deal?" David asked.

Oscar looked at Wally, and Wally looked at the wall. The two had not hired an associate in fifteen years, nor had they even considered doing so. David's presence had caught them by surprise.

As the senior partner, Oscar felt compelled to take the initiative. "We can pay a thousand bucks a month, and you keep half of what you bring in. After six months, we'll reevaluate."

Wally jumped in quickly with "It will be rough at first, lots of competition out there on the streets."

"We can toss some files your way," Oscar added.

"We'll give you a piece of the Krayoxx litigation," Wally said, as if they were already banking huge fees.

"The what?" David asked.

"Never mind," Oscar said with a frown.

"Look, guys," David said with a smile. He was far more at ease than they were. "I've made a very nice salary for the past five years. I've spent a lot, but there's a chunk in the bank. Don't worry about me. I'll take the deal." And with that he thrust out a hand, shaking Oscar's first, then Wally's.

CHAPTER 10

David cleaned for the next hour. He wiped dust from the desk and
chairs. He found an old Hoover in the kitchen and vacuumed the plank
floors. He filled three large bags with trash and put them on the small
porch out back. He stopped occasionally to admire the windows and
sunlight, something he'd never done at Rogan Rothberg. Sure, on a
clear day the view across Lake Michigan was captivating, but he had
learned during his first year with the firm that time spent gazing out
from the Trust Tower was time that could not be billed. Rookie associates were placed in bunker-like cubicles, where they toiled around
the clock and, with time, forgot about sunshine and daydreaming.
Now David couldn't stay away from the windows. The view, admit-
tedly, was not as captivating. Looking down, he could see the massage
parlor, and beyond it the intersection of Preston, Beech, and Thirty-
eighth, the very spot where he'd taken a piece of metal to the slimeball
Gholston and chased him away. Beyond the intersection was a block of
more converted bungalows.

Not much of a view, but David liked it anyway. It represented an
exciting change in his life, a new challenge. It meant freedom.

Wally dropped in every ten minutes to check on things, and it
became obvious he had something on his mind. Finally, after an hour,
he said, "Say, David, I'm due in court at eleven. Divorce court. I doubt
you've ever been there, so I was thinking you could tag along and I'll
introduce you to the judge."

The cleaning had become monotonous. David said, "Let's go."

As they were leaving through the back door, Wally said, "Is that your Audi SUV?"

"It is."

"Do you mind driving? I'll do the talking."

"Sure."

As they were pulling onto Preston, Wally said, "Look, David, the truth is that I got a DUI a year ago and my license is suspended. There, I said it. I believe in being honest."

"Okay. You've certainly seen me drunk enough."

"I have indeed. But your cute wife told me you're not much of a drinker. I, on the other hand, have quite a history. I'm sober for sixty-one days now. Every day is a challenge. I go to AA, and I've rehabbed several times. What else do you want to know?"

"I didn't bring this up."

"Oscar, he has a few strong ones every night. Believe me, with his wife, he needs them, but he keeps it under control. Some people are like that, you know. They can stop with two or three. They can skip a few days, even weeks, no problem. Others can't stop until they black out, kinda like you yesterday."

"Thanks, Wally. Where are we headed, by the way?"

"The Daley Center downtown, 50 West Washington. Me, I do fine for a while. I've quit four or five times, you know?"

"How would I know that?"

"Anyway, enough of the booze."

"What's wrong with Oscar's wife?"

Wally whistled and looked out the side window for a moment. "Tough woman, man. One of these people who grew up in a nicer part of town, father wore a suit and tie to work, as opposed to a uniform, so she was raised to believe she's better than most. A real snot. She made a major mistake when she married Oscar because she figured he was a lawyer, right? Lawyers make lots of money, right? Not exactly. Oscar has never made enough to satisfy her, and she hammers him relentlessly because she wants more money. I loathe the woman. You won't meet her, because she refuses to set foot in the office, which suits me just fine."

"Why not get a divorce?"

"That's what I've been saying for years. Me, I got no problem with divorce. Been down that road four times."

"Four times?"

"Yep, and every trip was worth the hassle. You know what they say—the reason divorce is so expensive is because it's worth it." Wally laughed at this stale punch line.

"Are you married now?" David asked, somewhat cautiously.

"Nope, back on the prowl," Wally said smugly, as if no woman were safe. David couldn't imagine a less attractive person hitting on females in bars and at parties. So, in less than fifteen minutes, he had learned Wally was a recovering alcoholic with four ex-wives, several trips through rehab, and at least one DUI. David decided to stop with the questions.

Over breakfast with Helen, he had dug a bit online and learned that (1) ten years earlier, Finley & Figg had settled a sexual harassment suit brought by a former secretary; (2) on one occasion, Oscar had been reprimanded by the state bar association for overcharging a client in a divorce case; (3) on two prior occasions, Wally had been reprimanded by the state bar association for "blatant solicitation" of clients who'd been injured in auto accidents, including an apparently messy affair involving Wally wearing doctor's scrubs and barging into the hospital room of a badly wounded teenager who died an hour later; (4) at least four former clients had sued the firm alleging malpractice, though it was unclear if any recovered damages; and (5) the firm had been mentioned in a scathing article written by a professor of legal ethics who was sick of lawyers' advertising. And all of this was just over breakfast.

Helen had been alarmed, but David took a hard, cynical line and argued that such dubious behavior couldn't touch the cutthroat brand of law practiced by the fine folks at Rogan Rothberg. He had only to mention the Strick River case to win the argument. The Strick River in Wisconsin had been thoroughly polluted by an infamous chemical company represented by Rogan Rothberg, and after decades of brutal litigation and skillful legal wrangling the dumping continued.

Wally was digging through his briefcase.

The skyline came into view, and David looked at the tall, majestic buildings crowded together in downtown Chicago. The Trust Tower was in the center. "I would be there right now," he said softly, almost to himself. Wally looked up, saw the skyline, and realized what David was thinking.

"Which one?" Wally asked.

"The Trust Tower."

"I was in the Sears Tower one summer, a clerk, after my second year of law school. Martin & Wheeler. And I thought that's what I wanted."

"What happened?"

"Couldn't pass the bar exam."

David added that to the growing list of defects.

"You're not going to miss it, are you?" Wally asked.

"No, I'm breaking into a sweat right now, just looking at the building. I don't want to get any closer."

"Take a left on Washington. We're almost there."

Inside the Richard J. Daley Center, they passed through security scanners and took the elevator to the sixteenth floor. The place was bustling with lawyers and litigants, clerks and cops, either hustling about or huddled in little pockets of serious conversations. Justice was looming, and everyone seemed to be dreading it.

David had no idea where he was going or what he was doing, so he stuck close to Wally, who seemed quite at home. David was carrying his briefcase, which held only a single legal pad. They passed courtroom after courtroom.

"Have you really never seen the inside of a courtroom?" Wally asked as they walked quickly, their shoes clicking along on the worn marble tile.

"Not since law school."

"Unbelievable. What have you been doing for the past five years?"

"You don't want to know."

"I'm sure you're right about that. This is us," Wally said, pointing to the heavy double doors of a courtroom. A sign said: "Circuit Court of Cook County—Divorce Division, Hon. Charles Bradbury."

"Who's Bradbury?" David asked.

"You're about to meet him."

Wally opened the door, and they stepped inside. There were a few spectators scattered through the rows of benches. The lawyers were seated up front, bored and waiting. The witness chair was empty; no trial was in progress. Judge Bradbury was reviewing a document and taking his time. David and Wally sat in the second row. Wally scanned the courtroom, saw his client, smiled, and nodded.

He whispered to David, "This is known as an open day, as opposed to a trial day. Generally speaking, you can get motions granted, routine matters approved, crap like that. That lady over there in the short yellow dress is our beloved client DeeAnna Nuxhall, and she thinks she's about to get another divorce."

"Another?" David asked as he glanced over. DeeAnna winked at him. Bleached blonde, huge chest, legs everywhere.

"I've done one already. This would be my second. I think she has a prior."

"Looks like a stripper."

"Nothing would surprise me."

Judge Bradbury signed some papers. Lawyers approached the bench, chatted with him, got what they wanted, and left. Fifteen minutes passed, and Wally was getting anxious.

"Mr. Figg," the judge said.

Wally and David walked through the bar, past the tables, and approached the bench, a low one that allowed the lawyers to almost see eye to eye with His Honor. Bradbury shoved the microphone away so they could chat without being heard. "What's up?" he said.

"We have a new associate, Your Honor," Wally said proudly. "Meet

David Zinc." David reached over and shook hands with the judge, who received him warmly. "Welcome to my courtroom," he said.

"David's been with a big firm downtown. Now he wants to see the real side of justice," Wally said.

"You won't learn much from Figg," Bradbury said with a chuckle.

"He went to Harvard Law School," Wally said, even prouder.

"Then what are you doing here?" the judge asked, and appeared to be dead serious.

"Got sick of the big firm," David said.

Wally was handing over some paperwork. "We have a slight problem here, Judge. My client is the lovely DeeAnna Nuxhall, fourth row left, in the yellow dress." Bradbury peered slightly over his reading glasses and said, "She looks familiar."

"Yep, she was here about a year ago, second or third divorce."

"Same dress, I think."

"Yes, I think so too. Same dress, but the boobs are new."

"You getting any?"

"Not yet."

David felt faint. The judge and the lawyer were discussing sex with the client in open court, though no one could hear.

"What's the problem?" Bradbury asked.

"I haven't been paid. She owes three hundred bucks, and I can't seem to squeeze it out of her."

"What parts have you squeezed?"

"Ha-ha. She refuses to pay, Judge."

"I need a closer look."

Wally turned and motioned for Ms. Nuxhall to join them at the bench. She stood and wiggled herself from between the benches, then proceeded to the front. The lawyers went mute. The two bailiffs woke up. The other spectators gawked. The dress was even shorter when she walked, and she wore platform spiked heels that would make a hooker blush. David eased as far away as possible when she joined the boys at the bench.

Judge Bradbury pretended not to notice her. He was far too occupied with the contents of the court file. "Basic no-fault divorce, right, Mr. Figg?"

"That's correct, Your Honor," Wally replied properly.

"Is everything in order?"

"Yes, except for the small matter of my fee."

"I just noticed that," Bradbury said with a frown. "It looks as though there is a balance of $300, right?"

"That's correct, Your Honor."

Bradbury peered over his reading glasses and took in the chest first, then the eyes. "Are you prepared to take care of the fee, Ms. Nuxhall?"

"Yes, Your Honor," she said in a squeaky voice. "But I'll have to wait until next week. You see, I'm getting married this Saturday, and, well, I just can't swing it right now."

His eyes dancing from her chest to her face, His Honor said, "It's my experience, Ms. Nuxhall, in divorce cases the fees are never paid after the fact. I expect my lawyers to be taken care of, to be paid, before I sign the final orders. What is the total fee, Mr. Figg?"

"Six hundred. She paid half up front."

"Six hundred?" Bradbury said, feigning disbelief. "That's a very reasonable fee, Ms. Nuxhall. Why haven't you paid your lawyer?"

Her eyes were suddenly wet.

The lawyers and spectators couldn't hear the details, but they nonetheless kept their eyes on DeeAnna, especially her legs and shoes. David backed away even more, shocked at this shakedown in open court.

Bradbury moved in for the kill. He raised his voice slightly and said, "I'm not granting this divorce today, Ms. Nuxhall. You get your lawyer paid, then I'll sign the papers. You understand this?"

Wiping her cheeks, she said, "Please."

"I'm sorry, but I run a tight ship. I insist that all obligations be met—alimony, child support, legal fees. It's just $300. Go borrow it from a friend."

"I've tried, Your Honor, but—"

"Please. I hear this all the time. You're excused."

She turned around and walked away, His Honor leering at every step. Wally watched too, shaking his head, marveling, as if ready to pounce. When the door closed, the courtroom breathed again. Judge Bradbury took a sip of water and said, "Anything else?"

"One more, Judge. Joannie Brenner. No-fault, complete property settlement, no children, and, most important, my fee has been paid in full."

"Get her up here."

"I'm not sure I'm cut out for divorce law," David admitted. They were back on the street, inching along in noon traffic, leaving the Daley Center behind.

"Great, you've been to court one time now, for less than an hour, and you're already streamlining your practice," Wally replied.

"Do most judges do what Bradbury just did?"

"What? You mean protect his lawyers? No, most judges have forgotten what it's like to be in the trenches. As soon as they put on the black robe, they forget. Bradbury, he's different. He remembers what a bunch of creeps we represent."

"So what happens now? Will DeeAnna get her divorce?"

"She'll stop by the office this afternoon with the money, and we'll get the divorce on Friday. She gets married on Saturday, and in six months or so she'll be back for another divorce."

"I rest my case. I'm not cut out for divorce work."

"Oh, it sucks all right. Ninety percent of what we do sucks. We hustle the nickel-and-dime stuff to pay the overhead and dream of the big case. But last night, David, I didn't dream, and I'll tell you why. Ever hear of a drug called Krayoxx, a cholesterol drug?"

"No."

"Well, you will. It's killing people right and left, no doubt the next big mass tort wave of litigation, and we gotta get in fast. Where are you going?"

"I need to run a quick errand, and since we're downtown, it won't take a second."

A minute later, David parked illegally outside of Abner's. "Ever been here?" he asked.

"Oh, sure. There aren't many bars with which I'm unacquainted, David. But it's been a while."

"This is where I spent yesterday, and I need to pay my bar bill."

"Why didn't you pay it yesterday?"

"Because I couldn't find my pockets, remember?"

"I'll wait in the car," Wally said, then took a long, lustful look at the door into Abner's.

Miss Spence was on her throne, eyes glazed, cheeks red, in another world. Abner was hustling around the bar, mixing drinks, pouring beer, sliding along platters of burgers. David caught him near the cash register and said, "Hey, I'm back."

Abner smiled and said, "So you're alive after all."

"Oh, sure. Just left court. You got my tab somewhere close?"

Abner fished through a drawer and pulled out a ticket. "Let's call it a hundred and thirty bucks."

"Is that all?" David handed over two $100 bills and said, "Keep it."

"Your chick is over there," Abner said, nodding at Miss Spence, whose eyes were temporarily closed.

"She's not as cute today," David said.

"I gotta friend in finance, he was in last night, says she's worth eight billion."

"On second thought."

"I think she likes you, but you'd better hurry."

"I'd better leave her alone. Thanks for taking care of me."

"No problem. Come back and see me sometime."

Highly unlikely, David thought as they quickly shook hands.

CHAPTER 11

For an unlicensed driver, Wally proved to be a skillful navigator. Somewhere near Midway Airport, he directed David through a series of quick turns onto short streets, delivered them from two impossible dead ends, insisted he drive two blocks the wrong way, and did it all with a nonstop monologue that included "I know this place like the back of my hand" several times. They parked at the curb in front of a sagging duplex with aluminum foil covering the windows, a barbecue grill on the front porch, and a huge orange cat guarding the front door.

"And who lives here?" David asked, taking in the run-down neighborhood. Two sketchy teenagers across the street seemed fascinated by his shiny Audi.

"Here liveth a lovely woman by the name of Iris Klopeck, widow of Percy Klopeck, who died about eighteen months ago at the age of forty-eight, died in his sleep. Very sad. They came to see me about a divorce one time but then changed their minds. As I recall, he was rather obese, but not nearly as large as she."

The two lawyers were sitting in the car talking, as if they did not want to get out. Only a couple of FBI agents in black suits and a black sedan could have been more conspicuous.

"So, why are we here?" David asked.

"Krayoxx, my friend, Krayoxx. I want to talk to Iris and see if by chance Percy had been on the drug when he died. If so, then voilà! We have another Krayoxx case, worth somewhere between two and four mill. Any more questions?"

Oh, dozens of questions. David's mind was spinning as he realized they were about to cold-call Ms. Klopeck to inquire about her dead husband. "Is she expecting us?" he asked.

"I haven't called, have you?"

"No, actually."

Wally yanked open the door and got out. David reluctantly did the same and managed to frown at the teenagers admiring his car. The orange cat refused to move from the doormat. The doorbell could not be heard from outside, so Wally commenced knocking. Louder and louder, while David continued to glance nervously at the street. Finally, a chain was heard, then a crack in the door.

"Who is it?" a woman asked.

"Attorney Wally Figg, looking for Ms. Iris Klopeck."

The door opened, and through the glass storm door Iris presented herself. As large as advertised, she wore what appeared to be a beige bedsheet with openings for her head and arms. "Who are you?" she asked.

"Wally Figg, Iris. I met you and Percy when you were thinking about a divorce. Probably three years ago. You guys came to my office over on Preston."

"Percy's dead," she said.

"Yes, I know. I'm sorry. That's why I'm here. I want to talk about his death. I'm curious about what medications he was taking when he died."

"Why does it matter?"

"Because there's a lot of litigation over cholesterol drugs and painkillers and antidepressants. Some of these drugs killed thousands of people. There could be a lot of money on the table."

A pause as she looked at them. "The house is a wreck," she said. What a surprise, thought David. They followed her inside to a narrow, dirty kitchen and sat at the table. She fixed instant coffee in three mix-matched Bears mugs, then sat across from them. David's chair was a flimsy wooden model that felt as though it might collapse any second. Hers appeared to be of the same variety. The trip to the door, then to the kitchen, along with the preparation of the coffee, had winded her. There was sweat on her spongy forehead.

Wally finally got around to introducing David to Ms. Klopeck. "David went to Harvard Law, and he's just joined our firm," Wally said. She did not offer a hand to shake, nor did Mr. Harvard. She could not have cared less where David, Wally, or anyone else went to college or law school. Her breathing was as noisy as an old furnace. The room smelled of dried cat urine and yesterday's nicotine.

Wally again expressed his phony condolences for dear Percy's demise, then quickly got to the point. "The main drug I'm after is called Krayoxx, a cholesterol drug. Was Percy taking it when he died?"

With no hesitation, she said, "Yes. He'd taken it for years. I used to take it, but I quit."

Wally was at once thrilled by Percy's usage and disappointed that Iris had given it up.

"Something wrong with Krayoxx?" she asked.

"Oh yes, very wrong," Wally said, rubbing his hands together. He launched into what was becoming a fluid and compelling case against Krayoxx and Varrick Labs. He cherry-picked facts and figures from the preliminary research that was being touted by the mass tort lawyers. He quoted heavily from the one-sided lawsuit filed in Fort Lauderdale. He made a convincing case that time was of the essence and Iris needed to sign on with Finley & Figg immediately.

"How much will it cost me?" she asked.

"Not a penny," Wally fired back. "We front the expenses of litigation and take 40 percent of the recovery."

The coffee tasted like saltwater. After one sip, David wanted to spit. Iris, though, seemed to savor it. She took a long drink, swirled it around her mammoth mouth, then swallowed. "Forty percent sounds like a lot," she said.

"This is very complicated litigation, Iris, against a corporation with a zillion dollars and a thousand lawyers. Look at it like this: Right now you have 60 percent of nothing. In a year or two, if you hire our firm, you could have 60 percent of something big."

"How big?"

"Tough question, Iris, but then I remember that you always ask the tough questions. That's what I always liked about you. Tough question, and to be honest, I can't answer it, because no one can predict what a jury might do. The jury might see the truth about Krayoxx and get ticked off at Varrick and give you five million bucks. Or, the jury might believe the lies put forth by Varrick and its shifty lawyers and give you nothing. Me, I tend to think the case will go for around a million bucks, Iris, but you gotta understand that I'm not making any promises." He looked at David and said, "Right, David, we can't make promises in cases like this? Nothing is guaranteed."

"That's right," David said convincingly, the new mass tort specialist.

She sloshed some more saltwater around her mouth and glared at Wally. "I could sure use some help," she said. "It's just me and Clint, and he's only working part-time these days." Wally and David were taking notes and nodding along as if they knew exactly who Clint was. She did not bother to elaborate. "I'm living off $1,200 a month Social Security, so anything you can get would be great."

"We'll get you something, Iris. I feel sure of it."

"When might this happen?"

"Another tough question, Iris. One theory is that Varrick will get hit so hard with Krayoxx cases that the company will surrender and negotiate a huge settlement. Most of the lawyers, including me, expect this to happen within the next twenty-four months. The other theory is that Varrick will take a few of these cases to trial, to sort of test the waters around the country, see what juries think about their drug. If this happens, it might take longer to force a settlement."

Even David, with a fine law degree and five years of experience, was beginning to believe Wally knew what he was talking about. The junior partner went on, "If a settlement occurs, and we certainly believe it will happen, the death cases will be negotiated first. Then Varrick will be desperate to settle all of the non-death cases, folks like you."

"I'm a non-death case?" she asked, confused.

"For now. The scientific evidence is not clear, but there appears to be a decent chance that Krayoxx is responsible for heart damage in many people who are otherwise healthy." How anyone could look at Iris Klopeck and deem her healthy was mind-blowing, at least to David.

"Mercy," she said as her eyes watered. "That's all I need—more heart problems."

"Don't worry about it now," Wally said, without the slightest trace of reassurance. "We'll get to your case later. The important thing is to get Percy signed up. You're his widow and his principal heir; therefore, you need to hire me and act as his representative." He produced a folded sheet of paper from his rumpled jacket and spread it before Iris. "This is a contract for legal services. You've signed one before, for the divorce, when you and Percy came to my office."

"I don't remember signing one," she said.

"We have it on file. You need to sign a new one before I can handle your claim against Varrick."

"And you're sure this is all legal and everything?" she asked, hesitant, uncertain.

It struck David as odd that the potential client would ask the lawyer if the document was "legal." Wally, though, did not inspire a sense of strict ethical standards. Her question did not faze him.

"All of our Krayoxx clients are signing these," he said, fudging a bit because Iris would technically be the first in her class to sign up. There were other fish in the pond, but no one had actually signed such a contract.

She read it and signed it.

As Wally stuffed it back into his pocket, he said, "Now, listen, Iris. I need your help. I need for you to scope out other Krayoxx cases. Friends, family members, neighbors, anyone else who may have been injured by this drug. Our firm is offering a referral fee of $500 for a death case and $200 for a non-death case. Cash."

Her eyes were suddenly dry. They narrowed, then a tiny smile formed at the corners of her lips. She was already thinking of others.

David managed to maintain a lawyerly frown as he scribbled useless drivel on a legal pad and tried to digest what he was hearing. Was this ethical? Legal? Cash bribes to bring in more cases?

"Do you happen to know of another death case involving Krayoxx?" Wally asked.

Iris almost said something but held her tongue. It was obvious she had a name. "Five hundred bucks, huh?" she said, her eyes suddenly darting from David's to Wally's.

"That's the deal. Who is it?"

"There's a man two blocks over, used to play poker with Percy, croaked last year in the shower two months after my Percy passed. I know for a fact he was on Krayoxx."

Wally's eyes were wild. "What's his name?"

"You said cash, right? Five hundred cash. I'd like to see it, Mr. Figg, before I give you another case. I sure need it."

Stung for a second, Wally rallied with a convincing lie. "Well, normally we make a withdrawal from the firm's litigation account, keeps the bean counters happy, you know?"

She folded her stump-like arms across her chest, stiffened her spine, narrowed her eyes, and said, "Fine. Go make your withdrawal and bring me the cash. Then I'll give you the name."

Wally was reaching for his wallet. "Well, I'm not sure I have that much cash on me. David, how liquid are you?"

David instinctively reached for his wallet. Iris watched with great suspicion as the lawyers scrambled to find cash. Wally produced three $20 bills and a $5 bill and looked hopefully at David, who found $220 in assorted denominations. If they had not stopped by Abner's to pay the tab, they could have come within $15 of covering Iris's referral fee.

"I thought lawyers had plenty of money," Iris observed.

"We keep it in the bank," Wally shot back, unwilling to concede an inch. "Looks like we have about $285. I'll stop by tomorrow with the rest."

Iris was shaking her head no.

"Come on, Iris," Wally pleaded. "You're now our client. We're on the same team. We're talking about a huge settlement one day, and you won't trust us with two hundred bucks?"

"I'll take an IOU," she said.

At this point, David preferred to stand his ground, show some pride, rake the cash off the table, and say good-bye. But David was anything but sure-footed, and he knew it was not his call. Wally, on the other hand, was a rabid dog. He quickly scribbled an IOU on his legal pad, signed his name, and slid it across the table. Iris read it slowly, disapproved, then handed it to David. "You sign it too," she said.

For the first time since his great escape, David Zinc questioned his wisdom. Approximately forty-eight hours earlier, he had been working on a complicated repackaging of high-grade bonds being sold by the government of India. All told, the deal involved around $15 billion. Now, in his new life as a street lawyer, he was being bullied by a four-hundred-pound woman who was demanding his signature on a worthless piece of paper.

He hesitated, took a deep breath, shot Wally a look of sheer bewilderment, then signed his name.

The run-down neighborhood got dramatically worse the deeper they drove into it. The "two blocks over" Iris had mentioned was more like five blocks, and by the time they found the house and parked on the street in front of it, David was worried about their safety.

The tiny home of the widow Cozart was a fortress—a small brick house on a narrow lot lined with eight-foot chain-link fencing. According to Iris, Herb Cozart was at war with the black teenage thugs who roamed the streets. He spent most of his days sitting on the front porch holding a shotgun, glaring at the punks and cursing them if they got too close. When he died, someone tied party balloons along the fence. Someone else tossed a string of firecrackers onto the front lawn in the middle of the night. Mrs. Cozart was planning to move, according to Iris.

As David turned off the ignition, he looked down the street and said, "Oh, boy."

Wally froze, looked in the same direction, and said, "This could be interesting."

Five black males, teenagers, all dressed in the appropriate rapper garb, had noticed the shiny Audi and were giving it the once-over from fifty yards away.

"I think I'll stay with the car," David said. "You can handle this one by yourself."

"Good call. I'll make it quick." Wally jumped out with his briefcase. Iris had called ahead, and Mrs. Cozart was standing on the porch.

The gang was moving toward the Audi. David locked the doors and thought of how nice it would be to have a pistol of some variety, just for protection. Something to show the boys so they would take their fun and games elsewhere. But armed only with a cell phone, he stuck it to his ear and pretended to be in deep conversation as the gang moved closer and closer. They surrounded the car, chatting nonstop, though David could not understand what they were saying. Minutes passed as David waited for a brick to crash through a window. They regrouped at the front bumper, and all five leaned back casually, as if they owned the car and needed to use it as a resting place. They rocked it gently, careful not to scratch or damage it. Then one of them lit a joint, and they passed it around.

David thought about starting the engine and attempting to drive away, but that would create several problems, not the least of which was poor Wally getting stranded. He thought about lowering a window and engaging the boys in friendly banter, but they did not appear friendly at all.

From the corner of his eye, David saw Mrs. Cozart's front door fly open and Wally storm out of the house. Wally reached into his briefcase, yanked out a very large black handgun, and yelled, "FBI! Get off the damn car!" The boys were too startled to move, or to move quickly enough, so Wally aimed at the clouds and fired a shot that sounded like a cannon. The five bolted, scattered, vanished.

Wally stuffed the pistol into his briefcase and jumped into the car. "Let's get outta here," he said.

David was already accelerating.

"Punks," Wally hissed.

"Do you always carry a gun?" David asked.

"I have a permit. Yes, I always carry a gun. In this business, you might need one."

"Do most lawyers carry guns?"

"I don't care what most lawyers do, okay? It's not my job to protect most lawyers. I've been mugged twice in this city, so I ain't getting mugged again."

David slid around a curve and sped through the neighborhood.

Wally continued, "Crazy woman wanted some money. Iris, of course, called and said we were coming over, and of course she told Mrs. Cozart about the referral fee, but since the old gal is nuts, all she heard was the part about the five hundred bucks."

"Did you sign her up?"

"No. She demanded cash, which is pretty stupid because Iris should know that she took all our cash."

"Where are we going now?"

"To the office. She wouldn't even tell me her husband's date of death, so I figure we'll run a search and find out. Why don't you do that when we get to the office?"

"But he's not our client."

"No, he's dead. And since his wife is crazy, and I mean this woman is really nuts, we can get a court-appointed administrator to approve his lawsuit. More ways than one to skin a cat, David. You'll learn."

"Oh, I'm learning. Isn't it against the law to discharge a firearm within the city limits?"

"Well, well, they did teach you something at Harvard. Yes, that's true, and it's also against the law to discharge a firearm with a bullet that goes into the head of another person. It's called murder, and it happens at least once a day here in Chicago. And since there are so many murders, the police are overworked and have no time to fool with firearms that discharge bullets that fly harmlessly through the air. You thinking about turning me in or something?"

"No. Just curious. Does Oscar carry a gun?"

"I don't think so, but he keeps one in a desk drawer. Oscar was assaulted once, in his office, by an irate divorce client. It was a simple no-fault divorce, uncontested on all issues, and Oscar somehow found a way to lose the case."

"How do you lose an uncontested divorce?"

"I don't know, but don't ask Oscar, okay? It's still a touchy subject. Anyway, he told the client that they would have to refile and go through the entire process again, and the client went crazy, beat the hell out of Oscar."

"Oscar looks like he can take care of himself. The guy must've been a bad dude."

"Who said it was a guy?"

"A woman?"

"Yep. A very large and angry woman, but a woman nonetheless. She got the drop on him by throwing her coffee cup—ceramic, not paper—and hitting him between the eyes. Then she grabbed his umbrella and started flailing away. Fourteen stitches. Vallie Pennebaker was her name, never forget her."

"Who broke it up?"

"Rochelle finally got back there—Oscar swears she took her time—and she pulled Vallie off and settled her down. Then she called the cops, and they hauled Vallie away, charged her with aggravated assault. She countered with a lawsuit for malpractice. Took two years and probably five thousand bucks to get it all settled. Now Oscar keeps a piece in his desk."

What would they think at Rogan Rothberg? David asked himself. Lawyers carrying guns. Lawyers claiming to be FBI agents and firing into the air. Lawyers being bloodied by unhappy clients.

He almost asked Wally if he'd ever been assaulted by a client, but bit his tongue and let it pass. He thought he knew the answer.

CHAPTER 12

They returned to the apparent safety of the office at 4:30. The printer was spitting out sheets of paper. Rochelle was at the table sorting and arranging stacks of letters. "What did you do to DeeAnna Nuxhall?" she growled at Wally.

"Let's just say her divorce has been postponed until she can find a way to pay her lawyer. Why?"

"She's called here three times, crying and carrying on. Wanted to know what time you'd be back. Really wants to see you."

"Good. That means she found the money."

Wally was scanning a letter from a stack on the table. He handed one to David, who took it and began reading. He was immediately hooked by the opening: "Beware of Krayoxx!"

"Let's start signing," Wally said. "I want these in the mail this afternoon. The clock is ticking."

The letters were on Finley & Figg stationery and sent by the Honorable Wallis T. Figg, Attorney and Counselor-at-Law. After the "Sincerely" sign-off, there was room for only one signature. "What am I supposed to do here?" David asked.

"Start signing my name," Wally replied.

"I'm sorry."

"Start signing my name. What, do you think I'm signing all three thousand of these?"

"So, I'm forging your name?"

"No. I hereby give you the authority to sign my name on these letters," Wally said slowly, as if speaking to an idiot. Then he looked at Rochelle and said, "And you too."

"I've already signed a hundred," she said as she handed another letter to David. "Look at that signature. A first grader could do better." And she was right. The signature was an effortless scrawl that began with a wavy roll that was probably meant to be a *W* and then spiked dramatically for either the *T* or the *F*. David picked up one of the letters Wally had just signed and compared his signature with Rochelle's forgery. They were slightly similar, but both were illegible and indecipherable.

"Yes, this is pretty bad," David observed.

"It doesn't matter what you fling down, can't nobody read it anyway," she added.

"I think it's very distinguished," Wally said, signing away. "Now, can we all get busy?"

David sat down and began experimenting with his scrawl. Rochelle was folding, stuffing, and putting on stamps. After a few minutes, David asked, "Who are these people?"

"Our client database," Wally replied with great importance. "Over three thousand names."

"Going back how far?"

"About twenty years," Rochelle said.

"So, some of these folks have not been heard from in many years, right?"

"That's right," she said. "Some are probably dead; some moved away. A lot of these folks won't be too happy to get a letter from Finley & Figg."

"If they're dead, let's hope Krayoxx got 'em," Wally blurted and followed it with a loud laugh. Neither David nor Rochelle saw the humor. A few minutes passed without a word. David was thinking about his room upstairs and all the work it needed. Rochelle was watching the clock, waiting on 5:00 p.m. Wally was happily casting a wider net for new clients.

"What kind of a response do you expect?" David asked. Rochelle rolled her eyes as if to say "Zero."

Wally paused for a second and shook the stiffness out of his signing hand. "Great question," he admitted, then rubbed his chin and gazed at the ceiling as if only he could answer such a complex question. "Let's assume that 1 percent of the adult population in this country is taking Krayoxx. Now—"

"Where did you get 1 percent?" David interrupted.

"Research. It's in the file. Take it home tonight and learn the facts. So, as I was saying, 1 percent of our pool is about thirty people. If 20 percent of the pool has had problems with heart attacks or strokes, then we're down to about, say, five or six cases. Maybe seven or eight, who knows. And if we believe, as I do, that each case, especially a death, is worth a couple mill, then we're looking at a very nice payday. I get the sense that nobody else around here believes me, but I'm not going to argue."

"I haven't said a word," Rochelle replied.

"Just curious. That's all," David said. A couple of minutes passed, then he asked, "So when do we file some big lawsuit?"

Wally, the expert, cleared his throat in preparation for a mini-seminar. "Very soon. We have Iris Klopeck signed up, so we could file tomorrow if we wanted. I plan to get Chester Marino's widow on board as soon as the funeral is over. These letters go out today; the phones'll start ringing in a day or so. With some luck, we might have half a dozen cases in hand within a week, then we'll file. I'll start drafting the lawsuit tomorrow. It's important to file quickly in these mass tort cases. We'll drop the first bomb here in Chicago, get the headlines, and every person on Krayoxx will toss the drug and give us a call."

"Oh, brother," Rochelle said.

" 'Oh, brother' is right. Wait till we get around to the settlement, and I'll show you another 'Oh, brother.' "

"State or federal court?" David asked, quick to throttle the bickering.

"Good question, and I'd like for you to research the issue. If we go into state court, we can also sue the doctors who prescribed Krayoxx to our clients. That's more defendants, but also more high-powered defense lawyers causing trouble. Frankly, there's enough money at Varrick Labs to make us all happy, so I'm inclined to keep the doctors out of it. On the federal side, because the Krayoxx litigation will go nationwide, we can plug into the mass tort network and ride their coattails. No one really expects these cases to go to trial, and when the settlement negotiations begin, we need to be hooked in with the big boys."

Again, Wally sounded so knowledgeable that David wanted to believe him. But he'd already been at the firm long enough to know that Wally had never handled a mass tort case. Nor had Oscar.

Oscar's door opened, and he emerged with his usual frown and look of fatigue. "What the hell is this?" he said pleasantly. No one responded. He walked to the table, picked up a letter, then dropped it. He was about to say something when the front door burst open and a tall, thick, burly, tattooed Philistine stomped in and yelled at the entire room, "Which one is Figg!?"

With no hesitation, Oscar and David and even Rochelle pointed at Wally, who was wild-eyed and frozen. Behind the intruder was a tart in a yellow dress, DeeAnna Nuxhall from divorce court, and she yelled, "That's him, Trip, the short fat one!"

Trip went straight for Wally as if he might kill him. The rest of the firm scrambled away from the table, leaving Wally to fend for himself. Trip made a couple of fists, hovered over Wally, and said, "Look, Figg, you little weasel! We're getting married Saturday, so my girl here needs her divorce tomorrow. What's the problem?"

Wally, still seated and hunkering down in anticipation of a beating, said, "Well, I would like to get paid."

"She promised to pay you later, didn't she?"

"I sure did," DeeAnna added helpfully.

"If you touch me, I'll have you arrested," Wally said. "You can't get married if you're in jail."

"I told you he was a smart-ass," DeeAnna said.

Because he needed to hit something but was not quite ready to slap Wally around, Trip backhanded a stack of Krayoxx letters and sent them flying. "Get the divorce, okay, Figg! I'll be there tomorrow, in court, and if my girl doesn't get her divorce then, I'll stomp your chubby little ass right there in the courtroom."

"Call the police," Oscar barked at Rochelle, who was too frightened to move.

Trip needed something with more drama, so he grabbed a thick law book off the table and tossed it through a front window. Glass shattered and rattled across the porch. AC yelped but retreated to a hiding place under Rochelle's desk.

Trip's eyes were shiny and glazed. "I'll snap your neck, Figg. You got that?"

"Hit him, Trip," DeeAnna urged.

David glanced at the sofa and saw Wally's briefcase. He eased closer to it.

"We'll be in court tomorrow, Figg. You gonna be there?" Trip took another step closer. Wally braced for the assault. Rochelle moved in the direction of her desk, and this upset Trip. "Don't move! You're not calling the cops!"

"Call the police," Oscar barked again, but made no effort to do so himself. David inched closer to the briefcase.

"Talk to me, Figg," Trip demanded.

"He embarrassed me in open court," DeeAnna whined. It was obvious she wanted bloodshed.

"You're a slimeball, Figg, you know that?"

Wally was about to say something clever when Trip finally made contact. He pushed Wally, a rather benign little shove that seemed tame in light of the buildup, but it was an assault nonetheless. "Hey, watch it!" Wally barked, slapping at Trip's hand.

David quickly opened the briefcase and withdrew the long black .44 Magnum Colt. He was not certain if he had ever touched a revolver, and he wasn't sure he could do so now without blowing his hand off, but he knew to avoid the trigger. "Here, Wally," he said as he placed the gun on the table. Wally snatched it and jumped from his chair, and the rules of engagement changed dramatically.

Trip blurted "Holy shit!" in a high-pitched voice and took a long step back. DeeAnna ducked behind him, whimpering. Rochelle and Oscar were as stunned as Trip was by the weapon. Wally did not aim the gun at anyone, not directly anyway, but he handled it in such a way that there was little doubt he could and would unload a few rounds in a matter of seconds.

"First, I want an apology," he said as he moved toward Trip, who had lost his swagger. "You got a lotta balls coming in here and making demands when your girl there won't pay her bills."

Trip, who no doubt had some experience in handguns, stared at the Colt and said meekly, "Yeah, sure, you're right, man."

"Call the police, Ms. Gibson," Wally said, and she dialed 911. AC poked his head out and growled at Trip.

"I want three hundred bucks for the divorce and two hundred bucks for the window," Wally demanded. Trip was still backing away, with DeeAnna practically unseen behind him.

"Be cool, man," Trip said, both palms facing Wally.

"Oh, I'm very cool."

"Do something, baby," DeeAnna said.

"Like what? You see the size of that thing?"

"Can't we just get outta here?" she asked.

"No," Wally replied. "Not until the cops get here." He raised the gun a few inches, careful not to point it directly at Trip.

Rochelle backed away from her desk and went to the kitchen.

"Be cool, man," Trip pleaded. "We're leaving."

"No you're not."

The police arrived in minutes. Trip was handcuffed and placed in the backseat of a patrol car. DeeAnna cried without effect, then she tried flirting with the cops, and this proved slightly more useful. In the end, though, Trip was hauled away to face charges of assault and vandalism.

When the excitement was over, Rochelle and Oscar went home, leaving Wally and David to sweep up the broken glass and finish signing the Krayoxx letters. They worked for an hour, mindlessly signing Wally's name and also discussing what to do about the broken window. It could not be replaced until the following day, and the office wouldn't survive the night with a missing window. Preston wasn't a dangerous neighborhood, but no one left keys in cars or doors unlocked. Wally had just made the decision to sleep at the office, on the sofa, next to the table, with AC nearby and the Colt within reach, when the front door swung open and dear DeeAnna popped in for the second time.

"What are you doing here?" Wally demanded.

"We need to talk, Wally," she said in a voice that was unsteady and much softer. She sat in a chair near Rochelle's desk and crossed her legs in such a way as to leave most of the flesh exposed. She had very nice legs and was wearing the same hooker's heels she had displayed in court that morning.

"Ooh la la," Wally said under his breath. Then, "And what would you like to talk about?" he asked.

"I think she's been drinking," David whispered as he kept signing.

"I'm not sure I should marry Trip," she announced.

"He's a brute, a real loser, DeeAnna. You can do better than that."

"But I really want my divorce, Wally, can't you help me out here?"

"Then pay me."

"I can't get the money before court tomorrow. I swear that's the truth."

"Then too bad."

David decided that, had the case been his, he would do whatever necessary to get the divorce so DeeAnna and Trip would be history. An extra $300 wasn't worth all the hassle.

She recrossed her legs, and her skirt inched up even higher. "I was thinking, Wally, that maybe we could make some other arrangements. You know, just me and you."

Wally sighed, looked at the legs, thought for a second, and said, "Can't do it. I gotta stay here tonight because some jackass knocked out the front window."

"Then I'll stay too," she cooed, licking her bright red lips.

Wally had never possessed the willpower to run from these situations, not that he encountered them all the time. Seldom had a client been so open and obvious. In fact, he could not, at that dreadful yet thrilling moment, remember one being so easy. "We might work something out," he said, leering at DeeAnna.

"I'm outta here," David said, jumping to his feet and grabbing his briefcase.

"You can hang around," she said.

The visual was instantaneous and ugly—happily married David romping around with a cute slut who'd had as many divorces as her chubby and naked lawyer. David ran for the door and slammed it behind him.

The favorite late-night bistro was within walking distance of their home in Lincoln Park. They had often met there for a quick dinner just before the kitchen closed at eleven, just as David staggered home from another crushing day at the office. Tonight, though, they arrived before nine and found the place bustling. Their table was in a corner.

At some point, about halfway through his five-year career at Rogan Rothberg, David had adopted the policy of not discussing his work, of never bringing it home. It was so unpleasant and distasteful, and boring to boot, he simply could not dump it on Helen. She happily went along with this policy, and so they usually talked about her studies or what their friends were doing. But things were suddenly different. The big firm was gone, as were the faceless clients and their tedious files. Now David worked with real people who did incredible things that had to be retold in great detail. Take, for example, the two near gunfights David had survived with his sidekick, Wally. At first, Helen flatly refused to believe that Wally had actually fired a shot in the air to scatter the street thugs, but she eventually softened under David's relentless narrative. Nor did she believe the Trip story on the first telling. She was equally skeptical of the Wally–Judge Bradbury shakedown of DeeAnna Nuxhall in open court. She was incredulous that her husband would fork over all of his cash to Iris Klopeck, then sign an IOU for more. Oscar getting mauled by an angry (female) divorce client was slightly more believable.

Saving the best for last, David wrapped up his unforgettable first day at Finley & Figg with: "And, dear, even as we speak, Wally and DeeAnna are naked on the sofa having a romp with the window open and the dog watching and the unpaid fee getting satisfied in spectacular fashion."

"You're lying."

"I wish. The $300 will be forgiven, and DeeAnna will be divorced by noon tomorrow."

"What a sleazeball."

"Which one?"

"How about both? Do most of your clients pay this way?"

"I doubt it. I mentioned Iris Klopeck. I suspect she's more in line with the firm's client profile. The fee couch couldn't hold up under the pounding."

"You can't work for these people, David. Come on. Quit Rogan if you want, but let's find a different firm somewhere. These two clowns are a couple of crooks. What about ethics?"

"I doubt if they spend much time discussing ethics."

"Why not look for a nice midsized firm somewhere, with nice people who don't carry guns and chase ambulances and swap labor for sex?"

"What's my specialty, Helen?"

"Something to do with bonds."

"Right. I know a lot about high-yield, long-term bonds issued by foreign governments and corporations. That's all I know about the law because that's all I've done for the past five years. Put that on a résumé, and the only people who might call are a handful of eggheads at other large firms, just like Rogan, who might be in need of someone like me."

"But you can learn."

"Of course I can, but no one will hire a five-year lawyer at a nice salary and put him in kindergarten. They demand experience, and I don't have it."

"So Finley & Figg is the only place you can work?"

"Or someplace like it. I'll treat it like a seminar for a year or two, then maybe open my own shop."

"Great. One day on the job and you're already thinking about leaving."

"Not really. I love the place."

"You've lost your mind."

"Yes, and it's so liberating."

CHAPTER 13

Wally's mass-mailing scheme proved futile. Half of the letters were returned by the postal service for a variety of reasons. Phone traffic spiked a bit in the week that followed, though most of the calls were from former clients who demanded to be removed from Finley & Figg's mailing list. Undaunted, Wally filed a lawsuit in the U.S. District Court for the Northern District of Illinois, naming Iris Klopeck and Millie Marino, as well as "others to be named later," and claimed their loved ones had been killed by the drug Krayoxx, manufactured by Varrick Labs. Throwing darts, Wally asked for an even $100 million in total damages, and he demanded a trial by jury.

The filing was not nearly as dramatic as he wished. He tried desperately to attract the media to the lawsuit he was brewing, but there was little interest. Instead of simply filing it online, he and David, both dressed in their finest dark suits, drove to the Everett M. Dirksen U.S. Courthouse in downtown Chicago and hand delivered the twenty-page lawsuit to the clerk. There were no reporters and no photographers, and this upset Wally. He harangued a deputy clerk into snapping a photograph of the two grim-faced lawyers as they filed the lawsuit. Once back at the office, he e-mailed the lawsuit and the photograph to the *Tribune*, the *Sun-Times*, the *Wall Street Journal*, *Time*, *Newsweek*, and a dozen other publications.

David prayed the photograph would go unnoticed, but Wally got lucky. A reporter from the *Tribune* called the office and was immediately put through to an ecstatic Attorney Figg. The avalanche of publicity began.

On the front page of Section B the following morning, a headline read: "Chicago Attorney Attacks Varrick Labs over Krayoxx." The article summarized the lawsuit and said local attorney Wally Figg was a "self-described mass tort specialist." Finley & Figg was a "boutique firm" with a long history of fighting big drug companies. The reporter, though, did some sniffing and quoted two well-known plaintiffs' lawyers as saying, in effect, we've never heard of these guys. And there was no record of similar lawsuits filed by Finley & Figg during the past ten years. Varrick responded aggressively by defending its product, promising a vigorous defense, and "looking forward to a fair trial before an impartial jury to clear our good name." The reproduced photograph was rather large. This tickled Wally and embarrassed David. They were quite a pair: Wally was balding, rotund, and badly dressed, while David was taller, trimmer, and much younger looking.

The story went wild on the Internet, and the phone rang nonstop. At times, Rochelle was overwhelmed and David helped out. Some of the callers were reporters, others were lawyers sniffing around for information, but most were Krayoxx users who were terrified and confused. David wasn't sure what to say. The firm's strategy, if it could be called that, was to pick through the net and take the death cases, then at some undefined point in the future corral the "non-death" clients and lump them into a class action. This was impossible to explain over the phone because David didn't quite grasp it himself.

As the phones rang and the excitement continued, even Oscar came out of his office and showed some interest. His little firm had never seen such activity, and, well, maybe this was indeed their big moment. Maybe Wally was finally right about something. Maybe, just maybe, this could lead to real money, which meant at long last the divorce he so fervently wanted, followed immediately by retirement.

The three lawyers met at the table late in the day to compare notes. Wally was wired, even perspiring. He waved his legal pad in the air and said, "We got four death cases here, brand-new ones, and we gotta sign 'em up right now. Are you in, Oscar?"

"Sure, I'll take one," Oscar said, trying to appear reluctant as always.

"Thank you. Now, Ms. Gibson, there's a black lady who lives on Nineteenth, not far from you, Bassitt Towers, number three. She says it's safe."

"I will not go to Bassitt Towers," Rochelle said. "I can practically hear the gunfire from my apartment."

"That's my point. It's right down the street from you. You could stop by on the way home."

"I will not."

Wally slammed his legal pad onto the table. "Can't you see what's happening here, damn it? These people are begging us to take their cases, cases that are worth millions of bucks. There could be a huge settlement within a year. We're on the verge of something big here, and you, as always, couldn't care less."

"I will not risk my neck for this law firm."

"Great. So when Varrick settles and the cash pours in, you will forgo your share of the bonus. That's what you're telling us?"

"What bonus?"

Wally walked to the front door and back to the table, pacing. "Well, well, how quickly we forget. Remember the Sherman case last year, Ms. Gibson? Nice little car wreck, a rear-ender. State Farm paid sixty grand. We took a third, a nice fee of twenty thousand for good ol' Finley & Figg. We paid some bills. I took seven grand, Oscar took seven, and we gave you a thousand bucks cash under the table. Didn't we, Oscar?"

"Yes, and we've done it before," Oscar said.

Rochelle was calculating as Wally was talking. It would be a shame to miss a piece of the lottery. What if Wally was right for a change? He shut up, and things were quiet and tense for a moment as the air cleared. AC rose to his feet and began growling. Seconds passed, then the distant sound of an ambulance could be heard. It grew louder, but, oddly, no one moved to the window or to the front porch.

Had they already lost interest in their bread and butter? Had the little boutique firm suddenly outgrown car wrecks and moved on to a far more lucrative field?

"How much of a bonus?" she asked.

"Come on, Ms. Gibson," Wally said, exasperated. "I have no idea."

"What do I tell this poor woman?"

Wally picked up his legal pad. "I talked to her an hour ago, name's Pauline Sutton, age sixty-two. Her forty-year-old son, Jermaine, died of a heart attack seven months ago, said he was a bit on the heavy side, took Krayoxx for four years to lower his cholesterol. A charming lady but also a grieving mother. Take one of our brand-new Krayoxx contracts for legal services, explain it to her, sign her up. Piece of cake."

"What if she has questions about the lawsuit and settlement?"

"Make an appointment and get her in here. I'll answer her questions. What's important is getting her signed up. We've created a hornet's nest here in Chicago. Every half-assed ambulance chaser in the business is now loose on the streets looking for Krayoxx victims. Time is of the essence. Can you do it, Ms. Gibson?"

"I suppose."

"Thank you so much. Now, I suggest we all hit the streets."

Their first stop was an all-you-can-eat pizza house not far from the office. The restaurant was owned by a chain, a somewhat infamous company that was suffering through a firestorm of bad press caused entirely by its menu. A leading health magazine had analyzed its food and declared it all hazardous and unfit for human consumption. Everything was drenched with grease, oils, and additives, and no effort was made to cook anything even remotely healthy. Once the food was ready, it was served buffet style and offered at ridiculously low prices. The chain had become synonymous with hordes of morbidly obese people feeding at its buffet troughs. Profits were soaring.

The assistant manager was a plump young man named Adam Grand, and he asked them to wait ten minutes before he could take a break. David and Wally found a booth as far away from the buffet tables as possible, which wasn't far at all. The booth was roomy and wide, and David realized that everything in the place was oversized—plates, glasses, napkins, tables, chairs, booths. Wally was on his cell phone, eagerly lining up another meeting with a potential client. David could not help but watch the enormous people digging through piles of thick pizza. He almost felt sorry for them.

Adam Grand slid in beside David and said, "You got five minutes. My boss is yelling back there."

Wally wasted no time. "You told me on the phone that your mother died six months ago, heart attack. She was sixty-six and took Krayoxx for a couple of years. How about your father?"

"Died three years ago."

"Sorry. Krayoxx, perhaps?"

"No, colon cancer."

"Brothers, sisters?"

"One brother who lives in Peru. He will not be involved in any of this."

David and Wally were scribbling away. David felt as though he should say something important, but had nothing on his mind. He was there as the chauffeur. Wally was about to ask another question when Adam threw a curveball. "Say, I just talked to another lawyer."

Wally's spine straightened; his eyes widened. "Oh, really. What's his name?"

"He said he was a Krayoxx expert, and he could get us a million bucks, no sweat. Is that true?"

Wally was ready for combat. "He's lying. If he promised you a million bucks, then he's an idiot. We can't promise anything in the way of money. What we can promise is that we'll provide the best legal representation you can find."

"Sure, sure, but I like the idea of a lawyer telling me how much I might get, know what I mean?"

"We can get you a lot more than a million bucks," Wally promised.

"Now we're talking. How long will this take?"

"A year, maybe two," Wally promised again. He was sliding across a contract. "Look this over. It's a contract between our firm and you as the legal representative of your mother's estate." Adam scanned it quickly and said, "Nothing up front, right?"

"Oh no, we front the litigation expenses."

"Forty percent for you guys is pretty steep."

Wally was shaking his head. "That's the industry average. All standard. Any lawyer doing mass torts who's worth his salt is getting 40 percent. Some want 50, but not us. I think 50's unethical." He looked at David for confirmation, and David nodded and frowned at the thought of those shady lawyers out there who possessed questionable ethics.

"I guess so," Adam said, then signed his name. Wally snatched the contract and said, "Great, Adam, good move and welcome aboard. We'll add this case to our lawsuit and kick things into high gear. Any questions?"

"Yeah, what should I tell this other lawyer?"

"Tell him you went with the best, Finley & Figg."

"You're in good hands, Adam," David said solemnly, and immediately realized he sounded like a bad commercial. Wally shot him a look that said, "Seriously?"

"I guess that remains to be seen, doesn't it?" Adam said. "We'll know when the big check gets here. You promised more than a million, Mr. Figg, and I take you at your word."

"You won't be sorry."

"See you," Adam said and disappeared.

Wally was stuffing his legal pad into his briefcase when he said, "That was easy."

"You just guaranteed the guy something over a million. Is that wise?"

"No. But if that's what it takes, then that's what it takes. Here's how it works, young David. You sign 'em up, get 'em on board, keep 'em happy, and when there's money on the table, they'll forget about what you said up front. Say, for example, a year from now Varrick gets sick of its Krayoxx mess and throws in the towel. Let's say our new pal Adam here is due less than a million, pick a number—$750,000. Now, do you really believe that loser will walk away from that much money?"

"Probably not."

"Exactly. He'll be one happy boy, and he'll forget about anything we said today. That's how it works." Wally took a long, hungry look at the buffet bars. "Say, you got plans for dinner? I'm starving."

David had no plans, but he would not be eating there. "Yeah, my wife's waiting for a late snack."

Wally looked again at the troughs and the hulking masses of people grazing there. He froze for a second, then cracked a smile. "What a great idea," he said, complimenting himself.

"I'm sorry."

"Look at those people. What's the average weight?"

"I have no idea."

"Neither do I, but if I'm a bit pudgy at 240, those folks are well over 400 pounds."

"You're losing me, Wally."

"Look at the obvious, David. This place is packed with grossly overweight people, half of whom are probably on Krayoxx. I'll bet if I yelled out right now, 'Who's on Krayoxx?' half of these poor bastards would raise their hands."

"Don't do that."

"I'm not, but don't you see my point?"

"You want to start handing out cards?"

"No, smart-ass, but there must be a way to screen these people for Krayoxx users."

"But they're not dead yet."

"It won't be long. Look, we can add them to our second lawsuit of non-death cases."

"I'm missing something here, Wally. Help me. Aren't we required to prove, at some point, that the drug actually causes some type of damage?"

"Sure, and we'll prove it later when we hire our experts. Right now, the important thing is to get everybody signed up. It's a horse race out here, David. We gotta figure out a way to screen these folks and sign them up."

Six o'clock was approaching, and the restaurant was packed. David and Wally had the only booth not being used for dinner. A large family of four approached, each holding two platters of pizza. They stopped at the booth and cast menacing looks at the two lawyers. This was serious business.

Their next stop was a duplex in a neighborhood near Midway Airport. David parked at the curb, behind an ancient Volkswagen Beetle on blocks. Wally was saying, "Frank Schmidt, age fifty-two when he succumbed last year to a massive stroke. I spoke with his widow, Agnes." But David was only half listening. He was trying to convince himself that he was really doing this—scrambling around the rough spots of Chicago's Southwest Side with his new boss, who couldn't drive because of problems, after dark, on the lookout for street thugs, knocking on strange doors of untidy homes, not knowing what was inside, all in an effort to hustle clients before the next lawyer came along. What would his friends from Harvard Law think about it? How hard would they laugh? But David decided he really didn't care. Any law job was better than his old one, and most of his friends from law school were miserable. He, on the other hand, had been liberated.

Agnes Schmidt was either hiding or not at home. No one came to the door, and the two lawyers hurried away. As he drove, David said, "Look, Wally, I really would like to get home and see my wife. I haven't seen her much in the past five years. Time to catch up."

"She's very cute. I don't blame you."

CHAPTER 14

Within a week of filing its lawsuit, the firm had a total of eight death cases, a respectable number and one that would certainly make them rich. Because Wally said it so often, it had become the accepted belief that each case meant roughly half a million dollars in net fees to Finley & Figg. His math was shaky and riddled with assumptions that had little basis in reality, at least at such a preliminary stage of the litigation, but the three lawyers and Rochelle began to think in terms of that kind of money. Krayoxx was making news around the country, none of it positive, and its future looked ominous, as far as Varrick Labs was concerned.

The firm had worked so hard to get the cases, it was a shock to realize they could actually lose one. Millie Marino arrived at the office one morning in a foul mood and demanded to see Mr. Figg. She had hired him to probate her husband's estate, and then she had reluctantly agreed to pursue a Krayoxx claim for his death. In Wally's office, behind closed doors, she explained she could not resolve the fact that one lawyer in the firm—Oscar—had prepared a will that kept a sizable asset—the baseball card collection—out of her reach, and now the other lawyer—Wally—was probating that same will. This, in her opinion, was a glaring conflict of interest, and downright sleazy to boot. She was upset and began crying.

Wally tried to explain that lawyers are bound by rules of confidentiality. When Oscar prepared the will, he had to do what Chester wanted, and since Chester wanted his baseball cards hidden until after his death, then given to his son, Lyle, so be it. Ethically, Oscar could not divulge any information to anyone about Chester and his will.

Millie didn't see it that way. As his wife, she had a right to know about all of his assets, especially something as valuable as his cards. She had already talked to a dealer, and the Shoeless Joe card alone was worth at least $100,000. The entire collection might fetch $150,000.

Wally really didn't give a damn about the baseball cards, or the estate for that matter. The $5,000 fee he had once contemplated was now peanuts. He had a Krayoxx case on the line here, and he would say or do anything to keep it. "Frankly," he said gravely as he glanced at his door, "between the two of us, I would have handled it differently, but Mr. Finley comes from the old school."

"Meaning what?" she asked.

"He's pretty chauvinistic. The husband is the head of the house, keeper of all assets, the only decision maker, you know the type. If the man wants to hide things from his wife, nothing wrong with that. Me, I'm much more liberated." He followed this with a nervous laugh that was confusing.

"But it's too late," she said. "The will has been written. Now it's going to probate."

"True, Millie, but things will work out. Your husband left his baseball cards to his son, but he left you with a beautiful lawsuit."

"A beautiful what?"

"You know, the Krayoxx thing."

"Oh, that. Yes, I'm not too happy with that either. I've talked to another lawyer, and he says you're in over your head, says you've never handled a case like this."

Wally gasped for air, then managed to ask, in a squeaky voice, "Why are you talking to other lawyers?"

"Because he called me the other night. I checked him out online. He's in a big firm with offices all over the country, and all they do is sue drug companies. I'm thinking about hiring him."

"Don't do that, Millie. These guys are famous for signing up a thousand cases, then screwing their clients. You'll never talk to him again, just some young paralegal in the back room. It's a scam, I swear it is. You can always get me on the phone."

"I don't want to talk to you on the phone, or in person either." She was on her feet, gathering her handbag.

"Please, Millie."

"I'll think about it, Figg, but I'm not happy."

Ten minutes after she left, Iris Klopeck called and asked to borrow $5,000 against her portion of the Krayoxx settlement. Wally sat at his desk with his head in his hands and wondered what might happen next.

Wally's lawsuit was assigned to the Honorable Harry Seawright, a Reagan appointee who had been on the federal bench for almost thirty years. He was eighty-one, anticipating retirement, and not too excited about a lawsuit that could take a few years to resolve and eat up his calendar in the process. But he was curious. His favorite nephew had been taking Krayoxx for several years, with great success and no side effects at all. Not surprisingly, Judge Seawright had never heard of the law firm of Finley & Figg. He directed his law clerk to check out the firm, and the clerk's e-mail read: "A 2 man ham and egg operation on Preston, Southwest Side; advertises for quickie divorces, DUIs, the usual criminal, domestic, injury practice; no record of any filings in federal court in the past 10 years; no record of jury trials in state court in past 10 years, no bar association activity; they do occasionally go to court—Figg has either 2 or 3 DUIs in past 12 years; firm was once sued for sexual harassment, settled."

Seawright was incredulous. He e-mailed his clerk: "These guys have no trial experience, yet they filed a $100 million lawsuit against the third-largest pharmaceutical company in the world?"

The clerk responded: "Correct."

Judge Seawright: "Insane! What's behind this?"

The clerk: "Krayoxx stampede. It's the latest and hottest bad drug in the country; mass tort bar is in frenzy. Finley & Figg probably hopes to ride coattails all the way to a settlement."

Judge Seawright: "Keep digging."

Later the clerk responded: "The lawsuit is signed by Finley & Figg, but also a third lawyer—David E. Zinc, former associate at Rogan Rothberg; I called a friend there—said Zinc cracked up, bolted ten days ago, somehow landed out there at FF; no litigation experience; guess he found the right place."

Judge Seawright: "Let's watch this case closely."

The clerk: "As always."

Varrick Labs was headquartered in a baffling series of glass and steel buildings in a forest near Montville, New Jersey. The complex was the work of a once famous architect who had since repudiated his own design. It was occasionally praised as daring and futuristic, but much more often it was denounced as drab, hideous, bunker-like, Soviet style, and a lot of other unkind words. In several ways it resembled a fortress, surrounded by trees, away from the traffic and crowds, protected. Because Varrick got sued so often, its headquarters seemed fitting. The company was hunkered down out there in the woods, braced for the next assault.

Its CEO was Reuben Massey, a company man who had led Varrick for many years, through turbulent times, and always to impressive profits. Varrick was in a constant state of war with the mass tort bar, and while other pharmaceuticals wilted or folded under waves of litigation, Massey managed to keep his stockholders happy. He knew when to fight, when to settle, how to settle cheap, and how to appeal to the lawyers' greed while saving his company tons of money. During his term, Varrick had survived (1) a $400 million settlement for a denture cream that caused zinc poisoning; (2) a $450 million settlement for a stool softener that backfired and clogged things up; (3) a $700 million settlement for a blood thinner that cooked a bunch of livers; (4) a $1.2 billion settlement for a migraine remedy that allegedly caused high blood pressure; (5) a $2.2 billion settlement for a high blood pressure pill that allegedly caused migraines; (6) a $2.3 billion settlement for a painkiller that was instantly addictive; and, worst of all, (7) a $3 billion settlement for a diet pill that caused blindness.

It was a long, sad list, and Varrick Labs had paid dearly in the court of public opinion. Reuben Massey, though, continually reminded his troops of the hundreds of innovative and effective drugs they created and sold to the world. What he did not talk about, except in the boardroom, was the fact that Varrick had profited from every drug that had been targeted by the plaintiffs' lawyers. So far, the company had won the battle, even after forking over huge settlements.

Krayoxx, however, could be different. There were now four lawsuits; the first one in Fort Lauderdale, the second in Chicago, and now two new ones in Texas and Brooklyn. Massey closely monitored the workings and dealings of the mass tort bar. He spent time each day with his in-house lawyers, studying the lawsuits, reading the bar journals and newsletters and blogs, and talking to his lawyers in big firms across the country. One of the most revealing signals in any looming war was TV advertising. When the lawyers began bombarding the airwaves with their sleazy, get-rich-quick come-ons, Massey knew Varrick was in for another expensive brawl.

Krayoxx ads were popping up everywhere. The frenzy had begun.

Massey had worried about a few of Varrick's other targets. The migraine pill was a huge blunder, and he still cursed himself for ramming it through research and approvals. The blood thinner almost got him fired. But he had never doubted Krayoxx, nor would he ever. Varrick had spent $4 billion developing the drug. It had been tested extensively in clinical trials in third-world countries; the results had been spectacular. Its research was thorough and immaculate. Its pedigree was flawless. Krayoxx caused no more strokes and heart attacks than the daily vitamin pill, and Varrick had a mountain of research to prove it.

The daily legal briefing was held at precisely 9:30 in the Varrick boardroom on the fifth floor of a building that resembled a Kansas wheat silo. Reuben Massey was a stickler for punctuality, and his eight in-house lawyers were in their seats by 9:15. The team was led by Nicholas Walker, a former U.S. attorney, former Wall Street litigator, and the current mastermind behind every defense Varrick erected to protect itself. When the lawsuits began dropping like cluster bombs, Walker and Reuben Massey spent hours together, coolly responding, analyzing, scheming, and directing counterattacks when necessary.

Massey entered the room at 9:25, picked up an agenda, and said, "What's the latest?"

"Krayoxx or Faladin?" Walker asked.

"Gee, I almost forgot about Faladin. Let's stick to Krayoxx for the moment." Faladin was an antiwrinkle cream that was allegedly causing wrinkles, according to a few loudmouthed lawyers on the West Coast. The litigation had yet to gain momentum, primarily because the lawyers were finding it difficult to measure wrinkleness, before and after.

Nicholas Walker said, "Well, the gates are open. Snowball's rolling down the mountain. Pick your metaphor. All hell's breaking loose. I chatted with Alisandros at Zell & Potter yesterday, and they're getting flooded with new cases. He plans to push hard to establish multidistrict in Florida and keep his finger on things."

"Alisandros. Why do the same thieves show up at every heist?" Massey asked. "Haven't we paid them enough over the past twenty years?"

"Evidently not. He's built his own golf course, for Zell & Potter lawyers only and a few lucky friends, and he invited me to come down and play. Eighteen holes."

"Please go, Nick. We need to see how wisely our money is being invested by these thugs."

"Will do. I got a phone call late yesterday afternoon from Amanda Petrocelli in Reno, says she's hooked her a few death clients, putting together a class, and will file suit either today or tomorrow. I told her it really didn't matter to us when she filed suit. We can expect more filings this week and next."

"Krayoxx is not causing strokes and heart attacks," Massey said. "I believe in this drug."

The eight lawyers nodded their heads in agreement. Reuben Massey was not one to make bold statements or false claims. He had doubts about Faladin, and Varrick would eventually settle for a few million, long before a trial.

Number two on the legal team was a woman named Judy Beck, another veteran of the mass tort wars. She said, "All of us feel the same, Reuben. Our research is better than theirs, if they actually have any. Our experts are better. Our proof is better. Our lawyers will be better. Perhaps it's time we counterattack and throw everything we have at the enemy."

"My thoughts exactly, Judy," Massey said. "You guys have a strategy?"

Nicholas Walker said, "It's evolving, but for now we go through the same motions, make the same public comments, watch and wait and see who files what and where. We look at the lawsuits, study the judges and the jurisdictions, and we pick our spot. When the stars are all aligned—the right plaintiff, the right city, the right judge—then we hire the hottest gunslinger in town and push hard for a trial."

"This has backfired, you know," Massey said. "Don't forget Klervex. That cost us two billion." Their miracle blood pressure pill was destined for greatness until thousands of its users developed horrific migraines. They—Massey and the lawyers—believed in the drug and rolled the dice with the first jury trial, which they fully expected to win in a slam dunk. An overwhelming victory would dampen the tort bar's enthusiasm and save Varrick a ton of money. The jury, though, felt otherwise and gave the plaintiff $20 million.

"This is not Klervex," Walker said. "Krayoxx is a much better drug, and the lawsuits are much weaker."

"I agree," Massey said. "I like your plan."

CHAPTER 15

At least twice a year, and more often if possible, the Honorable Anderson Zinc and his lovely wife, Caroline, drove from their home in St. Paul to Chicago to see their only son and his lovely wife, Helen. Judge Zinc was the chief justice of the Supreme Court of Minnesota, a position he had been honored to hold for fourteen years. Caroline Zinc taught art and photography at a private school in St. Paul. Their two younger daughters were still in college.

Judge Zinc's father, and David's grandfather, was a legend named Woodrow Zinc, who at the age of eighty-two was still hard at work managing the two-hundred-lawyer firm he'd founded fifty years earlier in Kansas City. The Zincs had deep roots in that city, but not deep enough to keep Anderson Zinc and his son from fleeing the harshness of working for old Woodrow. They wanted no part of his firm and left Kansas City, and this had caused a rift that was just beginning to mend.

Another rift was brewing. Judge Zinc did not understand his son's sudden career change and wanted to get to the bottom of it. He and Caroline arrived in time for a late lunch on Saturday afternoon and were pleasantly surprised to see their son at home. He was usually at the office, downtown in a tall building. On a visit the previous year, they had never actually laid eyes on him. He came home after midnight on a Saturday, then left to return to the office five hours later.

Today, though, he was on a ladder cleaning the gutters. He jumped down and hurried to greet them. "You look great, Mom," he said as he lifted her up and spun her around.

"Put me down," she said. David shook hands with his father, but there was no hug. The Zinc men did not hug each other. Helen appeared from the garage and greeted her in-laws. She and David were both grinning goofily about something. He finally said, "We have some big news."

"I'm pregnant!" Helen blurted.

"You two geezers are about to be grandparents," David said.

Judge and Mrs. Zinc took the news well. They were, after all, in their late fifties and many of their friends were already grandparents. Helen was thirty-three, two years older than David, and, well, it was certainly about time, wasn't it? They digested this amazing news, rallied nicely, then offered congratulations and wanted details. Helen gabbed away as David unloaded their luggage and everyone moved inside.

Over lunch, the baby talk eventually subsided, and Judge Zinc finally got down to business. "Tell me about your new firm, David," he said. David knew damn well his father had dug and dug and found what little there was to know about Finley & Figg.

"Oh, Andy, don't start that," Caroline said, as if "that" were a raw subject that should be avoided. Caroline agreed with her husband and believed David had made a serious mistake, but the news of Helen's pregnancy had changed everything, for the future grandmother anyway.

"I told you on the phone," David said quickly, anxious to have this discussion and get it over with. He was also prepared to defend himself, to fight if necessary. His father chose a career that was not what old Woodrow wanted. David had now done the same.

"It's a small two-man firm with a general practice. Fifty hours a week, which gives me time to fool around with my wife and keep the family name going. You should be proud."

"I'm delighted Helen is expecting, but I'm not sure I understand your decision. Rogan Rothberg is one of the most prestigious law firms in the world. They've trained judges, legal scholars, diplomats, and leaders of business and government. How can you just walk away from that?"

"I didn't walk away, Dad, I ran. And I'm not going back. I hate the memories of Rogan Rothberg, and I think even less of the people."

They were eating as they spoke. Things were cordial. Andy had promised Caroline he would not provoke a fight. David had promised Helen he would not engage in one.

"So, this new firm has two partners?" the judge asked.

"Two partners and now three lawyers. Plus Rochelle, the secretary, receptionist, office manager, and a lot of other things."

"Support staff? Clerks, paralegals, interns?"

"Rochelle handles all that. It's a small firm where we do most of our own typing and research."

"He's actually home for dinner," Helen added. "I've never seen him so happy."

"You look great," Caroline said. "Both of you."

The judge was not accustomed to being outnumbered or out-flanked. "These two partners, are they trial lawyers?"

"They claim to be, but I have my doubts. They're basically a couple of ambulance chasers who advertise a lot and survive on car wrecks."

"What made you choose them?"

David glanced at Helen, who looked away with a smile. "That, Dad, is a long story that I will not bore you with."

"Oh, it's not boring," Helen said, barely suppressing laughter.

"What kind of money do they make?" the judge asked.

"I've been there three weeks. They have not shown me the books, but they're not getting rich. And I'm sure you wanna know how much I'm making. Same answer. I don't know. I get a piece of what I bring in the door, and I have no idea what might walk in tomorrow."

"And you're starting a family?"

"Yes, and I'll be home for dinner with my family, and T-ball, and

Cub Scouts and school plays and all the other wonderful stuff parents are supposed to do with their kids."

"I was there, David, I missed very little."

"Yes, you were, but you never worked for a sweatshop like Rogan Rothberg."

A pause as everybody took a breath. David said, "We saved a lot. We'll survive nicely, just wait and see."

"I'm sure you will," his mother said, switching sides completely and now fully aligned against her husband.

"I haven't started the nursery yet," Helen said to Caroline. "If you'd like, we can go to a great shop around the corner and look at wallpaper."

"Perfect."

The judge touched the corners of his mouth with a napkin and said, "Associate boot camp is just part of the routine these days, David. You survive that, make partner, and life is good."

"I didn't sign up for the Marines, Dad, and life is never good at a huge law firm like Rogan because the partners never make enough money. I know these partners. I've seen them. For the most part, they're great lawyers and miserable people. I've quit. I'm not going back. Drop it." It was the first flash of anger during lunch, and David was disappointed in himself. He drank some mineral water and took a bite of chicken salad.

His father smiled, took a bite himself, and chewed for a long time. Helen asked about David's two sisters, and Caroline jumped at the chance to change the subject.

Over dessert, his father asked pleasantly, "What type of work are you doing?"

"Lots of good stuff. This week I prepared a will for a lady who's hiding her assets from her children. They suspect she inherited some money from her third husband, which she did, but they can't seem to find it. She wants to leave everything to her FedEx deliveryman. I represent a gay couple who are trying to adopt a child in Korea. I have two deportation cases involving illegal Mexicans who were caught in a drug ring. I represent the family of a fourteen-year-old girl who's been hooked on crack for two years and there's no place to lock her up for rehab. A couple of drunk-driving clients."

"Sounds like a bunch of riffraff," the judge observed.

"No, actually, they're real people with real problems who need help. That's the beauty of street law—you meet the clients face-to-face, you get to know them, and, if things work out, you get to help them."

"If you don't starve."

"I'm not going to starve, Dad, I promise. Besides, these guys do hit the jackpot every now and then."

"I know, I know. I saw them when I was practicing, and I see their cases now on appeal. Last week, we affirmed a $9 million jury verdict, a terrible case involving a brain-damaged kid who got lead poisoning from some toys. His lawyer was a sole practitioner who did a DUI for the mother. He got the case, called in a gunslinger to try it, now they're splitting 40 percent of $9 million."

Those numbers bounced around the table for a few minutes. "Coffee, anyone?" Helen asked. They all declined and moved to the den. After a few moments, Helen and Caroline left to inspect the guest room that was about to become a nursery.

When they were out of range, the judge mounted his final assault. "One of my law clerks came across a story about the Krayoxx litigation. Saw your picture online, the one from the *Tribune*, with Mr. Figg. Is he a straight-up guy?"

"Not really," David admitted.

"Doesn't look like."

"Let's just say that Wally's complicated."

"I'm not sure your career will be advanced if you hang around with these guys."

"You could be right, Dad, but for now I'm having fun. I look forward to getting to the office. I enjoy my clients, the few that I have, and I am enormously relieved to be out of the sweatshop. Just relax a bit, okay? If this doesn't work out, I'll try something else."

"How did you get involved in this Krayoxx litigation?"

"We found some cases." David smiled at the thought of his father's reaction if he told the truth about their search for clients. Wally and his .44 Magnum. Wally offering cash bribes for client referrals. Wally hitting the funeral home circuit. No, there were things the judge should never know.

"Have you researched Krayoxx?" the judge asked.

"I'm in the process. Have you?"

"Yes, as a matter of fact. The TV ads are running in Minnesota. The drug is getting a lot of attention. Looks like another mass tort scam to me. Pile on the lawsuits until the drugmaker is facing bankruptcy, then broker a huge settlement that makes the lawyers richer and allows the manufacturer to stay in business. Lost in the shuffle is the issue of liability, not to mention what's best for the clients."

"That's a pretty fair summary," David admitted.

"So you're not sold on the case?"

"Not yet. I've plowed through a thousand pages, and I'm still looking for the smoking gun, the research to prove that the drug hurts people. I'm not sure it does."

"Then why did you put your name on the lawsuit?"

David took a deep breath and thought for a moment. "Wally asked me, and since I'm new at the firm, I felt an obligation to join the fun. Look, Dad, there are some very powerful lawyers around the country who have filed this same lawsuit and who believe this is a bad drug. Wally does not inspire a lot of confidence, but other lawyers do."

"So you're just riding their coattails?"

"Hanging on for dear life."

"Don't get hurt."

The women were back and organizing a shopping trip. David jumped to his feet and claimed to be infatuated with wallpaper. The judge reluctantly tagged along.

David was almost asleep when Helen rolled over and said, "Are you awake?"

"I am now. Why?"

"Your parents are funny."

"Yes, and it's time for my parents to go home."

"That case your father mentioned, about the little boy and the lead poisoning—"

"Helen, it's five minutes after midnight."

"The lead came from a toy, and it caused brain damage, right?"

"As I recall, yes. Where is this going, dear?"

"There's a lady in one of my classes, Toni, and we had a quick sandwich last week in the student union. She's a few years older, kids in high school, and she has a housekeeper who is from Burma."

"This is fascinating. Can we get some sleep?"

"Just listen. The housekeeper has a grandson, a little boy, who's in the hospital right now with brain damage. He's comatose, on a respirator, things are desperate. The doctors suspect it's lead poisoning, and they've asked the housekeeper to search high and low for lead. One source might be the child's toys."

David sat up in bed and switched on a lamp.

CHAPTER 16

Rochelle was at her desk diligently tracking news of a bed linen sale at a nearby discount house when the call came. A Mr. Jerry Alisandros from Fort Lauderdale wanted to speak with Mr. Wally Figg, who was at his desk. She routed the call through and returned to her online work.

Moments later, Wally strutted out of his office with his patented look of self-satisfaction. "Ms. Gibson, could you check flights to Las Vegas this weekend, leaving midday Friday?"

"I suppose. Who's going to Las Vegas?"

"Well, who else has asked about going to Vegas? Me, that's who. There's an unofficial meeting of Krayoxx lawyers this weekend at the MGM Grand. That was Jerry Alisandros on the phone. Maybe the biggest mass tort operator in the country. Says I need to be there. Is Oscar in?"

"Yes. I think he's awake."

Wally tapped on the door as he shoved it open. He slammed it behind himself. "Come right in," Oscar said as he pulled himself away from the paperwork littering his desk.

Wally fell into a large leather chair. "Just got a call from Zell & Potter in Fort Lauderdale. They want me in Vegas this weekend for a Krayoxx strategy meeting, off the record. All the big boys will be there to plan the attack. It's crucial. They'll discuss multi-district litigation, which lawsuit goes first, and, most important, settlement. Jerry thinks that Varrick might want a quick endgame on this one." Wally was rubbing his hands together as he spoke.

"Jerry?"

"Alisandros, the legendary tort lawyer. His firm made a billion off Fen-Phen alone."

"So you want to go to Las Vegas?"

Wally shrugged as if he could take it or leave it. "I don't care anything about going, Oscar, but it's imperative that someone from our firm show up at the table. They might start talking money, settlement, big bucks, Oscar. This thing could be closer than we realize."

"And you want the firm to pay for your trip to Vegas?"

"Sure. It's a legitimate litigation expense."

Oscar ruffled through a pile of papers and found what he wanted. He lifted it and sort of waved it at his junior partner. "Have you seen David's memo? It came in last night. The one about the projected costs of our Krayoxx litigation."

"No, I didn't know he was—"

"The guy's very bright, Wally. He's doing the homework that you should be doing. You need to take a look at this because it's scary as hell. We need at least three experts on board now, not next week. In fact, we should've had them lined up before you filed suit. The first expert is a cardiologist who can explain the cause of death of each of our beloved clients. Estimated cost to hire one is $20,000, and that's just for the initial evaluation and deposition. If the cardiologist testifies at trial, add another $20,000."

"It's not going to trial."

"That's what you keep saying. Number two is a pharmacologist who can explain to the jury in great detail exactly how the drug killed our clients. What did it do to their hearts? This guy is even pricier— $25,000 initially and the same if he testifies at trial."

"That sounds high."

"All of it sounds high. Number three is a research scientist who can present to the jury the findings of his study that will show, by a preponderance of the evidence, that statistics prove you're much likelier to suffer heart damage while taking Krayoxx than some other cholesterol drug."

"I know just the guy."

"Is it McFadden?"

"That's him."

"Great. He wrote the report that started this frenzy, and now he's a bit reluctant to get involved in the litigation. However, if a law firm will fork over an initial retainer of $50,000, he might favor the law firm with a lending hand."

"That's outrageous."

"It's all outrageous. Please look at David's memo, Wally. He summarizes the backlash against McFadden and his work. There are some serious doubts about whether this drug actually causes harm."

"What does David know about litigation?"

"What do we know about litigation, Wally? You're talking to me, your longtime partner, not some prospective client. We bark and growl about hauling bad guys into the courtroom, but you know the truth. We always settle."

"And we're going to settle now, Oscar. Trust me. I'll know a whole lot more when I get back from Vegas."

"How much will that cost?"

"Peanuts, in the scope of things."

"We're in over our heads, Wally."

"No, we're not. We'll piggyback with the big boys and make a fortune, Oscar."

Rochelle found a much cheaper room at the Spirit of Rio Motel. The photos on its Web site were of stunning views of the Vegas Strip, and it was easy to get the impression that its guests were in the thick of things. They were not, as Wally realized when the airport shuttle van finally stopped. The tall, sleek casino-hotels were visible, but fifteen minutes away. Wally cursed Rochelle as he waited in the sauna-like lobby to check in. A standard room at the MGM Grand was $400 a night. At this dump it was $125, a two-night savings that almost covered his airfare. Pinching pennies while waiting on a fortune, Wally told himself as he climbed two flights of stairs to his rather small room.

He couldn't rent a car because of his DUI conviction and lack of a valid license. He asked around and learned that another shuttle ran from the Spirit of Rio to the Strip every thirty minutes. He played dollar slots in the lobby and won $100. Maybe this was his lucky weekend.

The shuttle was packed with overweight retirees. Wally couldn't find a seat, so he stood, clutched the handrails, rocked along in bodily contact with sweaty people, and, as he glanced around, he wondered how many might be Krayoxx victims. High cholesterol was definitely on display. He had business cards in his pockets, as always, but he let it pass.

He roamed the casino for a while, watching closely as an astonishing variety of people played blackjack, roulette, and craps, games he'd never played and had no desire to try now. He killed some time at a slot machine and twice said no thanks to a comely cocktail waitress. Wally was beginning to realize that a casino was a lousy place for a recovering drunk. At 7:00 p.m., he found his way to a banquet room on the mezzanine. Two security guards blocked the door, and Wally was relieved when they found his name on the list. Inside, there were two dozen or so well-dressed men, and three women, engaged in light chatter over drinks. A buffet dinner was being arranged along a far wall. Some of the lawyers knew each other, but Wally was not the only rookie in the crowd. They all seemed to recognize his name, and they all knew about his lawsuit. Before long, he was beginning to fit in. Jerry Alisandros sought him out, and they shook hands like old friends. Others crowded around, then little pockets of conversation peeled off here and there. They talked about lawsuits, politics, the latest in private jets, homes in the Caribbean, and who was getting divorced and remarried. Wally had little to add, but he gamely hung on and proved to be a good listener. Trial lawyers prefer to do all the talking, and at times they all talked at once. Wally was happy to just grin, listen, and sip his club soda.

After a quick dinner, Alisandros stood and began the conversation. The plan was to meet at nine the following morning, in the same room, and get down to business. They should be finished by noon. He had spoken several times with Nicholas Walker at Varrick, and obviously the company was shell-shocked. In its long and colorful history of litigation, it had never been hit so fast and so hard with so many lawsuits. It was scrambling to get some sense of the damage. According to experts hired by Alisandros, the potential pool of injured or dead could be as high as half a million.

This news—of so much misery and suffering—was well received around the table.

The potential cost to Varrick, according to yet another expert hired by Alisandros, was at least $5 billion. Wally was fairly certain he was not the only one at the table who did a quick multiplication: 40 percent of $5 billion. The others, though, seemed to take it all in stride. Another drug, another war with Big Pharma, another massive settlement that would make them even richer. They could buy more jets, more homes, more trophy wives, assets Wally cared nothing for. All he wanted was a chunk in the bank, enough cash to make life enjoyable and free from the daily grind.

In a roomful of considerable egos, it was only a matter of time before someone else wanted the floor. Dudley Brill, from Lubbock, boots and all, plunged into the retelling of a recent conversation with a high-ranking Varrick defense lawyer in Houston, who strongly implied that the company had no plans to settle until after the drug's liability was tested before a few juries. Therefore, based on Brill's analysis of a conversation no one else in the room knew about, he was of the firm opinion that he, Dudley Brill of Lubbock, Texas, should lead the first trial, and do so in his hometown, where the jurors had proven they loved him and would fork over huge sums if he asked for them. Brill had obviously been drinking, as had everybody else but Wally, and his self-serving analysis touched off a furious debate around the dinner table. Before long, several skirmishes were under way, with tempers flaring and insults being traded.

Jerry Alisandros managed to bring order. "I was hoping we could save all of this for tomorrow," he said diplomatically. "Let's retire now, go to our separate corners, and come back tomorrow all sobered up and rested."

From the looks of things the following morning, not all of the trial lawyers went to their rooms and to bed. Puffy eyes, red eyes, hands grabbing cold water and coffee—the signs were there. There was no shortage of hangovers. There were not as many lawyers either, and as the morning dragged on, Wally began to realize a lot of business had been conducted over drinks late the night before. Deals had been cut, alliances forged, backs stabbed. Wally wondered where he stood.

Two experts talked about Krayoxx and the most recent studies. Each lawyer spent a few minutes talking about his or her lawsuit—number of clients, number of potential client deaths versus injuries, judges, opposing counsel, and verdict trends in the jurisdiction. Wally winged it nicely and said as little as possible.

An incredibly boring expert dissected the financial health of Varrick Labs and deemed the company fit enough to sustain huge losses from a Krayoxx settlement. The word "settlement" was used frequently and was always ringing in Wally's ears. The same expert became even more tedious when analyzing the various insurance coverages Varrick had in force.

After two hours, Wally needed a break. He eased out and went to find a restroom. When he returned, Jerry Alisandros was waiting outside the door. "When are you headed back to Chicago?" he asked.

"In the morning," Wally replied.

"Flying commercial?"

Of course, Wally thought. I do not have my own jet, so like most poor Americans I'm forced to pay for a ticket on a jet owned by someone else. "Sure," he said with a smile.

"Look, Wally, I'm headed to New York this afternoon. Why don't you hitch a ride? My firm just bought a brand-new Gulfstream G650. We'll have lunch on the plane and drop you off in Chicago."

There would be a price to pay, a deal to be cut, but Wally was looking for one anyway. He had read about rich trial lawyers and their private jets, but it had never crossed his mind that he would see the inside of one. "That's very generous," he said. "Sure."

"Meet me in the lobby at 1:00 p.m., okay?"

"You got it."

There were a dozen or so private jets lined up on the deck at McCarran Field's general aviation center. As Wally followed his new pal Jerry past them, he wondered how many were owned by the other mass tort boys. When they got to Jerry's, he climbed the steps, took a breath, then stepped inside the gleaming G650. A striking Asian girl took his coat and asked what he wanted to drink. Just club soda.

Jerry Alisandros had a small entourage with him—an associate, two paralegals, and an assistant of some kind. They huddled briefly in the rear of the cabin as Wally settled into the rich leather seat and thought about Iris Klopeck and Millie Marino, and those wonderful widows whose dead husbands had led Wally into the world of mass torts, and now to this. The flight attendant handed Wally a menu. Down the aisle, far away, he could see a kitchen with a chef, just waiting. As they taxied, Jerry made his way to the front and sat down opposite Wally. "What do you think?" he asked, raising his hands to take in his latest toy.

"Sure beats commercial," Wally said. Jerry howled with laughter—no doubt the funniest thing he'd ever heard.

A voice announced takeoff, and they all buckled their seat belts. As the jet left the runway and shot upward, Wally closed his eyes and tried to savor the moment. It might never happen again.

As soon as they began to level off, Jerry came to life. He popped a switch and pulled a mahogany table out of the wall. "Let's talk business," he said.

It's your plane, Wally thought. "Sure."

"How many cases do you realistically expect to sign up?"

"We might get ten death cases; we have eight now. Non-death, I'm not sure. We have a pool of several hundred potential cases, but we haven't screened them yet." Jerry frowned as if this weren't enough, not worth his time. Wally wondered if he might order the pilot to turn around or open a hatch somewhere.

"Have you thought about teaming up with a bigger firm?" Jerry asked. "I know you guys don't do a lot of mass tort work."

"Sure, I'm open to that discussion," Wally replied, trying to conceal his excitement. That had been his plan since the beginning. "My contracts provide for a contingency fee of 40 percent. How much do you want?"

"In our typical deal, we front the expenses, and these are not cheap cases. We find the doctors, experts, researchers, whomever, and they cost a fortune. We take half the fee, 20 percent, but the expenses are paid back to us before any split of the fee."

"That sounds fair. What's our role in this?"

"Simple. Find more cases, death and non-death. Round 'em up. I'll send a draft of an agreement on Monday. I'm trying to piece together as many cases as possible. The next big step is the creation of an MDL—multi-district litigation. The court will appoint a plaintiff's trial committee, usually five or six seasoned lawyers who will control the litigation. That panel is entitled to an additional fee, usually around 6 percent, and this comes off the top and out of the lawyers' portion."

Wally was nodding along. He'd done some research and knew the ins and outs, most of them. "Will you be on the trial committee?" he asked.

"Probably, I usually am."

The flight attendant brought fresh drinks. Jerry took a sip of wine and continued. "When discovery starts, we'll send someone to help with the depositions of your clients. No big deal. Pretty routine legal work. Keep in mind, Wally, that the defense firms see this as a gold mine too, so they work the cases hard. I'll find a cardiologist we can trust, one who'll screen your clients for damage. We'll pay him out of the litigation fund. Any questions?"

"Not now," Wally said. He was not pleased to be giving away half the fee, but he was delighted to be in business with an experienced and deep-pocketed tort firm. There would still be plenty of money for Finley & Figg. He thought of Oscar and couldn't wait to tell him about the G650.

"What's your best guess for the timeline?" Wally asked. In other words, when can I expect some money?

A long, satisfying pull of the wine, and, "Based on my experience, which, as you know, Wally, is quite vast, I expect we'll reach a settlement in twelve months and start disbursing money right away. Who knows, Wally, in a year or so you might have your own airplane."

CHAPTER 17

Nicholas Walker flew with Judy Beck and two other Varrick lawyers to Chicago on one of the company's corporate jets, a Gulfstream G650 that was just as new as the one that had so thoroughly impressed Wally. The purpose of their trip was to fire their old law firm and hire a new one. Walker and his boss, Reuben Massey, had hammered out the details of a master plan to deal with their Krayoxx mess, and the first major battle would take place in Chicago. First, though, they had to get the right people in place.

The wrong people belonged to a firm that had represented Varrick Labs for a decade, and their work had always been considered top-notch. Their shortcoming was not their fault. According to the exhaustive research done by Walker and his team, there was another firm in the city with closer ties to Judge Harry Seawright. And this firm happened to have a partner who was the hottest defense lawyer in town.

Her name was Nadine Karros, a forty-four-year-old litigation partner who had not lost a jury trial in ten years. The more she won, the more difficult her cases became, and the more impressive her victories. After chatting with dozens of attorneys who had faced her in court, and lost, Nick Walker and Reuben Massey decided that Ms. Karros would lead the defense of Krayoxx. And they didn't care what it would eventually cost.

First, though, they had to convince her. During a long teleconference, she had seemed ambivalent about taking charge of a major case that was expanding daily. Not surprisingly, she already had too much work on her desk; her trial calendar was booked; and so on. She had never been involved in a mass tort case, though as a pure litigator this was not much of an obstacle. Walker and Massey knew her recent string of courtroom wins included a wide range of issues—groundwater contamination, hospital negligence, the midair collision of two commuter planes. As an elite courtroom advocate, Nadine Karros could handle any case before any jury.

She was a partner in the litigation section of Rogan Rothberg, on the eighty-fifth floor of the Trust Tower, with a corner office with a view of the lake, though she seldom enjoyed it. She met the Varrick crew in a large conference room on the eighty-sixth floor, and after everyone had a quick gawk at Lake Michigan, they settled in for what was expected to be a two-hour meeting, minimum. On her side of the table, Ms. Karros had the usual complement of young associates and paralegals, a veritable entourage of grim-faced minions ready to say "How high?" when she said "Jump!" To her right was a male litigation partner named Hotchkin, her right-hand man.

Later, in a phone call to Reuben Massey, Nicholas Walker would report, "She's very attractive, Reuben, long dark hair, strong chin and teeth, beautiful hazel eyes that are so warm and inviting you think this is the woman I want to take home to meet Momma. A very pleasant personality, quick with a nice smile. A deep, rich voice like one you'd expect from an opera singer. Easy to see why jurors are so taken with her. But she's tough, no doubt about that, Reuben. She takes charge and gives orders, and you get the impression that those around her are fiercely loyal. I'd hate to face this woman in court, Reuben."

"So, she's the one?" Reuben asked.

"No question. I found myself looking forward to the trial, just to watch her in action."

"Legs?"

"Oh yes. The package. Slender, dressed like something out of a magazine. You should meet her as soon as possible."

It was her turf, so Ms. Karros quickly assumed control of the meeting. She nodded to Hotchkin and said, "Mr. Hotchkin and I presented your proposal to our Fee Committee. My rate will be $1,000 an hour out of court, $2,000 in court, with an initial retainer of $5 million, nonrefundable of course."

Nicholas Walker had been negotiating fees with elite lawyers for two decades, and he was shockproof. "And how much for the other partners?" he asked calmly, as if his company could handle anything she threw at them, which in fact it could.

"Eight hundred an hour. Five hundred for associates," she replied.

"Agreed," he said. Everyone in the room knew the cost of defense would run into the millions. In fact, Walker and his team had already pegged their initial estimate at $25 to 30 million. Peanuts, when you're getting sued for billions.

With the air clear on what it would cost, they moved on to the next important matter. Nicholas Walker had the floor. "Our strategy is simple and it's complicated," he began. "Simple, in that we pick a case from the myriad of those filed against us, an individual case, not a class action, and we push hard for a trial. We want a trial. We are not afraid of a trial, because we believe in our drug. We believe, and we can prove, that the research being relied upon by the tort boys is deeply flawed. We are convinced that Krayoxx does what it is supposed to do, and it does not increase the risks of heart attack or stroke. We are certain of this, so certain that we want a jury, one right here in Chicago, to hear our evidence, and soon. We are confident the jury will believe us, and when the jury rejects the attack on Krayoxx, when the jury finds in our favor, the battlefield will change dramatically. Frankly, we think the tort bar will scatter like leaves in the wind. They'll cave. It might take another trial, another victory, but I doubt it. In short, Ms.

Karros, we hit them hard and fast with a jury trial, and when we win, they'll go home."

She listened without taking notes. When he finished, she said, "Indeed, that's pretty simple, and not altogether original. Why Chicago?"

"The judge. Harry Seawright. We've researched every judge in every Krayoxx case filed so far, and we think Seawright is our man. He's shown little patience for mass torts. He despises frivolous lawsuits and junk filings. He uses his Rocket Docket to ram cases through discovery and get them to trial. He refuses to allow cases to gather dust. His favorite nephew uses Krayoxx. And, most important, his close friend is former U.S. senator Paxson, who now has an office on, I believe, the eighty-third floor here at Rogan Rothberg."

"Are you suggesting we could somehow influence a federal judge?" she asked, with her left eyebrow slightly arched.

"Of course not," Walker said with a nasty grin.

"What's the complicated part of your plan?"

"Deception. We create the impression that we intend to settle the Krayoxx cases. We've been down this road before, believe me, so we know quite a lot about mass settlements. We understand the greed of the tort bar, and it is enormous beyond imagination. Once they believe that billions are about to hit the table, the frenzy will get much worse. With a settlement looming, the preparation for a major trial will become less important. Why bother to prepare when the cases are about to settle? We—you—on the other hand, are working diligently to get ready for the trial. In our scheme, Judge Seawright will crack the whip, and the case will move along quickly. At the perfect moment, the settlement negotiations will collapse, the mass tort bar will be in chaos, and we'll be staring at a trial date that Seawright will refuse to move."

Nadine Karros was nodding, smiling, enjoying the scenario. "I'm sure you have a case in mind," she said.

"Oh yes. There's a local divorce lawyer named Wally Figg who filed the first Krayoxx case here in Chicago. Not much of a lawyer, three-man firm, nickel-and-dime stuff down on the Southwest Side. Almost zero trial experience, and absolutely none in the mass tort arena. Now he's hooked up with a lawyer in Fort Lauderdale named Jerry Alisandros, a longtime nemesis whose goal in life is to sue Varrick at least once a year. Alisandros is a force."

"Can he try a case?" Nadine asked, already thinking about the trial.

"His firm is Zell & Potter, and they have some competent trial lawyers, but they rarely go to trial. Their specialty is forcing companies to settle and raking in enormous fees. At this point, we have no idea who would show up here and actually handle the trial. They might bring in a local lawyer."

To Walker's left, Judy Beck cleared her throat and began, somewhat nervously, "Alisandros has already filed a motion to consolidate every Krayoxx case into an MDL, multi-district litigation, and—"

"We understand MDL," Hotchkin broke in sharply.

"Of course. Alisandros has a favorite federal judge in southern Florida, and his MO is to create the MDL, get himself appointed to the plaintiff's steering committee, then control the litigation. He, of course, receives extra compensation for being on the committee."

Nick Walker took up the narrative. "Initially, we would resist all efforts to consolidate the cases. Our plan is to select one of Mr. Figg's clients and convince Judge Seawright to assign it to his Rocket Docket."

"What if the judge in Florida orders consolidation of all cases and wants them down there?" Hotchkin asked.

"Judge Seawright is a federal judge," Walker said. "The case has been filed in his court. If he wants to try it here, no one, not even the Supreme Court, can order him to do otherwise."

Nadine Karros was scanning a summary that had been passed around by the Varrick team. She said, "So, if I follow things, we select one of Mr. Figg's dead clients, and we convince Judge Seawright to extract this case from the group. Then, assuming the judge goes along, we respond rather softly to the lawsuit, admit nothing, issue bland denials, take an easy approach to discovery because we don't want to slow things down, take a few depositions, give them whatever documents they want, and sort of lead them down the primrose path until they wake up and realize they have a real trial on their hands. Meanwhile, you lull them into a false sense of security with the illusion of another jackpot."

"That's it," Nick Walker said. "Exactly."

They spent almost an hour discussing Mr. Figg's dead clients—Chester Marino, Percy Klopeck, Wanda Grand, Frank Schmidt, and four others. As soon as the lawsuit was properly answered, Ms. Karros and her team would depose the legal representatives of the dead eight. Once they had the opportunity to observe and learn, they would make the decision about which one to isolate and push toward a trial.

The matter of young David Zinc was dealt with quickly. Though he had worked at Rogan Rothberg for five years, he was no longer employed there. No conflict of interest existed because at the time the firm did not represent Varrick, and Zinc did not represent the dead clients. Nadine Karros had never met him; indeed, only one associate on her side of the table could recall ever knowing who he was. Zinc had worked in international finance, a world away from litigation.

Zinc was now working in the world of street law and happy to be even further away from international finance. Very much on his mind these days was the Burmese housekeeper and her lead-poisoned grandson. He had a name, a phone number, and an address, but making contact had proved difficult. Toni, Helen's friend, had suggested to the grandmother that the family consult a lawyer, but this had terrified the poor woman to the point of tears. She was emotionally spent, confused, and, for the moment, unapproachable. Her grandson remained on life support.

David had contemplated running the case by his two partners but quickly thought better of it. Wally might go charging into the hospital room and frighten someone to death. Oscar might insist on taking charge of the case and then want an extra percentage in the event of a settlement. As David was learning, his two partners did not split money equally and, according to Rochelle, fought over fees. Points were given for the lawyer who made initial contact, more for the lawyer who worked up the file, and so on. According to Rochelle, on almost every decent car wreck Oscar and Wally quibbled over the split.

David was at his desk drafting a simple will for a new client—typing it himself because Rochelle had informed him weeks earlier that three lawyers were far too many for one secretary—when his e-mail chimed with a note from the federal court clerk. He opened the e-mail and found an answer to their amended complaint. His eyes went straight to the attorney register, straight to the name of Nadine Karros of Rogan Rothberg, and he felt faint.

David had never met her, but he certainly knew her by reputation. She was famous throughout the entire Chicago bar. She tried and won the biggest cases of all. He had never uttered a recorded word in court. But there they were, names listed together as if they were equals. For the plaintiffs—Wallis T. Figg, B. Oscar Finley, David E. Zinc, of the firm of Finley & Figg, along with S. Jerry Alisandros of the firm of Zell & Potter. And for Varrick Laboratories, Nadine L. Karros and R. Luther Hotchkin of the firm of Rogan Rothberg. On paper, David looked as if he belonged in the game.

He read the answer slowly. The obvious facts were admitted; all liability was denied. Overall, it was a straightforward, almost benign response to a $100 million lawsuit, and it was not what they had antici- pated. According to Wally, the first response from Varrick would be a vicious motion to dismiss, accompanied by a weighty brief prepared by bright Ivy Leaguers who toiled in the firm's research department. The motion to dismiss would cause a significant skirmish, but they would prevail because such motions were rarely granted, according to Wally.

Along with the answer, the defense filed a set of basic interrogatories that sought personal information about each of the eight dead clients and their families, and requested the names and general testimonies of the expert witnesses. As far as David knew, they had yet to hire experts, though Jerry Alisandros was believed to be in charge of that. Ms. Karros also wanted to take the eight depositions as soon as possible.

According to the clerk, a hard copy of the answer and other filings was in the mail.

David heard heavy footsteps on the stairs. Wally's. He lumbered in, panting, and said, "You see what they filed?"

"Just read it," David answered. "Seems rather tame, don't you think?"

"What do you know about litigation?"

"Ouch."

"Sorry. Something's up. I gotta call Alisandros and figure this thing out."

"It's just a simple answer and some discovery. Nothing to panic over."

"Who's panicked? You know this woman—it is your old law firm?"

"Never met her, but she's supposed to be terrific in the courtroom."

"Yeah, well, so is Alisandros, but we ain't going to court." He said this with a noticeable lack of conviction. He left the office mumbling and stomped down the stairs. A month had passed since they had filed the lawsuit, and Wally's dreams of a quick gold strike were fading. It looked as though they would be required to do a little work before the settlement talks began.

Ten minutes later, David received an e-mail from the junior partner. It read: "Can you get started on those interrogatories? I gotta run down to the funeral home."

Sure, Wally. I'd love to.

CHAPTER 18

The minor charges against Trip were eventually dropped due to a lack of interest, though the court did require him to sign a statement promising to stay away from the firm of Finley & Figg and its lawyers. Trip vanished, but his ex-girlfriend did not.

DeeAnna arrived minutes before 5:00 p.m., her usual time. On this day, she was dressed like a cowgirl—skintight jeans, boots with pointed toes, a tight red blouse upon which she had neglected to fasten the top three buttons. "Is Wally in?" she cooed at Rochelle, who couldn't stand her. The cloud of perfume caught up with her and settled into the room, causing AC to sniff, then growl and retreat even farther under the desk.

"He's in," Rochelle said dismissively.

"Thanks, dear," DeeAnna said, trying to irritate Rochelle as much as possible. She strutted to Wally's office and entered without knocking. A week earlier, Rochelle had instructed her to sit and wait like all the other clients. It was becoming apparent, though, that she had far more clout than the other clients, at least as far as Wally was concerned.

Once inside the office, DeeAnna walked into the arms of her lawyer, and after a long kiss with an embrace and the obligatory fondle Wally said, "You look great, baby."

"All for you, baby," she said.

Wally checked to make sure the door was locked, then returned to his swivel chair behind his desk. "I need to make two calls, then we're outta here," he said, drooling.

"Anything, baby," she cooed, then she took a seat and pulled out a celebrity gossip magazine. She read nothing else and was as dumb as a rock, but Wally didn't care. He refused to judge her. She'd had four husbands. He'd had four wives. Who was he to pass judgment? Right now, they were in the process of trying to kill each other in bed, and Wally had never been happier.

Outside, Rochelle was tidying up her desk, anxious to leave now that "that hooker" was in Mr. Figg's office and who knew what they were doing in there. Oscar's door opened, and he emerged, holding some paperwork. "Where's Figg?" he asked, looking at Figg's closed door.

"In there with a client," Rochelle said. "Door's bolted and locked."

"Don't tell me."

"Yep. Third day in a row."

"Are they still negotiating his fee?"

"Don't know. He must've raised it."

Though the fee was small—just a typical no-fault divorce case—Oscar was due a portion of it, but he wasn't sure how to get his split when half was being paid on the sofa. He stared at Wally's door for a moment, as if waiting for the sounds of passion, and, hearing none, turned to Rochelle and waved the papers. "Have you read this?"

"What is it?"

"It's our agreement with Jerry Alisandros and Zell & Potter. Eight pages long, lots of fine print, already signed by my junior partner, obviously without being read in its entirety. Says here that we must contribute $25,000 to help front the litigation expenses. Figg never mentioned this to me."

Rochelle shrugged. It was lawyer business, not hers.

But Oscar was hot. "Further, it says that we get a fee of 40 percent on each case, half of which goes to Zell & Potter. But in the fine print it says that a fee of 6 percent is paid to the Plaintiffs' Litigation Committee, a little bonus to the big shots for their hard work, and the 6 per-cent comes off the top of the settlement and out of our portion. So, as I figure it, we lose 6 percent off the top, and that gives us 34 percent to split with Alisandros, who of course will get a chunk of the 6 percent. Does this make sense to you, Ms. Gibson?"

"No."

"That makes two of us. We're getting screwed right and left, and now we must put up $25,000 for litigation expenses." Oscar's cheeks were red, and he kept looking at Wally's door, but Wally was safe inside.

David came down the steps and walked into the conversation. "Have you read this?" Oscar asked angrily, waving the contract.

"What is it?"

"Our contract with Zell & Potter."

"I looked over it," David said. "It's pretty straightforward."

"Oh, it is? Did you read the part about the $25,000 up-front money for expenses?"

"Yes, and I asked Wally about that. He said we'd probably just go to the bank, hit the firm's line of credit, then pay it back when we settle."

Oscar looked at Rochelle, who looked back at Oscar. Both were thinking, What line of credit?

Oscar started to speak, then abruptly wheeled around and returned to his office, slamming the door after himself. "What's that all about?" David asked.

"We don't have a line of credit," Rochelle said. "Mr. Finley's wor-ried that the Krayoxx litigation will backfire and kill us financially. This wouldn't be the first time one of Figg's schemes blew up in our faces, but it could certainly be the biggest."

David glanced around and took a step closer. "Can I ask you some-thing, in confidence?"

"I don't know," she said, taking a cautious step back.

"These guys have been at this game for a long time. Thirty plus years for Oscar, twenty plus for Wally. Do they have some money stashed away somewhere? You don't see any around the office, so I figured they must have some buried."

Rochelle glanced around too, then said, "I don't know where the money goes when it leaves here. I doubt if Oscar has a dime because his wife spends everything. She thinks she's a cut or two above and wants to play that game. Wally, who knows? I suspect he's as broke as I am. But they do own the building free and clear."

David couldn't help but look at the cracks in the ceiling plaster. Let it go, he told himself.

"Just curious," David said.

There was a shriek of female laughter from deep inside Mr. Figg's office.

"I'm leaving," David said, grabbing his overcoat.

"Me too," Rochelle said.

Everyone was gone when Wally and DeeAnna emerged. They quickly turned off the lights, locked the front door, and got in her car. Wally was delighted to have not only a new squeeze but also one who was willing to drive. He had six weeks left on his suspension, and with Krayoxx so hot he needed to be mobile. DeeAnna had jumped at the chance to earn referral fees—$500 cash for a death case and $200 for a non-death—but what really thrilled her was listening to Wally's predictions of taking down Varrick Labs in a massive settlement that would bring in huge fees for him (and perhaps something for her as well, though this wasn't exactly out in the open yet). More often than not, their pillow talk drifted away to the world of Krayoxx and all it could mean. Her third husband had taken her to Maui, and she loved the beach. Wally had already promised a vacation in paradise.

At that stage of their involvement, Wally would have promised her anything.

"Where to, dear?" she said, racing away from the office. She was a dangerous driver in a little Mazda convertible, and Wally knew his chances would be slim in a collision. "Just take it easy," he said, ratcheting down the seat belt. "Let's go north, toward Evanston."

"Are we hearing from these people?" she asked.

"Oh yes. Lots of phone calls." And Wally wasn't lying—his cell phone rang constantly with inquiries from people who had picked up his little "Beware of Krayoxx!" brochure. He had printed ten thousand and was littering Chicago with them. He tacked them on bulletin boards in Weight Watchers meeting rooms, VFW posts, bingo parlors, hospital waiting rooms, and the restrooms of fast-food restaurants—anywhere the shrewd mind of Wally Figg thought there might be people battling high cholesterol.

"So how many cases do we have?" she asked.

Wally did not miss the "we" part of her question. He wasn't about to tell her the truth. "Eight death cases, several hundred non-death, but they have to be tested first. I'm not sure every non-death case is really a case. Gotta find some damage to the heart before we take on the case."

"How do you do that?" They were flying along the Stevenson, dodging traffic, most of which she didn't appear to notice. Wally was ducking with each near miss. "Take it easy, DeeAnna, we're not in a hurry," he said.

"You're always bitching about my driving," she said as she gave him a long, sad look.

"Just watch the road. And slow down."

She eased off the gas and pouted for a few minutes. "As we were saying, how do you know if these people have been damaged?"

"We'll hire a doctor to screen them. Krayoxx weakens the heart valves, and there are some tests that can tell us if a client has been harmed by the drug."

"How much are the tests?" she asked. Wally was noticing a growing curiosity into the economics of their Krayoxx litigation, and it was slightly irksome.

"About a thousand bucks a pop," he said, though he had no idea. Jerry Alisandros had assured him that Zell & Potter had already retained the services of several doctors who were screening potential clients. These doctors would be made available to Finley & Figg in the near future, and once the testing began, their pool of non-death clients would expand greatly. Alisandros was on a jet every day zipping across the country, meeting with lawyers like Wally, piecing together big lawsuits here and there, hiring experts, plotting trial strategies, and, most important, hammering away at Varrick and its lawyers. Wally felt honored to be a player in such a high-stakes game.

"That's a lot of money," DeeAnna said.

"Why are you so concerned about the money?" Wally snapped, glancing down at her unbuttoned cowgirl shirt.

"I'm sorry, Wally. You know I'm the nosy type. This is all so exciting and stuff, and, well, it'll be so awesome when Varrick starts writing those big checks."

"That could be a long way off. Let's just concentrate on rounding up the clients."

At the Finley home, Oscar and his wife, Paula, were watching a *M★A★S★H* rerun on cable when they were suddenly confronted with the shrill voice and anxious face of a lawyer named Bosch, who was no stranger to cable commercials in the Chicago market. For years, Bosch had been pleading for car wrecks and tractor-trailer accident victims and cases involving asbestos and other products, and now, evidently, Bosch had become an expert on Krayoxx. He thundered on about the dangers of the drug and said vile things about Varrick Labs, and throughout the entire thirty seconds his phone number was pulsating across the bottom of the screen.

Oscar watched with great curiosity but said nothing.

Paula said, "Have you ever thought about advertising on television, Oscar? Seems like your firm needs to do something to get more business."

This was not a new conversation. For thirty years, Paula had dispensed unsolicited advice on how to run the law office, a place that would never generate enough in revenue to satisfy her.

"It's very expensive," Oscar said. "Figg wants to pursue it. I'm skeptical."

"Well, you certainly couldn't put Figg on television, could you? That would scare away every potential client for a hundred miles. I don't know, the ads just seem so unprofessional."

Typical of Paula. TV advertising might bring in some business, and at the same time it was unprofessional. Was she for it or against it? Neither, or both? Oscar didn't know, and he'd stopped caring years earlier.

"Doesn't Figg have some Krayoxx cases?" she asked.

"A few, yes," Oscar grunted. She did not know that Oscar, as well as David, had signed the lawsuit and was responsible for its prosecution. She did not know that the firm was on the line for litigation expenses. Paula's only concern was the paltry monthly draw brought home by Oscar.

"Well, I discussed it with my doctor, and he says the drug is fine. It keeps my cholesterol under two hundred. I am not getting off the drug."

"Then you should not," he said. If Krayoxx did in fact kill people, he wanted her to keep taking the full daily dosage.

"But there are lawsuits everywhere, Oscar. I'm still not convinced. Are you?"

She's loyal to the drug, but she's worried about the drug.

"Figg is convinced the drug causes damages," Oscar said. "A lot of big law firms agree, and they're going after Varrick. The general feeling is that the company will settle before going to trial. Too much at risk."

"So, if there's a settlement, what happens to Figg's cases?"

"They're all death cases, so far. Eight of them. If they settle, then we'll collect some nice fees."

"How nice?"

"It's impossible to say." Oscar was already making plans. If and when the settlement talk became serious, he would move out, file for divorce, then try to keep her away from his Krayoxx money.

"But I doubt they'll settle," he said.

"Why not? Bosch here says there might be a big settlement."

"Bosch is an idiot, and he proves it every day. These big pharmaceuticals usually go to trial a few times to test the waters. If they get hammered by juries, then they start settling. If they win, they keep trying the cases until the plaintiffs' lawyers give up. This could take years."

Don't get your hopes up, dear.

David and Helen Zinc had been almost as amorous as Wally and DeeAnna. With David working shorter hours and their newfound energy, it had taken less than a week to become pregnant. Now that David was home at a decent hour every night, they made up for lost time. They had just finished a session and were lying in bed watching late-night TV when Bosch appeared on their screen.

When he was gone, Helen said, "Looks like a frenzy."

"Oh yes. Wally's out there somewhere right now, littering the streets with brochures. It would be easier to advertise on television, but we can't afford it."

"Thank God for that. I really don't want to see you on-screen fighting it out with the likes of Benny Bosch."

"I think I'd be a natural as a TV lawyer. 'Have you been injured?' 'We fight for you.' 'Insurance companies fear us.' Whatta you think?"

"I think your friends at Rogan Rothberg would howl with laughter."

"I have no friends there. Only bad memories."

"You've been gone, what, a month?"

"Six weeks and two days, and I have not, for one moment, wanted to go back."

"And how much have you earned with your new firm?"

"Six hundred and twenty dollars, and counting."

"Well, we do have an expansion under way. Have you thought about future earnings, things like that? You walked away from $300,000 a year, fine. But we can't live on $600 a month."

"Do you doubt me?"

"No, but a little reassurance would be nice."

"Okay. I promise you I'll make enough money to keep us happy and healthy. All three of us. Or four, or five, or whatever."

"And how do you plan to do this?"

"TV. I'll go on the air to find Krayoxx victims," David said, laughing. "Me and Bosch. Whatta you think?"

"I think you're crazy."

They were both laughing, then groping.

CHAPTER 19

The official name of the gathering was a discovery conference, and it was typically a brief lawyers' get-together in front of the judge to discuss the initial stages of the lawsuit. No record was kept, just informal notes taken by a clerk. Often, and especially in the courtroom of Harry Seawright, the judge himself begged off and sent a magistrate to pinch-hit.

Today, however, Judge Seawright was presiding. As the senior judge in the Northern District of Illinois he had a large courtroom, a splendid and spacious layout on the twenty-third floor of the Dirksen Federal Building on Dearborn Street in downtown Chicago. The courtroom was lined with dark, oak-paneled walls, and there were plenty of thick leather chairs for the various players. On the right side, and to the judge's left, was the plaintiffs' team of Wally Figg and David Zinc. On the left side, and to the judge's right, was the team of about a dozen or so Rogan Rothberg lawyers toiling away on behalf of Varrick Laboratories. Their leader, of course, was Nadine Karros, the only female lawyer present, and for the occasion she was modeling a classic Armani navy suit, skirt just above the knees, nude legs, and designer platform pumps with four-inch heels.

Wally couldn't take his eyes off the shoes, the skirt, the entire package. "Maybe we should come to federal court more often," he'd quipped to David, who was in no mood for humor. Nor was Wally, to be honest. For both of them, it was their first venture into a federal courtroom. Wally claimed he handled cases in federal court all the time, but David was doubtful. Oscar, senior partner, who was supposed to be there with them, taking on the twin Goliaths of Rogan Rothberg and Varrick, had called in sick.

Oscar wasn't the only no-show. The great Jerry Alisandros and his team of world-class litigators were all lined up to blast into Chicago for an impressive display of strength, but a last-minute emergency hearing in Boston had become more important. Wally freaked out when he got the call from one of Alisandros's underlings. "It's just a discovery conference," the young man said. Driving to court, Wally had expressed skepticism about Zell & Potter.

For David, the moment was extremely uncomfortable. He was sitting in a federal courtroom for the first time knowing that he would not say a word because he had no idea what to say, and his opposition was a team of well-dressed and highly skilled lawyers from a firm he'd once been loyal to, a firm that had recruited him, trained him, paid him a top salary, and promised him a long career, and a firm that he had jilted, rejected. In favor of . . . Finley & Figg? He could almost hear them snickering behind their legal pads. David, with his pedigree and Harvard diploma, belonged over there, where they billed by the hour, not on the plaintiffs' side, where you beat the streets looking for clients. David did not want to be where he was. Nor did Wally.

Judge Seawright settled himself into his perch and wasted no time. "Where's Mr. Alisandros?" he growled in the direction of Wally and David.

Wally jumped to his feet, offered a greasy smile, and said, "He's in Boston, sir."

"So he will not be here today?"

"That's right, Your Honor. He was on his way but got sidetracked with some emergency in Boston."

"I see. He's an attorney of record for the plaintiffs in this case. The next time we get together, tell him to be here. I will fine him $1,000 for missing the conference."

"Yes sir."

"And you're Mr. Figg?"

"That's correct, Your Honor, and this is my associate, David Zinc." David tried to smile. He could almost see every Rogan Rothberg lawyer craning to have a look.

"Welcome to federal court," the judge said sarcastically. He looked at the defense and said, "I suppose you're Ms. Karros?"

She stood, and every eye in the courtroom locked onto her. "I am, Your Honor, and this is my co-counsel, Luther Hotchkin."

"Who are all of those other people?"

"This is our defense team, Your Honor."

"Do you really need all these people for a simple discovery conference?"

Give 'em hell, Wally thought, still staring at the skirt.

"We do indeed, Your Honor. This is a large and complicated case."

"So I've heard. You may keep your seats for the remainder of this hearing." Judge Seawright picked up some notes and adjusted his reading glasses. "Now, I've spoken to two of my colleagues in Florida, and we are not sure if these cases will proceed in a multi-district litigation. It appears as if the plaintiffs' lawyers are having some difficulty getting themselves organized. Many, it seems, want a bigger piece of the pie, which is not surprising. At any rate, we have no choice but to proceed with discovery in this case. Mr. Figg, who are your experts?"

Mr. Figg had no experts and had no idea when he might retain them. He was relying on the increasingly unreliable Jerry Alisandros to find the experts because that's what he promised to do. Wally stood slowly, knowing that any hesitation would look bad. "We'll have them next week, Your Honor. As you know, we are partnering with the law firm of Zell & Potter, a well-known firm specializing in mass torts, and with the flurry of activity around the country it's been difficult to lock up the best experts. But we're definitely making progress."

"That's nice. Please sit down. So you actually filed this lawsuit before you consulted with any experts?"

"Well, yes, Your Honor, and that's not unusual."

Judge Seawright doubted if Mr. Figg knew what was usual or

unusual, but he decided not to embarrass the guy this early in the game. He picked up a pen and said, "You have ten days to designate your experts, then the defense will be allowed to depose them without delay."

"Yes sir," Wally said, falling back into his chair.

"Thank you. Now, we have eight death cases here, so we're dealing with eight families. To start with, I want you to take the depositions of the personal representatives of all eight. Mr. Figg, when can you make these people available?"

"Tomorrow," Wally said.

The judge turned to Nadine Karros and said, "That soon enough?"

She smiled and said, "We prefer reasonable notice, Your Honor."

"I'm sure you have a busy trial calendar, Ms. Karros."

"As always, yes."

"And you also have unlimited resources. I count eleven lawyers taking notes right now, and I'm sure there are hundreds more back at the firm. These are just depositions, nothing complicated, so on Wednesday of next week you're going to depose four of the plaintiffs, and on Thursday you'll do the other four. Two hours max per plaintiff; if you need more time, we'll do them later. If you can't be there, Ms. Karros, just pick out five or six from your squad, and I'm sure they can handle the depositions."

"I'll be there, Your Honor," she said coolly.

"Mr. Figg?"

"We'll be there."

"I'll get my clerk to arrange the time, schedule, details, and we'll e-mail it to you by tomorrow. Then, as soon as Mr. Figg designates his experts, we will schedule their depositions. Ms. Karros, when your experts are in place, please provide the necessary information, and we'll go from there. I want these initial depositions out of the way within sixty days. Any questions?" There were none.

He continued: "Now, I have reviewed three other lawsuits involving this defendant and its products, and, frankly, I'm not impressed with Varrick's integrity or its ability to abide by the rules of discovery. The company, it seems, has a great deal of trouble turning over documents to the other side. It has been caught red-handed concealing documents. It has been sanctioned by judges at the state and federal levels. It has been embarrassed before juries and paid dearly with large verdicts, yet it continues to hide documents. At least three times, its executives have been charged with perjury. Ms. Karros, how can you assure me that your client will play by the rules?"

She glared at the judge, paused for a moment in a stare-down, then said, "I was not the attorney for Varrick Labs in those other cases, Your Honor, and I don't know what happened there. I will not be tainted by lawsuits I had nothing to do with. I know the rules inside and out, and my clients always play by the rules."

"We'll see. Your client needs to be warned that I am watching closely. At the first hint of a discovery violation, I will haul the CEO into this courtroom and draw blood. Do you understand me, Ms. Karros?"

"I do."

"Mr. Figg, you have not yet made a request for documents. When might this happen?"

"We're working on that now, Your Honor," Wally said with as much confidence as possible. "We should have it in a couple of weeks." Alisandros had promised an exhaustive list of documents to be sought from Varrick but had yet to come through.

"I'm waiting on you," Seawright said. "This is your lawsuit. You filed it, now let's get going."

"Yes sir," Wally replied anxiously.

"Anything else?" he asked.

Most of the lawyers shook their heads. His Honor seemed to relax somewhat as he chewed on the cap of his pen. He said, "I'm thinking this case might do well under Local Rule 83:19. Have you considered this, Mr. Figg?"

Mr. Figg had not, because Mr. Figg was not aware of Local Rule 83:19. He opened his mouth, but only dry came forth. David quickly picked up the flag and spoke his first words in court: "We've considered that, Your Honor, but we have not yet discussed it with Mr. Alisandros. We should make a decision within the week."

Seawright looked at Nadine Karros and said, "And your response?"

"We are the defense, Your Honor, and we are never eager to go to trial." Her candor amused the judge.

Wally whispered to David, "What the hell's Rule 83:19?"

David whispered back, "The Rocket Docket. Streamline the case. Balls to the wall."

"We don't want that, do we?" Wally hissed.

"No. We want to settle and cash in."

"No need to file a motion, Mr. Figg," His Honor said. "I'm placing this case in 83:19 status. On the fast track, Mr. Figg, so let's get things moving along."

"Yes sir," Wally managed to mumble.

Judge Seawright tapped his gavel and said, "We'll meet again in sixty days, and I expect Mr. Alisandros to be here. Adjourned."

As David and Wally were stuffing files and notepads into their briefcases in hopes of a fast exit, Nadine Karros sauntered over for a quick hello. "Nice to meet you, Mr. Figg, Mr. Zinc," she said with a smile that made Wally's nervous heart skip another beat.

"A pleasure," he said. David returned the smile as he shook her hand.

"This promises to be a long, bruising fight," she said, "with a lot of money on the table. I try to keep things on a professional level and hard feelings at a minimum. I'm sure your firm feels the same way."

"Oh yes," Wally gushed, and almost asked her to go have a drink. David wasn't as easily manipulated. He saw her as a pretty face and a warm facade, but just below the surface was a ruthless combatant who would enjoy watching you bleed in open court.

"I guess I'll see you next Wednesday," she said.

"If not sooner," Wally said, a lame attempt at humor.

As she stepped away, David grabbed Wally by the arm and said, "Let's get out of here."

CHAPTER 20

Now that Helen was expecting and her future would be consumed with the baby, her studies at Northwestern seemed less important. She dropped one class because of morning sickness, and she was struggling with motivational problems in most of her others. David was pushing her, delicately, but she wanted to take a break. She was almost thirty-four, thrilled at the prospect of becoming a mother, and losing interest quickly in a doctorate in art history.

On a frigid day in March, they were having lunch in a café near the campus when Toni Vance, Helen's friend from class, happened to drop by. David had met her only once. She was ten years older and had two teenagers and a husband who had something to do with containerized shipping. She also had the Burmese housekeeper with a grandson who was alive but probably brain damaged. David had urged Helen to push Toni to arrange a meeting, but the housekeeper had not been cooperative. Snooping, without violating laws or anyone's privacy, David had learned that the little boy was five years old and for the past two months had been in intensive care at the Lakeshore Children's Hospital on Chicago's North Side. His name was Thuya Khaing, and he had been born in Sacramento, so he was a U.S. citizen. As for his parents, David had no way of knowing their immigration status. Zaw, the housekeeper, supposedly had a green card.

"I think Zaw would talk to you now," Toni said as she sipped an espresso.

"When and where?" David asked.

She glanced at her watch. "My next class is over at two, then I'll go home. Why don't you guys stop by?"

At 2:30, David and Helen parked behind a Jaguar in the driveway of a striking contemporary house in Oak Park. Whatever Mr. Vance did with containerized cargo, he did it well. The house jutted here and there, up and down, with lots of glass and marble and no discernible design. It tried desperately to be unique, and it succeeded greatly. They finally located the front door and were met by Toni, who'd found time to change outfits and was no longer trying to look like a twenty-year-old student. She led them to a sunroom with full views of the sky and clouds, and moments later Zaw entered with a tray of coffees. Introductions were made.

David had never met a Burmese woman, but he guessed her age at sixty. She was petite in her maid's uniform, with short, graying hair and a face that seemed locked into a perpetual smile.

"Her English is very good," Toni said. "Please join us, Zaw." Zaw awkwardly sat on a small stool near her boss.

"How long have you been in the United States?" David asked.

"Twenty year."

"And you have family here?"

"My husband is here, work for Sears. My son too. Work for tree company."

"And he's the father of the grandson who's in the hospital?"

She nodded slowly. The smile vanished at the mention of the boy. "Yes."

"Does the boy have brothers and sisters?"

She flashed two fingers and said, "Two sister."

"Have they been sick too?"

"No."

"Okay, can you tell me what happened when the boy got sick?"

She looked at Toni, who said, "It's okay, Zaw. You can trust these people. Mr. Zinc needs to hear the story."

Zaw nodded and began talking, her eyes glued to the floor. "He get real tired all the time, sleep a lot, then bad pain here." She tapped her stomach. "He cry so hard because of the pain. Then he start to vomit, every day he vomit, and he lose weight, get real skinny. We take him to doctor. They put him in hospital and he go to sleep." She touched her head. "They think he has brain problem."

"Did the doctor say it was lead poisoning?"

She nodded. "Yes." No hesitation.

David nodded too as he let this soak in. "Does your grandson live with you?"

"Next door. Apartment."

He looked at Toni and asked, "Do you know where she lives?"

"Rogers Park. It's an old apartment complex. I think everyone there is from Burma."

"Zaw, is it possible for me to see the apartment where the boy lives?"

She nodded. "Yes."

"Why do you need to see the apartment?" Toni asked.

"To find the source of the lead. Could be in the paint on the walls or in some of his toys. It might be in the water. I should have a look."

Zaw rose quietly and said, "Excuse me, please." A few seconds later, she was back with a small plastic bag, from which she removed a set of pink plastic teeth, complete with two large vampire fangs. "He like these," Zaw said. "He scare his sisters, make funny noise."

David held the cheap toy. The plastic was hard, and some of the coloring, or paint, had chipped off. "Did you see him play with these?"

"Yes. Many time."

"When did he get these?"

"Last year. Halloween," she said, without the *H* sound. "I don't know if it make him sick, but he use them all the time. Pink, green, black, blue, many color."

"So there's a whole set of these?"

"Yes."

"Where are the others?"

"Apartment."

———

It was spitting snow when David and Helen found the apartment complex after dark. The buildings were 1960s-style blocks of plywood and tar paper, a few bricks on the steps, a few shrubs here and there. All the units were two stories, some with boarded windows and obviously abandoned. There were a few vehicles, all ancient imports from Japan. It was easy to get the impression that the place would have been condemned, with bulldozers to follow, but for the heroic efforts of the Burmese immigrants.

Zaw was waiting at 14B and led them a few steps to 14C. Thuya's parents looked to be about twenty years old, but were really closer to forty. They looked exhausted, sad eyed, and as frightened as any parents would be. They were appreciative that a real lawyer would come to their home, though they were terrified of the legal system and understood nothing about it. The mother, Lwin, hurried about preparing and serving tea. The father, Zaw's son, went by Soe and, as the man of the house, did most of the talking. His English was good, much better than his wife's. As Zaw had said, he worked for a company that did all manner of tree work. His wife cleaned offices downtown. It was obvious to both David and Helen that there had been a lot of discussion before their arrival.

The apartment was sparsely furnished but neat and clean. The only effort at decor was a large photograph of Aung San Suu Kyi, the 1991 Nobel Peace Prize winner and most famous dissident in Burma. Something was on the stove in the kitchen, and its pungent aroma reeked of onions. In the car, the Zincs had vowed not to stay for dinner in the unlikely event they were invited. Thuya's two sisters were not to be seen or heard.

The yellowish tea was served in tiny cups, and after a sip or two Soe said, "Why do you want to talk to us?"

David took his first sip, hoped it would be his last, and said, "Because if your son has in fact been poisoned by lead, and if the lead came from a toy or something here in the apartment, then you may—and I emphasize the word 'may'—have a case against the maker of the dangerous product. I would like to investigate this matter, but I am making no promises."

"You mean we could get money?"

"Possibly. That's the purpose of the case, or lawsuit, but first we need to dig a little deeper."

"How much money?"

Here, of course, Wally would promise them anything. David had heard him promise—or practically guarantee—a million or more to several of his Krayoxx clients.

"I can't answer that," David said. "It's too early. I would like to investigate, see if we can put together a case, and take it one step at a time."

Helen was watching her husband with admiration. He was doing a fine job in an arena where he knew nothing and had no experience. He'd never seen a lawsuit at Rogan Rothberg.

"Okay," Soe said. "What now?"

"Two things," David said. "First, I'd like to have a look at his things—toys, books, bed—anything that might be a source of lead. Second, I need for you to sign some papers that will allow me to begin accumulating his medical records."

Soe nodded at Lwin, who reached into a small box and removed a plastic ziploc bag. She opened it and on the small coffee table lined up five pairs of fake teeth and fangs—blue, black, green, purple, and red. Zaw added the pink ones from the afternoon visit, and the set was complete.

"These called Nasty Teeth," Soe said.

David stared at the row of Nasty Teeth and for the first time felt the twinge of excitement of a big lawsuit. He picked up the green ones—hard but pliable plastic, flexible enough to open and close easily. He had no trouble seeing a pesky little brother with these in his mouth, growling and snapping at his sisters.

"Your son played with these?" David asked. Lwin nodded sadly.

Soe said, "He like them, kept them in his mouth. Tried to eat dinner with them one night."

"Who bought them?" David asked.

"I did," Soe said. "I bought a few things for Halloween. Cost not too much."

"Where did you buy them?" David asked, almost holding his breath. He hoped for an answer like Walmart, Kmart, Target, Sears, Macy's—some chain with deep pockets.

"At market," Soe said.

"What market?"

"Big mall. Near Logan Square."

Helen said, "Probably the Mighty Mall," and David's excitement waned a bit. The Mighty Mall was a hodgepodge of cavernous metal buildings housing a maze of cramped stalls and booths where one could find almost anything of legal value and many items from the black market. Cheap clothing, household goods, old albums, athletic gear, counterfeit CDs, used paperbacks, fake jewelry, toys, games, a million things. The low prices attracted large crowds. Virtually all business was in cash. Record keeping and receipts were not priorities.

"Did these come in a package?" David asked. A package would provide the name of the manufacturer and maybe the importer.

"Yes, but it gone," Soe said. "In garbage, long time ago."

"No package," Lwin added.

The apartment had two bedrooms—one used by the parents, the other by the children. David followed Soe as the women stayed in the den. Thuya's bed was a small mattress on the floor near his sisters'. The children had a small, cheap bookcase filled with coloring books and paperbacks. Next to it was a plastic tub filled with boy toys.

"This his," Soe said, pointing to the tub.

"May I look through it?" David asked.

"Yes, please."

David dropped to his knees and slowly went through the box— action figures, race cars, airplanes, a pistol, and handcuffs, the usual assortment of inexpensive toys for a five-year-old boy. When he stood, he said, "I'll look at these later. For now, just make sure that everything stays here."

Back in the den, the Nasty Teeth were ziplocked again. David explained that he would send them to an expert on lead poisoning and have them evaluated. If the teeth did indeed contain unsuitable levels of lead, then they would meet again and discuss the lawsuit. He cautioned that it might be difficult to pin down the maker of the toys, and he tried to dampen any enthusiasm for the thought of one day collecting money. The three—Zaw, Lwin, and Soe—seemed as puzzled and apprehensive when the Zincs were leaving as they'd been when they arrived. Soe was on his way to the hospital to spend the night with Thuya.

The following morning, David sent by overnight parcel the set of Nasty Teeth to a lab in Akron. Its director, Dr. Biff Sandroni, was a leading expert on lead poisoning in children. He also sent a check for $2,500, not from Finley & Figg, but from his personal bank account. David had yet to discuss the case with his two bosses and planned to avoid doing so until more was known.

Sandroni called two days later to say he had received the package, and the check, and that it would be a week or so before he could get around to testing the teeth. He was keenly interested because he had never seen a toy designed to be placed in the mouth. Virtually every toy he examined was one that a child chewed on for whatever reasons. The likely sources of the toy were China, Mexico, and India, and without the package it would be virtually impossible to determine the importer and manufacturer.

Sandroni was a big talker and went on about his most significant cases. He testified all the time—"love the courtroom"—and took full responsibility for several million-dollar verdicts. He called David "David" and insisted on being called Biff. As David listened, he could not remember another conversation with someone named

Biff. The bluster would have worried David but for his research into lead-poisoning experts. Dr. Sandroni was a warrior with impeccable credentials.

At 7:00 the next Saturday morning, David and Helen found the Mighty Mall and parked in a crowded lot. Traffic was thick; the place already busy. It was thirty degrees outside and not much warmer inside. They waited in a long line for beverages, bought two tall cups of hot cocoa, then began roaming. As chaotic as the market appeared, there was some semblance of organization. The food vendors were near the front, with such takeaway delicacies as Pronto Pups, doughnuts, and cotton candy drawing fans. Then a stretch of booths offering inexpensive clothing and shoes. Another long aisle was lined with books and jewelry, then furniture and auto parts.

The shoppers, as well as the vendors, were of all shades and colors. Along with English and Spanish, there were many other languages: Asian tongues, something from Africa, then a loud voice that was probably Russian.

David and Helen moved with the crowd, stopping occasionally to inspect something of interest. After an hour, and with the hot cocoa growing cooler, they found the household goods section, then the toys. There were three booths offering thousands of cheap gadgets and playthings, none of which resembled a set of Nasty Teeth. The Zincs were well aware they were months away from Halloween and were unlikely to find costumes and such.

David picked up a package containing three different dinosaurs, all small enough for a toddler to chew on but too large to swallow. All three were painted shades of green. Only a scientist like Sandroni could scrape off the paint and test for lead, but after a month of exhaustive research David was convinced that most of the cheapest toys were contaminated. The dinosaurs were sold by Larkette Industries, Mobile, Alabama, and made in China. He had seen the name Larkette as a defendant in several lawsuits.

As he held the dinosaurs, his mind was carried away by the absurdity of it all. A cheap toy is made five thousand miles away, for pennies, decorated with lead paint, imported into the United States, passed along the distribution system until it lands here, in a giant flea market, where it's offered for $1.99, where it's purchased by the poorest customers, taken home, presented to the child, who chews on it, then ends up in a hospital, brain damaged and ruined for life. Where are all of those consumer protection laws, inspectors, bureaucrats?

Not to mention the hundreds of thousands of dollars required to treat the child and support him for his lifetime.

"You buy?" the tiny Hispanic woman barked.

"No thanks," David said, coming back to reality. He placed the toys back in the pile and turned away.

"Any sign of Nasty Teeth?" he asked as he stepped behind Helen.

"Not a thing."

"I'm freezing. Let's get out of here."

CHAPTER 21

As scheduled by Judge Seawright's clerk, the depositions of Finley & Figg's Krayoxx clients began promptly at 9:00 a.m. in a ballroom of the Downtown Marriott. Since the defendant, Varrick Labs, was picking up the tab for the depositions, there was a generous spread of rolls and pastries, along with coffee, tea, and juice. A long table had been arranged with a video camera at one end and a witness chair at the other.

Iris Klopeck was the first witness. She had called 911 the day before and rode in an ambulance to the hospital, where they treated her for arrhythmia and hypertension. Her nerves were shot, and she told Wally several times she could not go through with the lawsuit. He mentioned, more than once, that if she could tough it out, she would soon be receiving a large check, "probably a million bucks," and this helped somewhat. Also helping was a supply of Xanax, so when Iris took the witness chair and looked at the legion of lawyers, she was fairly glassy-eyed and drifting off to la-la land. Still, she at first froze and looked helplessly at her lawyer.

"It's just a deposition," Wally had repeated. "There'll be a lot of lawyers there, but they're nice people, for the most part."

They didn't look nice. To her left was a line of intense young men in dark suits and frowns. They were already scratching away on their yellow legal pads, and she hadn't said a word. The nearest lawyer to her was an attractive woman who smiled and helped Iris settle down. To her right were Wally and his two sidekicks.

The woman said, "Ms. Klopeck, my name is Nadine Karros, and I'm the lead lawyer for Varrick Labs. We're going to take your deposition over the next two hours, and I want you to try to relax. I promise I will not try to trick you. If you don't understand a question, don't answer it. I'll just repeat it. Are you ready?"

"Yes," Iris said, seeing double.

Next to Iris was a court reporter who said, "Raise your right hand." Iris did so, then swore to tell the truth.

Ms. Karros said, "Now, Ms. Klopeck, I'm sure your attorneys have explained that we are making a video of your deposition, and this might be used in court if for some reason you're unable to testify. Do you understand this?"

"I think so."

"So if you'll look at the camera when you talk, we'll do just fine."

"I'll try, yes, I can do that."

"Great. Ms. Klopeck, are you currently taking any medication?"

Iris stared at the camera as if waiting for it to tell her what to say. She took eleven pills a day for diabetes, blood pressure, cholesterol, erratic heartbeat, arthritis, kidney stones, and a few other ailments, but the one she worried about was Xanax because it could affect her mental state. Wally had suggested she skip any discussion about Xanax if asked the question, and here, right off the bat, Ms. Karros was digging.

She giggled. "Sure, I'm on a lot of meds."

It took fifteen minutes to straighten them out, with no help from the Xanax, and just when Iris got to the bottom of the list, she remembered another one and blurted, "And I used to take Krayoxx but not anymore. That stuff'll kill you."

Wally roared with laughter. Oscar thought it was funny too. David suppressed a chuckle by looking directly across the table at the stone-faced boys from Rogan Rothberg, not a single one of whom would allow himself even a grin. But Nadine smiled and said, "Is that all, Ms. Klopeck?"

"I think so," she said, still not sure.

"So, you're taking nothing that would affect your judgment, memory, or ability to give truthful answers?"

Iris glanced at Wally, who hid behind a legal pad, and for a second it was obvious that something was going unsaid. "That's correct," Iris said.

"Nothing for depression, stress, panic attacks, anxiety disorders?"

It was as if Ms. Karros were reading Iris's mind and knew she was lying. Iris was about to choke when she said, "Not normally."

Ten minutes later they were still grappling with "not normally," and Iris finally admitted that she popped a Xanax "every now and then." She proved sufficiently elusive, though, when Ms. Karros tried to pin her down on her Xanax use. She stumbled when she referred to the drug as her "happy pills," but plowed on. In spite of her thick tongue and drooping eyelids, Iris assured the wall of lawyers to her left that she was clearheaded and ready to roll.

Address, birth dates, family members, employment, education, the deposition quickly sank into tedium as Nadine and Iris fleshed out the Klopeck family, with emphasis on Percy, the departed. Iris, with increasing lucidity, managed to choke up twice when talking about her beloved husband, dead now for almost two years. Ms. Karros probed into Percy's health and habits—drinking, smoking, exercise, diet—and as much as she tried to whip the old boy into shape, Iris did a fair job of portraying him with accuracy. Percy came across as a fat, sick man who ate bad food, drank too much beer, and rarely left the sofa. "But he quit smoking," Iris added at least twice.

They took a break after an hour, and Oscar excused himself, saying he had to be in court, but Wally was suspicious. He had arm-twisted his senior partner to show up at the depositions, sort of a show of force in the face of the ground troops Rogan Rothberg would send in, though it was doubtful the presence of Oscar Finley would rattle the defense. When fully manned, the Finley & Figg side of the table had three lawyers, now minus one. Ten feet away, on the other side, Wally counted eight.

Seven lawyers to sit and take the same notes while one did the talking? Ridiculous. But then Wally began thinking, as Iris droned on, that perhaps the show of force was a good thing. Perhaps Varrick was so worried that they had instructed Rogan Rothberg to spare no expense. Maybe Finley & Figg had them on the ropes and didn't realize it.

When they resumed the deposition, Nadine prompted Iris to begin talking about Percy's medical history, and Wally zoned out. He was still irritated that Jerry Alisandros had once again skipped the proceedings. At first, Alisandros had big plans to attend the depositions with his entourage, to make his first dramatic entrance into the case, to do battle with Rogan Rothberg and stake out some turf. But another last-minute urgency, this one in Seattle, proved more important. "It's only depositions," Alisandros told an agitated Wally on the phone the day before. "Pretty basic stuff."

Basic indeed. Iris was talking about one of Percy's old hernias.

David's role was limited. He was there as a warm body, a real lawyer taking up space, but with little to do but scribble and read. He was reviewing an FDA study on lead poisoning in children.

Occasionally, Wally would politely say, "Objection. Calls for conclusion."

The lovely Ms. Karros would stop and wait to make sure Wally was finished, then she would say, "You may answer, Ms. Klopeck." And by then, Iris would tell her all she wanted to hear.

Judge Seawright's strict two-hour time limit was obeyed. Ms. Karros asked her last question at 10:58, then graciously thanked Iris for being such a good witness. Iris was going for her purse where the Xanax was kept. Wally walked her to the door and assured her she had done a superb job.

"When do you think they'll want to settle?" she whispered.

Wally put a finger to his lips and shoved her out.

Next up was Millie Marino, widow of Chester and stepmother of Lyle, the inheritor of the baseball card collection and Wally's initial source of information about Krayoxx. Millie was forty-nine, attractive, somewhat fit, reasonably well dressed, and apparently unmedicated, a far cry from the last witness. She was there for her depo, but she was still not a believer in the lawsuit. She and Wally were still bickering over her late husband's estate. She was still threatening to pull out of the lawsuit and find another lawyer. Wally had offered to guarantee, in writing, a million-dollar settlement.

Ms. Karros asked the same questions. Wally made the same objections. David read the same memo and thought, Only six more after this one.

After a quick lunch, the lawyers reconvened for the deposition of Adam Grand, the assistant manager of an all-you-can-eat pizza house whose mother had died the previous year after taking Krayoxx for two years. (It was the same pizza house Wally now frequented, but only to secretly leave copies of his "Beware of Krayoxx!" brochures in the restrooms.)

Nadine Karros took a break, and her number two, Luther Hotchkin, handled the deposition. Nadine, though, apparently loaned him her questions because he asked the same ones.

During his insufferable career at Rogan Rothberg, David had heard many tales about the boys in litigation. The litigators were a breed apart, wild men who gambled with huge sums of money, took enormous risks, and lived on the edge. In every large law firm, the litigation section was the most colorful and filled with the biggest characters and egos. That was the urban legend anyway. Now, as he glanced occasionally across the table at the solemn faces of his adversaries, he had serious doubts about the legend. Nothing he had ever experienced in his career was as monotonous as sitting through depositions. And this was only his third one. He almost missed the drudgery of plodding through the financial records of obscure Chinese corporations.

Ms. Karros was taking a break, but she missed nothing. This early round of depositions was nothing more than a little contest, a pageant to provide her and her client the opportunity to meet and examine the eight contestants and select a winner. Could Iris Klopeck withstand the rigors of an intense two-week trial? Probably not. She was stoned during her depo, and Nadine had two associates already working on her medical records. On the other hand, some jurors might have great sympathy for her. Millie Marino would make an impressive witness, but her husband, Chester, could potentially have the strongest link to heart disease and death.

Nadine and her team would finish the depos, watch them again and again, and slowly eliminate the better ones. They and their experts would continue to dissect the medical records of the eight "victims" and eventually select the one with the weakest claim. When they picked their winner, they would race to court with a thick, cold-blooded, and well-reasoned motion to separate. They would ask Judge Seawright to take the single case they wanted, place it on his Rocket Docket, and clear all obstacles between it and a trial by jury.

Minutes after 6:00 p.m., David bolted from the Marriott and almost ran to his car. He was punch-drunk and needed his lungs full of cold air. Leaving downtown, he stopped at a Starbucks in a strip mall and ordered a double espresso. Two doors down was a party store that advertised costumes and favors, and, as had become his habit, he wandered over for a look. No party store was safe from him, or Helen, these days. They were searching for a set of Nasty Teeth, in the wrapper, with names of corporations in fine print. This one had the usual inventory of cheap costumes, gag gifts, decorations, glitter, toys, wrapping paper. There were several sets of vampire teeth, made in Mexico and sold by a company called Mirage Novelties of Tucson.

He was familiar with Mirage, even had a small file on the company. Privately owned, sales last year of $18 million, most of its products along the same lines of what David was now inspecting. He had files on dozens of companies that specialized in cheap toys and gadgets, and his research was growing daily. What he had not found was another set of Nasty Teeth.

He paid three bucks for a set of fangs, to add to his growing collection, then drove to the Brickyard Mall, where he met Helen at a Lebanese restaurant. Over dinner, he refused to describe his day—the same ordeal was planned for tomorrow—so they chatted about her classes and, not surprisingly, the coming addition to their family.

Lakeshore Children's Hospital was nearby. They found the ICU, then found Soe Khaing in a visitors' room. He had relatives with him, and introductions were made, though neither David nor Helen caught a single name. The Burmese were visibly touched that the Zincs would stop by and say hello.

Thuya's condition had changed little in the past month. The day after their visit to the family's apartment, David had contacted one of the doctors. After he e-mailed the paperwork signed by Soe and Lwin, the doctor was willing to talk. The boy's outlook was bleak. The level of lead in his body was highly toxic, with substantial damage to his kidneys, liver, nervous system, and brain. He was in and out of consciousness. If he survived, it would take months or years to gauge the level of impaired brain activity. Normally, though, with this much lead, children did not survive.

David and Helen followed Soe down the hall, past a nurse's station, and to a window where they could see Thuya strapped to a small bed and hooked to an astonishing assortment of tubes, lines, and monitors. His breathing was aided by a respirator.

"I touch him once a day. He hear me," Soe said, then wiped the moisture from his cheeks.

David and Helen stared through the window but could think of nothing to say.

CHAPTER 22

Another aspect of big-firm life that David had learned to despise was the endless meetings. Meetings to evaluate and review, to discuss the firm's future, to plan everything, to greet new lawyers, to say good-bye to old ones, to stay current on the law, to mentor rookies, to get mentored by senior partners, to talk about compensation, labor issues, and an endless list of other incredibly boring topics. The Rogan Rothberg culture was nonstop work and nonstop billing, but there were so many useless meetings that the making of money was actually often impeded.

With that in mind, David reluctantly suggested his new firm have a meeting. He'd been there four months and had settled into a comfortable routine. He was worried, though, about the lack of civility and communication among the other members of the firm. The Krayoxx litigation was dragging on. Wally's dreams of a quick jackpot were fading, and revenue was down. Oscar was increasingly more irritable, if that was possible. In gossiping with Rochelle, David learned that the partners never sat around the table to think strategically and to air complaints.

Oscar said he was too busy. Wally said such a meeting was a waste. Rochelle thought the idea was awful until she realized she would be invited, then she became enamored with the idea. As the only non-lawyer employee, she thought the idea of being allowed a soapbox was appealing. With time, David was able to cajole the senior and junior partners, and Finley & Figg scheduled its inaugural firm meeting.

They waited until 5:00 p.m., then locked the front door and put the phones on hold. After a few awkward moments, David said, "Oscar, as the senior partner, I think you should run the meeting."

"What do you want to talk about?" Oscar shot back.

"Glad you asked," David said as he quickly passed around an agenda. Number 1: Fee Schedule. Number 2: Case Review. Number 3: Filing. Number 4: Specialization.

"This is just a suggestion," David said. "Frankly, I don't care what we talk about, but it's important for each of us to be able to unload."

"You spent too much time in a big firm," Oscar said.

"So what's bugging you?" Wally asked David.

"Nothing's bugging me. It's just that I think we could do a better job of keeping our fees uniform and reviewing each other's cases. The filing system is twenty years out of date, and as a firm we're not going to make money if we don't specialize."

"Well, speaking of money," Oscar said, picking up a notepad. "Since we filed these Krayoxx cases, our gross has declined for three straight months. We're spending far too much time on those cases, and our cash is getting low. That's what's bugging me." He was staring at Wally.

"The payoff's coming," Wally said.

"That's what you keep saying."

"We'll settle the Groomer car wreck next month and net around twenty grand. It's not unusual to go through a dry period, Oscar. Hell, you've been doing this a long time. You know the ups and downs. Last year we lost money nine months outta twelve, and we still showed a nice profit."

There was a loud knock on the front door. Wally jumped to his feet and said, "Oh no, it's DeeAnna. Sorry, guys, I told her to take the day off." He raced to the door and opened it. She made her entrance—skintight black leather pants, hooker's heels, tight cotton sweater. Wally said, "Hey, honey, we're having a little meeting. What say you wait in my office?"

"How long?" she asked.

"Not long."

DeeAnna smiled like a tart at Oscar and David as she strutted by. Wally led her to his office and closed her inside. He sat down at the table, slightly embarrassed.

"Know what's bugging me?" Rochelle asked. "Her." She nodded toward Wally's office. "Why does she have to stop by every afternoon?"

"You used to see clients after five," Oscar jumped in. "Now you're just locked in there with her."

"She's not bothering anyone," Wally said. "And not so loud."

"She bothers me," Rochelle said.

Wally raised both palms, arched his eyebrows, and was instantly ready for a brawl. "Look, she and I are getting serious, and it's none of your business. Got that? I'm not going to discuss it further."

There was a pause as everyone took a breath, then Oscar launched another round. "I suppose you've told her about Krayoxx and the big settlement that's just around the corner, so it's not surprising she's hanging around. Right?"

"I don't talk about your women, Oscar," Wally fired back. Women? More than one? Rochelle's eyes widened, and David remembered all the good reasons for hating firm meetings. Oscar glared at Wally in disbelief for several seconds. Both men appeared stunned at their exchange.

"Let's move along," David said. "I'd like permission to study our fee structure and attempt to come up with a proposed schedule that will aim for uniformity. Any objections?"

There were none.

On a roll, David quickly passed around some sheets of paper. "This is a case I've stumbled across, and it has great potential."

"Nasty Teeth?" Oscar said, looking at a color photo of the collection.

"Yep. The client is a five-year-old boy in a coma from lead poisoning. His father purchased this set of teeth and fangs last Halloween, and the kid kept them in his mouth for hours. The various paint colors are loaded with lead. Page 3 is a preliminary report from a lab in Akron where one Dr. Biff Sandroni examined the teeth. His conclusion is at the bottom—all six sets of plastic teeth are coated with lead. Dr. Sandroni is an expert on lead poisoning, and he says this is one of the worst products he's come across in the last twenty-five years. He thinks the teeth were probably made in China and imported by one of the many low-end toy companies here in the States. Chinese factories have a terrible history of coating a million different products with lead paint. The Food and Drug Administration and the Bureau of Consumer Protection scream and order recalls, but it's impossible to monitor everything."

Rochelle, looking at the same handout as Oscar and Wally, said, "That poor child. Is he gonna make it?"

"The doctors think not. There's substantial damage to his brain, nervous system, and many of his organs. If he lives, he'll be a very sad sight."

"Who's the manufacturer?" Wally asked.

"That's the big question. I've been unable to find another set of Nasty Teeth in Chicago, and Helen and I have been poking around for a month. Nothing online. Nothing in suppliers' catalogs. So far, no clue. It's possible that the product shows up at Halloween only. The family did not keep the package."

"There must be similar products," Wally said. "I mean, if the company makes crap like this, then surely it makes crap like fake mustaches and such."

"That's my theory. I'm accumulating a nice collection of similar items, and I'm researching the importers and manufacturers."

"Who paid for this report?" Oscar asked, suspiciously.

"I did. Twenty-five hundred bucks."

This caused a gap in the conversation as all four looked at the report. Finally, Oscar asked, "Have the parents signed a contract with our firm?"

"No. They've signed a contract with me so I could get the medical records and begin the investigation. They'll sign one with the firm if I ask them to. The question is simply this: Does Finley & Figg take this case? If the answer is yes, then we need to spend some money."

"How much?" Oscar asked.

"The next step is to hire Sandroni's outfit to go into the apartment where the boy and his family live and look for lead. It could be in other toys, paint on the walls that's chipping, even in the drinking water. I've been to the apartment, and it's at least fifty years old. Sandroni needs to isolate the source of the lead. He's fairly confident we have the source, but he wants to exclude everything else."

"And how much does that cost?" Oscar asked.

"Twenty thousand."

Oscar's jaw dropped, and he shook his head. Wally whistled and scattered the sheets of paper. Only Rochelle was hanging on, and she really didn't have a vote when the issue was spending money.

"With no defendant, there's no lawsuit," Oscar said. "Why burn cash investigating this when you don't know who to sue?"

"I'll find the manufacturer," David said.

"Great, and when you do, then we have ourselves a lawsuit, maybe."

The door to Wally's office rattled, then opened. DeeAnna took a step out and said, "Wally, how much longer, baby?"

"Just a few minutes," Wally said. "We're almost finished here."

"But I'm tired of waiting."

"Okay, okay. I'll be there in a minute." She slammed the door and the walls shook.

"I guess she's now running the firm meeting," Rochelle observed.

"Knock it off," Wally said to Rochelle, then to David he continued: "I like this case, David, I really do. But with the Krayoxx litigation in full swing, we can't commit to spending big money on another case. I say you put this on hold, maybe keep looking for the importer, and after we settle Krayoxx, we'll be in a great position to pick and choose. You've got this family signed up. This kid ain't going anywhere. Let's keep it on a leash and crank it up next year."

David was in no position to argue. Both partners had said no. Rochelle would say yes if she had a vote, but she was losing interest. "Fair enough," David said. "Then I would like to pursue it myself, in my spare time, with my own money, and under the protection of my own malpractice policy."

"You have your own policy?" Oscar asked.

"No, but I'll get one easy enough."

"What about the twenty grand?" Wally asked. "According to the financials here, you've grossed less than $5,000 in the last four months."

"True, but each month has exceeded the prior one. Plus, I have a little cash in the bank. I'm willing to roll the dice and try to help this little boy."

"It's not about helping a little boy," Oscar shot back. "It's about financing the lawsuit. I agree with Wally. Why not put it off for a year?"

"Because I don't want to," David replied. "This family needs help now."

Wally shrugged and said, "Then go for it. I have no objections."

"Fine with me," Oscar said. "But I want to see an increase in your monthly gross."

"You'll see one."

Wally's door opened again, and DeeAnna stormed out. She stomped across the room, hissed the word "Bastard!" under her breath, then yanked open the front door, snarled "Don't call me!" in the general direction of the table, and shook the walls again when she slammed the door behind her.

"She has a temper," Wally observed.

"What a class act," Rochelle said softly.

"You can't be getting serious with her, Wally," Oscar said, almost pleading.

"She falls under the category of my business and not yours," Wally said. "Anything left on the agenda? I'm tired of this meeting."

"Nothing else from me," David said.

"Meeting adjourned," the senior partner announced.

CHAPTER 23

The great Jerry Alisandros finally made his appearance on the Chicago stage of his grand war against Varrick, and his arrival was impressive. First, he landed in the Gulfstream G650 that Wally was still dreaming of. Second, he brought with him an entourage that rivaled the one that surrounded Nadine Karros when she went to court. With Zell & Potter front and center, the playing field seemed level. Third, he had the skill, experience, and national reputation one would never find at Finley & Figg.

Oscar skipped the hearing because he wasn't needed. Wally couldn't wait to get there so he could strut in with his stud co-counsel. David tagged along out of curiosity.

Nadine Karros, her team, and her client had selected Iris Klopeck as their guinea pig, though neither her attorneys nor Iris herself had the slightest whiff of the master scheme. Varrick had filed a motion to separate the plaintiffs' cases, to make eight different lawsuits out of one, and to keep the litigation in Chicago instead of having it lumped with thousands of other cases in the brand-new multi-district litigation in southern Florida. The plaintiffs' lawyers opposed these motions strenuously. Thick briefs had been swapped. The mood was tense when the squads of lawyers gathered in Judge Seawright's courtroom.

As they waited, a clerk came forth and announced that the judge was delayed by some urgent matter but should be out in half an hour. David was loitering near the plaintiffs' table, chatting with a Zell &

Potter associate, when a defense lawyer slid over for a contrived hello. David vaguely recognized him from somewhere in the halls of Rogan Rothberg, but he had tried hard to forget those people. "I'm Taylor Barkley," the guy said on top of a quick handshake. "Harvard, two years ahead of you."

"A pleasure," David said, then introduced Barkley to the Zell & Potter lawyer he had just met. For a few minutes they chatted about the Cubs and the weather and finally got around to the issue at hand. Barkley claimed to be working around the clock as Rogan was getting slammed with Krayoxx work. David had lived that life, and survived it, and he had no desire to hear it again.

"Should be a hell of a trial," David said to fill in a gap.

Barkley snorted as if he had the inside scoop. "What trial?" he said. "These cases will never get near a jury. You know that, don't you?" he asked, looking at the Zell & Potter associate.

Barkley continued, half under his breath because the place was crawling with wired lawyers. "We'll defend like hell for a while, pad the file, rack up some obscene fees, then advise our dear client to settle. You'll figure out this game, Zinc. If you stay in it long enough."

"I'm catching on," David said, watching every word. He and the Zell & Potter associate were both on their heels, absorbing but not believing.

"For what it's worth," Barkley said, in a whisper, "you're almost a legend around Rogan these days. A guy with the balls to walk away, go find an easier job, now sitting on a pile of cases that are a gold mine. We're still slaving away by the hour."

David just nodded, hoping he would go away.

The courtroom deputy suddenly came to life and ordered everyone to stand. Judge Seawright swept in from behind the bench and ordered everyone to sit. "Good morning," he said into his mike as he arranged his papers. "We have a lot of ground to cover in the next two hours, and, as always, brevity with words will be appreciated. I am monitoring discovery, and it appears as though things are proceeding on course. Mr. Alisandros, do you have any complaints about discovery?"

Jerry stood proudly because everyone was watching. He had long gray hair swept back over his ears and bunched around his neck. His skin was well tanned, and his custom-tailored suit hung perfectly on his lean frame. "No sir, Your Honor, not at this time. And I am delighted to be in your courtroom."

"Welcome to Chicago. Ms. Karros, do you have any complaints with discovery?"

She stood, in her light gray silk and linen dress, V-neck, Empire waist, tight down the slender legs, long below the knee, with black platform pumps, and all eyes feasted upon her. David was looking forward to the trial just to watch the fashion show. Wally was drooling.

"Your Honor, we exchanged lists of experts this morning, so everything is in order," she said, her voice rich, her diction perfect.

"Very well," Seawright said. "That leads to the biggest issue of the day—that of where these cases will be tried. The plaintiffs have filed a motion to move all the cases, to join the multi-district litigation in federal court in Miami. The defendant objects, and not only prefers to keep the cases here in Chicago, but also to separate them, try them one at a time, beginning with the estate of one Percy Klopeck, now deceased. These issues have been thoroughly and exhaustively briefed. I've read every word. At this point, I'll allow remarks by both sides, beginning with the attorneys for the plaintiffs."

Jerry Alisandros walked with his notes to a small podium in the center of the courtroom, directly in front of and several feet below Judge Seawright. He carefully arranged his papers, cleared his throat, and began with the typical "If it pleases the court."

For Wally, it was the most exciting moment in his career. To think he, a hustler from the Southwest Side, was sitting in federal court watching great lawyers do battle over cases he had found and filed, cases he was responsible for, cases he had created—it was almost too much to behold. As he suppressed a grin, he felt even better when he touched his midsection and slid a finger under his belt. Down fifteen pounds.

Sober for 195 days. The lost weight and clear head were no doubt linked to the indescribable fun he and DeeAnna were having in bed. He was eating Viagra, driving a new convertible Jaguar (new to him but slightly used and financed over sixty months), and feeling twenty years younger. As he buzzed around Chicago with the top down, he dreamed endlessly of his Krayoxx money and the glorious life ahead. He and DeeAnna would travel and lie on beaches, and he would work only when necessary. He had already decided that he would specialize in mass torts, forget the humdrum of the street, the cheap divorces and drunk drivers, and go for the big money. He was certain he and Oscar would split. Frankly, after twenty years, it was time. Though he loved him like a brother, Oscar had no ambition, no vision, no real desire to step up his game. He and Oscar had already had a conversation about how to hide their Krayoxx money so his wife would see little of it. Oscar would go through a bad divorce, and Wally would be there to support him, but when it was over, the partners would split. It was sad but inevitable. Wally was going places; Oscar was too old to change.

Jerry Alisandros got off to a bad start when he tried to argue that Judge Seawright had no choice but to transfer the cases to Miami. "These cases were filed in Chicago, not Miami," the judge reminded Alisandros. "No one made you file them here. I suppose you could've filed them anywhere you can find Varrick Labs, which I presume is in any of the fifty states. I'm having trouble understanding why a federal judge in Florida thinks he can order a federal judge in Illinois to transfer his cases down there. Can you help me here, Mr. Alisandros?"

Mr. Alisandros could not. He tried valiantly to suggest that nowadays in mass tort litigation it is customary to establish multi-district litigation and have only one judge preside over all the cases.

Customary, but not mandatory. Seawright seemed irritated that someone, anyone would suggest that he was required to move the cases. They were his!

David sat behind Wally in a row of chairs in front of the bar. He was enthralled by the drama of the courtroom, the pressure, the high stakes, but he was also worried because it was apparent Judge Seawright was against them on this issue. However, Alisandros had assured their team that winning these initial motions was not crucial. If Varrick Labs wanted to try a single test case in Chicago, and to do so quickly, then so be it. He had never run away from a trial in his career. Bring it on!

The judge, though, seemed hostile. Why was David worried? There would be no trial, right? All the lawyers on his side of the aisle believed secretly, fervently, that Varrick Labs would settle its Krayoxx mess long before the trials started. And if Barkley on the other side could be believed, the defense lawyers were also thinking settlement. Was it a rigged game? Was this how the mass tort business really worked? A bad drug gets discovered; the plaintiffs' lawyers go into a frenzy rounding up the cases; lawsuits are filed; the big defense firms respond with an endless supply of expensive legal talent; both sides slug it out until the drugmaker gets tired of writing fat checks to its lawyers; then everything gets settled; the plaintiffs' lawyers rake in huge fees, and their clients get far less than they expected. When the dust settles, the lawyers on both sides are richer; the company cleans up its balance sheet and develops a replacement drug.

Was this nothing more than good theater?

Just as Jerry Alisandros began to repeat himself, he sat down. The lawyers perked up as Nadine Karros stood and walked to the podium. She had a few notes but didn't use them. Since it was obvious the judge agreed with her, she kept her arguments brief. She spoke in long eloquent sentences, as if they had been written down with plenty of forethought. Her words were clear, her voice carried nicely around the courtroom. Nothing was wasted—no extra verbiage, no useless gestures. The woman was meant for the stage. From several angles, she made the point that there was no case, no rule of procedure, no precedent anywhere that required a federal judge to transfer one of his cases to another federal judge.

After a few moments, David was wondering if he would actually get to watch Ms. Karros in action before a jury. Did she know, at that very moment, there would be no trial? Was she just going through the motions, at $2,000 an hour?

A month earlier Varrick Labs reported its quarterly earnings, which were down significantly. The company surprised analysts by writing off $5 billion for the projected costs of ongoing litigation, primarily Krayoxx. David was following this closely in financial publications and blogs. Opinion was split between those who thought Varrick Labs would hurry and clean up its mess through a massive settlement and those who thought the company might try to weather the storm through hardball litigation. The stock price ping-ponged between $35 and $40 per share, so the stockholders seemed reasonably calm.

He was also studying the history of mass tort litigation and found it surprising the number of times that a defendant corporation's stock rose impressively when it settled and got rid of a bunch of lawsuits. There was normally a dip in the stock price with the first wave of bad news and hysterics from the plaintiffs' bar, but as battle lines were formed and the numbers became firm, Wall Street seemed to prefer a good settlement. What Wall Street hated was "squishy liability," the kind that was often seen when a big case was handed over to a jury and the results were unpredictable. In the past ten years, virtually all of the major mass tort cases involving pharmaceuticals had been settled, and for billions.

On one hand, David was finding comfort in the research. But on the other, it had turned up little in the way of credible proof that Krayoxx did all the terrible things it was accused of doing.

———

After a thorough and fair debate, Judge Seawright had heard enough. He thanked the lawyers for their preparation and promised a ruling within ten days. The extra time was not needed—he could have ruled immediately from the bench. There was little doubt he would keep the cases in Chicago, and he seemed to favor the idea of a "show trial."

The plaintiffs' lawyers retired to the Chicago Chop House, where Mr. Alisandros had reserved the back room for a private lunch. Including Wally and David, there were seven lawyers and two paralegals (all men), and they all took their places around an oblong table. Jerry had preordered wine, and it was poured as soon as they sat down. Wally and David declined.

"A toast," Jerry announced as he tapped his wineglass. Silence. "I propose a toast to the Right Honorable Harry Seawright and his famous Rocket Docket. The trap has been laid, and the fools at Rogan Rothberg think we're blind. They want a trial. Old Harry wants one too, so by God let's give 'em a trial."

Everyone took a sip, and within seconds the conversation spiraled down to an analysis of the legs and backside of Nadine Karros. Wally, who had the right-hand seat to the throne of Mr. Alisandros, offered comments that were deemed hilarious. Over salads, the chatter quite naturally made its way to their second favorite subject—settlement. David, who was saying as little as possible, was coaxed into telling the story of his encounter with Taylor Barkley just before the hearing. His narrative was received with great interest—too much, in his opinion.

It was Jerry's stage, and he did most of the talking. In equal parts, he was enthusiastic about a big trial with a big verdict, but he was also supremely confident Varrick would buckle and put billions on the table.

Hours later, David was still confused, but he was also comforted by the presence of Jerry Alisandros. The man had fought the wars, inside the courtroom and out, and he almost never lost. According to *Lawyers Weekly*, the thirty-five partners at Zell & Potter split $1.3 billion in net profits the previous year. Net, after new jets, a firm golf course, and every other lavish expense allowed by the IRS. According to *Florida Business* magazine, Jerry's net worth was somewhere around $350 million.

Not a bad way to practice law.

David had not shown these numbers to Wally.

CHAPTER 24

For almost thirty years, Kirk Maxwell represented Idaho in the U.S. Senate. He was generally well regarded as a steady hand who shunned publicity and preferred to work off camera to get things done. He was quiet, unassuming, and one of the more popular members of Congress. However, his sudden death was nothing short of spectacular.

Maxwell had the Senate floor, microphone in hand, arguing fiercely with a colleague from the other side of the aisle, when he suddenly clutched his chest, dropped his mike, opened his mouth in horror, and crashed forward into the back of the desk in front of his. He died instantly of cardiac arrest, and it was all captured on the official Senate camera, released without proper authorization, and seen by the world on YouTube before his wife could get to the hospital.

Two days after his funeral, his wayward son mentioned to a reporter that the senator had been taking Krayoxx and the family was considering a lawsuit against Varrick Labs. By the time this was digested through the 24/7 news cycle, there was little doubt that the drug had killed the senator. Maxwell was only sixty-two, in fine health, but with a family history of high cholesterol.

An angry colleague announced a subcommittee hearing into the hazards of Krayoxx. The Food and Drug Administration was besieged with demands that the drug be pulled. Varrick Labs, hunkered down in the hills outside of Montville, offered no comment. It was another dark day for the company, but Reuben Massey had seen worse.

Such a lawsuit would be ironic for two reasons. First, in his thirty years in Washington, Senator Maxwell had taken millions from Big Pharma and, as far as the industry was concerned, had a perfect voting record. Second, the senator was an ardent tort reformer who had voted for years to place severe restrictions on the filing of lawsuits. But in the aftermath of a tragedy, irony is often lost on those left behind. His widow hired a noted plaintiffs' lawyer in Boise, but for "consultation only."

With Krayoxx on the front page, Judge Seawright decided a trial might be interesting after all. He ruled against the plaintiffs on all issues. The lawsuit Wally had filed and then amended would be broken up into separate pieces, with the case of the late Percy Klopeck being the first to get slotted into the fury of Local Rule 83:19, the Rocket Docket.

Wally was panic-stricken when he received notice of the ruling, but he began to settle down during a long and soothing conversation with Jerry Alisandros. Jerry explained that the death of Senator Maxwell was a gift from heaven—in more ways than one because a rabid tort reformer had been silenced—and would only increase the pressure on Varrick to begin settlement talks. And besides, as Jerry kept saying, he would welcome the chance to be on center stage versus the lovely Ms. Karros in a packed Chicago courtroom. "The last place they want to see me is in a courtroom," Jerry said again and again. His "Klopeck trial unit" was hard at work at that very moment. His firm had dealt with many egocentric federal judges with their own special versions of their own little Rocket Dockets.

"Seawright didn't create the Rocket Docket?" Wally asked, innocently.

"Heavens, no, Wally. I heard that term thirty years ago in upstate New York." Jerry went on to encourage Wally to continue combing the streets for more Krayoxx cases. "I'm about to make you rich, Wally," he said again and again.

Two weeks after Senator Maxwell's death, the FDA caved and ordered Krayoxx off the market. The mass tort bar was orgasmic, and lawyers in a dozen cities issued statements to the press, most of the same variety: Varrick will have to answer for its gross negligence. A federal investigation should be launched. The FDA should never have approved the drug. Varrick knew it had problems but had rushed the drug to market, where, in six years, it had grossed over $30 billion for the company. Who knows what's really buried in the Varrick research.

Oscar was conflicted by the news. On one hand, he, obviously, wanted the drug to generate as much bad press as possible to force the company to come to the table. But on the other hand, he was secretly, fervently hoping the drug would take care of his wife. Pulling it would ratchet up the pressure on Varrick, but it would also remove the drug from her medicine cabinet. Actually, Oscar's perfect outcome would be breaking news of a pending settlement at about the same time his wife croaked on the drug. He could keep all the money, avoid a messy divorce, then file suit on behalf of his dear departed wife and nail Varrick yet again.

He dreamed of such things behind his locked door. The phone lines were blinking nonstop, but he refused to pick up. Most of the calls were from Wally's "non-death cases," folks Wally had tracked down through his various schemes. Let Rochelle, Wally, and young David worry about the calls and the frantic clients. Oscar planned to stay in his office and avoid the frenzy, if possible.

Rochelle was ready to quit, and she demanded another firm meeting. "See what you've started," Oscar sneered at David as all four gathered around the table late one afternoon.

"What's on the agenda?" Wally asked, though everyone knew.

Rochelle had twisted David's arm to the point where he was willing to run interference. He cleared his throat and got right to the point.

"We have to get these Krayoxx cases organized. Since the drug was pulled, the phones are ringing like crazy with people who either are already signed up or want to jump on board."

"Ain't it great?" Wally said with a wide, satisfied grin.

"Maybe, Wally, but this is not a mass tort firm. We're not equipped to handle four hundred cases at a time. Your big mass tort boys have dozens of associates and even more paralegals, lots of bodies to handle the work."

"We have four hundred cases?" Oscar asked, and it wasn't clear if he was pleased or overwhelmed.

Wally slurped down some diet soda and said, proudly, "We have the eight death cases, of course, and 407 non-death cases, and counting. And I'm sorry that these minor cases are causing so much trouble, but when it's time to settle, and when we get to plug these guys into the compensation grid hammered out by Jerry Alisandros, we'll probably learn that each non-death is worth a paltry hundred thousand bucks or so. Times 407. Anybody here want to do the math?"

"That's not the issue, Wally," David countered. "We get the math. What you're missing is the fact that these cases may not be cases. Not a single one of these non-death clients has been evaluated by a doctor. We don't know if they have actually been harmed, do we?"

"No, not yet, and we have not filed suit for these clients either, have we, now?"

"No, but these people certainly believe they're full-fledged clients and they're about to be compensated. You've painted a rosy picture."

"When will they see a doctor?" Oscar asked.

"Soon," Wally shot in his direction. "Jerry is in the process of hiring an expert doctor here. He will examine each patient and give a report."

"And you're assuming that everyone has a legitimate claim?" David asked.

"I'm not assuming anything."

"How much will each exam cost?" Oscar asked.

"We don't know until we find the doctor."

"Who's paying for the exams?" Oscar asked.

"The Krayoxx Litigation Group. KLG for short."

"Are we on the hook?"

"No."

"Are you sure?"

"What is this?" Wally growled angrily. "Why is everybody hammering me? The first firm meeting was all about my girlfriend. This one is all about my cases. I'm starting to dislike firm meetings. What's wrong with you guys?"

"I'm fed up with these people on the phone," Rochelle said. "It's nonstop. Everybody's got a story. Some are crying because you've scared them to death, Wally. Some even stop by and want me to hold their hands. They all think they got bad hearts because of you and the FDA."

"What if they do have bad hearts, and their bad hearts are caused by Krayoxx, and we're able to get them some cash? Isn't that what lawyers are supposed to do?"

"What if we hire a paralegal for a few months?" David suggested, rather abruptly, then braced for the reactions. When the other three didn't speak quickly enough, he plowed on. "We can stick him or her in the junk room upstairs and send all the Krayoxx cases up there. I'll help him or her set up the litigation software and filing systems so that he or she is on top of every case. I'll supervise the project if you want. All phone calls dealing with Krayoxx can be routed to the new office. We take the pressure off Rochelle, and Wally can keep doing what he does best—hustle cases."

"We're not in a position to hire anyone," Oscar said, predictably. "Our cash flow is far below normal, thanks to Krayoxx. And, since you're not paying the bills yet, and not even close to doing so, I might add, I don't think you're in a position to suggest spending more money."

"I understand," David said. "I was just suggesting a way for the firm to get itself organized."

Actually, you're quite lucky we decided to hire you, Oscar thought to himself and almost said aloud.

Wally liked the idea but, at the moment, didn't have the spine to take on his senior partner. Rochelle admired David for his boldness, but she wasn't about to comment on an issue dealing with the overhead.

"I have a better idea," Oscar said to David. "Why don't you become the Krayoxx paralegal? You're already upstairs. You know something about litigation software. You're always squawking about getting organized around here. You've been wanting a new filing system. Judging by your monthly grosses, it looks as though you have some spare time. It'll save us some dough. Whatta you say?"

It was all true, and David wasn't about to back down. "Okay, what's my cut of the settlement?"

Oscar and Wally looked at each other, all four eyes narrowing as this rattled around their brains. They had not yet decided how they themselves would split the money. There had been some loose chatter about a bonus for Rochelle and one for David, but as for the real division of the spoils, not a word.

"We'll have to talk about that," Wally said.

"Yes, this is a matter for the partners," Oscar added, as if being a partner in their firm were akin to belonging to an exclusive and powerful club.

"Well, hurry up and decide something," Rochelle said. "I can't answer all these calls and do all the filing."

There was a knock on the door. DeeAnna was back.

CHAPTER 25

Reuben Massey's master plan to deal with his company's latest drug mess had been upended by the death of Senator Kirk Maxwell, who was now derisively known in the Varrick hallways as Jerk Maxwell. His widow had not filed suit, but her windbag of a lawyer was thoroughly savoring his fifteen minutes in the spotlight. He was readily available for interviews, even got himself on a few of the cable yak fests. He colored his hair, bought some new suits, and was living the dream of so many lawyers.

Varrick's common stock had dipped to $29.50, its lowest price in six years. Two Wall Street analysts, two men loathed by Massey, had issued sell recommendations. One wrote: "After only six years on the market, Krayoxx accounts for one-quarter of Varrick's revenue. With it off the market, the company's near-term forecast is quite uncertain." The other wrote: "The numbers are frightening. With one million potential Krayoxx plaintiffs, Varrick will be mired in the cesspool of mass tort litigation for the next ten years."

At least he got the word "cesspool" right, Massey mumbled to himself as he flipped through the morning financials. It was not yet 8:00 a.m. The sky over Montville was cloudy, the mood inside his bunker was somber, but, oddly, he was in good spirits. At least once a week, and more often if possible, Mr. Massey allowed himself the pleasure of eating someone for breakfast. Today's meal would be especially delightful.

———

As a young man Layton Koane had served four terms in the U.S. House before he was called home by the voters after a messy affair with a female staffer. Disgraced, he was unable to find meaningful work back home in Tennessee, and as a college dropout he possessed no real talents or skills. His résumé was embarrassingly thin. Divorced, unemployed, bankrupt, and only forty years old, he drifted back to the Capitol and decided to venture down the yellow brick road traveled by so many washed-up politicians. He embraced one of Washington's time-honored traditions. He became a lobbyist.

Unburdened by ethical considerations, Koane quickly became a rising star in the game of pork. He could find it, smell it, dig it out, and deliver it to clients willing to pay his constantly rising fees. He was one of the first lobbyists to understand the intricacies of earmarks, those addictive little dishes of lard so craved by members of Congress and paid for by unwitting factory workers back home. Koane first got noticed in his new trade when he collected a $100,000 fee from a well-known public university in need of a new basketball arena. Uncle Sam pitched in $10 million for the project, an appropriation found in the fine print of a three-thousand-page bill passed at midnight. When a rival school heard about it, a brouhaha ensued. But it was too late.

The controversy put Koane on the map, and other clients came running. One was a real estate developer in Virginia who envisioned the damming of a river, thus creating a lake, thus allowing lakefront lots to be sold at hefty prices. Koane charged the developer $500,000 and instructed him to drop another $100,000 into the PAC of the congressman who represented the district where the dam was not needed. Once everyone was paid and on board, Koane went to work on the federal budget and found some spare change—$8 million—in a defense appropriation to the Army Corps of Engineers. The dam was built. The developer made a bundle. Everyone was happy but the environmentalists, conservationists, and the communities downstream.

This was business as usual in Washington and would have gone unnoticed but for a persistent reporter from Roanoke. Embarrassment and black eyes all around—the congressman, the developer, Koane—but in the lobbying trade there is no shame, and all publicity is good. Koane's business soared. After five years in the game, he opened his own shop—The Koane Group, Specialists in Governmental Affairs. After ten years, he was a multimillionaire. After twenty, he was annually ranked as one of the three most powerful lobbyists in Washington. (Does any other democracy rank its lobbyists?)

Varrick paid The Koane Group a flat retainer of $1 million per year, and much more when actual work was done. For that kind of money, Mr. Layton Koane would come running when his client said so.

As witnesses to the bloodbath, Reuben Massey decided to use his most trusted lawyers—Nicholas Walker and Judy Beck. The three were in place when Koane arrived, alone, as per Massey's instructions. Koane now owned a jet, had a chauffeur, and liked to travel with an entourage, but not today.

Things got off to a cordial start as they exchanged pleasantries and nibbled on croissants. Koane had gained even more weight, and his tailored suit was pulling at the seams. It was shiny gray, with a sheen similar to that usually seen on suits worn by television evangelists. His well-starched white shirt was bulging around the waist. His fleshy triple neck was straining under his collar. As always, he wore an orange tie and orange pocket square. Regardless of his wealth, he had never learned how to dress.

Massey loathed Layton Koane and viewed him as a rube, a dope, a hack, a huckster who was lucky enough to be in the right place at the right time. But then, Massey loathed almost everything about Washington: the federal government and its stifling regulations; the horde of staffers who wrote them; the politicians who approved them; the bureaucrats who enforced them. To survive in such a dysfunctional place, he figured, one had to be as greasy as Layton Koane.

"We're getting hammered in Washington," Massey said, stating the obvious.

"Not just Washington," Koane replied with his twang. "I own forty thousand shares of your stock, remember?"

True, Varrick Labs had once paid The Koane Group with stock options.

Massey picked up some notes and peered over his reading glasses. "Last year we paid your company over $3 million."

"Three million two," Koane said.

"And we contributed the maximum amount to either the reelection campaign or the PAC of eighty-eight out of a hundred members of the U.S. Senate, including, of course, the late great Maxwell, may he rest in peace. We maxed out to over three hundred members of the House. In both houses, we maxed out to both parties' central slush funds, whatever the hell they're called. We maxed out to no fewer than forty PACs, all supposedly doing God's work down there. In addition, two dozen of our senior executives did their own version of maxing out, all under your guidance. And now, thanks to the wisdom of the Supreme Court, we are able to funnel into the electoral system vast sums of cash that cannot be detected. Over $5 million last year alone. If you tally all this up, and you include all payments of all types, reported and unreported, above the table and below, Varrick Laboratories and its executives forked over almost $40 million last year to keep our great democracy on the right track."

Massey dropped the papers and glared at Koane. "Forty million to buy one thing, Layton, the one and only product you have to sell. Influence."

Koane was nodding slowly.

"So please tell us, Layton, with all this influence that we've purchased over the years, how in hell does the FDA pull Krayoxx off the market?"

"The FDA is the FDA," Koane replied. "It's a world of its own, immune from political pressure, or so we're led to believe."

"Political pressure? Everything was fine until a politician died. It looks to me like his buddies in the Senate pressured the hell out of the FDA."

"Of course they did."

"Then where were you? Don't you have former FDA commissioners on your payroll?"

"We have one, but the important word is 'former.' He no longer gets a vote."

"So, it appears to me as if you got outpoliticked."

"Perhaps for now, Reuben. We've lost the first battle, but we can still win the war. Maxwell's gone and he's being forgotten by the minute. That's what happens in Washington—they forget about you real fast. They're already campaigning in Idaho to replace him. Give it some time and his death will be forgotten."

"Time? We're losing $18 million a day in sales because of the FDA. Since you arrived here this morning and parked your car, we've lost $400,000 in sales. Don't talk to me about time, Layton."

Nicholas Walker and Judy Beck were, of course, taking notes. Or at least scribbling something on their yellow legal pads. Neither looked up, but both were enjoying this little workout.

"Are you blaming me, Reuben?" Koane asked, almost desperately.

"Yes. Absolutely. I don't understand how that rotten place works down there, so I hire and pay you a bloody fortune to guide my company through the minefield. So, yes, Layton, when something goes wrong, I blame you. A perfectly safe drug has been yanked off the market for no valid reason. Explain that to me, can you?"

"I can't explain it, but it's not fair to blame me. We've been on top of this matter since the first lawsuits were filed. We had solid contacts up and down the line, and the FDA showed little interest in pulling the drug, regardless of how loud the trial lawyers were screaming. We were safe. And then Maxwell collapsed in fine fashion, on video. That changed everything."

There was a pause as all four reached for their coffee cups.

Koane never failed to bring along some gossip, some inside knowledge that was passed along in whispers, and he couldn't wait to share it. "A source tells me the Maxwell family does not want to file a lawsuit. A very good source."

"Who?" Massey demanded.

"Another member of the club, another senator who's very close to Maxwell and his family. He called me yesterday. We had a drink. Sherry Maxwell does not want a lawsuit, but her lawyer does. He's pretty shrewd, realizes he's got Varrick in his crosshairs. If the lawsuit is filed, it's another round of bad news for the company, more pressure on the FDA to keep the drug off the market. But if the lawsuit goes away, then Maxwell will soon be forgotten. One headache down, more to follow."

Massey flipped his right hand in circles. "Keep going. Spill it."

"For $5 million, the lawsuit will go away. I'll handle it through my office. It will be a confidential settlement, no details whatsoever."

"Five million? For what? For a drug that did no harm?"

"No. Five million to soothe a big headache," Koane replied. "He was a senator for almost thirty years, an honest one, so his estate is not too impressive. The family needs a little cash."

"Any news of a settlement will trigger an avalanche with the tort boys," Nicholas Walker said. "You can't keep this quiet. There are too many reporters watching."

"I know how to manipulate the press, Nick. We shake hands on a deal now, sign the papers behind locked doors, and wait it out. The Maxwell family and their lawyer will have no comment, but I'll make sure there's a nice leak to the effect that the family has chosen not to file suit. Look, there's no law, not even in this country, that they have to sue. People walk away from lawsuits all the time for all sorts of reasons. We cut the deal, sign the papers, promise them the money in two years, plus interest. I can sell it."

Massey stood and stretched his back. He walked to a tall window and surveyed the fog and mist seeping through the woods. Without turning around, he said, "What do you think, Nick?"

Thinking out loud, Walker said, "Well, it would certainly be nice to get the Maxwell matter out of the way. Layton's right. His pals in the Senate will forget about him quickly, especially if there's no lawsuit on page 2. Five million sounds like a bargain, in the scheme of things."

"Judy?"

"Agreed," she said without hesitation. "The priority is getting the drug back on the market. If making the Maxwell family happy speeds this along, I say go for it."

Massey slowly returned to his seat, cracked his knuckles, rubbed his face, sipped his coffee, obviously a man in deep thought. But he was anything but indecisive. "Okay, Layton, do the deal. Get rid of Maxwell. But if this settlement blows up in our faces, I'm terminating our relationship immediately. Right now, I'm not happy with you and your firm, and I'm looking for a reason to shop around."

"No need to do that, Reuben. I'll make Maxwell go away."

"Super. Now, how long before Krayoxx is back on the market? How long and how much?"

Koane gently rubbed his forehead and removed a few tiny beads of sweat. "I can't answer that, Reuben. We need to go one step at a time and run out some clock. I'll shove Maxwell under the rug, then let's meet again."

"When?"

"Thirty days?"

"Great. Thirty days is $540 million in lost revenue."

"I got the math, Reuben."

"I'm sure you do."

"I got it, Reuben, okay?"

Massey's eyes were flashing, and his right index finger was jabbing through the air, in the direction of his lobbyist. "Listen to me, Layton. If this drug is not back on the market in the very near future, I'm coming to Washington to fire you and your firm, then I'll hire a whole new bunch of 'government affairs specialists' to protect my company. I can get a meeting with the vice president and the Speaker of the House. I can have drinks with a dozen or so senators. I'll take my checkbook and a truckful of cash, and if I have to, I'll take a carload of hookers to the FDA and turn 'em loose."

Koane offered a fake smile as if he'd heard something funny. "No need for that, Reuben. Just give me a little time."

"We don't have a little time."

"The quickest way to get Krayoxx back on the market is to prove it's not harmful," Koane said coolly, wanting to divert the chatter away from being fired. "Any ideas?"

"We're working on it," Nicholas Walker said.

Massey stood again and returned to his favorite window. "Meeting's over, Layton," he growled, and did not turn around to say good-bye.

As soon as Koane was gone, Reuben relaxed and felt better about the morning. Nothing like a human sacrifice to get a hard-nosed CEO in good spirits. As Nick Walker and Judy Beck checked their e-mails on their smartphones, Reuben waited. When he had their attention, he said, "I suppose we should discuss our settlement strategy. What's the timeline now?"

"The Chicago trial is on track," Walker said. "There is no trial date, but we should hear something soon. Nadine Karros is watching Judge Seawright's calendar, and there's a nice gap in late October. With some luck, it might happen then."

"That's less than a year after the lawsuit was filed."

"Yes, but we've done nothing to slow it down. Nadine's putting up a stiff defense, going through all the motions, but no real obstacles. No motion to dismiss. No plans for summary judgment. Discovery is proceeding nicely. Seawright seems to be curious about the case and wants a trial."

"Today is June 3. They're still filing lawsuits. If we start talking settlement now, can we string it out until October?"

Judy Beck responded. "No problem at all. Fetazine took three years to settle, and there were half a million claims. Zoltaven took even longer. The tort bar is thinking about one thing—the $5 billion we charged off last quarter. They're dreaming of that much money hitting the table."

"It will be another frenzy," Nick said.

"Let's get it started," Massey said.

CHAPTER 26

Wally was sitting in divorce court on the sixteenth floor of the Richard J. Daley Center, downtown. On tap for the morning was *Strate v. Strate*, one of a dozen or so miserable little divorces that would forever (hopefully) separate two people who had no business getting married in the first place. To untangle things, they had hired Wally, paid him $750 in full for an uncontested divorce, and after six months were now in court, on opposite sides of the aisle, anxious for their case to be called. Wally waited too, waited and watched the procession of scarred and warring spouses trek meekly to the bench, bow at the judge, speak when their lawyers told them to, avoid eye contact with each other, and after a few somber minutes leave, unmarried again.

Wally was in a group of lawyers, all waiting impatiently. He knew about half of them. The other half he'd never seen before. In a city with twenty thousand lawyers, the faces were always changing. What a rat race. What a grinding treadmill.

A wife was crying in front of the judge. She didn't want the divorce. Her husband did.

Wally could not wait until these scenes were history. One day soon he would spend his time in a swanky office closer to downtown, far away from the sweat and stress of street law, behind a wide marble desk with two shapely secretaries answering his phones and fetching his files and a paralegal or two doing his grunt work. No more divorces, DUIs, wills, cheap estates, no more clients who couldn't pay. He would pick and choose the injury cases he wanted and make big money in the process.

The other lawyers were watching him warily. He knew this. They mentioned Krayoxx from time to time. Curious, envious, some hoping Wally would strike gold because that would give them hope. Others, though, were eager to see him fall flat because that would prove their drudgery was what they were meant to do. Nothing more.

His cell phone vibrated in his coat pocket. He grabbed it, focused on the name and number of the caller, then jumped from his seat and sprinted from the courtroom. As soon as he cleared the doors, he said, "Jerry. I'm in court. What's up?"

"Big news, Brother Wally," Alisandros sang. "I played eighteen holes of golf yesterday with Nicholas Walker. Ring a bell?"

"No, yes. I'm not sure. Who?"

"We played on my course. I shot a 78. Poor Nick was 20 strokes back. Not much of a golfer, I'm afraid. He's the chief in-house lawyer for Varrick Labs. Known him for years. Prince of an asshole, but honorable."

There was a gap Wally needed to fill here, but he could think of nothing helpful. "So, Jerry, you didn't call to brag about your golf game, right?"

"No, Wally. I'm calling to inform you that Varrick wants to open a dialogue on the issue of settlement. Not actual negotiations, mind you, but they want to start talking. This is the way it usually happens. They crack the door. We get a foot in. They tap-dance. We tap-dance. And before you know it, we're talking money. Big money. Are you with me, Wally?"

"Oh yes."

"I thought so. Look, Wally, we have a long way to go before your cases are in a posture to be settled. Let's get to work. I'll line up the doctors to do the exams—that's the crucial part. You need to jack up your efforts to find more cases. We'll probably settle the death cases first—how many do you have now?"

"Eight."

"Is that all? Thought it was more."

"It's eight, Jerry, with one on the fast track, remember? Klopeck."

"Right, right. With that hot chick on the other side. Frankly, I'd like to try that one just to stare at her legs all day."

"Anyway."

"Anyway, let's kick into high gear. I'll call later this afternoon with a game plan. Lots of work to do, Wally, but the fix is in."

Wally returned to the courtroom and resumed his wait. He kept repeating, "The fix is in. The fix is in." Game's up. Party's over. He'd heard it all his life, but what did it mean in the context of high-powered litigation? Was Varrick throwing in the towel, surrendering so quickly, cutting its losses? Wally assumed so.

He glanced at the haggard, beaten-down lawyers around him. Ham-and-eggers just like himself who spent their days trying to squeeze fees out of working stiffs with no money to spare. You poor bastards, he thought.

He couldn't wait to tell DeeAnna, but first he had to talk to Oscar. And not at Finley & Figg, where no conversation was ever private.

They met for lunch two hours later at a spaghetti house not far from the office. Oscar had had a rough morning trying to referee six grown children fighting over their dead mother's estate, in which there was virtually nothing of value. He needed a drink and ordered a bottle of inexpensive wine. Wally, at 241 days sober, had no trouble sticking with water. Over Caprese salads, Wally quickly recapped his conversation with Jerry Alisandros and ended with a dramatic "This is the moment, Oscar. It's finally going to happen."

Oscar's mood changed as he listened and gulped down the first glass. He managed a smile, and Wally could almost see the skepticism evaporating. He took out a pen, shoved the salad aside, and began scratching. "Let's run through the math again, Wally. Is a death case really worth $2 million?"

Wally glanced around to make sure no one was listening. The coast was clear. "I've done a ton of research, okay? I've looked at dozens of settlements in mass tort drug cases. There are too many unknowns right now to predict how much each case is worth. You gotta determine liability, cause of death, medical history, age of the deceased, income-earning potential, stuff like that. Then we gotta find out how much Varrick is tossing in the pot. But a million bucks is the floor, I think. We have eight. Fees are at 40 percent. Half to Jerry, plus a stroke for his expertise, and we're looking at a net to our firm of something like $1.5 mill."

Oscar was scribbling with a fury, though he'd heard these numbers a hundred times. "They're death cases. They gotta be worth more than a mill each," he said, as if he'd handled dozens of these large cases.

"Maybe two," Wally said. "Then we got all the non-death cases, 407 as of now. Let's say only half can qualify after a medical exam. Based on somewhat similar cases—the mass drug variety—I think $100,000 is a reasonable figure for a client whose heart valve has been slightly damaged. That's $20 million, Oscar. Our cut is something in the neighborhood of $3.5 million."

Oscar wrote something, then stopped, took a long drink of wine, and said, "So, we should talk about our split, right? Is that where this is going?"

"The split is one of several pressing issues."

"Okay, what's wrong with fifty-fifty?" All fee fights began with an even split.

Wally stuffed a slice of tomato into his mouth and chewed it fiercely. "What's wrong with fifty-fifty is that I discovered Krayoxx, rounded up the cases, and so far I've done about 90 percent of the work. I have the eight death cases in my office. David has the other four hundred upstairs. You, if I'm not mistaken, have no Krayoxx cases in your office."

"You're not asking for 90 percent are you?"

"Of course not. Here's my suggestion. We have a ton of work to do. All of these cases have to be screened by a doctor, evaluated, and so on. Let's put everything else aside—me, you, David—and get to work. We prep the cases while we're also looking for new ones. Once the settlement news breaks, every lawyer in the country will go crazy over Krayoxx, so we gotta get even busier. And once the checks arrive, I think a sixty-thirty-ten split is fair."

Oscar had ordered the lasagna special, and Wally the stuffed ravioli. When the waiter was gone, Oscar said, "Your fee is twice mine? That's never happened before. I don't like it."

"What do you like?"

"Fifty-fifty."

"And what about David? We promised him a cut when he agreed to take the non-death cases."

"Okay, fifty for you, forty for me, ten for David. Rochelle gets a nice bonus but no piece of the pie."

With so much money on the way, it was easy to toss around the numbers, even easier to cut a deal. There had been nasty fights over $5,000 fees, but not today. The money soothed them and took away any desire to squabble. Wally slowly reached across, and Oscar did the same. They quickly shook hands and plunged into their entrées.

After a few bites, Wally said, "How's the wife?"

Oscar frowned, grimaced, and looked away. Paula Finley was a subject completely off-limits because no one at the firm could stand her, including Oscar.

Wally pressed on. "You know, Oscar, this is the moment. If you're ever going to ditch her, do it now."

"Marital advice from you?"

"Yes, because you know I'm right."

"I assume you've been thinking about this."

"Yes, because you have not, and that's because you've never believed in these cases, until now perhaps."

Oscar poured more wine and said, "Let's hear it."

Wally leaned in closer again, as if they were swapping nuclear secrets. "File for divorce now, immediately. No big deal. I've done it four times. Move out, get an apartment, cut all ties. I'll handle it on your end, and she can hire whomever she wants. We'll draw up a contract, date it six months ago, and it'll say that I get 80 percent of the Krayoxx settlements, if any, and you and David split 20 percent. You gotta show some income from Krayoxx; otherwise her lawyer will go nuts. But most of the money can stay in a slush fund for, I don't know, a year or so, until the divorce is over. Then, at some unknown point in the future, you and I settle up."

"That's a fraudulent transfer of assets."

"I know. I love it. I've done it a thousand times, though on a much smaller scale. I suspect you have too. Pretty clever, don't you think?"

"If we get caught, we could both get thrown in jail for contempt of court, with no hearing."

"We will not get caught. She thinks Krayoxx is all mine, right?"

"Right."

"So, it'll work. It's our law firm, and we make the rules on how the money gets split. Completely within our discretion."

"Her lawyers won't be stupid, Wally. They'll know all about the big Krayoxx settlement as soon as it happens."

"Come on, Oscar, it ain't like we hit these licks all the time. Over the last ten years I suspect your adjusted gross has averaged, what, $75,000?"

Oscar shrugged. "About the same as yours. Pretty pathetic, don't you think? Thirty years in the trenches."

"Not the point, Oscar. The point is that in a divorce, they'll look at what you've earned in the past."

"I know."

"If the Krayoxx money is mine, then we can argue, with evidence, that your income hasn't changed."

"What will you do with the money?"

"Bury it offshore until the divorce is over. Hell, Oscar, we could leave it offshore and pop down to Grand Cayman once a year to check on it. Believe me, there's no way they'll ever know. But you gotta file now and get out."

"Why are you so keen on me getting a divorce?"

"Because I loathe that woman. Because you've been dreaming of a divorce since your honeymoon. Because you deserve to be happy, and if you sack this bitch and hide the money, your life will take a dramatic turn for the better. Think of it, Oscar, single at sixty-two with cash in the bank."

Oscar couldn't suppress a smile. He drained his third glass. He took a few bites. He was obviously struggling with something, so he finally asked, "How do I break it to her?"

Wally dabbed the corners of his mouth, stiffened his spine, and assumed the voice of authority. "Well, there are many ways to do it, and I've tried them all. Have you two ever talked about splitting up?"

"Not that I recall."

"I assume it would be easy to start a big fight."

"Oh, so easy. She's always unhappy about something, usually money, and we fight almost every day."

"That's what I figured. Do it like this, Oscar. Go home tonight and drop the bomb. Tell her you're unhappy and you want out. Plain and simple. No fighting, no bickering, no negotiating. Tell her she can have the house, the car, the furniture, she can have it all if she'll agree to a no-fault."

"And if she won't agree?"

"Leave anyway. Come stay at my place until we can find you an apartment. Once she sees you walk out the door, she'll get angry and start scheming, especially Paula. It won't take long for her to blow up. Give her forty-eight hours and she'll be a cobra."

"She's already a cobra."

"And she has been for decades. We'll file the papers, have them served on her, and that'll send her over the edge. She'll have a lawyer by the end of the week."

"I've given this advice before, just never thought I'd do it myself."

"Oscar, sometimes it takes balls to walk away. Do it now while you can still enjoy life."

Oscar poured the last of the wine into his glass and started smiling again. Wally could not remember the last time he'd seen his senior partner so content.

"Can you do it, Oscar?"

"Yep. In fact, I think I'll go home early, start packing, and get it over with."

"Awesome. Let's celebrate with dinner tonight. On the firm."

"A deal, but that bimbo won't be around, right?"

"I'll lose her."

Oscar downed the wine like a shot of tequila and said, "Damn, Wally, I haven't been this excited in years."

CHAPTER 27

It had been difficult to convince the Khaing family that they sincerely wanted to help, but after a few weeks of Big Mac dinners a high level of trust developed. Each Wednesday, after an early dinner of something healthier, David and Helen pulled through the same McDonald's, ordered the same burgers and fries, and drove to the apartment complex in Rogers Park to visit the family. Zaw, the grandmother, and Lu, the grandfather, joined in because they were also fond of fast food. For the rest of the week they lived on a diet that was primarily rice and chicken, but on Wednesday the Khaings ate like real Americans.

Helen, seven months pregnant and looking every day of it, was initially hesitant about the weekly visits. If there was lead in the air, she had an unborn baby to protect. So David checked everything. He badgered Dr. Biff Sandroni until he cut his fee from $20,000 to $5,000, with David doing most of the legwork. David went through the apartment himself and collected samples of wall paint, water, ceramic coatings, cups and saucers, plates, mixing bowls, family photo albums, toys, shoes, clothing, virtually anything and everything the family came into contact with. He drove this collection to Sandroni's lab in Akron, dropped it off, then picked it up two weeks later and returned it to the family. According to Sandroni's report, there were only traces of lead, acceptable levels and nothing for the family to worry about. Helen and the baby were safe in the Khaing apartment.

Thuya had been poisoned by the Nasty Teeth, and Dr. Sandroni was prepared to say so, under oath, in any court in the country. David was sitting on a promising lawsuit, but they had yet to find a defendant. He and Sandroni had a short list of four Chinese companies known to make similar toys for American importers, but they had not been able to pinpoint the manufacturer. And, according to Sandroni, there was a good chance they would never identify it. The set of Nasty Teeth could have been made twenty years earlier, then stored in a warehouse for a decade before being shipped to the U.S., where it could have spent another five years languishing in the supply chain. The manufacturer and the importer could still be in business, or they might have gone bust years ago. The Chinese were under constant pressure from U.S. watchdogs to monitor the amount of lead used in a thousand products, and it was often impossible to determine who made what in the maze of cheap factories scattered around the country. Dr. Sandroni had an endless list of sources, he'd been involved in hundreds of lawsuits, but after four months of digging, he was empty-handed. David and Helen had been to every flea market and toy store in Greater Chicago, and they had put together an astonishing collection of fake teeth and vampire fangs, but nothing exactly like Nasty Teeth. Their search wasn't over, but it had lost steam.

Thuya was home now, alive but grievously wounded. The brain damage was severe. He could not walk without assistance, speak clearly, feed himself, or control his bodily functions. His vision was limited, and he could barely respond to basic commands. Ask him his name and he would open his mouth and emit a sound similar to "Tay." He spent most of his time in a special bed with guardrails, and keeping it clean was a difficult task. Caring for the boy was a daily struggle that involved everyone in the family and many of the neighbors. The future was beyond contemplation. His condition was not likely to improve, according to the rather tactful statements of his doctors. Off the record and away from the family, they told David in confidence that Thuya's body and mind would not grow normally, and there was nothing else they could do. And there was no place to put him—no facility for brain-damaged children.

Thuya was spoon-fed a special formula that was a mix of finely ground fruit and vegetables and loaded with daily nutrients. He wore diapers made especially for such children. The formula, diapers, and medications were running $600 a month, of which David and Helen had pledged half. The Khaings had no health insurance, and had it not been for the generosity of the Lakeshore Children's Hospital he would not have received such high-quality care. He would probably be dead. In short, Thuya was now a burden that was almost inconceivable.

Soe and Lwin insisted that he sit at the table for dinner. He had a special chair, also donated by the hospital, and when properly belted and latched down, he sat straight and expected his food. While the family devoured the burgers and fries, Helen carefully fed Thuya with a baby spoon. She said she needed the practice. David sat on the other side with a paper towel, chatting with Soe about work and life in America. Thuya's sisters, who chose to use the American names of Lynn and Erin, were eight and six, respectively. They said little during dinner, but it was obvious they were thrilled with real fast food. When they did speak, it was with perfect, unaccented English. According to Lwin, they were making straight A's in school.

Perhaps it was the gloomy prospect of an uncertain future, or maybe it was just the meager existence being carved out by desperate immigrants, but the dinners were solemn and subdued. At various times, the parents, grandparents, and sisters looked at Thuya as if they wanted to cry. They remembered the noisy, hyper little boy with the quick smile and easy laugh, and they were struggling to accept the truth that he would never return. Soe blamed himself for buying the fake teeth. Lwin blamed herself for not being more diligent. Lynn and Erin blamed themselves for encouraging Thuya to play with the teeth and scare them. Even Zaw and Lu blamed themselves; they should have done something, though they had no idea what.

After dinner, David and Helen walked Thuya out of the apartment, down the short sidewalk, and, with the entire family watching, strapped him into the rear seat of their car and drove away. For emergencies, they brought along a small bag with extra diapers and cleaning supplies.

They drove twenty minutes to the lakefront and parked near Navy Pier. David took his left hand, Helen his right, and they began a slow, plodding walk that was almost painful to watch. Thuya moved like a ten-month-old attempting his first steps, but there was no hurry and he wasn't about to fall. They eased along the boardwalk, passing all kinds of boats. If Thuya wanted to stop and inspect a forty-foot ketch, they did so. If he wanted to look at a large fishing boat, they stopped and talked about it. David and Helen chattered nonstop, like two proud parents with a toddler. Thuya jabbered back, an incomprehensible stream of utterings and noises that they pretended to understand. When he grew tired, they pushed him to keep walking. It was important, according to the rehab specialist at the hospital. His muscles could not get soft.

They had taken him to parks, carnivals, malls, ball games, and street parties. The Wednesday night excursions were important to him, and the only break during the week for his family. After two hours, they returned to the apartment.

Three new faces were waiting. In the past months, David had handled several minor legal matters for the Burmese who lived in the complex. There were the usual immigration matters, and he was becoming adept in that growing specialty of the law. There had been a near divorce, but the spouses reconciled. There was an ongoing lawsuit over the purchase of a used car. His reputation was growing among the Burmese immigrants, and he was not convinced that was altogether a good thing. He needed clients who could pay.

They stepped outside and leaned on the cars. Soe explained that the three men were working for a drainage contractor. Because they were illegals, and the contractor knew this, he was paying them $200 a week in cash. They were working eighty hours a week. To make matters worse, their boss had not paid them a dime in three weeks. They spoke little English, and because David could not believe what he was hearing, he asked Soe to carefully go through it a second time.

This version was the same as the first. Two hundred dollars a week, straight pay for overtime, no pay in three weeks. And they were not the only ones. There were others from Burma and a whole truckload from Mexico. All illegals, all working like dogs, all getting screwed.

David took notes and promised to look into the situation.

Driving home, he described the case to Helen. "But does an illegal worker have the right to sue a crooked employer?" she asked.

"That's the question. I'll find out tomorrow."

After lunch, Oscar did not return to the office. To do so would have been fruitless. He had far too much on his mind to waste time puttering around his desk. He was half drunk, and he needed to sober up. He filled his tank at a convenience store, bought a tall cup of black coffee, then headed south on I-57 and was soon outside of Chicago and passing through farmland.

How many times had he advised his clients to file for divorce? Thousands. It was so easy to do, under the circumstances. "Look, there comes a time in some marriages when a spouse needs to get out. For you, that time is now." He'd always felt so wise, even smug when dispensing such advice. Now he felt like a fraud. How could a person give such counsel unless he'd been through it himself?

He and Paula had been together for thirty unhappy years. Their only child was a twenty-six-year-old divorcée named Keely who was becoming more and more like her mother. Keely's divorce was still fresh, primarily because she enjoyed reveling in her misery. She had a job that paid little, lots of contrived emotional problems that required pills, and her principal source of therapy was nonstop shopping with her mother at Oscar's expense.

"I'm sick of both of them," Oscar said loudly and boldly as he passed the exit signs at Kankakee. "I'm sixty-two years old, in good health, with a life expectancy now of twenty-three more years, and I have the right to pursue happiness. Right?"

Of course he did.

But how to break the news? That was the question. What should he say to drop the bomb? He thought of old clients, old divorces he'd handled over the years. At the extreme end of the spectrum, the bomb was dropped when the wife caught the husband in bed with another woman. Oscar could think of three, maybe four cases where this had happened. That was a bomb dropper all right. The marriage is over, honey, I've found someone else. At the other end, he'd once handled a divorce for a couple who never fought, never discussed separation or divorce, and had just celebrated their thirtieth wedding anniversary and purchased a retirement home on a lake. Then the husband came home from a business trip and the house was deserted. All of his wife's clothes and half the furnishings were gone. She moved out, said she had never loved him. She soon remarried, and he killed himself.

It was never difficult provoking a fight with Paula; the woman loved to bicker and brawl. Perhaps he should drink some more, go home half drunk, get her started on his drinking, push back hard with her endless shopping, keep throwing gas on the fire until they were both screaming. He could then pack some clothes in a huff and storm out.

Oscar had never found the courage to walk out. He should have, dozens of times, but he always slunk down the hall, went to the guest bedroom, locked the door, and slept alone.

As he approached Champaign, he settled on his plan. Why go through the ruse of starting a fight so he could pin blame on her? He wanted out, so be a man and admit it. "I'm unhappy, Paula, and I've been unhappy for years. There's no doubt you're unhappy too; otherwise you wouldn't bitch and quarrel all the time. I'm leaving. You can have the house and everything in it. I'm taking my clothes. Goodbye." He turned around and headed north.

Ultimately, it was quite simple, and Paula took it well enough. She cried a little, and called him a few names, but when Oscar refused to take the bait, she locked herself in the basement and refused to come out. Oscar loaded his car with clothes and a few personal items, then sped away, smiling, relieved, growing happier with each passing street.

Sixty-two, about to be single for the first time in forever, about to be rich, if he could trust Wally, which he did at the moment. In fact, he was placing an enormous amount of trust in his junior partner.

Oscar wasn't sure where he was going, but he wasn't about to stop by Wally's apartment and spend the night. He saw enough of the guy at the office; besides, the bimbo was apt to drop in, and Oscar couldn't stand her. He drove around for an hour, then checked in to a hotel near O'Hare. He pulled a chair to the window and watched the takeoffs and landings in the distance. One day soon he would be jetting here and there—islands, Paris, New Zealand—with a pleasant lady at his side.

He felt twenty years younger already. He was going places.

CHAPTER 28

At 7:30 the following morning, Rochelle arrived nice and early with plans to enjoy her yogurt and newspaper with no one but AC around, but AC was already playing with someone else. Mr. Finley was there and quite chipper. Rochelle could not remember the last time he had arrived before she did.

"Good morning, Ms. Gibson," he said in a warm, hearty voice, his lined and craggy face full of joy.

"What are you doing here?" she asked suspiciously.

"I happen to own the building," Oscar said.

"Why are you so happy?" she asked, dropping her purse on her desk.

"Because last night I slept in a hotel, alone."

"Maybe you should do it more often."

"Don't you want to know why?"

"Sure. Why?"

"Because I left Paula last night, Ms. Gibson. I packed up, said good-bye, walked out, and I'm never going back."

"Praise the Lord," she said, wide-eyed and wonder-struck. "You didn't?"

"Yes, I did. After thirty miserable years, I'm a free man. This is why I'm so happy, Ms. Gibson."

"Well, I'm happy too. Congratulations." In her eight and a half years at Finley & Figg, Rochelle had never met Paula Finley in person, and she was delighted about this. According to Wally, Paula refused to set foot on the property because it was beneath her dignity. She was quick to tell folks her husband was a lawyer, with the requisite implications of money and power, but was also secretly humiliated by the low standing of his firm. She spent every dime he earned, and if not for some mysterious family money on her side, they would have gone broke years earlier. On at least three occasions, she had demanded that Oscar fire Rochelle, and he had tried twice. Twice he'd limped back to his office, locked the door, and licked his wounds. On one noted occasion, Ms. Finley called and wanted to talk to her husband. Rochelle politely informed her he was with a client. "I don't care," she said. "Put me through." Rochelle declined again and instead put her on hold. When Rochelle picked up again, Paula was cursing, near cardiac arrest, and threatened to march right down there and straighten things out at the office. To which Rochelle responded: "Do so at your own risk. I live in the projects and I don't scare too easy." Paula Finley did not appear, but she did berate her husband.

Rochelle took a step over and gave Oscar a firm hug. Neither could remember the last time they had touched for any reason. "You're gonna be a new man," she said. "Congratulations."

"Should be a simple divorce," he said.

"You're not using Figg, are you?"

"Well, yes. He works cheap. I saw his name on a bingo card." They shared a laugh, then began swapping gossip at the table.

An hour later, during the third firm meeting, Oscar repeated the news for the benefit of David, who seemed a bit confused by the enthusiasm the news was generating. Not a trace of sadness anywhere. It was obvious that Paula Finley had made plenty of enemies. Oscar was almost giddy at the thought of shedding her.

Wally summed up his conversations with Jerry Alisandros and spun the news in such a way that it seemed as though big checks were practically in the mail. As he rambled on, David suddenly figured out the divorce. Unload the wife now, and quickly, before serious money rolled in. Whatever the scheme was, David smelled trouble. Hiding assets, rerouting funds, setting up bogus bank accounts—he could almost hear the conversations between the two partners. Warning flags went up. David would be curious and vigilant.

Wally exhorted the firm to kick into high gear, to get the files in order, find new cases, set aside everything else, and so on. Alisandros promised to provide medical screeners, cardiologists, all manner of logistical support to prepare his clients for the settlement. Every current case was worth serious cash; every prospective case could be worth even more.

Oscar just sat there and grinned. Rochelle listened intently. David found the news exciting, but he was also cautious. So much of what Wally said was hyperbole, and David had learned to cut it in half. Still, half would be a wonderful payday.

The Zinc family balance sheet had dipped under $100,000 in buried cash, and while David refused to worry, he was thinking about it more and more. He'd paid Sandroni $7,500 for a case that was probably worthless. He and Helen had committed $300 a month to Thuya's support, which would hopefully go on for years. They had not hesitated to do this, but reality was setting in. His monthly gross from the firm was rising steadily, though it was unlikely he would ever earn what he'd made at Rogan. That was not his benchmark. With a new child, he figured he needed $125,000 a year to live comfortably. Krayoxx just might shore up the balance sheet, though he and the two partners had not discussed his slice of the pie.

The third firm meeting ended abruptly when a woman the size of a linebacker, in sweats and flip-flops, barged through the front door and demanded to speak to a lawyer about Krayoxx. She had taken it for two years, could actually feel her heart getting weaker, and wanted to sue the company that very day. Oscar and David vanished. Wally welcomed her with a smile and said, "Well, you've certainly come to the right place."

The family of Senator Maxwell hired a Boise trial lawyer by the name of Frazier Gant, the number one man in a mildly successful firm that handled mostly tractor-trailer accidents and medical malpractice. Boise is not exactly on the big-verdict circuit. It rarely sees the liberal awards common in Florida, Texas, New York, and California. Idaho frowns on tort litigation, and juries there are generally conservative. But Gant could put together a case and get a verdict. He was someone to reckon with, and at the moment he happened to have the biggest tort case in the country. A dead senator, stricken on the Senate floor, and the cause of death pinned squarely on a huge corporation. It was a trial lawyer's dream.

Gant insisted on meeting in Washington, as opposed to Boise, though Layton Koane was perfectly willing to meet anywhere. In fact, Koane preferred anywhere but Washington because that would bring Gant into his office. The Koane Group leased the top floor of a brand-new sleek, shiny ten-story building on K Street, that stretch of asphalt packed with the real power brokers in Washington. Koane had paid a fortune to a New York designer to project the image of pure wealth and prestige. It worked. Clients—current and prospective—were awed by marble and glass the moment they stepped off the private elevator. They were in the midst of power, and they were certainly paying for it.

With Gant, though, the tables were turned. It was the lobbyist who would be handing over the money, and he preferred a more low-key meeting place. But Gant insisted, and some nine weeks after the senator's death, and, more important, at least to Koane and Varrick, almost seven weeks after the FDA yanked Krayoxx, they introduced themselves and settled around a small conference table at the far end of Koane's personal office. Since he was not interested in impressing a client, and he found this particular task distasteful, Koane didn't waste time.

"I have a source who tells me the family will settle for five million without a lawsuit," he said.

Gant frowned, a quick sharp grimace as if a hemorrhoid had twitched. "We can negotiate," he said, a throwaway line that meant nothing. He'd flown in from Boise to negotiate and nothing more. "But I think five is on the low side."

"What's on the high side?" Koane asked.

"My client doesn't have a lot of money," Gant said sadly. "As you know, the senator devoted his life to public service and sacrificed a lot. His estate is only half a million, but the family has needs. Maxwell is a big name out in Idaho and the family would like to maintain a certain lifestyle."

One of Koane's specialties was the shakedown, and he found it somewhat amusing to be on the other end of one. The family consisted of a widow, a very nice, low-key woman of sixty whose tastes were not expensive, a forty-year-old daughter who was married to a Boise pediatrician and maxed out credit-wise on all fronts, a thirty-five-year-old daughter who taught school for $41,000 a year, and a thirty-one-year-old son who was the problem. Kirk Maxwell Jr. had been battling drugs and alcohol since he was fifteen, and he was not winning. Koane had his research, and he knew more about the family than Gant.

"Why don't you suggest a figure?" he said. "I mentioned five, now it's your turn."

"Your client is losing about twenty million a day in revenue because Krayoxx is no longer on the market," Gant said smartly, as if dealing in inside information he'd cleverly gathered.

"It's more like eighteen, but let's not nitpick."

"Twenty has a nice ring to it."

Koane glared over his reading glasses. His jaw dropped slightly. In this business nothing surprised him, and he was faking it now. "Twenty million bucks?" he repeated, as if dumbfounded.

Gant gritted his teeth and nodded.

Koane recovered quickly and said, "Let me get this straight. Senator Maxwell was here for thirty years, and during that time he received at least $3 million from Big Pharma and its related PACs, much of it from the pockets of Varrick and its executives, and he also took about $1 million from folks like the National Tort Reform Initiative and other groups seeking to severely restrict lawsuits, bogus and otherwise. He took another $4 million from doctors, hospitals, banks, manufacturers, retailers, a very long list of good-government groups determined to cap damages, limit lawsuits, and basically slam the courthouse door on anyone with a claim of injury or death. When it came to tort reform and Big Pharma, the dear late senator had a perfect voting record. I doubt if you ever supported him."

"Occasionally," Gant said without conviction.

"Well, we couldn't find any record of any contribution from you or your firm to any of his campaigns. Face it, you guys were on opposite sides of the street."

"Okay, why is that relevant now?"

"It's not."

"Then why are we discussing it? He, like every other member of the Senate, raised a lot of money. It was all legal, and the money was always spent to get him reelected. Surely you understand this game, Mr. Koane."

"Indeed I do. So he drops dead and now blames Krayoxx. Are you aware that he had stopped using the drug? His last prescription was in October of last year, seven months before he succumbed. His autopsy revealed significant heart disease, congestion, blockage, none of which was caused by Krayoxx. You take this case to trial and you'll get buried."

"I doubt that, Mr. Koane. You've never seen me in the courtroom."

"I have not." But Koane had the research. Gant's largest verdict was $2 million, half of which was set aside on appeal. His previous year's IRS 1040 listed an adjusted gross of just under $400,000. Chump change compared with the millions Koane raked in. Gant was paying $5,000 in alimony and $11,000 a month on a highly mortgaged golf course home that was underwater. The Maxwell case was, without a doubt, his ship coming in. Koane did not know the specific terms of his contingency fee, but according to a Boise source Gant would get 25 percent of a settlement and 40 percent of a jury verdict.

Gant leaned forward on his elbows and said, "You and I both know this case is not about liability, and it's not really about damages. The only real issue here is how much Varrick is willing to pay to keep me from filing a big, splashy lawsuit. Because if I do, then we keep the pressure on the FDA, don't we, Mr. Koane?"

Koane excused himself and went into another room. Reuben Massey was waiting in his office at Varrick Labs. Nicholas Walker was also at the table. They were using a speakerphone. "They want $20 million," Koane said, then braced for the attack.

But Massey received the news without emotion. He believed in using his products and had just popped a Plazid, his company's version of the daily happy pill. "Wow, Koane," he said calmly. "You're doing a helluva job at the negotiating table, old boy. Start at five, now you're up to twenty. We'd better grab the twenty before you get it up to forty. What the hell's happening down there?"

"Nothing but greed, Reuben. They know they have us over a barrel. This guy freely admits the lawsuit is not about liability or damages. We can't take any more bad press, so how much are we willing to pay to make Maxwell's case go away? It's that simple."

"I thought you had some great source whispering in your ear to the tune of $5 million."

"I thought so too."

"This is not litigation. This is armed robbery."

"Yes, Reuben, I'm afraid so."

"Layton, Nick here. Have you countered?"

"No. My authority was five. Until you say so, I cannot go higher."

Walker was smiling as he spoke. "This is the perfect time to walk away. This guy Gant is already counting his money, several million, he thinks. I know the species, and they're very predictable. Let's send him back to Idaho with empty pockets. He won't know what hit him, neither will the family. Koane, tell him your limit is five and the CEO is out of the country. We'll have to meet and discuss all of this, which could take a few days. Warn him, though, that if he fires off a lawsuit, then all settlement talk goes away."

"He won't do that," Koane said. "I think you're right. I think he's counting his money."

"I like it," Massey said, "but it would be nice to wrap this up. Go to seven, Layton, but that's all."

Back in his office, Koane settled into his chair and said, "My authority is seven. I can't go higher today and I can't get the CEO. I think he's traveling in Asia, probably on a plane."

"Seven is a long way from twenty," Gant replied with a frown.

"You're not getting twenty. I spoke with in-house counsel, who's also on the board."

"Then we'll see you in court," Gant said, zipping up a thin brief-case he hadn't used.

"That's a pretty lame threat, Mr. Gant. No jury in the country will give you $7 million for a death that was caused by heart disease completely unrelated to our drug. And the way we litigate, a trial is three years away. That's a long time to sit and think about $7 million."

Gant abruptly stood and said, "Thank you for your time, Mr. Koane. I'll see myself out."

"When you leave, Mr. Gant, our offer of $7 million comes off the table. You go home with zero."

Gant stutter-stepped slightly, then regained his stride. "See you in court," he said, tight-lipped, and left through the door.

Two hours later, Gant called on his cell. Seemed the Maxwell family had reconsidered, came to its senses, at the prodding of their trusted lawyer, of course, and, well, $7 million sounded pretty damn good after all. Layton Koane carefully walked him through each issue at stake, and Gant was happily on board with all of it.

After the call, Koane relayed the news to Reuben Massey.

"I doubt if he ever talked to the family," Koane said. "I think he assured them of $5 million, said what the hell and rolled the dice with twenty, and is a happy boy going home with a settlement of $7 million. He'll be a hero."

"And we've dodged a bullet, the first one to miss in a long time," Massey said.

CHAPTER 29

In federal court, David filed a lawsuit alleging all manner of fair labor violations by a shady drainage contractor called Cicero Pipe. The job was a large water-treatment plant on the South Side, of which the defendant had a $60 million piece. The plaintiffs were three undocumented workers from Burma and two from Mexico. The violations covered many more workers, but most refused to join the lawsuit. There was too much fear of coming forward.

According to David's research, the Department of Labor (DOL) and the U.S. Immigration and Customs Enforcement (ICE) had reached an uneasy truce regarding the mistreatment of illegal immigrants. The steadfast principle of unhindered access to justice overrode (slightly) the country's need to regulate immigration. Therefore, an undocumented worker courageous enough to fight a crooked employer would not be subjected to scrutiny by ICE, at least not while engaged in the labor dispute. David explained this repeatedly to the workers, and the Burmese, with Soe Khaing's prodding, eventually found the nerve to file suit. Others, from Mexico and Guatemala, were too frightened by the idea of risking what little money they were being paid. One of the Burmese workers estimated there were at least thirty men, all of them thought to be undocumented, being paid $200 a week in cash for eighty hours or more of hard labor.

The potential damages were impressive. The minimum wage was $8.25, and federal law also required $12.38 for any hour over forty per week. For eighty hours, each worker was due $825.20 per week, or $625.20 more than he was being paid. Though exact dates were hard to pin down, David's best guess was that the current scam by Cicero Pipe had been under way for at least thirty weeks. The law allowed liquidated damages of twice the unpaid wages, so each of his five clients was entitled to about $37,500. The law also allowed the judge to impose court costs and attorneys' fees on a defendant found liable.

Oscar reluctantly agreed to allow David to file the lawsuit. Wally could not be found. He was burning up the streets looking for large people.

Three days after the lawsuit was filed, an anonymous caller threatened to cut David's throat if the lawsuit was not dismissed immediately. David reported the call to the police. Oscar advised him to purchase a handgun and keep it in his briefcase. David refused. The following day, an anonymous letter threatened his life and named his pals—Oscar Finley, Wally Figg, even Rochelle Gibson.

The thug walked briskly along Preston as if hurrying home at such a late hour. It was just after 2:00 a.m., the late July air still thick and warm. Male, white, age thirty, an impressive rap sheet, and not much between the ears. Slung over his shoulder was a cheap gym bag, and inside was a two-liter plastic jug of gasoline, tightly sealed. He took a quick right and darted low onto the narrow porch of the law office. All lights were off, inside and out. Preston was asleep; even the massage parlor had finally wound down.

If AC had been awake, he might have heard the slight rattle of the doorknob as the thug gently checked to see if someone had forgotten to lock up. The lock had not been forgotten. AC was asleep in the kitchen. Oscar, though, was awake on the sofa, in his pajamas, under a quilt, thinking about how happy he'd become since moving out.

The thug eased along the front porch, stepped down, and scooted low around the building until he came to the back door. His strategy was to get inside and detonate his crude little bomb. Two liters of gasoline on a wooden floor with curtains and books nearby would gut the old house before a fire crew got there. He shook the door—it too was locked—then quickly jimmied it with a screwdriver. It swung open as he took one step inside. Everything was dark.

A dog growled, then two extremely loud shots rang out. The thug screamed and fell off the back steps into a small neglected flower bed. Oscar stood over him. A quick glance revealed a wound just above his right knee.

"Don't! Please!" the thug begged.

Carefully, coldly, Oscar shot him in the other leg.

Two hours later, Oscar, partially dressed now, was chatting with two policemen at the table. All three were sipping coffee. The thug was at the hospital, in surgery—two damaged legs but no chance of dying. His name was Justin Bardall, and when he wasn't playing with fire and getting shot, he operated a bulldozer for Cicero Pipe. "Idiots, idiots, idiots," Oscar kept saying.

"But he wasn't supposed to get caught," said one of the cops, laughing.

At that moment, two detectives were in Evanston knocking on the door of the man who owned Cicero Pipe. It was the beginning of a long day for him.

Oscar explained that he was going through a divorce and looking for an apartment. When he wasn't at a hotel, he slept on the office sofa. "I've owned this place for twenty-one years," he said. He knew one of the cops and had seen the other one around. Neither had the slightest concern over the shooting. It was a clear-cut case of protecting one's property, though Oscar's narrative omitted the unnecessary wounding of the second leg. In addition to the two-liter bottle of gas, the gym bag contained a strip of cotton cloth doused with what appeared to be kerosene and several strips of cardboard. It was a modified Molotov cocktail, but not one to be tossed. The police guessed that the cardboard was to be used as kindling. It was a laughable effort at arson, but then it doesn't take a genius to start a fire.

While they chatted, a television news van parked on the street in front of the office. Oscar put on his tie and got himself filmed.

A few hours later, during the fourth firm meeting, David took the news hard but still insisted he would not carry a gun. Rochelle kept a cheap pistol in her purse, so three of the four were armed. Reporters were calling. The story was growing by the moment.

"Remember," Wally repeated to his colleagues, "we're a boutique firm specializing in Krayoxx cases. Everybody got that?"

"Yeah, yeah," Oscar chimed in. "And what about Burmese labor law violations?"

"That too."

The meeting broke up when a reporter banged on the front door.

It was soon evident that no law would be practiced that day at Finley & Figg. David and Oscar talked to the *Tribune* and the *Sun-Times*. Details were being passed along. Mr. Bardall was out of surgery, locked in his room, and not talking to anyone but his lawyer. The owner of Cicero Pipe and two of his superintendents had been arrested and released on bail. The general contractor on the water-treatment project was a blue-chip firm out of Milwaukee, and it was promising to investigate matters quickly and thoroughly. The job site was shut down. No undocumented worker would go near it.

David finally left before noon, quietly informing Rochelle he was needed in court somewhere. He drove home, collected Helen, who was looking more pregnant by the day, and took her to lunch. He explained recent events—the death threats, the thug and his intentions, Oscar and his defense of the firm, and the growing interest from the press. He downplayed any danger and assured her the FBI was on top of things.

"Are you worried?" she asked.

"Not at all," he said, unconvincingly. "But there could be something in the papers tomorrow."

———

Indeed there was. Big photos of Oscar in the metro sections of both the *Tribune* and the *Sun-Times*. In all fairness to the press, how many stories do you get wherein an old lawyer is bunking at his office and shoots an intruder who is carrying a Molotov cocktail designed to burn down the building in retaliation for the firm's filing of a wage dispute involving undocumented workers who are being abused by a company that, years ago, had links to organized crime? Oscar was being portrayed as a fearless gunslinger from the Southwest Side, and, by the way, one of the country's leading mass tort specialists in the assault on Varrick Labs and its dreadful drug Krayoxx. The *Tribune* ran a smaller photo of David, as well as shots of the owner of Cicero Pipe and his lieutenants as they were being hauled into jail.

The entire alphabet was rushing in—FBI, DOL, ICE, INS, OSHA, DHS (Homeland Security), OFCCP (Office of Federal Contract Compliance Programs)—and most had something to say to the reporters. The job site was shut down for the second day, and the prime contractor was screaming. Finley & Figg was again besieged by reporters, investigators, Krayoxx hopefuls, and more than the usual riffraff from the street. Oscar, Wally, and Rochelle kept their weapons close. Young David remained blissfully naive.

Two weeks later, Justin Bardall left the hospital in a wheelchair. He and his boss, along with one other, had been indicted on numerous charges by a federal grand jury, and their lawyers were already discussing the possibility of plea bargains. His left fibula was shattered and more surgery would be needed, but his doctors expected a full recovery with time. He had mentioned to his lawyers, his boss, and the police that the shattering of his left fibula had been unnecessary; the shot was taken after he'd been wounded and was no longer a threat, but he found no sympathy. The general reaction could be summed up by a detective who said, "You're lucky he didn't blow your head off."

CHAPTER 30

Jerry Alisandros finally made good on a promise. He was extremely busy organizing the settlement negotiations, and according to the associate Wally spoke to, he, Jerry, simply didn't have the time to spend on the phone with the dozens of lawyers he was juggling. But in the third week of July, he finally sent in the experts.

The company's name was meaningless—Allyance Diagnostic Group, or ADG, as it preferred to be called. As best Wally could tell, ADG was an Atlanta-based team of medical technicians who did nothing but travel the country running tests on people who were clamoring to profit from Jerry's latest mass tort attack. As instructed, Wally rented two thousand square feet in a dingy strip mall, a space that had once housed a low-end pet supply store. He hired a contractor to erect walls and doors and a cleaning service to fix things up. The front windows were covered with brown paper; there was no signage. He rented a few cheap chairs and tables and a desk and installed a phone and a copier. All bills were sent by Wally to an assistant in Jerry's firm who did nothing but keep the books dealing with the Krayoxx litigation.

When the space was ready, ADG moved in and went to work. Its team consisted of three technicians, all properly attired in aqua surgical scrubs. Each had a stethoscope. They looked so official that even Wally at first figured they were highly skilled and credentialed. They were not, but they had tested thousands of potential plaintiffs. Their leader was Dr. Borzov, a cardiologist from Russia who had made a lot of money diagnosing patients/clients for Jerry Alisandros and a dozen other trial lawyers around the country. Dr. Borzov rarely saw an obese person who wasn't suffering from a significant medical problem that could be pinned on the mass-tort-drug-of-the-month. He never testified in court—his accent was too thick and his résumé was too thin—but he was worth his weight in gold in the screening rooms.

David, because he was the de facto paralegal for all (now) 430 non-death Krayoxx clients, and Wally, because he had hustled them all together, were both present when ADG began its assembly line. On schedule, three clients arrived at 8:00 a.m. and were greeted with coffee, Wally, and a cute ADG technician in scrubs and white rubber hospital clogs. The paperwork took ten minutes and was primarily designed to ensure that the client had indeed taken Krayoxx for more than six months. The first client was led into another room where ADG had installed its own echocardiogram and two other technicians were waiting. One explained the procedure—"We're just taking a digital picture of your heart"—while the other helped the client onto an official, heavily fortified hospital bed that ADG hauled around the country, along with the echocardiogram. As they probed the patient's chest with the sonar, Dr. Borzov entered the room and nodded slightly at the patient. His bedside manner was never reassuring, but then he had no real patients. He wore a full-length white exam coat, had his name stenciled above the left pocket, and had his own stethoscope for good measure and effect, and when he spoke, his accent conveyed a sense of expertise. He studied the screen, frowned because he always frowned, then left the room.

The assault on Krayoxx was fueled by research purporting to show that the drug weakened the seals around the aortic valve, thus causing a decrease in mitral valve regurgitation. The echocardiogram measured aortic sufficiency, and a decrease of 30 percent was excellent news for the lawyers. Dr. Borzov reviewed the graphs immediately, always eager to find another weakened aortic valve.

Each exam took twenty minutes, so they did three per hour, about twenty-five each day, six days a week. Wally had leased the space for a month. ADG billed the Zell & Potter, Finley & Figg litigation account $1,000 for each exam, with the bills going to Jerry in Florida.

Before that stop, ADG and Dr. Borzov had been in Charleston and Buffalo. From Chicago, they were headed to Memphis, then Little Rock. Another ADG unit was covering the West Coast with a Serbian doctor reading the graphs. Another was harvesting gold in Texas. The Zell & Potter Krayoxx web covered forty states, seventy-five lawyers, and almost 80,000 clients.

To avoid the chaos of the office, David hung around the strip mall and chatted with his clients, none of whom he'd ever met. Generally speaking, they were happy to be there, worried about whatever damage the drug had done to their hearts, hopeful of some type of recovery, overweight and terribly out of shape, but pleasant enough. Black, white, old, young, male, female—obesity and high cholesterol ran the gamut. Every client he spoke to had been thrilled with the drug, delighted with its results, and was now anxious about finding a replacement. Gradually, David chatted up the ADG technicians and learned something of their work, though they were fairly closemouthed. Dr. Borzov would hardly speak to him.

After hanging around for three days, David could tell that the ADG team was not pleased with their testing. Their $1,000 exams were producing little evidence of aortic insufficiency, but there were a few potential cases.

On the fourth day, the air-conditioning system crashed, and Wally's rented space turned into a sweatshop. It was August, temperature above ninety, and when the landlord refused to return calls, the ADG crew threatened to leave. Wally hauled in box fans and ice cream and begged them to stay and finish the screening. They plowed on, the twenty-minute exams becoming fifteen, then ten, with Borzov barely scanning the graphs on the sidewalk while he smoked cigarettes.

Judge Seawright set the hearing for August 10, the last possible date on any judge's calendar before the system shut down for summer vacation. There were no motions pending, no fights brewing, all discovery had proceeded with remarkable cooperation. Varrick Labs, so far, had been unduly forthcoming with documents, witnesses, and experts. Nadine Karros had filed only a handful of benign motions, all of which the judge quickly dispensed with. On the plaintiff's side, the Zell & Potter lawyers had been remarkably efficient with their requests and filings.

Seawright was monitoring the settlement gossip. His clerks scoured the financial press and watched the serious bloggers. Varrick Labs had issued no formal statement regarding settlement, but it was obvious the company knew how to leak. Its share price dipped as low as $24.50, but the buzz about a massive settlement had moved it back to $30.00.

When the two packs of lawyers were in place, Judge Seawright assumed the bench and welcomed everyone. He apologized for calling the hearing in August—"the most difficult month of the year for busy people"—but he felt strongly that the two sides should get together before everyone scattered. He quickly went through his discovery checklist to make sure both sides were behaving. There were no complaints.

Jerry Alisandros and Nadine Karros were so polite to each other it was almost silly. Wally sat to Jerry's right, as if he would be the go-to guy in a courtroom brawl. Behind him, and wedged among a group of Zell & Potter lawyers, were David and Oscar. Since the shooting and the publicity, Oscar was getting out more, enjoying the attention. He was also smiling and already considered himself a bachelor.

Changing subjects, Judge Seawright said, "I'm hearing a lot of chatter about a settlement, one big global settlement, as they're called these days in this business. I want to know what's going on. As fast as this particular case has come together, it is now in a posture to be placed on my trial calendar. However, if a settlement is likely, then why bother? Can you shed any light on this issue, Ms. Karros?"

She stood, all eyes on her, and took a few elegant steps to the podium. "Your Honor, as you probably know, Varrick Labs has been involved in a number of complicated lawsuits, and the company has its own way of approaching a settlement that involves many plaintiffs. I have not been authorized to initiate negotiations in the Klopeck case, nor have I been authorized by my client to make public statements on the issue of settlement. As far as I'm concerned, we are preparing for trial."

"Fair enough. Mr. Alisandros?"

They exchanged places at the podium, and Jerry offered up a sappy smile. "Likewise, Your Honor, we are preparing for trial in this case. However, I must say that I, as a member of the Plaintiffs' Litigation Committee, have had several informal and quite preliminary conversations with the company regarding a global settlement. I believe Ms. Karros is aware that these conversations are taking place, but, as she said, she has not been authorized to discuss them. I don't represent Varrick so I am not burdened with such constraints. However, the company has not requested that I remain silent about our discussions. In addition, Your Honor, if we reach the point of formal negotiations, I doubt that Ms. Karros will be involved. I know from prior experience that Varrick handles these in-house."

"Do you anticipate formal negotiations?" asked Seawright.

There was a long pause as many held their breath. Nadine Karros managed to look curious, though she had a clear view of the big picture. No one else in the courtroom did. Wally's heart was racing as he tasted the words "formal negotiations."

Jerry shifted weight a few times, then finally said, "Judge, I don't want to get quoted, so I'll go the safe route and say that I'm not sure."

"So you, and Ms. Karros, cannot give me any guidance on the issue of settlement?" Seawright said with a hint of frustration.

Both lawyers shook their heads. Nadine knew damn well the case wouldn't be settled. Jerry was almost positive that it would. Neither, though, could play his or her hand. And, truthfully and ethically, the judge did not have the right to know their strategies outside the courtroom. His job was to referee a fair trial, not monitor settlements.

Jerry returned to his seat, and Judge Seawright changed subjects again. "I'm looking at October 17, a Monday, as a trial date. I anticipate the trial will last no longer than two weeks." A dozen lawyers were instantly looking at their calendars, all frowning.

"If you have a conflict, it had better be a good one," he said. "Mr. Alisandros?"

Jerry stood slowly, holding a small leather appointment book. "Well, Judge, that would mean that we're going to trial ten months after the lawsuit was filed. That's pretty quick, don't you think?"

"Indeed it is, Mr. Alisandros. Eleven months is about my average. I don't allow my cases to grow stale. What's your conflict?"

"No conflict, Judge, but I'm more concerned with having sufficient time to prepare. That's all."

"Hogwash. Discovery is almost complete. You have your experts. The defendant has its experts. God knows both sides have enough legal talent. October 17 is sixty-eight days away. That should be a piece of cake for a litigator of your reputation, Mr. Alisandros."

What a show, thought Wally. This case, and all the others, would be settled in a month.

"What about the defense, Ms. Karros?" Seawright asked.

"We have some conflicts, Your Honor," she said. "But nothing that we cannot work around."

"Very well. The case of Klopeck versus Varrick Labs is hereby set for jury trial on October 17. Pending a disaster, there will be no delays, no continuances, so don't even bother to ask." He tapped his gavel on the bench and said, "Court's adjourned. Thank you."

CHAPTER 31

News of the trial date swept through the financial press and was all over the Internet. The story was spun various ways, but in general it looked as though Varrick was being frog-marched into a federal courtroom to answer for its multitude of sins. Reuben Massey did not care how the story was told, nor did he care what the public thought at that moment. To the tort bar, it was important to react as if his company was shaken and frightened. He understood trial lawyers.

Three days after the hearing in Chicago, Nicholas Walker phoned Jerry Alisandros and suggested they arrange a secret meeting between the company and the biggest tort firms involved with Krayoxx. The purpose of the meeting would be to throw open the door to full-scale negotiations. Alisandros jumped at the idea and gravely vowed total silence. From the twenty or so years he'd been dealing with trial lawyers, Nicholas knew the meeting would not be a secret because one (or more) of the lawyers would tip the press.

The following day, a blurb in the *Wall Street Journal* reported that Cymbol, Varrick's principal insurance company, had been put on notice by the company that its reserve fund was about to be activated. Citing an anonymous source, the story went on to speculate that the only reason for such an action was to settle its "Krayoxx mess." Other leaks followed, and the bloggers were soon declaring another victory for consumers.

Since every trial lawyer worth his salt owned his own jet, the destination was no problem. With New York City deserted in August, Nicholas Walker secured a large meeting room on the fortieth floor of a half-empty midtown hotel. Many of the trial lawyers were out of the office, off somewhere dodging the heat, but not a single invitation was declined. A large settlement was far more important than a few days of vacation. When they convened, eight days after Judge Seawright set the date for the first trial, there were the six members of the Plaintiffs' Litigation Committee, plus another thirty trial lawyers, each with thousands of Krayoxx cases. Those as insignificant as Wally Figg did not even know of the meeting.

Large young men in dark suits guarded the door to the meeting room and checked credentials. After a quick breakfast the first morning, Nicholas Walker welcomed everyone as if they were all salesmen for the same company. He even cracked a joke and got a laugh, but just under the surface there was tension. An avalanche of money was about to be unleashed, and the lawyers in the room were seasoned brawlers, ready for hand-to-hand combat.

So far, there were eleven hundred death cases. Or in other words, eleven hundred cases in which the dead person's estate claimed Krayoxx was the cause. The medical proof was not exactly ironclad, though it was probably sufficient to become a question for a jury. Going along with their master plan, Nicholas Walker and Judy Beck spent almost no time discussing the basic issue of liability. They presumed, as did the horde on the other side, that the drug was responsible for eleven hundred deaths and thousands of other injuries.

After the formalities, Walker began by saying that Varrick would like to nail down the value of each death case. Assuming that could be done, they would then move on to the non-death cases.

Wally was on the shore of Lake Michigan, in a small rental a block off the water, with his darling DeeAnna, who was a knockout in a bikini, and he had just finished some pasta salad when his cell phone chirped. He saw the number, snatched the phone, and said, "Jerry, my man, what's going on?" DeeAnna, topless in a nearby lounge chair, perked up too. She knew that any call from dear Jerry could be thrilling.

Jerry explained that he was back in Florida after two days in New York, secret meeting and all, hammering things out with Varrick, tough bunch, just the death cases, you know, but anyway, lots of progress, no deal, no handshake, certainly nothing in writing, but it looks as though each death case will be somewhere around $2 million.

Wally hummed along with an occasional smile at DeeAnna, who had inched closer. "Good news, Jerry, nice work. Let's chat next week."

"What's up?" she cooed when the call was over.

"Nothing, really. Just an update from Jerry. Varrick has filed a bunch of motions and he wants me to take a look."

"No settlement?"

"Nope."

All she talked about now was the settlement. Sure, it was his fault for running his big mouth, but the woman was obsessed with the settlement. She didn't have enough sense to play along as though she couldn't have cared less. No. She wanted details.

She wanted money, and this was worrying Wally. He was already thinking of an exit strategy, just like his new hero Oscar. Ditch the women before the money arrives.

Sixteen million dollars. Seventeen percent of which would flow into the coffers of Finley & Figg, a total of $2.7 million, of which Wally would take 50 percent. He was a millionaire.

He crawled onto an air mattress and floated across the pool. He closed his eyes and tried not to grin. Soon DeeAnna was next to him, floating on the water, still topless, touching him occasionally to make sure he still needed her. They had been together for many months now, and Wally was finally getting bored. He was finding it more difficult to keep up with her constant demands for sex. He was, after all, forty-six, ten years older than DeeAnna, though her actual birth date was a moving target. The day and month had been nailed down, but the year kept inching forward. He was tired and needed a break, and he was also concerned about her fascination with his Krayoxx money.

It would be in his best interests to ditch her now, do the breakup routine, one he knew well, and get her out of his life and away from the money. This would not be easy and would take some time. Such a strategy would work well for Oscar too. Paula Finley had hired an obnoxious divorce lawyer named Stamm, and he was banging the war drums. During their first phone chat, Stamm expressed surprise at how little money Oscar cleared from his law practice and went on to imply that money was being hidden. He probed into the murky world of fees paid in cash, but he got nothing from Wally, who knew that territory well. Stamm mentioned the Krayoxx litigation, but got stiff-armed by Wally's well-rehearsed denials that Oscar was involved.

"Well, it looks suspicious," Stamm had said. "Mr. Finley is willing to walk away with nothing but his car and clothes after thirty years of marriage."

"Oh no," Wally had protested. "It makes perfect sense if you really got to know Paula Finley, your client." They bickered for a while, as divorce lawyers do, then promised to talk later.

As bad as Wally wanted the money, he decided to delay the actual receipt of the cash for several months. Do the paperwork now, or in the next few weeks, keep it under wraps in court, then get rid of the women.

For what was supposed to be the slowest month of the year, August was proving to be quite productive. On August 22, Helen Zinc gave birth to an eight-pound girl, Emma, and for a couple of days her parents acted as though they had produced the first baby in history. Mother and child were in perfect health, and when they arrived home, all four grandparents were waiting, along with two dozen friends. David took a week off and found it impossible to stay out of the little pink nursery.

He was called back into action by an angry federal judge, one who evidently did not believe in vacations and was rumored to work ninety hours a week. Her name was Sally Archer, or Sudden Sal, as she had been aptly nicknamed. She was young and brash, extremely bright, and in the process of driving her staff into the ground. Sudden Sal ruled quickly and wanted every lawsuit settled the day after it was filed. David's labor case had been assigned to Archer, who had minced no words in voicing her low opinion of Cicero Pipe and its sleazy practices.

Under pressure from multiple arms of the federal government, and Sudden Sal as well, the prime contractor convinced its sub, Cicero Pipe, to clean up its labor mess and legal problems and get on with its portion of the water-treatment plant. The criminal charges against the would-be arsonist, Justin Bardall, and others at the company would take months to untangle, but the wage-and-hour dispute could, and would, be wrapped up quickly.

Six weeks after filing the lawsuit, David hammered out a settlement that was hard for him to believe. Cicero Pipe agreed to pay to each of his five clients the lump sum of $40,000. In addition, the company would pay $30,000 each to another three dozen undocumented workers, most Mexican and Guatemalan, who had been paid $200 a week for at least eighty hours.

Because of the notoriety of the case, said notoriety being greatly enhanced by Oscar's vigorous defense of his own property and the ensuing arrest of the wealthy owner of Cicero Pipe, the hearing before Sudden Sal attracted some reporters. Judge Archer began by recapping the lawsuit, and in doing so guaranteed she would be quoted by describing Cicero Pipe's abuses as "slave labor." She lashed out at the company, rebuked its lawyers, who were actually pretty nice guys in David's opinion, and in general grandstanded for thirty minutes as the reporters scribbled away.

"Mr. Zinc, are you satisfied with this settlement?" Her Honor inquired. The agreement was in writing. The deal had been cut a week earlier; the only remaining issue was attorneys' fees.

"Yes, Your Honor," David said quietly. The three lawyers for Cicero Pipe hunkered down, almost afraid to look up.

"I see that you have submitted a request for attorneys' fees," Sudden Sal observed as she looked at some paperwork. "Fifty-eight hours. I would say, in light of what you have accomplished and the money you've obtained for all these workers, that your time has been well spent."

"Thank you, Your Honor," David said. He was standing at his table.

"What is your hourly rate, Mr. Zinc?"

"Well, Your Honor, I have been anticipating that question, and the truth is that I really don't have an hourly rate. My clients can't afford to pay by the hour."

Judge Archer nodded. "In the past year, have you billed anyone by the hour?"

"Oh sure. Until last December, I was a senior associate at Rogan Rothberg."

The judge laughed into her microphone and said, "Oh boy. Talk about experts at the hourly rate. What were you worth back then, Mr. Zinc?"

David shifted uncomfortably and shrugged. "Judge, the last time I worked on the clock, the client was billed $500 an hour."

"Then you're worth $500 an hour." Sudden Sal scribbled for a few seconds, then announced, "Let's round it off to $30,000. Any objections, Mr. Lattimore?"

The defendant's chief counsel stood and paused and pondered what to say. Objecting would do no good because the judge was clearly in the other camp. His client was getting clobbered so badly anyway, what was another $30,000? And if Lattimore expressed misgivings about the fees, he knew that Sudden Sal would hit him with a quick "Well, then, Mr. Lattimore, what's your hourly rate?"

"Sounds reasonable," Lattimore said.

"Good. I want all funds exchanged within thirty days. Court's adjourned."

Outside the courtroom, David spent time with three reporters, patiently answering their questions. When he was finished, he drove to the apartment of Soe and Lwin, where he met with his three Burmese clients and broke the news that they would soon receive checks for $40,000 each. The message wasn't clear in translation, and Soe repeated himself several times to convince the men. They laughed and thought it was all a joke, but David refused to laugh along. When reality set in, two of the three began crying. The third was too shocked. David tried to make the point that they had earned the money with their sweat and labor, but this, too, did not translate well.

David was in no hurry. He had been away from his new daughter for all of six hours, a record, but she wasn't going anywhere. He sipped tea from a tiny cup and chatted with his clients, glowing in his first major victory. He had taken a case that most lawyers would refuse. His clients had bravely stepped out from the shadows of illegal immigration to confront a wrong, and David had coaxed them into it. Three little guys a million miles from home, abused by a big company with plenty of big friends, nothing between them and more abuse except a young attorney and a court of law. Justice, with its flaws and ambiguities, had prevailed in a magnificent way.

Driving to the office, alone, David was filled with immense pride and a sense of accomplishment. He hoped to have many great wins in the future, but this one would always be special. Never, in five years with the big firm, had he ever felt so proud of being a lawyer.

It was late and the office was deserted. Wally was on vacation, checking in occasionally with the latest Krayoxx update. Oscar was AWOL for a few days, not even Rochelle knew where he'd gone. David checked his phone messages and mail, puttered around his desk for a few minutes, then got bored with it. As he locked the front door, a police car pulled to a stop in front of the building. Friends of Oscar's, keeping an eye on the place. David waved at the two officers and headed home.

CHAPTER 32

Fresh from a long Labor Day weekend, Wally wrote to his client Iris Klopeck:

> *Dear Iris:*
>
> *As you know, our trial is set for next month, October 17 to be exact, but this is not something to worry about. I spent most of last month negotiating with the attorneys at Varrick, and we have arrived at a very favorable settlement. The company is in the process of offering a sum in the neighborhood of $2 million for the wrongful death of your husband, Percy. This offer is not official, but we expect to receive it in writing within the next fifteen days. I know this is considerably more than the $1 million I promised, but, nonetheless, I need your approval to accept this offer when it is formally put on the table. I'm quite proud of our little boutique firm. We are like David battling Goliath, but right now we're winning.*
>
> *Please sign the attached form authorizing the settlement and mail it back.*
>
> *Sincerely,*
> *Wallis T. Figg*
> *Attorney and Counselor-at-Law*

He sent similar letters to the other seven clients in his wonderful little class of death cases, and when he finished, he kicked back in his swivel rocker, placed his shoeless feet on his desk, and once again contemplated the money. His dreams were interrupted, though, when Rochelle buzzed in with a curt "That woman is on the phone. Please talk to her. She's driving me crazy."

"Okay," Wally snapped and stared at the phone. DeeAnna was not going away quietly. During the drive home from Lake Michigan, he had picked a fight with her and managed to escalate it to the level of some serious name-calling. In the heat of the battle, he had announced that they were through, and for two tranquil days thereafter they did not speak. Then she showed up at his apartment, drunk, and he relented and allowed her to sleep on the sofa. She was apologetic, even pitiful, and managed to offer some manner of sexual adventure every five minutes. Wally had declined, so far. Now she was calling at all hours and had even appeared at the office several times. But Wally was determined. It had become clear to him that his Krayoxx money wouldn't last three months with DeeAnna in the picture.

He picked up the phone and offered a brusque "Hello." She was already crying.

The windy, gloomy Monday would long be remembered at Zell & Potter as the Labor Day Massacre. No holiday was being observed— they were professionals, not laborers, not that it mattered. Holidays were often ignored, as were weekends. The building was open early, and by 8:00 a.m. the halls were buzzing with lawyers eagerly pursuing a variety of defective drugs and the companies that made them.

Occasionally, though, a pursuit yielded nothing. A chase went nowhere. A well was dry.

The first blow landed at 9:00 a.m., when Dr. Julian Smitzer, the firm's director of medical research, insisted on seeing Jerry Alisandros, who really didn't have the time but couldn't say no, especially when the matter was described by his secretary as "urgent."

Dr. Smitzer had completed an illustrious career as a cardiologist and researcher at Mayo Clinic in Rochester, Minnesota, and with an ailing wife headed for the sunshine of south Florida. After a few months, he was bored. By chance he met Jerry Alisandros. One meeting led to another, and for the past five years Dr. Smitzer had supervised the law firm's medical research, at an annual salary of $1 million. It was a natural fit because he had spent most of his career writing about the evils of Big Pharma.

In a law firm full of hyperaggressive lawyers, Dr. Smitzer was a revered figure. No one questioned his research or his opinions, and his work was far more valuable than what he was paid.

"We have a problem with Krayoxx," he said not long after he'd taken a seat in Jerry's grand office.

After a deep, painful breath, Jerry said, "I'm listening."

"We've spent the past six months analyzing the McFadden research, and I am now of the opinion that it is flawed. There is no credible statistical evidence that the consumers of the drug have a higher risk of stroke and heart attack. Frankly, McFadden fudged his results. He's an excellent doctor and researcher, but he obviously became convinced the drug was dangerous, then tweaked his findings to fit his conclusions. The people who take this drug have many other problems— obesity, diabetes, hypertension, atherosclerosis, to name a few. Many are in terrible health, and elevated cholesterol can be expected. Typically, they take a handful of pills several times a day, Krayoxx being just one, and so far it has been impossible to determine the effects of the combinations of all these drugs. Statistically, there might, and I emphasize that word, be a slight increased chance for a heart attack or stroke by Krayoxx users, but then again there may not be. McFadden studied three thousand subjects over a two-year period—a small pool in my opinion—and found only a 9 percent higher chance of stroke and heart attack."

"I've read the report, Julian, many times," Jerry said, interrupting. "I practically memorized it before we jumped into this litigation."

"You jumped in too fast, Jerry. There's nothing wrong with this drug. I've spoken with McFadden at length. You know how heavily he was criticized when the report came out. He's taken the heat, and now he's backing off the drug."

"What?"

"Yes. McFadden admitted to me last week that he should have included more subjects. He's also concerned with the fact that he did not spend the time studying the effects of the combinations of multiple drugs. He is planning to reverse himself and try to salvage his reputation."

Jerry was pinching the bridge of his nose as if he might crush it. "No, no, no," he kept mumbling.

Smitzer pressed on. "Yes, yes, and his repair work will be forthcoming."

"When?"

"Roughly ninety days. And it gets worse. We've studied, thoroughly, the effects of the drug on the aortic valve. As you know, the Palo Alto study seemed to link the leakage in the valve to a deterioration caused by the drug. This now looks doubtful, highly so."

"Why are you telling me this now, Julian?"

"Because the research takes time, and we are just now learning a few things."

"What does Dr. Bannister say?"

"Well, for starters, he says he's not willing to testify."

Jerry rubbed his temples and stood, glaring at his friend. He walked to a window and looked out, at nothing. Since Dr. Smitzer was on the firm's payroll, he was precluded from testifying in any Zell & Potter litigation, either in discovery or at trial. An important part of his job was maintaining a network of expert witnesses—hired guns willing to take the stand for huge fees. Dr. Bannister was a professional testifier with a thick résumé and a fondness for mixing it up with hotshot lawyers in big trials. The fact that he was now backing down seemed fatal.

The second blow landed an hour later with Jerry already on the ropes and bleeding. A young partner named Carlton arrived with a thick report and some grim news. "Things are not going well, Jerry," he began.

"I know."

Carlton was supervising the screening of thousands of potential clients, and his thick report was filled with terrible numbers. "We're not seeing the damage, Jerry. Ten thousand exams so far, and the results are not impressive. Maybe 10 percent have some loss of aortic pressure, but nothing to get excited about. We're seeing all sorts of heart disease, hypertension, clogged arteries, and the like, but nothing we can link to the drug."

"Ten million bucks on screenings and we have nothing?" Jerry said, thumbs on temples, eyes closed.

"At least ten million, and, yes, we have nothing. I hate to say this, Jerry, but this drug looks harmless. I think we're drilling a dry hole here. I'd say we cut and run."

"I didn't ask for advice."

"No, you didn't." Carlton left the office and closed the door. Jerry locked it and went to a sofa where he stretched out and stared at the ceiling. He had been there before—caught with a drug that wasn't quite as bad as he had claimed it to be. There was still a chance Varrick was a step or two behind. Perhaps the company didn't know what Jerry now knew. With all the settlement buzz, its share price had moved steadily up, closing the Friday before at $34.50. Maybe, just maybe, the company could be bluffed into an even quicker settlement. He had seen it before. A company with plenty of cash and a ton of bad press wants the lawsuits and lawyers to simply go away.

As the minutes passed, he managed to relax. He couldn't think of all the Wally Figgs out there—they were big boys who had made their own decisions to file suit. And he couldn't think of all the clients who were expecting a sizable check, and soon. Nor was he too concerned with saving face—he was obscenely rich, and the money had long since toughened his skin.

What Jerry was really thinking about was the next drug, the one after Krayoxx.

The third blow, and the knockout punch, arrived in a scheduled 3:00 p.m. phone conference with another member of the Plaintiffs' Litigation Committee (PLC). Rodney Berman was a flamboyant New Orleans trial lawyer who had made and lost several fortunes gambling with juries. Thanks to an oil spill in the Gulf, he was currently in the money and had managed to piece together even more Krayoxx clients than Zell & Potter.

"We're up shit creek," he began pleasantly.

"It's been a bad day, Rodney, so go ahead and make it worse."

"Inside scoop from a very confidential, and very well-paid, I might add, spook who has laid eyes on a preliminary report headed for the *New England Journal of Medicine* next month. Researchers at Harvard and Cleveland Clinic will declare that our beloved Krayoxx is as healthy as wheat germ and causes no problems whatsoever. No increased risk of heart attack or stroke. No damage to the aortic valve. Nothing. And these boys have résumés that make our guys look like witch doctors. My experts are running for the hills. My lawyers are hiding under their desks. According to one of our lobbyists, the FDA is considering putting the drug back on the market. Varrick is dropping cash all over Washington. What else do you want to hear, Jerry?"

"I think I've heard enough. I'm looking for a bridge."

"I can see one from my office," Rodney said, somehow managing a laugh. "It's beautiful, spanning the Mississippi and just waiting on me. The Rodney Berman Memorial Bridge. They'd find me in the Gulf one day, covered in crude oil."

Four hours later, all six of the PLC members were linked into a conference call Jerry organized from his office. After he summarized the grim news of the day, Berman delivered his version. Each of the six took a turn, and there was not a single piece of good news. The litigation was crumbling on all fronts, on all theories, from coast to coast. There was a lengthy debate over how much Varrick knew at the moment, and the general feeling was that they, the lawyers, were far ahead of the company. But that would change quickly.

They agreed to stop the screening immediately. Jerry volunteered to contact Nicholas Walker at Varrick and attempt to speed up settlement talks. Each of the six agreed to begin buying huge chunks of Varrick common stock in an effort to drive up the price. It was a public corporation, after all, and its share price meant everything. If Varrick believed a settlement would soothe Wall Street, it might decide to get rid of its Krayoxx mess, however harmless the drug might be.

The conference call lasted two hours and ended with a tone that was slightly more optimistic than when it began. They would continue pushing hard for a few more days, maintain their poker faces, play the game, and hope for a miracle, but under no circumstances would they continue spending money on their own Krayoxx mess. It was over; they would cut their losses and move on to the next battle.

Almost nothing was said about the Klopeck trial six weeks away.

CHAPTER 33

Two days later, Jerry Alisandros made a seemingly routine phone call to Nicholas Walker at Varrick Labs. They went through the weather and some football, then Jerry got around to business. "I'm in your neck of the woods next week, Nick, and I'd like to stop by for a meeting, if you're in and have the time."

"Maybe," Walker said cautiously.

"Our numbers are coming together nicely and we've made progress, at least on the death cases. I've spent hours with the PLC and we're ready to enter into a formal settlement agreement, round one, of course. Let's get the big cases out of the way and then slog through the small ones."

"That's our plan, Jerry," Walker said, in full agreement, and Jerry finally managed to breathe. "I'm taking heat from Reuben Massey to get this stuff out of the way. He chewed me for breakfast this morning and I was planning to call you. Massey has instructed me to get down there with our in-house team and our Florida firms and hammer out a settlement along the same lines as what we have already discussed. I suggest we meet in Fort Lauderdale a week from today, sign the agreement, present it to the judge, and move on. The non-death cases will take longer, but let's get the big ones closed. Agreed?"

Agreed? You have no idea, Jerry thought. "A great idea, Nick. I'll set it up down here."

"But I insist that all six PLC members be in the room."

"I can arrange that, no problem."

"And can we get a magistrate or someone from the judge's office to be present? I'm not leaving there until we have a deal, in writing and approved by the court."

"Excellent idea, Nick." Jerry was grinning like an idiot.

"Let's get it done."

After the call, Jerry checked the market. Varrick was trading at $36, and the only plausible reason for its uptick was the good spin about the settlement.

The phone conversation had been recorded by a company specializing in truth and deception. It was a firm Zell & Potter used frequently to secretly record conversations in an effort to determine the level of veracity on the other end. Thirty minutes after Jerry hung up, two experts entered his office with some graphs and charts. They had camped out in a small conference room down the hall with their staff and machines. They had measured the stress of both voices and had easily determined that both men were lying. Jerry's lies had been planned, of course, in an effort to prompt Walker.

Walker's voice-stress analysis showed a high level of deception. When he spoke of Reuben Massey and the company's desire to get rid of the litigation, he was telling the truth. But when he spoke of the big plans for a settlement summit next week in Fort Lauderdale, he was clearly being deceptive.

Jerry gave the impression of taking the news in stride. Such evidence was never admissible in court because it was so wildly unreliable. He had often asked himself why he even bothered with voice-stress analysis, but after using it for years, he almost believed it. Anything to give him a slight edge. Such recordings were highly unethical anyway, and even illegal in some states, so it was easy to bury the information.

For most of the past fifteen years, he had kept Varrick on the run with one lawsuit after another. And in doing so, he had learned much about the company. Its research was always better than that of the plaintiffs. It hired spies and invested heavily in corporate espionage. Reuben Massey loved hardball and usually found a way to win the war, even after losing most of the battles.

Alone in his office, Jerry typed an entry into his private daily log: "Krayoxx is evaporating before my eyes. Just spoke with N. Walker who plans to be here next week to sign a deal. 80–20 chance he doesn't show."

Iris Klopeck shared Wally's letter with several friends and family members, and the imminent arrival of $2 million was already causing problems. Clint, her deadbeat son, who routinely went days without offering her as much as a rude grunt or two, was suddenly showing all manner of affection. He was cleaning his room, washing dishes, running errands for his dear mother, and chattering away nonstop, his favorite topic being his desire for a new car. Iris's brother, fresh from his second stint in prison for stealing motorcycles, was painting her house (with no charge for the labor) and dropping hints about his longtime dream of owning a used motorcycle business. He knew of one on the market for only $100,000. "A steal," he said, at which her son whispered behind his back, "He should know a steal when he sees one." Percy's wretched sister Bertha was letting it be known that she was entitled to a chunk of the money because she was "blood." Iris loathed the woman, as had Percy, and Iris had already reminded Bertha that she had not attended Percy's funeral. Bertha was now claiming she had been hospitalized on that day. "Prove it," Iris said, and so they bickered.

On the day Adam Grand received his letter from Wally, he was hustling around the all-you-can-eat pizza house when his boss barked at him for no apparent reason. Adam, the assistant manager, returned the favor, and a nasty row ensued. When the shouting and cursing ended, Adam either quit or was fired, and for several minutes both men argued over the exact nature of Adam's departure. Not that it mattered—he was gone. And that didn't matter to Adam either, because he was about to be rich.

Millie Marino had the good sense to show her letter to no one. She read it several times before the words began to sink in, and she felt a twinge of guilt for doubting Wally's ability. He still failed to inspire confidence, and she was still angry over her late husband Chester's will and estate, but those issues were now of fading importance. Chester's son, Lyle, would be entitled to his portion, and for that reason he had been monitoring the litigation. If he knew how close they were to pay dirt, he might become a nuisance. So Millie put the letter under lock and key and told no one.

On September 9, five weeks after being shot in both legs, Justin Bardall filed a lawsuit against Oscar individually and Finley & Figg as a partnership. He alleged Oscar used "excessive force" in the shooting and, in particular, deliberately fired the third shot into the left leg after Bardall was seriously wounded and no longer posed a threat. The lawsuit demanded $5 million in actual damages and $10 million in punitive damages for Oscar's malicious conduct.

The lawyer who filed the case, Goodloe Stamm, was the same lawyer hired by Paula Finley to handle her divorce. Evidently, at some point Stamm tracked down Bardall and convinced him to sue, in spite of his criminal activities and the fact that he was about to spend time in prison for attempted arson.

The divorce was proving to be more contentious than Wally or Oscar had expected, especially in light of the fact that Oscar was basically walking away with nothing but his car and clothes. Stamm kept chirping about the big Krayoxx money and smelled a conspiracy to hide it.

Oscar was furious over the $15 million lawsuit and blamed everything on David. Had it not been for the wage case filed against Cicero Pipe, he and Bardall would have never met. Wally managed to broker a truce, and the yelling stopped. He contacted their insurance company and insisted it provide a defense and coverage.

With the big settlement so close, it was much easier to make peace, to smile, even to joke about the image of that little thug Bardall limping into court and trying to convince a jury he, an incompetent arsonist, should be made rich because he failed to burn down a law office.

CHAPTER 34

The e-mail was prefaced with the standard warnings of confidentiality and protected with encryption codes. It was written by Jerry Alisandros and sent to about eighty lawyers, one of whom was Wally Figg. It read:

> I regret to inform you that tomorrow's settlement conference has been canceled by Varrick Labs. This morning I had a lengthy phone conversation with Nicholas Walker, chief in-house counsel for Varrick, during which I was advised that the company has decided to temporarily postpone settlement negotiations. Their strategy has changed somewhat, especially in light of the fact that the Klopeck trial is scheduled to begin in Chicago in four weeks. Varrick now thinks it's wise to sort of test the waters with an initial trial, see how the facts play out, determine liability, and roll the dice with a real jury. While this is not unusual, I had some very harsh words for Mr. Walker and his company's rather abrupt change of plans. I suggested they had negotiated in bad faith, and so on, but there is little to be gained by arguing at this point. Since we did not quite reach the point of agreeing on the specifics of a settlement, there is nothing to enforce. It looks as though all eyes will be on the courtroom in Chicago. I'll keep you posted. JA

Wally printed the e-mail—it weighed a ton—walked it into Oscar's office, and placed it on his desk. Then he fell into a leather chair and almost began weeping.

Oscar read it slowly, the wrinkles across his forehead growing thicker with each sentence. He was breathing through his mouth, heavily. Rochelle buzzed in with a call for Oscar, but he did not respond. They heard her heavy footsteps as she walked to his office door, tapped it, and when neither lawyer responded, she peeked inside and said, "Mr. Finley, it's Judge Wilson."

Oscar shook his head and said, "I can't talk now. I'll call him back."

She closed the door. Minutes passed, then David knocked on the door, came inside, looked at the two partners, and knew the world was coming to an end. Oscar handed him the e-mail, which he read as he paced in front of the bookshelves.

"There's more," David said.

"What do you mean, there's more?" Wally asked, his voice weak and dry.

"I was just online, looking at a discovery filing, when I saw the notice that a motion had been filed. Not twenty minutes ago. Jerry Alisandros, on behalf of Zell & Potter, filed a motion to withdraw as counsel in the Klopeck case."

Wally's entire body slumped a good six inches. Oscar grunted as if trying to say something.

David, himself pale and stunned, continued: "I called my contact at Zell & Potter, guy named Worley, and he tells me off the record that it's a full retreat. The experts—our experts—have all collapsed on the drug and no one is willing to testify. The McFadden report won't stand up in court. Varrick has known this for some time and has been stringing out the settlement talks so they could yank the rug out right before the Klopeck trial. Worley says the Zell & Potter partners are at war but Alisandros gets the last word. He isn't coming to Chicago because he doesn't want such a notorious loss on his great record. With no experts, the case is hopeless. Worley says there's a good chance that there was nothing wrong with the drug to begin with."

"I knew these cases were a bad idea," Oscar said.

"Oh shut up," Wally hissed.

David sat in a wooden chair as far from the two partners as possible. Oscar had both elbows on his desk with his head between his forearms, as if in a vice, as if a lethal migraine were forming. Wally's eyes were closed and his head twitched. Because they seemed unable to speak, David felt compelled to attempt conversation. "Can he withdraw this close to trial?" he asked, fully aware that his two partners knew virtually nothing about the rules of federal court procedure.

"That's up to the judge," Wally said. "What are they going to do with all their cases?" he asked David. "They have thousands, tens of thousands."

"Worley thinks that everybody will just sit tight and see what happens here, with Klopeck. If we win, then I guess Varrick will resume settlement talks. If we lose, I guess the Krayoxx cases are worthless."

The idea of winning seemed quite remote. Minutes passed with no words. The only sounds were the labored breathing of three bewildered men. The distant sound of an ambulance approached on Beech Street, but none of the three reacted.

Finally, Wally sat erect, or tried to, and said, "We'll have to ask the court for a continuance, for additional time, and we'll probably want to oppose this motion to withdraw."

Oscar managed to dislodge his head. He glared at Wally as if he could shoot him too. "What you need to do is call your buddy Jerry and find out what the hell's going on. He can't run away with the trial this close. Tell him we'll file an ethics complaint. Tell him we'll leak it to the press—the great Jerry Alisandros afraid to come to Chicago. Tell him anything, Wally, but he has to come try this case. God knows we can't do it."

"If there's nothing wrong with the drug, why even think about going to trial?" David asked.

"It's a bad drug," Wally said. "And we can find an expert who'll say so."

"For some reason I'm having trouble believing you," Oscar said.

David stood and headed for the door. "I suggest we go to our rooms, think about the situation, and reconvene here in an hour."

Wally said, "Good idea," and staggered to his feet. He got to his office, to his phone, and began calling Alisandros. Not surprisingly, the great man was unavailable. Wally began sending him e-mails— long, scorching messages filled with threats and invective.

David scoured the blogs—financial, mass tort, legal watchdogs— and found confirmation that Varrick had called off settlement talks. Its share price was down for the third day in a row.

By late afternoon, the firm had filed a motion for a continuance and a response to Jerry's motion to withdraw. Virtually all the work was done by David because Wally had fled the office and Oscar was not functioning well. David had briefed Rochelle on the disaster, and her first concern was Wally's drinking. He'd been sober for almost a year, but she had witnessed his earlier relapses.

The following day, in an unusually prompt move, Nadine Karros filed a response in opposition to the request for more time. And, in a move that was easily predictable, she had no problem with Zell & Potter making an exit. A long trial against a pro like Jerry Alisandros would be a tremendous challenge, but Nadine was confident she could make quick work of either Finley or Figg, or both.

The following day, in a response that was almost dizzying in its speed, Judge Seawright denied the request for additional time. The trial had been set for October 17, and it would go on. He had cleared his calendar for two weeks, and it would be unfair to other litigants to change the schedule. Mr. Figg had filed the lawsuit ("with as much noise as possible"), and he'd had ample time to prepare for trial. Welcome to the Rocket Docket.

Judge Seawright had harsh words for Jerry Alisandros but in the end granted his motion to withdraw. Procedurally, such a motion was almost always granted. The judge noted that the client, Iris Klopeck, would still have adequate legal representation after the departure of

Mr. Alisandros. The word "adequate" could have been debated, but the judge took the high ground and did not comment on the complete lack of federal trial experience by Mr. Figg, Mr. Finley, and Mr. Zinc.

The only remaining option was for Wally to file a motion to dismiss the Klopeck case, along with the other seven. His fortune was slipping away, and he was close to a nervous breakdown, but as painful as a dismissal would be, he could not imagine the horror of walking into Seawright's courtroom, practically alone, with the unbearable weight of thousands of Krayoxx victims on his back, and pursuing a case that even the great trial lawyers were now dodging. No sir. He, along with what appeared to be everyone else who'd stepped into the pit, was scrambling to get out of it. Oscar was adamant that the clients should first be notified. David was of the opinion that Wally should obtain their consent before he killed their cases. Wally halfheartedly agreed with both, but he could not bring himself to inform his clients that he was dismissing their cases only days after he'd sent his jolly letters virtually promising $2 million each.

He was already working on his lies. He planned to tell Iris, then the rest of them, that Varrick had successfully managed to get the cases kicked out of federal court and that he and the other lawyers were considering refiling them in state court, and this would take time, and so on. Wally needed to burn some clock, let a few months go by, stall, procrastinate, lie, blame the delays on big bad Varrick Laboratories. Let the dust settle. Let the dreams of quick money fade away. After a year or so he would conjure up some more lies, and with the passage of time all would be forgotten.

He typed the motion himself, and when it was finished, he stared at it for a long time on his desktop. Finally, with his door locked and his shoes off, Wally punched the Send button and said farewell to his fortune.

He needed a drink. He needed oblivion. Alone, broker than ever, his dreams dashed, his pile of debts higher, Wally finally cracked and started crying.

CHAPTER 35

Not so fast, said Ms. Karros. Her prompt and sharply worded response to what Wally thought was a routine motion to dismiss was startling. She began by declaring that her client insisted upon a trial. She went into great detail describing the torrent of bad press Varrick Labs had endured for over a year—much of it created and fanned by the plaintiffs' bar—and she attached to her motion a binder three inches thick and filled with press clippings from around the country. Every story was driven by some loudmouthed lawyer (including Wally) flaying Varrick over Krayoxx and screaming for millions. It was now grossly unfair to allow these same lawyers to cut and run without a word of apology to the company.

Her client really didn't want an apology; it wanted justice. It demanded a fair trial before a jury. Varrick Labs didn't start this fight, but it certainly planned to finish it.

Along with her response she included her own motion, one that had never been seen around the offices of Finley & Figg. Its title—Rule 11 Motion for Sanctions—was frightening; its language was enough to send Wally back to rehab, David back to Rogan Rothberg, and Oscar into an early, unfunded retirement. Ms. Karros argued, quite persuasively, that if the court granted the plaintiff's motion to dismiss the case, then the filing of the case was purely frivolous in the first place. The fact that the plaintiff now wanted to dismiss was a clear sign the case had no merit and should never have been filed. However, it was filed, some nine months earlier, and the defendant, Varrick, had no alternative but to vigorously defend itself. Therefore, under the sanctions provision of Rule 11 of the Federal Rules of Civil Procedure, the defendant was entitled to be reimbursed for the costs of fighting back.

So far, and Ms. Karros was blunt about the fact that the meter was still running at full throttle, Varrick Labs had spent approximately $18 million defending itself, with at least half of that attributable to the Klopeck case. A huge sum no doubt, but she was quick to point out that the plaintiff had demanded $100 million when the lawsuit was filed. And given the nature of mass tort litigation, with all the elements of a stampede, it was, and still is, imperative that Varrick Labs successfully defend the first trial at all costs. The law does not require a party to select the cheapest law firm or look for a bargain. With so much at stake, Varrick Labs wisely chose a law firm with a long history of success in the courtroom.

She went on for pages giving details of other frivolous cases in which federal judges had thrown the book at the less than scrupulous lawyers who filed all this junk, including two from the sacred courtroom of the Honorable Harry L. Seawright.

Rule 11 provides that sanctions, if granted by the court, are to be borne equally by the lawyers and their client.

"Hey, Iris, guess what? You owe half of $9 million," David mumbled to himself, hoping to find a bit of humor in another depressing day. He read it first, and by the time he finished, he was sweating around the neck. Nadine Karros and her small army at Rogan Rothberg had cranked it out in less than forty-eight hours, and David could visualize the young grunts pulling all-nighters and sleeping at their desks.

When Wally read it, he quietly left the office and was not seen for the rest of the day. When Oscar read it, he shuffled to a small sofa in his locked office, eased off his shoes, and stretched out, his eyes covered with an arm. After a few minutes, he not only appeared to be dead; he was actually praying for the end.

———

Bart Shaw was a lawyer who specialized in suing other lawyers for malpractice. This little niche in the crowded market had earned him the reputation, among the bar, as a pariah. He had few friends in the profession, but he had always considered that to be a good thing. He was smart, talented, and aggressive, just the man Varrick needed for a job that appeared to be a bit shady but was actually well within ethical guidelines.

After a series of phone conversations with Judy Beck, Nick Walker's cohort in the legal department at Varrick, Shaw agreed to the terms of a confidential representation. His retainer was $25,000 and his hourly rate was $600. Any fees earned from the potential malpractice cases would be kept by Shaw.

His first call was to Iris Klopeck, who, with a month to go before trial, was drifting in and out of a state that vaguely resembled emotional stability. She wanted no part of a conversation with another lawyer, a stranger, but did admit she wished she had never met that other one. After she abruptly hung up, Shaw waited an hour and tried again. After a cautious "Hello," Shaw plunged in.

"Are you aware that your attorney is trying to dismiss your case?" he asked. When she couldn't respond immediately, he continued. "Ms. Klopeck, my name is Bart Shaw. I'm a lawyer and I represent people who get screwed by their own lawyers. Legal malpractice. It's all I do, and your lawyer, Wally Figg, is trying to weasel out of your case. I think you may have a lawsuit against him. He has malpractice insurance coverage and you might be entitled to recover some money."

"I've heard that somewhere before," she said softly.

It was Shaw's game, and he talked nonstop for the next ten minutes. He described the motion to dismiss and Wally's efforts to unload not just her case but seven others as well. When she finally spoke, she said, "But he promised me a million dollars."

"He promised?"

"Oh yes."

"That's highly unethical, but then I doubt if Mr. Figg worries too much about ethics."

"He's pretty sleazy," she observed.

"How, exactly, did he promise you a million dollars?"

"Right here at the kitchen table, first time I laid eyes on him. Then he put it in writing."

"He what? You have it in writing?"

"Got a letter from Figg a week or so ago. Said they were about to agree on a $2 million settlement, which was a lot more than the $1 million he had promised. Got the letter right here. What happened to the settlement? What's your name again?"

Shaw kept her on the phone for an hour, and both were exhausted when the conversation was over. Millie Marino was next, and, unmedicated, she grasped the issues much more quickly than poor Iris. She knew nothing about the collapse of the settlement plan, or the dismissal, nor had she spoken with Wally in several weeks. As with Iris, Shaw convinced her to hold off contacting Wally right away. It was more important for Shaw to do so, at the right moment. Millie was thoroughly bewildered by the conversation and the turn of events and said she needed some time to gather her thoughts.

Adam Grand needed no such time. He began cursing Wally immediately. How could the little worm try to dismiss the case without telling him? Last he heard they were about to settle for $2 million. Hell yes, Grand was ready to go after Figg. "How much malpractice insurance coverage does he have?" he asked.

"The standard policy is $5 million, but there are many variations," Shaw explained. "We'll know soon enough."

The fifth firm meeting took place after dark on a Thursday night, and Rochelle skipped it. She could not handle more bad news, and there was nothing she could do to help the miserable situation.

The letter from Bart Shaw had arrived that afternoon and was now lying in the center of the table. After explaining that he was "in consultation with six of your clients who were involved in the Krayoxx litigation, including Ms. Iris Klopeck," he went on to clearly state that he had not been retained by any of the six. Not yet. They were waiting to see what happened next with their cases. However, he, Shaw, was gravely concerned with Finley & Figg's efforts to unload the cases, and without notifying the clients. Such behavior breached all manner of professional conduct. In stiff but lucid language, he lectured the firm on a variety of topics: (1) its ethical duty to diligently protect its clients' interests; (2) its duty to keep the clients informed of all developments; (3) the unethical payment of referral fees to clients; (4) the outright guarantee of a favorable outcome in order to induce a client to sign up; and on and on. He sternly warned them that further lapses in their conduct would lead to unpleasant litigation.

Oscar and Wally, who had survived numerous charges of unethical behavior, were not as bothered by the allegations as they were terrified of the letter's overall message; to wit, the firm would be immediately sued for malpractice if the cases were dismissed. David was upset over every word in Shaw's letter.

They sat around the table, all three subdued and thoroughly defeated. There was no cursing or shouting. David knew the fighting had already taken place when he was away from the office.

There was no way out. If the Klopeck lawsuit was dismissed, Ms. Karros would castrate them with her demand for sanctions, and old Seawright would go right along with it. The firm could face millions in fines. On top of that, this shark Shaw would pile on with a malpractice claim and drag them through the mud for the next two years.

If they withdrew their motion to dismiss, they would be staring at a trial date that was now only twenty-five days away.

While Wally doodled on a legal pad as if he were heavily medicated, Oscar did most of the talking. "So, either we get rid of these cases and face financial ruin, or we march into federal court three weeks from Monday with a case that no lawyer in his right mind would try before a jury, a case with no liability, no experts, no decent facts, a client who's crazy half the time and stoned the other half, a client whose dead husband weighed 320 pounds and basically ate himself to death, a veritable platoon of highly paid and very skilled lawyers on the other side with an unlimited budget and experts from the finest hospitals in the country, a judge who strongly favors the other side, a judge who doesn't like us at all because he thinks we're inexperienced and incompetent, and, well, what else? What am I leaving out here, David?"

"We have no cash for litigation expenses," David said, but only to complete the checklist.

"Right. Helluva job, Wally. As you used to say all the time, these mass tort cases are a gold mine."

"Come on, Oscar," Wally pleaded softly. "Give me a break. I take full responsibility. It's all my fault. Flog me with a bullwhip, whatever. But allow me to suggest we limit our discussions to something that might be productive, okay, Oscar?"

"Sure. What's your plan? Dazzle us some more, Wally."

"We have no choice but to go fight," Wally said, his voice still hoarse, his delivery slow. "We try to piece together some proof. We go to court and fight like hell, and when we lose we can tell our clients, and this scumbag Shaw, that we fought the good fight. In every lawsuit, somebody wins, somebody loses. Sure, we'll get our butts kicked, but at this point I'd rather walk out of the courtroom with my head up than deal with sanctions and malpractice claims."

"Have you ever faced a jury in federal court, Wally?" Oscar asked.

"No. Have you?"

"No," Oscar said and looked at David. "Have you, David?"

"No."

"That's what I thought. The three stooges bumbling into the courtroom with the lovely Iris Klopeck and no clue about what to do next. You mentioned piecing together some proof. Care to enlighten us, Wally?"

Wally glared at him for a moment, then said, "We try to find a couple of experts, a cardiologist and maybe a pharmacologist. There are a lot of experts out there who'll say anything for a fee. We pay them, put them on the witness stand, hope like hell they survive."

"There's no way they'll survive, because they would have to be bogus in the first place."

"Right, but at least we're trying, Oscar. At least we're putting up a fight."

"How much do these quacks cost?"

Wally looked at David, who said, "I caught up with Dr. Borzov this afternoon, the guy who was here screening our clients. He's back home in Atlanta now that the screening has come to a sudden halt. He said he would consider testifying in the Klopeck case for a fee of, uh, I think he said $75,000. His accent is pretty thick."

"Seventy-five thousand?" Oscar repeated. "And you can't even understand him?"

"He's Russian and his English is not too refined, which may work to our advantage in a trial because we might want the jury to be thoroughly confused."

"I'm sorry, you're losing me."

"Well, you gotta figure that Nadine Karros will batter the guy on cross-examination. If the jury understands how lame he is, then our case is weakened. But if the jury isn't sure because they cannot understand him, then maybe, just maybe, the damage is lessened."

"And they taught you this at Harvard?"

"I really don't remember what they taught me at Harvard."

"So how did you become an expert on trial practice?"

"I'm not an expert, but I am reading a lot, and watching *Perry Mason* reruns. Sweet little Emma is not sleeping well and I'm roaming around at night."

"I feel better."

Wally said, "With some luck, we can find a bogus pharmacologist for $25,000 or so. There will be a few more expenses, but Rogan has not put up much of a fight."

"And now we know why," Oscar said. "They want a trial, and fast. They want justice. They want a quick, clear verdict that they can take and broadcast around the world. You guys fell for their trap, Wally. Varrick started talking settlement, and the mass tort boys started buying new jets. They strung you along until the first trial was only a month away, then they pulled the rug. Your close friends at Zell &

Potter hit the back door, and here we are, with nothing but financial ruin."

"We've had this conversation, Oscar," Wally said firmly.

A thirty-second time-out was observed as things settled down somewhat. Wally calmly said, "This building is worth $300,000 and debt free. Let's go to the bank, put up the building for a line of credit, cap it at $200,000, and go search for experts."

"I was expecting this," Oscar said. "Why should we throw good money after bad?"

"Come on, Oscar. You know more about litigation than I do, which isn't much, but—"

"You're right about that."

"It's not enough to simply walk into court, start the trial, pick a jury, then duck for cover when Nadine starts firing cannons at us. We won't even get to the trial if we don't find a couple of experts. That in itself is malpractice."

David tried to help. "You can bet this guy Shaw will be in the courtroom, watching us."

"Right," said Wally. "And if we don't at least try to put on a case, Seawright might consider it frivolous and hit us with sanctions. As crazy as it seems, spending some money might save us a bundle down the road."

Oscar exhaled and clasped his hands behind his head. "This is insanity. Complete insanity."

Wally and David agreed.

Wally withdrew his motion to dismiss his cases and sent copies to Bart Shaw for good measure. Nadine Karros withdrew her response and Rule 11 Motion for Sanctions. When Judge Seawright signed both orders, the boutique firm of Finley & Figg breathed easier. For the moment, the three lawyers were not in her gun sights.

After reviewing the firm's financials, the bank was reluctant to make the loan, even with the office building free and clear. Unknown to Helen, David signed a personal guaranty for the line of credit, as did his two partners. With $200,000 now available, the firm kicked into high gear, which was made complicated by the fact that none of the three was clear on what needed to be done.

Judge Seawright and his clerks reviewed the file daily, and with growing concern. On Monday, October 3, all lawyers were summoned to chambers for an informal update session. His Honor began the meeting by stating, unequivocally, that the trial would begin in two weeks and nothing could change this. Both sides claimed to be ready for trial.

"Have you retained experts?" he asked Wally.

"Yes sir."

"And when do you think you might share this information with the court and with the other side? You are months past due on this, you know?"

"Yes, Your Honor, but we've had a few unexpected events in our timeline," Wally said beautifully, like a real smart-ass.

"Who's your cardiologist?" Nadine Karros fired from the other side of the table.

"Dr. Igor Borzov," Wally shot back confidently, as if Borzov were known as the greatest heart expert in the world. Nadine did not flinch, nor did she smile.

"When can he be here for a deposition?" the judge asked.

"Whenever," Wally said. No problem. The truth was that Borzov was having a difficult time making a decision about walking into a buzz saw, even for $75,000.

"We won't be deposing Dr. Borzov," Ms. Karros said, quite dismissively. In other words, I know he's a quack, don't care what he says in a depo, because I will annihilate him in front of the jury. She made this decision on the spot, with no need to confer with her minions or ponder things for twenty-four hours. Her iciness was indeed chilling.

"Do you have a pharmacologist?" she asked.

"We do," Wally lied. "Dr. Herbert Threadgill." Wally had actually spoken to this guy, but no agreement had been reached. David got his name from his pal Worley at Zell & Potter, who described Threadgill as "a nut job who'll say anything for a buck." But it was proving not to be that easy. Threadgill was asking for $50,000 to compensate for some of the humiliation he would undoubtedly face in open court.

"We don't need his deposition either," she said, with a slight flip of the hand that conveyed a thousand words. He'll be dog meat too.

When the meeting ended, David insisted that Oscar and Wally follow him to a courtroom on the fourteenth floor of the Dirksen building. According to the federal court's Web site, an important trial was getting started. It was a civil case involving the death of a seventeen-year-old high school senior who'd been killed instantly when a tractor-trailer rig blew through a red light and hit the kid broadside. The rig was owned by an out-of-state company, thus the federal jurisdiction.

Since no one at Finley & Figg had ever tried a case in federal court, David felt strongly that they should at least watch one.

CHAPTER 36

Five days before the trial, Judge Seawright reconvened the lawyers in his courtroom for the final pretrial conference. The three stooges looked remarkably put together and professional, thanks to David's efforts. He had insisted they wear dark suits, white shirts, ties that were anything but flashy, and black shoes. For Oscar, this had not been a serious problem since he had always dressed the part of a lawyer, albeit one from the streets. For David, it was second nature because he had a closet full of expensive suits from his days at Rogan Rothberg. For Wally, though, it had been more of a challenge. David found a men's store with moderately priced clothing, and he had actually gone with Wally to make selections and supervise the fitting. Wally had bitched and bickered throughout the ordeal, and he nearly bolted when the final tally came to $1,400. Eventually, he put it on a credit card, and he and David both held their breath when the clerk processed it. The charges cleared, and they hurried away with bags of shirts, ties, and one pair of black wing tips.

On the other side of the courtroom, Nadine Karros, in Prada, was surrounded by half a dozen of her attack dogs, all spiffed up in Zegna and Armani suits and looking like ads from glossy magazines.

As was his custom, Judge Seawright had not released the list of prospective jurors. The other judges released their lists weeks before trial, and this invariably set in motion a frenzied investigation by highly paid jury consultants for both sides. The bigger the case, the more money was spent probing into the backgrounds of the jury pool. Judge Seawright detested these shadowy maneuverings. Years earlier, in one of his cases, there had been allegations of improper contact by investigators. Prospective jurors had complained of being watched, followed, photographed, and even approached by smooth-talking strangers who knew too much about them.

Judge Seawright called the meeting to order, and his clerk handed one list to Oscar and another to Nadine Karros. There were sixty names, all of which had been prescreened by the judge's staff to eliminate any juror who (1) was taking or had ever taken Krayoxx or any other cholesterol medication; (2) had a family member, relative, or friend who was taking or had ever taken Krayoxx; (3) had ever been represented by a lawyer remotely connected to the case; (4) had ever been involved in a lawsuit involving a drug or product alleged to be defective; (5) had read a newspaper or magazine article about Krayoxx and the litigation surrounding it. The four-page questionnaire went on to cover other areas that might disqualify a prospective juror.

In the next five days, Rogan Rothberg would spend $500,000 delving into the backgrounds of the jury pool. Once the trial started, they would have three highly paid consultants scattered around the courtroom observing the jury as it reacted to the testimony. Finley & Figg's consultant cost $25,000 and was brought on board only after another firm fight. She and her associates would do their best to check backgrounds and profile the model juror, and she would observe the selection process. Her name was Consuelo, and she quickly realized that she had never worked with such inexperienced attorneys.

It had been determined, through an unpleasant and often testy process, that Oscar would take the role of lead counsel and do most of the footwork in the courtroom. Wally would observe, offer advice, take notes, and do whatever the second-in-command was supposed to do, though none of them were certain what this would entail. David would be in charge of the research, a monumental task since this was the first federal trial for all three and everything had to be researched. Through the course of numerous arduous strategy sessions around the table, David had learned that Oscar's last jury trial had been in state court eight years earlier, a relatively simple who-ran-the-red-light car accident that he had lost. Wally's record was even more modest—a slip-and-fall case against a Walmart in which the jury deliberated fifteen minutes before finding for the store, and an almost forgotten car wreck up in Wilmette that had also ended badly.

When Oscar and Wally locked horns over strategy, they had turned to David because he was the only one there. His votes had been crucial, a fact that disturbed him greatly.

After the lists were handed over, Judge Seawright delivered a stern lecture about getting close to the jury pool. He explained that when the prospective jurors arrived Monday morning, he would grill them on the subject of improper contact. Did they feel as if someone had been prying into their lives, their backgrounds? Had they been followed, photographed? Any violations, and he would be a very unhappy judge.

Moving on, he said, "No *Daubert* challenges have been filed, so it's safe to say that neither side wishes to challenge the other's experts, am I correct?"

Neither Oscar nor Wally was aware of the *Daubert* rule, which had been around for years. *Daubert* allowed each side to challenge the admissibility of the other's expert testimony. It was standard procedure in federal cases and was followed in about half of the states. David had stumbled across it ten days earlier when he was watching a trial down the hall. After some quick research, he realized that Nadine Karros could probably exclude their experts before the trial even started. The fact that she had not requested a *Daubert* hearing meant only one thing—she wanted their experts on the stand so she could castigate them before the jury.

After David explained the rule to his partners, the three made the decision not to file *Daubert* challenges against the experts for Varrick. Their reason was as simple as Nadine's but on the reverse side. Her experts were so experienced, credentialed, and qualified that a *Daubert* challenge would be fruitless.

"That's correct, Your Honor," she replied.

"That's correct," Oscar said.

"Unusual, but then I'm not looking for any extra work." The judge shuffled some papers and whispered to a clerk. "I see no pending motions, nothing left to do but start the trial. The jurors will be here at 8:30 Monday morning and we will begin promptly at 9:00 a.m. Anything else?"

Nothing from the lawyers.

"Very well. I commend both sides on an efficient discovery process and unusual cooperation. I intend to oversee a fair and speedy trial. Court's adjourned."

The Finley & Figg team quickly gathered its files and papers and left the courtroom. On the way out, David tried to imagine what the place would look like in five days, with sixty prospective and nervous jurors, moles from other mass tort law firms on hand for a bloodletting, reporters, stock analysts, jury consultants trying to blend in, smug corporate honchos from Varrick, and the usual courthouse observers. The knot in his stomach made breathing difficult. "Just survive it," he kept telling himself. "You're only thirty-two years old. This will not be the end of your career."

In the hallway, he suggested they split up and spend a few hours watching other trials, but Oscar and Wally just wanted to leave. So David did what he'd been doing for the past two weeks; he eased into a tense courtroom and took a seat three rows behind the lawyers.

The more he watched, the more fascinated he became with the art of a trial.

CHAPTER 37

In the matter of *Klopeck v. Varrick Labs,* the first crisis was the failure of the plaintiff to show up for court. When informed of this in chambers, Judge Seawright was less than pleased. Wally tried to explain that Iris had been rushed to the hospital in the middle of the night, complaining of shortness of breath, hyperventilation, hives, and one or two other afflictions.

Three hours earlier, as the Finley & Figg lawyers worked frantically around the table in a predawn session, a call came on Wally's cell. It was Bart Shaw, the malpractice lawyer who was threatening to sue if the Krayoxx cases were mishandled. Apparently, Iris's son, Clint, had found a lawyer's phone number and called to say his mother was in the ambulance and headed for the hospital. She would not be able to attend the trial. Clint had called the wrong lawyer, and Shaw was just passing along the news.

"Gee thanks, asshole," Wally had said as he punched the disconnect.

"When did you first learn that she was taken to the hospital?" Judge Seawright was now asking.

"A few hours ago, Judge. We were at the office preparing, and her lawyer called."

"Her lawyer? I thought you were her lawyer."

David and Oscar wanted to slide under the table. Wally's brain was already fried and he had taken two sedatives. He looked upward at the ceiling and tried to think of a quick way out of this blunder. "Yes, well, you see, Judge, it's complicated. But she's at the hospital. I'll go see her during the lunch break."

Across the table, Nadine Karros maintained a look of casual concern. She knew everything about Bart Shaw's bullying of Finley & Figg. In fact, she and her associates had located Shaw and recommended him to Nicholas Walker and Judy Beck.

"You do that, Mr. Figg," Seawright said sternly. "And I want to see some report from her doctors. I suppose if she's unable to testify, then we'll be forced to use her deposition."

"Yes sir."

"Jury selection should move right along. I anticipate seating the jury by late this afternoon, so you're first up in the morning, Mr. Figg. Ideally, the plaintiff begins its case by taking the stand and talking about the dearly departed."

It was certainly thoughtful of Judge Seawright to tell them how to try their case, Wally thought, but his tone was condescending.

"I'll talk to her doctors," Wally said again. "That's the best I can do."

"Anything else?"

All the lawyers shook their heads, then left the chambers. They filed into the courtroom, which had filled up nicely in the past fifteen minutes. To the left, behind the plaintiff's counsel table, a bailiff was herding the sixty jurors into the long, padded benches. To the right, several groups of spectators were milling about, waiting, whispering. Seated near the back, together, were Millie Marino, Adam Grand, and Agnes Schmidt, three of Finley & Figg's other victims, present out of curiosity and perhaps looking for answers since their guaranteed $1 million jackpots had suddenly vanished. They were with Bart Shaw, the vulture, the pariah, the lowest scum to be found in the legal profession. Two rows in front of them sat Goodloe Stamm, the divorce lawyer hired by Paula Finley. Stamm had already heard the gossip and knew the serious trial lawyers had jumped ship. Still, he was curious about the case and even hopeful Finley & Figg could pull off a miracle and generate some money for his client.

Judge Seawright called things to order and thanked the jurors for their patriotic duty. He gave a thirty-word summary of the case, then introduced the lawyers and the courtroom personnel who would take part in the trial—the court reporter, the bailiffs, the clerks. He explained the absence of Iris Klopeck and introduced Nicholas Walker, the corporate representative for Varrick Laboratories.

After thirty years on the bench, Harry Seawright knew a thing or two about selecting juries. The most important element, at least in his opinion, was to keep the lawyers as quiet as possible. He had his own list of questions, one tweaked over the years, and allowed the lawyers to submit inquiries to him. But he did the bulk of the talking.

The extensive screening questionnaire streamlined the process. It had already eliminated jurors who were over sixty-five, blind, or suffering from a disability that would affect their service, and those who had served in the past twelve months. It had flagged those who claimed to know something about the case, or the lawyers, or the drug. As the judge went through his questions, an airline pilot stood and asked to be excused because of his schedule. This prompted a surprisingly harsh lecture from Judge Seawright about civic duty. When the pilot sat down, adequately scorched, no one else dared to claim they were too busy to serve. A young mother with a Down's child was excused.

In the previous two weeks, David had talked to at least a dozen lawyers who had tried cases before Seawright. Every judge has his quirks, especially federal ones because they are appointed for life and their actions are seldom questioned. Every lawyer had told David to just lie low during jury selection. "The old man will do a thorough job for you," they said, over and over.

When the pool was down to fifty, Judge Seawright picked twelve names at random. They were directed by a bailiff to the jury box, where they filled the comfortable chairs. Every lawyer was scribbling away. The jury consultants were on the edges of their seats, practically gawking at the first twelve.

The great debate had been, what's the model juror for this case? On the plaintiff's side, the lawyers preferred heavy people with habits as slovenly as the Klopecks', preferably folks battling high cholesterol and other lifestyle-inflicted health problems. Across the aisle, the defense lawyers preferred lean, hard, youthful bodies with little patience and sympathy for the obese and afflicted. In the first batch, there was the inevitable mix, though only a couple appeared to spend much time in the gym. Judge Seawright zeroed in on Number 35 because she had admitted reading several articles about the drug. However, it became clear that she was open-minded and could be fair. Number 29's father was a doctor, and she grew up in a house where "lawsuit" was a dirty word. Number 16 had once filed a lawsuit over a bad roofing job, and this was discussed to the point of forcing yawns. But the judge plowed ahead with his endless questions. When he finished, he invited the plaintiff to quiz the prospective jurors, but only on topics that had not been covered.

Oscar walked to the podium, which had been turned to face the jury box. He offered a warm smile and said good morning to the jurors. "I have just a couple of questions," he said softly, as if he had done this many times.

Since the eventful day David Zinc had stumbled, literally, into the offices of Finley & Figg, Wally had said on numerous occasions that Oscar was not easily intimidated. Perhaps it was his rough childhood, his days as a tough street cop, or his long career representing freaked-out spouses and injured workers, or maybe it was just his pugnacious, Irish composition, but whatever the mix Oscar Finley had a very thick skin. Perhaps, too, it was the Valium, but when Oscar chatted with the twelve potential jurors, he managed to hide the jitters and nerves and outright fear and convey an air of calm and confidence. He asked a few benign questions, solicited a few feeble responses, then sat down.

The firm had taken a first baby step in court without a disaster, and David relaxed a little. He was comforted by the fact that he was third down the line—not that he had much confidence in the two in front of him—but at least they were on the firing line and he was partially hidden back in the trenches. He refused to glance over at the gang from Rogan Rothberg, and they seemed genuinely unconcerned about him.

This was game day and they were the players. They knew they would win. David and his partners were going through the motions, stuck with a case that no one wanted, and dreaming of the end.

Nadine Karros addressed the potential jurors and introduced herself. There were five men and seven women in the jury box. The men, ages twenty-three to sixty-three, sized her up and approved. David concentrated on the women's faces. It was Helen's theory that the women would have mixed and complicated feelings about Nadine Karros. First, and most important, there would be pride that a woman was not only in charge but, as they would soon realize, also the best lawyer in the courtroom. For some, though, the pride would soon yield to envy. How could one woman be so beautiful, stylish, thin, yet intelligent and successful in a man's world?

The first impressions were generally good, judging from the faces of the women. The men were all in.

Nadine's questions were more involved. She talked about lawsuits, the culture of litigation in our society, and the routine news of outrageous verdicts. Did this ever bother any of the jurors? For a few, yes, and so she probed deeper. Number 8's husband was a union electrician, generally a safe bet for any plaintiff suing a large corporation, and Nadine seemed to take a special interest in her.

The Finley & Figg lawyers watched Nadine carefully. Her striking appearance would probably be the only highlight of the trial for them, and even that would get old.

After two hours, Judge Seawright ordered a thirty-minute recess so the lawyers could compare notes, meet with their consultants, and start making selections. Each side could assert that any juror should be excluded for good cause. For example, if a juror claimed to be biased for some reason, or had once been represented by one of the law firms, or claimed to hate Varrick, then the juror would be excused for good cause. Beyond that, each side had three peremptory challenges that could be used to exclude a juror for any reason, or no reason.

After thirty minutes, both sides requested more time, and Judge Seawright adjourned the proceedings until 2:00 p.m. "I assume you will check on your client, Mr. Figg," he said. Wally assured him that he would.

Outside the courtroom, Oscar and Wally quickly decided that David would be sent to find Iris and determine if she was able, and willing, to testify first thing Tuesday morning. According to Rochelle, who had spent the morning haggling on the phone with hospital receptionists, Iris had been taken to the emergency room at Christ Medical Center. When David arrived there at noon, he learned that she had left an hour earlier. He raced away, in the direction of her home near Midway Airport, and he and Rochelle called her home number every ten minutes. There was no answer.

The same monstrous orange cat was curled up at the front door, one sleepy eye watching David as he cautiously approached along the sidewalk. He remembered the barbecue grill on the front porch. He remembered the aluminum foil covering the windows. He had made this same walk ten months earlier, the day after his escape from Rogan Rothberg, following Wally and wondering if he'd lost his mind. He now asked himself that again, but there was little time for navel-gazing. He banged on the front door and waited for the cat to either move or attack.

"Who is it?" came a male voice.

"David Zinc. Your lawyer. Is that you, Clint?"

It was. Clint opened the door and said, "What are you doing here?"

"I'm here because your mother is not in court. We're in the process of picking a jury, and there is a federal judge who's somewhat upset because Iris skipped court this morning."

Clint waved him in. Iris was laid up on the sofa, under a stained and tattered quilt, eyes closed, a beached whale. The coffee table next to her was covered in gossip magazines, an empty pizza box, empty bottles of diet soda, and three jars of prescription drugs. "How is she?" David whispered, though he had a general idea.

Clint shook his head gravely. "Not good," he said, as if she would die any minute.

David backed into a dirty chair covered in orange cat fur. He had no time to waste and despised being there anyway. "Iris, can you hear me?" he said at full volume.

"Yes," she answered without opening her eyes.

"Listen, the trial is under way, and the judge really needs to know if you plan to show up tomorrow. We need you to testify and tell the jury about Percy. It's sort of your job as the representative of his estate and spokesman for the family, you know?"

She grunted and exhaled, a painful racket that came from deep in her lungs. "Didn't want this lawsuit," she said, her words slurred. "That creep Figg came here and talked me into it. Promised me a million dollars." She managed to open her right eye and attempted to look at David. "You came with him, now I remember. I was just sitting here minding my own business, and Figg promised me all that money."

Her right eye closed. David pressed on: "You saw a doctor this morning at the hospital. What did he say? What's your condition?"

"You name it. Mainly nerves. I can't go to court. Might kill me."

The obvious finally occurred to David. Their case, if it could still be called that, would be damaged even more if Iris made an appearance before the jury. The rules of procedure allowed that in the event a witness cannot testify for some reason—death, sickness, imprisonment—the deposition could be edited and presented to the jury. As weak as her depo was, nothing could be as bad as Iris live and in person.

"What's your doctor's name?" David asked.

"Which one?"

"I don't know, pick one. The one you saw this morning at the hospital."

"I didn't see one this morning. Got tired of waiting at the emergency room, and so Clint brought me home."

"That's about five times in the past month," Clint said, with an edge.

"Not so," she fired back.

"She does it all the time," Clint explained to David. "She'll walk to the kitchen, claim she's tired and short of breath, next thing you know she's on the phone calling 911. I'm pretty sick of it, myself. It's always me who has to drive to the damn hospital and haul her back here."

"Well, well," Iris said, both eyes open, glazed but angry. "He was a lot nicer when all that money was on the way. Couldn't have been sweeter. Now look at him, beating up his poor sick momma."

"Just stop calling 911," Clint said.

"Are you going to testify tomorrow?" David asked firmly.

"No, I can't. I can't leave this house, otherwise my nerves will melt down."

"It won't do any good, will it?" Clint asked. "The lawsuit is a loser. That other lawyer, Shaw, says you guys have messed up the case so bad can't nobody win it."

David was about to return fire when he realized that Clint was right. The lawsuit was a loser. Thanks to Finley & Figg, the Klopecks were now in federal court with a case that was hopeless, and he along with his partners was simply going through the motions and looking forward to the end.

David said good-bye and left as quickly as possible. Clint followed him outside, and as they walked to the street, he said, "Look, if you need me, I'll come to court and speak for the family."

If an appearance by Iris was the last thing their case needed, a cameo by Clint was certainly next to last. "Let me think about it," David said, but only to be nice. The jury would get more than enough of the Klopecks through Iris's video deposition.

"Any chance we're gonna get some money?" Clint asked.

"We're fighting, Clint. There's always a chance, but no guarantees."

"Sure would be nice."

At 4:30, the jury was selected, seated, sworn, and sent home with instructions to return at 8:45 the following morning. Of the twelve, there were seven women, five men, eight whites, three blacks, and one Hispanic, though the jury consultants felt as if race would not be a factor. One woman was moderately obese. The rest were in reasonably good shape. Their ages ranged from twenty-five to sixty-one, all had finished high school, and three had college degrees.

The Finley & Figg lawyers piled into David's SUV and headed back to the office. They were exhausted, but oddly satisfied. They had gone toe-to-toe with the power of corporate America and, so far, had not crumbled under the pressure. Of course, the trial hadn't really started. No witness had been sworn. No evidence had been offered. The worst was yet to come, but for the moment they were still in the game.

David gave a detailed account of his visit to see Iris, and all three agreed she should be kept away from the courtroom. Their first task of the evening was to somehow obtain a letter from a doctor that would satisfy Seawright.

There was much to be done that evening. They bought a pizza and took it to the office.

CHAPTER 38

Monday's brief respite from the fear of annihilation was long forgotten by Tuesday morning. By the time the boutique team walked into the courtroom, the pressure was back in spades. This was the real beginning of the trial, and a heavy tension filled the air. "Just get through it," David repeated each time his stomach turned flips.

Judge Seawright offered an abrupt good morning, welcomed his jury, then explained, or tried to explain, the absence of Ms. Iris Klopeck, widow and personal representative of Percy Klopeck. When he finished, he said, "At this time, each party will make an opening statement. Nothing you are about to hear is evidence; rather, it's what the lawyers think they will prove during this trial. I caution you to take it lightly. You may proceed, Mr. Finley, for the plaintiff."

Oscar stood and walked to the podium with his yellow legal pad. He placed it on the podium, smiled at the jurors, looked at his notes, smiled again at the jurors, then, oddly, stopped smiling. Several awkward seconds passed, as if Oscar had lost his train of thought and could think of nothing to say. He wiped his forehead with the palm of his hand and fell forward. He ricocheted off the podium and landed hard on the carpeted floor, still groaning and grimacing as if in enormous pain. There was a wild scramble as Wally and David sprinted for him, as did two uniformed bailiffs and a couple of the Rogan Rothberg attorneys. Several of the jurors stood as if they wanted to help in some way. Judge Seawright was yelling, "Call 911! Call 911!" Then, "Is there a doctor here?"

No one claimed to be a doctor. One of the bailiffs took charge, and it wasn't long before it was clear that Oscar had not merely fainted. In the chaos, and as a crowd hovered over Oscar, someone said, "He's barely breathing." There was more scurrying about, more calls for help. A paramedic assigned to the courthouse arrived within minutes and knelt over Oscar.

Wally stood and backed away and found himself near the jury box. Without thinking, and in an incredibly stupid effort at humor, he looked at the jurors, pointed to his fallen partner, and said, in a voice that was heard by many, words that would be repeated by other lawyers for years to come, "Oh, the wonders of Krayoxx."

"Your Honor, please!" Nadine Karros shrieked. Several of the jurors found it funny; others did not.

Judge Seawright said, "Mr. Figg, get away from the jury."

Wally scampered away. He and David waited across the courtroom.

The jury was removed and sent back to the jury room. "Court's in recess for an hour," Seawright said. He walked down from the bench and waited near the podium. Wally eased over and said, "Sorry about that, Judge."

"Silence."

A team of paramedics arrived with a stretcher. Oscar was strapped down and wheeled out of the courtroom. He did not appear to be conscious. He had a pulse, but it was dangerously low. As the lawyers and spectators mingled about, uncertain as to what they should be doing, David whispered to Wally, "Any history of heart trouble?"

Wally shook his head. "Nothing. He's always been lean and healthy. Seems like his father may have died young from something. Oscar never talked about his family, though."

A bailiff approached and said, "The judge wants to see the lawyers in chambers."

———

Fearing that he was on the hot seat, Wally decided he had nothing to lose. He went into Judge Seawright's chambers with an attitude. "Judge, I need to get to the hospital."

"Just a moment, Mr. Figg."

Nadine was standing and not happy. She said, in her best courtroom voice, "Your Honor, based solely on the improper comments made by Mr. Figg directly to the jurors, we have no choice but to move for a mistrial."

"Mr. Figg?" His Honor demanded in a tone that clearly conveyed the message that a mistrial was only minutes, perhaps seconds away.

Wally was standing too and could think of no response. David instinctively said, "How is the jury prejudiced? Mr. Finley did not take the drug. Sure, it was a stupid comment, made in the chaos of the moment, but there is no prejudice."

"I disagree, Your Honor," Nadine shot back. "Several of the jurors thought it was funny and were actually on the verge of laughing. Calling it stupid is an understatement. It was clearly an improper and very prejudicial comment."

A mistrial would mean a delay, something that the plaintiff's team needed. Hell, they were willing to delay it for a decade.

"Motion granted," His Honor announced. "I declare a mistrial. Now what?"

Wally had fallen into a chair and looked pale. David said the first thing that came to his mind. "Well, Judge, we obviously need more time. How about a continuance or something like that?"

"Ms. Karros?"

"Judge, this is certainly a unique situation. I suggest we wait twenty-four hours and monitor Mr. Finley's condition. I think it's fair to point out that Mr. Figg filed this lawsuit and was lead counsel until just a few days ago. I'm sure he could try this case as well as his senior partner."

"Good point," Judge Seawright agreed. "Mr. Zinc, I think it best if you and Mr. Figg hustle on down to the hospital and check on Mr. Finley. Keep me posted by e-mail, with copies to Ms. Karros."

"Will do, Judge."

Oscar suffered acute myocardial infarction. He was stable and expected to survive, but the early scans revealed substantial blockage in three coronary arteries. David and Wally spent a miserable day in the ICU waiting room at the hospital, killing time, talking trial strategy, e-mailing Judge Seawright, eating food from a machine, and walking the halls out of boredom. Wally was certain that neither Paula Finley nor their daughter, Keely, was at the hospital. Oscar had moved out three months earlier and was already seeing someone else, on the sly of course. There were rumors that Paula had also found someone new. At any rate, the marriage was happily over with, though the divorce had a ways to go.

At 4:30, a nurse led them to Oscar's bed for a brief hello. He was awake, thoroughly covered with tubes and monitors, and breathing on his own. "Great opening statement," Wally said and got a weak smile in return. They were not about to mention the mistrial. After a few awkward efforts at conversation, they realized Oscar was too fatigued to chat, so they said good-bye and left. On the way out, a nurse informed them that surgery was scheduled for 7:00 the following morning.

At 6:00 the following morning, David, Wally, and Rochelle surrounded Oscar's bed for a final round of well-wishing before he went to the OR. When a nurse asked them to leave, they went to the cafeteria for a hearty breakfast of watery eggs and cold bacon.

"What happens to the trial?" Rochelle asked.

David gnawed a piece of bacon and eventually replied, "Not sure, but I have a hunch we won't be getting much of a continuance."

Wally was stirring his coffee and observing two young nurses. "And it looks like we're both getting promotions. I'll have the lead, and you're getting moved to the second chair."

"So the show goes on?" Rochelle asked.

"Oh yes," David said. "We have very little control over what's happening now. Varrick is calling the shots. The company wants a trial because the company wants vindication. A huge victory. Headlines. Proof that its wonderful drug is not so bad after all. And, most important, the judge is clearly on their side." Another bite of bacon. "So, they have the facts, the money, the experts, the legal talent, and the judge."

"What do we have?" she asked.

Both lawyers thought about that for a while, then both began shaking their heads. Nothing. We have nothing.

"I guess we have Iris," Wally finally said and got a laugh. "Lovely Iris."

"And she's gonna testify in front of the jury?"

"No. One of her doctors e-mailed a letter saying she is physically unable to testify in court," David said.

"Thank God for that," Wally said.

After an hour of killing time, the three voted unanimously to return to the office and try to pursue something productive. David and Wally had a dozen things to do for the trial. A nurse called at 11:30 with the welcome news that Oscar was out of surgery and doing well. He could not see visitors for twenty-four hours, which was also well received. David e-mailed the latest update to Judge Seawright's clerk and fifteen minutes later got a reply requiring all lawyers to be in his chambers at 2:00 p.m.

"Please give my regards to Mr. Finley," His Honor said indifferently as soon as the lawyers were seated, David and Wally on one side and Nadine and four of her henchmen on the other.

"Thanks, Judge," Wally said, but only because a response was required.

"Our new plan is as follows," Seawright said without breaking stride. "There are thirty-four jurors left in the pool. I will summon them back Friday morning, October 21, three days from today, and we will select a new jury. Next Monday, October 24, we will start the retrial. Any comments or concerns?"

Oh, lots of them, Wally wanted to say. But where should I begin? Nothing from the lawyers.

The judge continued: "I realize this does not give the plaintiff's lawyers much time to regroup, but I'm convinced that Mr. Figg will do as well as Mr. Finley. Frankly, neither has any experience in federal court. Substituting one for the other will not damage the plaintiff's case in any way."

"We are ready for trial," Wally said loudly, but only to retaliate and defend himself.

"Good. Now, Mr. Figg, I will not tolerate any more of your ridiculous comments in court, regardless of whether the jury is present."

"I apologize, Your Honor," Wally said with a phoniness that was obvious.

"And your apology is accepted. However, I am levying a fine of $5,000 against you and your firm for such reckless and unprofessional behavior in my courtroom, and I'll do it again if you step out of line."

"That's a bit steep," Wally blurted.

So the hemorrhaging continues, David thought to himself. Seventy-five thousand to Dr. Borzov; $50,000 to Dr. Herbert Threadgill, their expert pharmacologist; $15,000 to Dr. Kanya Meade, their expert economist; $25,000 to Consuelo, their jury consultant. Throw in another $15,000 to get all the experts to Chicago, feed them, put them up in nice hotels, and Iris Klopeck and her dead husband were costing Finley & Figg at least $180,000. Now, thanks to Wally's big mouth, they had just lost another $5,000.

Bear in mind, David kept telling himself, this was supposedly cheap money being thrown up as a defense. Otherwise, they would be sued for malpractice and face some rather terrifying sanctions for filing such a frivolous case. In effect, they were burning serious cash to make their frivolous case appear less frivolous.

Such maneuverings had never been mentioned during law school at Harvard, nor had he ever heard of such insanity during his five years at Rogan Rothberg.

On the subject of sanctions, Ms. Karros took charge and said, "Your Honor, this is a Rule 11 motion we are filing at this time." Copies were slid across the table as she continued, "We are requesting sanctions on the grounds that Mr. Figg's reckless actions in court yesterday caused a mistrial, resulting in unnecessary expense to our client. Why should Varrick Labs pay for the plaintiff's unprofessional behavior?"

Wally shot back, "Because Varrick has a book value of $48 billion. My net worth is substantially less." Humorous, but no laughs.

Judge Seawright read the motion carefully, and when David and Wally realized this, they began reading too. After ten minutes of silence, the judge said, "Your response, Mr. Figg?"

Wally tossed his copy of the motion onto the table as if it were filthy. "You know, Judge, I can't help the fact that these guys charge a zillion dollars an hour. They are obscenely expensive, but that should not be my problem. If Varrick wants to burn its cash, then it certainly has plenty to burn. But don't get me in the middle of it."

"You miss the point, Mr. Figg," Nadine replied. "We wouldn't be doing the extra work if not for you and the mistrial you created."

"But $35,000? Come on. Do you people really think you're that valuable?"

"Depends on the outcome of the trial, Mr. Figg. When you filed this lawsuit you asked for, what, a hundred million or so? Don't criticize my client for putting up a vigorous defense with good legal talent."

"So, let me get this straight. During this trial, if you and your client do something to sort of string things along, you know, drag out the trial, God forbid make a mistake, anything like that, then I can file a quick motion for sanctions and collect some money? Am I right about this, Judge?"

"No. That would be a frivolous motion, subject to Rule 11."

"Of course it would!" Wally said with a belly laugh. "You guys make a great tag team."

"Watch it, Mr. Figg," Judge Seawright growled.

"Knock it off," David whispered. A few seconds of silence followed as Wally settled down. Finally, the judge said, "I agree that the mistrial could have been avoided, and that it has caused additional expense. However, I think $35,000 is somewhat on the excessive end. Sanctions are in order, but not to that extent. Ten thousand dollars is a more reasonable sum. It is so ordered."

Wally exhaled—another shot to the gut. David's next thought was to try to speed things along so the meeting could come to a merciful end. Finley & Figg couldn't afford much more. He offered a lame "Judge, we need to get back to the hospital."

"Adjourned, until Friday morning."

CHAPTER 39

The second jury was comprised of seven men and five women. Of the twelve, half were white, three were black, two were Asian, one was Hispanic. It was slightly more blue-collar and slightly heavier as a whole. Two of the men were uncomfortably obese. Nadine Karros had decided to use her peremptory challenges to exclude fatties instead of minorities, but she had been overwhelmed by the sheer abundance of girth. Consuelo was convinced that this jury was far more to their liking than the first.

Monday morning, as Wally stood and made his way to the podium, David held his breath. He was on deck, and another heart attack would force him into the lineup against overwhelming competition. He was pulling mightily for the junior partner. Though Wally had lost a few pounds frolicking with DeeAnna, he was still pudgy and unkempt. As far as heart attacks go, he appeared to be a much likelier candidate than Oscar.

Come on, Wally, you can do it. Give 'em hell and please don't collapse.

He did not. He did a passable job of outlining their case against Varrick Labs, the third-largest drugmaker in the world, a "mammoth corporation" based in New Jersey, a company with a long, deplorable history of littering the market with bad drugs.

Objection by Ms. Karros. Sustained from the bench.

But Wally was careful, and with good reason. When a stray word or two can cost you upward of $10,000, you tiptoe lightly around anything you're not sure of. He repeatedly referred to the medicine not as Krayoxx but rather as "this bad drug." He rambled at times but for the most part stayed on script. When he finished thirty minutes after he started, David was breathing again and whispered, "Nice job."

Nadine Karros wasted no time in defending her client and its product. She began with a lengthy, detailed, but quite interesting list of all the fabulous drugs Varrick Labs had brought to the market over the past fifty years, drugs that every American knew and trusted, and some that most had never heard of. Drugs that we give to our children. Drugs we consume with confidence every day. Drugs synonymous with good health. Drugs that prolong lives, kill infections, prevent diseases, and so on. From sore throats and headaches to cholera outbreaks and AIDS epidemics, Varrick Labs had been on the front lines for decades, and the world was a better, safer, and healthier place because of it. By the time she finished with Act One, many of those in the courtroom would have taken a bullet for Varrick.

Switching gears, she dwelled on the drug at hand, Krayoxx, a drug so effective that it was prescribed by doctors—"your doctors"—more than any other cholesterol drug in the world. She detailed the extensive research that had gone into developing Krayoxx. Somehow, she made clinical trials sound interesting. Study after study had proven the drug to be not only effective but safe. Her client had spent $4 billion and eight years researching and developing Krayoxx, and it stood proudly behind this wonderful product.

Without staring, David watched the faces of the jurors. All twelve followed every word. All twelve were becoming believers. David himself was being persuaded.

She talked about the experts she would call to testify. Eminent scholars and researchers, from such places as Mayo Clinic, Cleveland Clinic, and Harvard Medical School. These men and women had spent years studying Krayoxx and knew it far better than the "lightweights" the plaintiff would present.

Wrapping up, she was confident that when all the proof had been

heard, they, the jurors, would have no trouble understanding and believing there was absolutely nothing wrong with Krayoxx, and they would
retire and reach a quick verdict for her client, Varrick Laboratories.

David watched the seven men as she walked away. All fourteen eyes
followed her closely. He glanced at his watch—fifty-eight minutes—
and the time had flown.

Two large screens were erected by technicians, and as they worked,
Judge Seawright explained to the jury they were about to watch the
deposition of the plaintiff, Ms. Iris Klopeck, who could not attend
due to health reasons. Her deposition had been taken and recorded
by video on March 30 in a hotel in downtown Chicago. The judge
assured the jury this was not unusual and should not influence their
opinion in any way.

The lights were dimmed, and suddenly there was Iris, much larger
than life, frowning at the camera, frozen, clueless, stoned. The depo
had been heavily edited to remove what was objectionable and the
squabbles between the lawyers. After breezing through all the background material, Iris got to the topic of Percy. His role as a father, his
work history, his habits, his death. Exhibits were offered and flashed
onto the screen: a photo of Iris and Percy splashing in the water with
little Clint, both parents already morbidly obese; another photo of
Percy at the grill with friends around, all preparing to devour brat-
wurst and burgers on July 4; another of him sitting in a rocker with
that orange cat in his lap—rocking, it seemed, was his only exercise.
The images soon ran together and formed a picture of Percy that was
accurate but not pretty. He'd been a very large man who ate too much,
never broke a sweat, was a slob, died too young, with the cause of death
fairly obvious. At times, Iris became emotional. At times, she was practically incoherent. The video did little to arouse sympathy. But as her
trial team knew so well, it was a much better presentation than having
her there in person. Edited, it ran for eighty-seven minutes, and everyone in the courtroom was relieved when it was over.

When the lights came on, Judge Seawright declared it was time for lunch and they would reconvene at 2:00 p.m. Without a word, Wally vanished with the crowd. He and David had planned to have a quick sandwich in the building and plot strategy, but David gave up after fifteen minutes and left to eat alone in the café on the second floor of the building.

Oscar was out of the hospital and convalescing in Wally's apartment. Rochelle checked on him twice a day—still no sign of his wife or daughter. David called him with a brief update on the start of the trial and put a positive spin on things. Oscar feigned interest, but it was obvious he was happy to be where he was.

At 2:00 p.m., the courtroom came to order. The bloodletting was about to begin, and Wally seemed remarkably at ease. "Call your next witness," the judge said, and Wally reached for his notepad. "This will be ugly," he whispered, and David caught the unmistakable odor of freshly consumed beer.

Dr. Igor Borzov was led to the witness stand, where the bailiff presented a Bible to help with the swearing in. Borzov looked at the Bible and began shaking his head. He refused to touch it. Judge Seawright asked if there was a problem, and Borzov said something about being an atheist. "No Bible," he said. "I don't believe it."

David watched in horror. Come on, you quack, for a $75,000 fee the least you can do is play along. After an awkward delay, Judge Seawright told the bailiff to lose the Bible. Borzov raised his right hand and swore to tell the truth, but by then the jury had already been lost.

Working from a carefully worded script, Wally led him through the rituals of qualifying an expert. Education—college and med school in Moscow. Training—a residency in cardiology in Kiev, a couple of hospitals in Moscow. Experience—a brief stint on staff at a community hospital in Fargo, North Dakota, and private practice in Toronto and Nashville. The night before, Wally and David had rehearsed with him for hours, and they had pleaded with him to speak as slowly and clearly as possible. In the privacy of their office, Borzov was somewhat comprehensible. On center stage, though, and in a tense courtroom, Borzov forgot their pleas and delivered his rapid-fire responses in an accent so thick it barely resembled English. Twice the court reporter called time-out for clarification.

Court reporters are brilliant in their ability to digest mumblings, speech impediments, accents, slang, and technical vocabulary. The fact that she couldn't follow Borzov was devastating. The third time she interrupted, Judge Seawright said, "I can't understand him either. Do you have an interpreter, Mr. Figg?"

Thanks, Judge. Several of the jurors were amused by the question.

Wally and David had actually discussed the hiring of a Russian interpreter, but that discussion had been part of a broader plan to forget Borzov, forget any expert, forget all witnesses as a whole, and simply not show up for the trial.

After a few more questions, Wally said, "We tender Dr. Igor Borzov as an expert witness in the field of cardiology."

Judge Seawright looked at the defense table and said, "Ms. Karros?"

She stood and with a wicked smile replied, "We have no objections."

In other words, we'll help feed him all the rope he needs.

Wally asked Dr. Borzov if he had reviewed the medical records of Percy Klopeck. He replied with a clear yes. For half an hour, they discussed Percy's dismal medical history, then began the tedious process of admitting the records into evidence. It would have taken hours if not for the remarkable cooperation of the defense. Ms. Karros could have objected to a lot of the material, but she wanted everything laid out for the jurors. By the time the four-inch-thick file was admitted, several of them were struggling to stay awake.

The testimony improved dramatically with the aid of a greatly enlarged diagram of a human heart. It was presented on a large screen, and Dr. Borzov was given wide latitude in describing it for the jury. Walking back and forth in front of the screen, and with the aid of a pointing stick, he did a decent job of describing the valves, chambers, and arteries. When he said something that no one understood, Wally helpfully repeated it for the benefit of the others. Wally knew this would be the easy portion of his testimony, and he took his time. The good doctor seemed to know his stuff, but then any second-year med student was well versed in this material. When the tutorial was finally finished, Borzov returned to the witness stand.

Two months before he died in his sleep, Percy had undergone his annual physical, complete with EKG and echocardiogram, thus providing Dr. Borzov with something to talk about. Wally handed him the echo report, and the two spent fifteen minutes discussing the basics of an echocardiogram. Percy's showed a marked decrease in the regurgitation of blood from the left ventricle chamber.

David took a deep breath as lawyer and witness waded into the minefield of technical, medical jargon. It was a disaster from the very beginning.

Krayoxx supposedly damaged the mitral valve in such a way that it impeded the flow of blood as it was being pumped out of the heart. In an attempt to explain this, Borzov used the term "left ventricle ejection fraction." When asked to clarify this for the jury, Borzov said: "The ejection fraction is actually the ventricular volume at end-diastole minus end-systole, the ventricle volume, and that divided by the total volume times one hundred is the ejection fraction." Such language was incomprehensible to laymen when delivered in slow, precise English. Out of Dr. Borzov's mouth, it was nothing but gibberish and sadly comical.

Nadine Karros rose and said, "Your Honor, please."

Judge Seawright shook his head as if he'd been slapped and said, "Come on, Mr. Figg."

Three of the jurors were glaring at David as if he had insulted them. A couple were suppressing chuckles.

Treading water, Wally asked his witness to speak slowly, clearly, and, if possible, in easier language. They plodded along, Borzov trying his best, Wally repeating virtually everything he said until some clarity was achieved, but not much and not nearly enough. Borzov discussed the grading of mitral insufficiency, the regurgitation of the left atrial area, and the level of severity of the mitral regurgitation.

Long after the jury gave up, Wally asked a series of questions about the interpretation of the echocardiogram, and it prompted this response: "If the ventricle was totally symmetrical and had no discrepancies in the wall motion or geometry, it would be a prolate ellipsoid. Just defines flat end and pointed end and gentle curve, an ellipsoid fraction. So the ventricle would contract down, would still be a prolate ellipsoid, but all walls would move except the plane of mitral valve."

The court reporter raised her hand and blurted, "I'm sorry, Your Honor, but I'm not getting this." Judge Seawright's eyes closed, his head was down, as if he, too, had given up and just wanted Borzov to finish and get out of the courtroom.

"Fifteen-minute recess," he mumbled.

Wally and David sat silent before two untouched cups of coffee in the small café. It was 4:30 Monday afternoon, and both felt as though they'd spent a month in Seawright's courtroom. Neither wanted to see it again.

While David was stunned by Borzov's thoroughly discreditable performance, he was also thinking about Wally's drinking. He wasn't drunk and didn't appear under the influence, but any return to the bottle for an alcoholic was troubling. He wanted to quiz him, to see if he was okay, but the place and time seemed inappropriate. Why bring up such a dreadful subject under such miserable circumstances?

Wally stared at a spot on the floor, motionless, off in another world.

"I don't think the jury is with us," David said offhandedly, no effort at humor. But Wally smiled and said, "The jury hates us and I don't blame them. We won't make it past summary judgment. As soon as we finish our case, Seawright will throw us out of court."

"So a quick end? Can't blame him for that."

"A quick and merciful end," Wally said, still staring at the floor.

"What will it mean for the other issues, like sanctions and malpractice?"

"Who knows? I think the malpractice cases will go away. You can't get sued just because you lose a case at trial. Sanctions, though, could be another story. I can see Varrick going for our jugulars, claiming the case had no merit."

David finally took a sip of coffee. Wally said, "I keep thinking about Jerry Alisandros. I'd like to catch him in an alley and beat him senseless with a baseball bat."

"Now that's a pleasant thought."

"We'd better go. Let's finish with Borzov and get him out of here."

For the next hour, the courtroom suffered through the tortuous process of watching the video of Percy's echocardiogram while Dr. Borzov attempted to describe what they were seeing. With the lights dimmed, several of the jurors began to nod off. When the video ended, Borzov returned to the witness chair.

"How much longer, Mr. Figg?" the judge asked.

"Five minutes."

"Proceed."

Even the flimsiest of cases require certain magical language. Wally wanted to slip it in quickly while the jury was comatose and, just maybe, the defense was ready to go home. "Now, Dr. Borzov, do you have an opinion, based on a reasonable degree of medical certainty, as to the cause of the death of Mr. Percy Klopeck?"

"I do."

David was watching Nadine Karros, who with little effort could have excluded any and all expert opinions from Borzov on numerous grounds. She seemed to have no interest in doing so.

"And what is that opinion?" Wally asked.

"My opinion, based on a reasonable degree of medical certainty, is that Mr. Klopeck died of acute myocardial infarction, or heart attack." Borzov offered this opinion slowly, his English much clearer.

"And do you have an opinion as to the cause of his heart attack?"

"My opinion, based on a reasonable degree of medical certainty, is that the heart attack was caused by an enlarged left ventricle chamber."

"And do you have an opinion as to what caused the enlargement of the left ventricle chamber?"

"My opinion, based on a reasonable degree of medical certainty, is that the enlargement was caused by the ingestion of the cholesterol drug Krayoxx."

At least four of the jurors were shaking their heads. Two others looked as though they wanted to stand and yell obscenities at Borzov.

At 6:00 p.m., the witness was finally excused and the jury sent home.

"Adjourned until nine o'clock in the morning," Judge Seawright said.

Riding back to the office, Wally fell asleep in the passenger's seat. Stuck in traffic, David checked his cell phone, then went online to check the market. Varrick's stock had jumped from $31.50 to $35.00.

News of the company's imminent victory was spreading fast.

CHAPTER 40

During her first two months on earth, little Emma had yet to sleep through the night. Down by eight, she was usually up by eleven for a quick snack and a clean diaper. A lengthy session of floor walking and chair rocking knocked her out by midnight, but by 3:00 a.m. she was hungry again. At first, Helen gamely clung to the plan of breast-feeding, but after six weeks she was exhausted and introduced the bottle. Emma's father was not sleeping much either, and they usually had a quiet chat during the predawn meals while Momma stayed under the covers.

Tuesday, around 4:30 a.m., David gently placed her back in the crib, turned off the light, and eased from the room. He went to the kitchen, made coffee, and as it brewed, he went online to check the news, weather, and law blogs. One blog in particular had followed the Krayoxx litigation and the Klopeck trial, and David was tempted to ignore it. But he could not.

The headline read: "Mauling in Courtroom 2314." The blogger, known as the Hung Juror, obviously had too much time on his hands, or perhaps he was one of the Rogan Rothberg grunts. He wrote: "For those with a morbid sense of curiosity, hustle on over to Courtroom 2314 in the Dirksen Federal Building today for round two of the world's first, and probably only, Krayoxx trial. For those of you who cannot attend, it's like watching a train wreck in slow motion, and a helluva lot of fun to boot. Yesterday, opening day, the jurors and spectators were treated to the gruesome sight of the widow Iris Klopeck testifying by video. Supposedly, she cannot attend the trial for medical reasons, though one of my spies saw her shopping for groceries yesterday at the Dominick's on Pulaski Road (click here for photos). This gal is one heavy woman, and when her face hit the screen yesterday, it was quite a shock. At first she seemed, well, rather stoned, but as the deposition wore on the drugs seemed to wear off. She even managed a few tears when talking about her beloved Percy, who died at forty-eight years and 320 pounds. Iris wants the jury to give her a truckload of cash and she tried her best to evoke sympathy. Didn't work. Most of the jurors were thinking the same thing I was thinking—if you people weren't so big, you wouldn't have so many health problems.

"Her dream team, now minus its leader, who had a heart attack of his own last week when he came face-to-face with a real jury, has made only one brilliant move so far, and that was to keep Iris out of the courtroom and away from the jury. No more brilliance is expected from these two lightweights.

"Their second witness was their star expert, a certified quack from Russia who has, so far, after fifteen years in this country, failed to master the most rudimentary elements of the English language. His name is Igor, and when Igor speaks, no one listens. Igor could easily have been bounced by the defense on the grounds that he is unqualified— his deficiencies are too numerous to mention—but it seems as though the defense has adopted a strategy of allowing the plaintiff's lawyers all the room they need to prove they have no case whatsoever. The defense wants Igor on the stand—he helps their side!"

Enough! David closed his laptop and went for the coffee. He showered and dressed quietly, kissed Helen good-bye, peeked in on Emma, then headed out. When he turned onto Preston, he noticed the lights were on at Finley & Figg. It was 5:45, and Wally was hard at work. Good, thought David, maybe the junior partner had discovered some new theory they could spring on Nadine Karros and Harry Seawright and reduce some of the humiliation. But Wally's car was not parked behind the building. The rear door was unlocked, as was the front. AC was prowling around the first floor, agitated. Wally was not in his office; he was not to be found. David locked the doors and went to his office upstairs, followed by AC. There were no messages on his desk, no e-mails. He called Wally's cell and got voice mail. Strange, but then Wally's routine often varied. However, neither he nor Oscar had ever left the office unlocked and the lights on.

David tried to review some materials but couldn't concentrate. His nerves were edgy because of the trial, and now there was a nagging sense that something else was wrong. He walked downstairs and had a quick look around Wally's office. The wastebasket next to his credenza was empty. David hated to do it, but he pulled open a few drawers and found nothing of interest. In the kitchen, next to the narrow fridge, there was a tall round wastebasket where the coffee grounds were dumped along with food containers and empty bottles and cans. David removed the white plastic liner, opened it wide, and found what he was afraid he might find. To one side, lying on top of a yogurt container, was an empty pint bottle of Smirnoff vodka. David removed it, rinsed it in the sink while he washed his hands, and took it upstairs, where he sat it on his desk and stared at it for a long time.

Wally had a few beers during lunch, then spent part of the night at the office, drinking vodka, and at some point decided to leave. Evidently he was drunk, because he left the lights on and the doors unlocked.

They had agreed to meet at 7:00 a.m. for coffee and a work session. By 7:15, David was worried. He called Rochelle and asked if she had heard from Wally. "No, is something wrong?" she asked, as if a bad phone call about Wally was never unexpected.

"No, just looking for him, that's all. You'll be in at eight, right?"

"I'm leaving the apartment now. I'll run by and check on Oscar, then come to the office."

David wanted to call Oscar but could not bring himself to do so. His triple bypass had been six days earlier, and David was not about to upset him. He paced the floor, fed AC, and tried Wally's cell again.

Nothing. Rochelle arrived promptly at eight with the news that Oscar was doing okay and had not seen Wally.

"He didn't come home last night," she said.

David pulled the empty pint bottle out of his back pants pocket and said, "I found this in the kitchen wastebasket. Wally got drunk last night, here, and left the doors unlocked and the lights on when he left."

Rochelle stared at the bottle and wanted to cry. She had nursed Wally through his previous battles and she had cheered him on through his rehabs. She had held his hand, prayed for him, cried for him, and celebrated with him as he joyfully counted the days of sobriety. One year, two weeks, and two days, and now they were looking at an empty bottle.

"I guess the pressure got to him," David said.

"When he falls, he falls hard, David, and each one is worse than the last."

David set the bottle on the table. "But he was so proud of being sober," he said. "I can't believe this." What he really couldn't believe was that the dream team (or the three stooges) was down to its last man standing. And though his partners were woefully lacking in trial experience, they were seasoned veterans compared with him.

"You think he'll show up in court?" David asked.

No, she did not, but Rochelle didn't have the heart to be blunt. "Probably so. You need to get on the road."

It was a long drive downtown. David called Helen and broke the news. She was as bewildered as her husband and offered the opinion that the judge would have no choice but to postpone the proceedings. David liked the sound of that, and by the time he parked, he was convinced that if Wally didn't show, he could prevail upon Judge Seawright to grant a continuance. In all fairness, losing the two lead lawyers in a case was surely grounds for either a mistrial or a postponement.

Wally was not in the courtroom. David sat alone at counsel table as the Rogan Rothberg team filed in and the spectators took their seats. At 8:50, David eased over to a bailiff and said he needed to see Judge Seawright, and it was urgent. "Follow me," the bailiff said.

Judge Seawright had just put on his black robe when David entered his chambers. Skipping the greetings, David said, "Judge, we have a problem. Mr. Figg is AWOL. He's not here and I don't think he'll show up."

The judge exhaled in frustration and continued to slowly zip up his robe. "You don't know where he is?"

"No sir."

Judge Seawright looked at the bailiff and said, "Go fetch Ms. Karros."

When Nadine arrived, alone, she and David sat with the judge at the end of his long conference table. David told them all that he knew and pulled no punches about Wally's history with alcohol. They were sympathetic and uncertain about what this meant for the trial. David confessed that he felt thoroughly unprepared and inadequate to handle whatever was left to be done, but at the same time he could not imagine the firm attempting to try the case again.

"Let's face it," he said, holding nothing back, "we don't have much of a case and we knew that when we started. We've pushed this thing about as far as we can, and we've done so only to avoid sanctions and malpractice suits."

"You want a continuance?" the judge asked.

"Yes. I think it's only fair under the circumstances."

Nadine said, "My client will resist any effort to delay matters, and I'm certain it will push hard to finish this trial."

Judge Seawright said, "I'm not sure a continuance will work. If Mr. Figg is back on the booze, and drinking so much he fails to show up for court, it might take some time to get him detoxed again and ready for action. I am not inclined to consider a continuance."

David could not argue with this logic. "Judge, I have no idea what to do out there. I've never tried a case before."

"I have not detected a great deal of experience on the part of Mr. Figg. You can certainly perform at his level."

There was a long pause as the three contemplated their rather unique dilemma. Finally, Nadine said, "I have a deal. If you will finish the trial, I will convince my client to forget Rule 11 sanctions."

Judge Seawright chimed in quickly, "Mr. Zinc, if you will finish the trial, I guarantee there will be no sanctions against you or your client."

"Great, but what about the malpractice claims?"

Nadine said nothing, but the judge replied, "I doubt you'll be in trouble there. I'm not aware of a successful malpractice action against a lawyer who simply lost a trial."

"Nor am I," Nadine added. "There's a winner and a loser in every trial."

Of course, David thought, and it must be nice to win every time.

"Let's do this," the judge said. "We'll stand in recess today—I'll send the jury home—and you do your best to find Mr. Figg. If by chance he shows up tomorrow, we'll continue as if nothing happened, and I will not punish him for today. If you don't find him, or if he's unable to continue, then we'll resume the proceedings at nine in the morning. You do your best, and I'll help you as much as I possibly can. We'll finish the trial, and that will be the end of it."

"What about an appeal?" Nadine asked. "Losing the two lead lawyers might make a convincing argument for a new trial."

David managed a smile and said, "I promise you there will be no appeal, not that I'm involved in. This case could very well bankrupt our little firm. We borrowed money to litigate this far. I can't imagine my partners wasting another moment fooling with an appeal. If they were to somehow win one, then they would be forced to come back here and try the case again. That's the last thing they want."

"All right, so we have a deal?" the judge asked.

"As far as I'm concerned we do," replied Nadine.

"Mr. Zinc?"

David had no choice. Continue, alone, and he would save the firm from the threat of sanctions, and probably malpractice as well. His only other option would be to demand a continuance and, when that was denied, refuse to participate in the trial.

"Sure, it's a deal."

He took his time driving back to the office. He continually reminded himself that he was only thirty-two, that this would not ruin his career as a lawyer. Somehow, he would survive the next three days. A year from now, it would almost be forgotten.

Still no sign of Wally. David locked himself in his office and spent the rest of the day reading transcripts of other trials, poring over the depositions from other cases, studying the rules of procedure and evidence, and fighting the urge to throw up.

Over dinner, he poked at his food as he replayed everything for Helen.

"How many attorneys are on the other side?" she asked.

"I don't know, too many to count. At least six, with another row of paralegals packed behind them."

"And you'll be alone at your table?"

"That's the scenario."

She chewed on a bite of pasta, then said, "Does anyone check the credentials of the paralegals?"

"I don't think so. Why?"

"Just thinking. Maybe I should be a paralegal for the next few days. I've always wanted to watch a trial."

David laughed for the first time in hours. "Come on, Helen. I'm not sure I want you, or anyone else, to witness the slaughter."

"What would the judge say if I showed up with a briefcase and a legal pad and started taking notes?"

"At this point, I think Judge Seawright would cut me a lot of slack."

"I can get my sister to keep Emma."

David laughed again, but the idea was gaining momentum. What was there to lose? It could well be the first and last trial of his career as a litigator, why not have a little fun? "I like it," he said.

"Did you say there are seven men on the jury?"

"Yes."

"Short skirt, or long?"

"Not too short."

CHAPTER 41

The Hung Juror blogged on: "A brief day in the Klopeck-Krayoxx trial as the dream team had trouble getting itself together. Word on the street is that the lead lawyer, the Honorable Wallis T. Figg, failed to answer the bell, and his rookie sidekick was sent to look for him. Figg wasn't seen in the courtroom just before 9:00 a.m. Judge Seawright sent the jury home with instructions to return this morning. Repeated calls to the Finley & Figg office went straight to voice mail; none returned by the staff, if the firm does indeed have a staff. Wonder if Figg is on a bender? Fair question in light of the fact that he's had at least two DUIs in the past twelve years, the last one a year ago. My records show that Figg has been married and divorced four times. I tracked down wife number 2, and she recalled that Wally's always battled the bottle. When contacted at her home yesterday, the plaintiff, Iris Klopeck, who is still allegedly too sick to come to court, replied, 'I'm not surprised,' when told that her lawyer had failed to show. Then she hung up. Noted legal malpractice lawyer Bart Shaw has been seen sneaking around the courtroom—rumor is that Shaw might pick up the pieces of the Krayoxx mess and go after Finley & Figg for botching the cases. So far, the Klopeck case has not been botched, in theory. The jury has not decided. Stay tuned."

David scanned other blogs as he ate a granola bar at his desk and waited for Wally, though he really didn't expect him. No one had heard a word—Oscar, Rochelle, DeeAnna, a couple of lawyer buddies from his former poker club. Oscar had called a pal at the police station for an informal inquiry, though neither he nor David suspected foul play. According to Rochelle, Wally once disappeared for a week without a peep, then called Oscar from a motel in Green Bay, pickled. David was getting a lot of Wally the Drunk stories, and he found them odd because he had known only the sober Wally.

Rochelle arrived early and climbed the stairs, something she rarely did. She was concerned about David and offered to help in any way. He thanked her and began packing files in his briefcase. She fed AC, got her yogurt, and was arranging her desk when she looked at her e-mails. "David!" she yelled.

It was from Wally, dated October 26, 5:10 a.m., sent from his iPhone: "RG: Hey, I'm alive. Don't call the police and don't pay the ransom. WF."

"Thank heavens," Rochelle said. "He's okay."

"He doesn't say he's okay. He just says he's alive. I suppose that's a good thing."

"What does he mean by 'ransom'?" she wondered.

"Probably his effort to be funny. Ha-ha."

David called Wally's cell phone three times as he drove downtown. His voice mail was full.

In a room filled with somber men in dark suits, a beautiful woman attracts far more attention than she would by simply walking down a busy street. Nadine Karros had used her looks like a weapon as she had risen to the top of the elite courtroom advocates in the Chicago area. On Wednesday, she had some competition.

Finley & Figg's new paralegal arrived at 8:45 and, as planned, went straight to Ms. Karros and introduced herself as Helen Hancock (maiden name), one of the part-time paralegals at Finley & Figg. Then she introduced herself to several of the other defense lawyers, causing all of them to stop whatever they were working on, stand awkwardly,

shake hands, smile, and be nice. At five feet eight inches and wearing four-inch heels, Helen was a few inches taller than Nadine, and
she looked down on some of the others as well. With her hazel eyes
and chic designer frames, not to mention the slender figure and skirt
six inches above the knees, Helen succeeded in slightly disrupting the
pregame rituals, if only for a moment. The spectators, almost all men,
looked her over. Her husband, who was ignoring all of this, pointed to
a chair behind his and said in a lawyerly fashion, "Get me those files."
Then, in a lower voice, he said, "You look spectacular, but don't smile
at me."

"Yes, boss," she said, unfastening a briefcase, one of several in his
collection.

"Thanks for coming."

An hour earlier, from his desk, David had e-mailed Judge Seawright and Nadine Karros with the news that Mr. Figg had been heard
from but would not be in court. They did not know where he was or
when they might actually see him. For all David knew, Wally could be
back in Green Bay, in a motel, comatose and pickled, though he kept
this to himself.

Dr. Igor Borzov was reintroduced to the proceedings and took the
stand with the look of a leper about to be stoned. Judge Seawright said,
"You may cross-examine, Ms. Karros."

She walked to the podium in another killer outfit—a lavender knit
dress that fit snug and did an outstanding job of showcasing her shapely
and quite firm backside, and a thick brown leather belt that was pulled
tight to announce "Yes, I'm in a size 4." She began by offering the
expert a lovely smile and asking him to speak slowly because she had
trouble understanding on Monday. Borzov mumbled incoherently in
return.

With so many obvious targets, it was impossible to predict where
she might attack first. David had been unable to prepare Borzov, not
that he wanted to spend another minute with the man.

"Dr. Borzov, when was the last time you treated a patient of your
own?"

He had to think for a moment and eventually said, "About ten year." This led to a series of questions about what, exactly, he had been doing for the past ten years. He had not been seeing patients, nor teaching, nor researching, nor doing all the things one would expect a doctor to do. Finally, when she had excluded virtually everything, she asked: "Isn't it true, Dr. Borzov, that for the past ten years you have worked exclusively for various trial lawyers?" Borzov squirmed a bit. He wasn't so sure about that.

Nadine was. She had the facts, all gleaned from a deposition given by Borzov in another case one year earlier. Armed with the details, she took him by the hand and led him down the path of destruction. Year by year, she went through the lawsuits, the screenings, the drugs, and the lawyers, and when she finished an hour later, it was clear to everyone in the courtroom that Igor Borzov was nothing but a rubber-stamper for the mass tort bar.

On her legal pad, the paralegal slipped David a note: "Where did you find this guy?"

David wrote back: "Impressive, huh? And his fee is only $75,000."

"Paid by whom?"

"You don't want to know."

Evidently, the hot seat affected his diction, or perhaps Borzov did not wish to be understood. At any rate, he became increasingly more difficult to understand. Nadine kept her cool, so much so that David seriously doubted if she ever lost it. He was watching a master, and he was taking notes, not to help resuscitate his witness, but on effective cross-examination techniques.

The jurors could not have cared less. They were gone, checked out, already waiting for the next witness. Nadine sensed this and began culling her list of problem areas. At 11:00 a.m., Judge Seawright needed a potty break and called a twenty-minute recess. When the jury left the courtroom, Borzov approached David and asked, "How much longer?"

"I have no idea," David replied. The doctor was sweating and breathing heavy; his armpits were wet. Too bad, David wanted to say. At least you're getting paid.

During the recess, Nadine Karros and her team made the tactical decision to stay away from a replaying of Percy's echocardiogram. With Borzov bloodied and on the ropes, the echo might allow him to regain some footing since he could once again lose the jury with medical jargon. After the recess, when Borzov slowly returned to the witness chair, she began chipping away at his education, with a heavy emphasis on the differences between med school here and med school in Russia. She went through a list of courses and lectures, standard here but unheard-of "over there." She knew the answer to every question she asked, and Borzov, by now, knew this. He became increasingly more hesitant to give a response directly, knowing that any discrepancy, however slight, would be pounced upon, dissected, and slung back at him.

She hammered away at his training and managed to trip him a few times. By noon, the jurors, those still watching the mayhem, had the clear impression of a doctor they wouldn't trust to prescribe lip balm.

Why had he never written any papers? He claimed there had been some in Russia but was forced to admit they had not been translated. Why had he never taught or joined a faculty? The classroom bored him, he tried to explain, though it was painful to imagine Borzov attempting to communicate with a group of students.

During lunch, David and his paralegal hustled out of the building and went to a deli around the corner. Helen was fascinated by the proceedings but still stunned by Dr. Borzov's pathetic showing. "Just for the record," she said over a spring salad, "if we ever reach the point of a divorce, I'm hiring Nadine."

"Oh, really. Well, then, I'll be forced to hire Wally Figg, if I can keep him sober."

"You're toast."

"Forget the divorce, baby, you're too cute and you have great potential as a courtroom paralegal."

Helen grew serious and said, "Look, I realize you have a lot on your mind right now, but you must be thinking about the future. You can't stay at Finley & Figg. What if Oscar can't come back? What if Wally can't kick the booze? And assuming they can, why would you want to stay there?"

"I don't know. I haven't had much time to think about it." He had shielded her from the twin nightmares of the Rule 11 sanctions and the potential malpractice cases, and he had decided not to tell her about the $200,000 line of credit he had guaranteed along with the two partners. Leaving the firm in the near future was not likely.

"Let's talk about it later," he said.

"I'm sorry. It's just that I think you can do so much better, that's all."

"Thank you, dear. What—you're not impressed with my court-room skills?"

"You're brilliant, but I suspect one big trial might be enough for you."

"By the way, Nadine Karros doesn't do divorces."

"Then that settles it. I guess I'll just tough it out."

At 1:30, Borzov tottered to the witness stand for the last time, and Nadine began her final assault. Since he was a cardiologist who didn't treat patients, it was safe to assume he never treated Percy Klopeck. True, plus Mr. Klopeck had been dead a long time before Borzov was hired as an expert. But surely he had consulted the doctors who did treat him. No, Borzov admitted, he had not. Feigning disbelief, she began hammering away at this incredible oversight. His responses grew slower, his voice weaker, his Russian thicker, until finally, at 2:45, Borzov pulled a white handkerchief from a coat pocket and began waving it.

Such drama was not contemplated by the wise folks who wrote the rules of federal trial procedure, and David was uncertain about what he should do. He stood and said, "Your Honor, I think this witness has had enough."

"Dr. Borzov, are you okay?" Judge Seawright asked. The answer was obvious.

The witness shook his head no.

"Nothing further, Your Honor," Ms. Karros announced and left the podium, another impressive annihilation under her belt.

"Any redirect, Mr. Zinc?" the Judge asked.

The last thing David wanted to do was to try to revive a dead witness. "No sir," he said quickly.

"Dr. Borzov, you're excused."

He staggered away with the aid of a bailiff, $75,000 richer but with another black mark on his résumé. Judge Seawright recessed court until 3:30.

Dr. Herbert Threadgill was a pharmacologist of dubious reputation. He, like Borzov, was spending the waning days of his career living the easy life, away from the rigors of real medicine, doing nothing but testifying for lawyers who needed his notoriously pliant opinions to fit their version of the facts. The paths of both professional testifiers crossed occasionally, and they knew each other well. Threadgill had been reluctant to sign on for the Klopeck case for three reasons: the facts were lousy; the case was weak; and he had no desire to face Nadine Karros in a courtroom. He had finally said yes for only one reason—$50,000 plus expenses, for only a few hours of work.

During the recess, he saw Dr. Borzov outside the courtroom and was appalled at his appearance. "Don't do it," Borzov said as he shuffled toward the elevators. Threadgill hurried to the men's room, splashed some water in his face, and decided to flee. Screw the case. Screw the lawyers, they were not major players anyway. He had been paid in full, and if they threatened to sue, he might consider returning a portion of his fee, or not. He would be on an airplane in an hour. In three hours he would be having a drink with his wife on the patio. He wasn't committing a crime. He was under no subpoena. If necessary, he would never return to Chicago.

At 4:00 p.m., David returned to the judge's chambers and said, "Well, Judge, looks like we've lost another one. I can't find Dr. Threadgill, and he won't answer his phone."

"When did you last speak to him?"

"During lunch. He was all set, or at least he said so."

"Do you have another witness, one who is here and has not gotten lost?"

"Yes sir, my economist, Dr. Kanya Meade."

"Then put her on, and we'll see if the lost sheep somehow find their way home."

Percy Klopeck worked for twenty-two years as a dispatcher for a freight company. It was a sedentary job, and Percy did nothing to break the monotony of sitting in a chair for eight straight hours. Non-union, he was earning $44,000 a year when he died and could have reasonably expected to work for seventeen more years.

Dr. Kanya Meade was a young economist at the University of Chicago, and she moonlighted occasionally as a consultant to pick up a few bucks—$15,000 in the Klopeck case. The math was straightforward: $44,000 a year for seventeen years, plus anticipated annual increases based on the historical trend, plus a retirement based on a fifteen-year life expectancy beyond the age of sixty-five, at 70 percent of his highest salary. In summary, Dr. Meade testified that Percy's death had cost his family $1.51 million.

Since he had died peacefully in his sleep, there would be no claim for pain and suffering.

On cross-examination, Ms. Karros took exception to the numbers of Percy's life expectancy. Since he had died at forty-eight, and early deaths were common among his male blood relatives, it was unrealistic to suggest that he would have lived to age eighty. Nadine was careful, though, not to spend much time debating damages. To do so would lend credence to the numbers. The Klopecks were not due a penny, and she would not give the impression she was worried about the alleged damages.

When Dr. Meade finished at 5:20, Judge Seawright adjourned court until nine the following morning.

CHAPTER 42

After a hard day in court, Helen was in no mood to cook. She picked up Emma at her sister's home in Evanston, thanked her sister profusely and promised to debrief later, and raced away to the nearest fast-food restaurant. Emma, who slept in moving vehicles much better than in her own crib, dozed peacefully as Helen inched along in the drive-thru. She ordered more burgers and fries than usual because she and David were both hungry. It was raining, and the late-October days were growing shorter.

Helen drove to the Khaings' apartment near Rogers Park, and by the time she arrived, David was there. The plan was to have a quick dinner and hustle home for an early bedtime—Emma, of course, holding the key to that. David had no more witnesses to present for the plaintiff, and he was not sure what to expect from Nadine Karros. In the pretrial order, the defense had listed twenty-seven expert witnesses, and David had read every one of their reports. Only Nadine Karros knew how many to call to the stand, and in what order. There was little for David to do but sit, listen, object occasionally, pass notes to his comely paralegal, and try to give the impression he knew what was going on. According to a friend from law school, a litigator in a Washington firm, there was an excellent chance the defense would move for summary judgment, convince Seawright that the plaintiff had failed to provide even the bare bones of a proper case, and win outright without presenting a single witness. "It could be over tomorrow," he said as he sat in traffic in Washington and David did the same in Chicago.

Since Thuya had been released from the hospital five months earlier, the Zincs had missed only a few of their Wednesday night fast-food dinners. The arrival of Emma had briefly interrupted things, but before long they were packing her along for the visits. A ritual had clearly been established. As Helen approached the apartment building with the baby, Lwin and Zaw, mother and grandmother, bolted from the door and raced to see the baby. Inside, Lynn and Erin, Thuya's two older sisters, sat side by side on the sofa, waiting eagerly to get their hands on Emma. Helen would place her gently in one of the laps, and the girls and their mother and grandmother would chatter and squeal and act as if they had never before seen an infant. They gently passed her around, back and forth with great care. This would go on for a long time while the men were starving.

Thuya watched it from his high chair and seemed amused. Each week David and Helen hoped to see some tiny sign of improvement in his condition, and each week they were disappointed. As his doctors predicted, progress was highly unlikely. The damage was, after all, permanent.

David sat by him, rubbed his head as always, and handed him a French fry. He chatted with Soe and Lu as the women formed a gaggle around the baby. Eventually, they made their way to the table, where they were delighted to learn that David and Helen would be eating with them. They usually avoided burgers and fries, but not tonight. David explained that they were a bit rushed and would not have time to take Thuya out for a drive.

Halfway through a cheeseburger, David's cell phone vibrated in his coat pocket. He looked at it, jumped to his feet, whispered "It's Wally" to Helen, and stepped outside the front door.

"Where are you, Wally?"

In a weak, dying voice, the reply came, "I'm drunk, David. So drunk."

"That's what we figured. Where are you?"

"You gotta help me, David. There's no one else. Oscar won't talk to me."

"Sure, Wally, you know I'll help, but where are you?"

"At the office."

"I'll be there in forty-five minutes."

He was on the sofa next to the table, snoring, AC nearby watching him with great suspicion. It was Wednesday night, and David assumed, correctly, that Wally's last shower had been bright and early Monday morning, the day the retrial commenced, six days after Oscar's dramatic collapse, and six days after Wally's legendary mistrial. No shower, no shave, no change of clothes—he was wearing the same navy suit and white shirt as when David had last seen him. The tie was missing. The shirt was heavily stained. There was a slight tear on the right leg of his trousers. Dried mud caked the soles of his new black wing tips. David tapped his shoulder and called his name. Nothing. His face was red and puffy, but there were no bruises, cuts, or scrapes. Perhaps he had not been brawling in bars. David wanted to know where he had been, but then he didn't. Wally was safe. There would be time for questions later, one being "How'd you get here?" His car was nowhere in sight, which was somewhat of a relief. Maybe, drunk as he was, Wally had the presence of mind not to drive. On the other hand, his car could have been wrecked, stolen, or repossessed.

David punched him on the biceps and yelled from six inches away. Wally's heavy breathing paused for a second, then continued. AC was whining, so David let him out for a pee and made a pot of coffee. He sent a text to Helen: "Drunk as a skunk but alive. Not sure what's next." He called Rochelle and passed along the news. A call to Oscar's cell went straight to voice mail.

Wally rallied an hour later and took a cup of coffee. "Thanks, David," he said over and over. Then, "Have you called Lisa?"

"And who might Lisa be?"

"My wife. You need to call her, David. That sonofabitch Oscar won't talk to me."

David decided to play along, to see where the chatter might go. "I did call Lisa."

"You did? What did she say?"

"Said you guys got a divorce years ago."

"That sounds just like her." He was staring at his feet, glassy-eyed, unable or unwilling to make eye contact.

"She said she still loves you, though," David said, just for the fun of it.

Wally started crying, the way drunks do when they cry over nothing and everything. David felt a little lousy but a lot more amused.

"I'm sorry," Wally said, wiping his face with a forearm. "I'm so sorry, David, thank you. Oscar won't talk to me, you know. Laid up in my apartment, hiding from his wife, cleaning out my refrigerator. I came home, had the door locked and chained. We had a big fight, neighbors called the police, I barely got away. Running away from my own apartment now, what kinda deal is that?"

"When did this happen?"

"I don't know. An hour ago, maybe. Not real sharp on times and days right now for some reason. Thank you, David."

"You're welcome. Look, Wally, we need to put together a plan. Sounds like your apartment is off-limits. If you want to sleep here tonight and sober up, I'll pull up a chair and keep you company. AC and I will get you through this."

"I need help, David. Ain't just a matter of sobering up."

"Okay, but getting sober will be an important first step."

Wally suddenly burst into laughter. He threw his head back and laughed as loud as humanly possible. He shook, squealed, gyrated, coughed, lost his breath, wiped his cheeks, and when he couldn't laugh anymore, he sat and chuckled for several minutes. When things were under control, he glanced at David and laughed again.

"Got something you'd like to share, Wally?"

Working hard to suppress more laughter, he said, "I just thought of the first time you came here, remember?"

"I remember some of it."

"I've never seen anybody drunker. All day in a bar, right?"

"Yep."

"Falling-down drunk, then you took a swing at that prickhead Gholston across the street, almost hit him too."

"That's what I've heard."

"I looked at Oscar, he looked at me, we said, 'This guy has potential.'" A pause as he drifted away for a moment. "You threw up twice. Now who's drunk and who's sober?"

"We're gonna get you sober, Wally."

His body was no longer shaking, and he was silent for a long time. "Do you ever wonder what you got yourself into here, David? You had it all, big firm, big salary, life in the lawyers' fast lane."

"I have no regrets, Wally," David said. For the most part, it was a true statement.

Another long pause and Wally cradled his coffee cup with both hands and stared into it. "What's gonna happen to me, David? I'm forty-six years old, broker than ever, humiliated, a drunk who can't stay away from the sauce, a washed-up street lawyer who thought he could play in the big leagues."

"Now is not the time to ponder the future, Wally. What you need is a good detox, get all the alcohol out of your system, then you can make decisions."

"I don't want to be like Oscar. He's seventeen years older than me, and in seventeen years I don't want to be here doing the same shit we do every day, you know, David? Thank you."

"You're welcome."

"Do you wanna be here in seventeen years?"

"I really haven't thought about it. I'm just trying to get through this trial."

"What trial?"

He didn't appear to be joking or pretending, so David let it pass. "You went through rehab a year ago, didn't you, Wally?"

He grimaced as he struggled to remember his last rehab. "What's today?"

"Today is Wednesday, October 26."

Wally began nodding. "Yes, October of last year. In for thirty days, a great time."

"Where was the rehab?"

"Oh, Harbor House, just north of Waukegan. My favorite. It's right on the lake, beautiful. I guess we should call Patrick." He was reaching for his wallet.

"And who's Patrick?"

"My counselor," Wally said, handing over a business card. *Harbor House—Where a New Life Begins. Patrick Hale, Team Leader.* "You can call Patrick any time of the day. It's part of his job."

David left a message on Patrick's voice mail, said he was a friend of Wally Figg's and it was important that they speak soon. Moments later, David's cell vibrated. It was Patrick, truly sorry to hear the bad news about Wally, but ready to help immediately. "Don't let him out of your sight," Patrick said. "Please, bring him in now. I'll meet you at the House in an hour."

"Let's go, big boy," David said, grabbing Wally by the arm. He stood, found his balance, and they walked arm in arm out of the building to David's SUV. By the time they accelerated onto I-94 North, Wally was snoring again.

With the help of his GPS, David found Harbor House an hour after they left the office. It was a small, private treatment facility, tucked away in the woods just north of Waukegan, Illinois. David was unable to rouse Wally, so he left him and went inside, where Patrick Hale was waiting in the reception room. Patrick sent two white-robed orderlies with a stretcher out to fetch Wally, and five minutes later they wheeled him in, still unconscious. David followed Patrick to a small office where paperwork was waiting.

"How many times has he been here?" David asked in an effort to make conversation. "He seems to know the place well."

"I'm afraid that's confidential, at least on our end." His warm smile had vanished when he closed the office door.

"Sorry."

Patrick was looking at some papers on a clipboard. "We have a slight problem with Wally's account, Mr. Zinc, and I'm not sure what to do about it. You see, when Wally checked out a year ago, his insurance would pay only $1,000 a day for his treatment here. Because of our exceptional treatment, and results, and facilities and staff, we charge $1,500 a day. Wally left here owing slightly less than $14,000. He's made a few payments, but his balance is still at $11,000."

"I am not responsible for his medical bills or his treatment for alcoholism. I have nothing to do with his insurance."

"Well, then, we will not be able to keep him."

"You can't make money charging $1,000 a day?"

"Let's not get into that, Mr. Zinc. We charge what we charge. We have sixty beds and none are empty."

"Wally's forty-six years old. Why does he need someone to co-sign?"

"Normally, he wouldn't, but he's not good at paying his bills."

And that was before Krayoxx, David thought to himself. You should see his balance sheet now.

"How long do you plan to keep him this time?" David asked.

"His insurance will cover thirty days."

"So it's thirty days, regardless of how much progress is made with your patient. It's all driven by the insurance company, right?"

"That's the reality of it."

"That sucks. What if a patient needs more time? I have a friend from high school who crashed and burned on cocaine. Did the thirty-day gig a few times, never stuck. It finally took a hard year in a locked-down facility to get him clean and committed."

"We can all tell stories, Mr. Zinc."

"I'm sure you can." David threw up his hands. "Okay, Mr. Hale, what's the deal? You and I both know he's not leaving here tonight because he'll hurt himself."

"We can forgive the past-due account, but we will require someone to co-sign for the uninsured portion going forward."

"And that's $500 a day? Not a penny more."

"Correct."

David yanked out his wallet, removed a credit card, and tossed it on the desk. "Here's my American Express. I'm good for ten days max. I'll come get him in ten days, and then I'll think of something else to do."

Patrick quickly scribbled down the credit card info and handed back the card. "He needs more than ten days."

"Of course he does. He's proven that thirty is not enough."

"Most alcoholics require three or four efforts, if they are in fact ultimately successful."

"Ten days, Mr. Hale. I don't have much money, and practicing law with Wally is proving to be less than profitable. I don't know what you do here, but do it faster. I'll be back in ten days."

As he approached the intersection of the Tri-State Tollway, a dashboard warning light flashed red. He was almost out of gas. For the past three days, he had never once checked his fuel gauge.

The truck stop was crowded, grungy, in need of a renovation. There was a diner on one side and a convenience store on the other. David filled his tank, paid by credit card, and went inside to buy a soft drink. There was only one cashier and a line of waiting customers, so he took his time, found a Diet Coke and a bag of peanuts, and was headed to the front of the store when he stopped dead cold.

The rack was crammed with cheap Halloween toys, gadgets, and trinkets. In the middle, at eye level, was a clear plastic container with brightly colored . . . Nasty Teeth. He grabbed it and went straight for the fine print on the label. Made in China. Imported by Gunderson Toys, Louisville, Kentucky. He collected all four packets, evidence of course, but he also wanted to yank the crap off the market before another kid got sick. The cashier gave him a weird look as she rang up his purchases. He paid in cash and hustled back to his SUV. He pulled away from the pumps and parked under a bright overhanging light near the 18-wheelers.

Using his iPhone, he Googled Gunderson Toys. The company was forty years old and had once been privately owned. Four years earlier, it had been purchased by Sonesta Games Inc., the third-largest toy company in America.

He had a file on Sonesta.

CHAPTER 43

Reuben Massey arrived after dark on a Varrick Gulfstream G650. He landed at Midway Airport and was immediately scooped up by an entourage that sped away in black Cadillac Escalades. Thirty minutes later he entered the Trust Tower and was whisked high into the sky to the 101st floor, where Rogan Rothberg kept an elegant private dining room that was used by only the most senior partners and their most important clients. Nicholas Walker and Judy Beck were waiting, along with Nadine Karros and Marvin Macklow, the managing partner of the law firm. A waiter wearing a white tux brought cocktails as everyone was properly introduced and became comfortable with each other. Reuben had been wanting to meet, and examine, Nadine Karros for many months. He was not disappointed. She turned on the charm, and after the first cocktail Reuben was thoroughly smitten. He ran the ladies hard and was always on the prowl, and, well, you never know what might happen with a new acquaintance. However, according to the scouting report, she was happily married, and her only diversion was working. In the ten months Nick Walker had known Nadine, he had seen nothing less than a complete devotion to professionalism. "It's not going to work," he said to his boss back at the home office.

Per Reuben's preference, dinner was a lobster salad with pasta shells. He sat next to Nadine and hung on her every word. He went heavy on the praise for her handling of the case and the trial. He, along with everyone around the table, was anxiously awaiting a momentous verdict.

"We're here to have a conversation," Nick said after the dessert plates were removed and the door closed. "But first, I would like Nadine to tell us what's up next in the courtroom."

Without hesitation, she began her summary. "We are presuming the plaintiff has no more witnesses. If the pharmacologist were to appear in the morning, he would be allowed to testify, but according to our sources Dr. Threadgill is still hiding at home in Cincinnati. So, the plaintiff should rest its case at 9:00 a.m. At that point, we have a choice. First, and obvious, is to move for summary judgment. Judge Seawright allows this to be done both orally and in writing. We'll do both at the same time, if we choose to go that route. In my opinion, which is shared by my trial team, there is an excellent chance Judge Seawright will grant our motion immediately. The plaintiff has failed to establish even the most basic elements of a case, and everyone, including the plaintiff's lawyer, knows this. Judge Seawright has never liked this case, and, frankly, I get the impression he can't wait to toss it."

"What's his history with summary judgment motions made after the plaintiff rests?" Reuben asked.

"In the past twenty years, he's granted more than any other federal judge in Chicago and the State of Illinois. He has zero patience with cases that cannot reach even the lowest standard of proof."

"But I want a verdict," Reuben said.

"Then we will forget summary judgment and start putting on witnesses. We have a lot, you've paid for them, and they will be unimpeachable. But I have a strong feeling that this jury is fed up."

"Absolutely," said Nick Walker, who had been in the courtroom for every word. "I suspect they've already started their deliberations, in spite of Judge Seawright's admonitions."

Judy Beck added, "Our consultants feel strongly that we should finish the case as soon as possible, definitely before the weekend. The verdict is all but in."

Reuben smiled at Nadine and said, "So, Counselor, what's your advice?"

"For me, a win is a win. Summary judgment is a slam dunk. If it goes to the jury, there's always the risk of a freak accident. I would take the easy way out, but then I understand there's more in play here than a ruling by a judge."

"How many cases do you try each year?"

"Six is the average. I can't prepare for more than that, regardless of staff."

"And you haven't lost in how many years?"

"Eleven. Sixty-four wins in a row, but who's counting?" This tired line drew laughs far louder than it deserved, but everyone needed the humor.

"Have you ever felt this confident about a trial and a jury?" Reuben asked.

She took a sip of wine and thought for a moment, then shook her head. "Not that I remember."

"If we go all the way to the verdict, what are our chances of winning?"

Everyone watched her as she took another tiny sip. "A lawyer is not supposed to make these predictions, Mr. Massey."

"But you're not a typical lawyer, Ms. Karros."

"Ninety-five percent."

"Ninety-nine," Nick Walker said with a laugh.

Reuben took a gulp of his third Scotch, smacked his lips, and said, "I want a verdict. I want the jury to deliberate briefly and walk back into that courtroom with a verdict for Varrick Laboratories. To me, a verdict is repudiation, it's revenge, retribution, it's a lot more than victory. I'll take the verdict and splash it all over the world. Our PR people and ad agencies are ready and itching to go. Koane, our man in Washington, assures me that a verdict will break the logjam at the FDA and get a reversal. Our lawyers from coast to coast are convinced a verdict will even further frighten the tort boys and send them running for the hills. I want a verdict, Nadine. Can you deliver it?"

"As I said, Reuben, I'm 95 percent sure."

"Then that settles it. No summary judgment. Let's bury these bastards."

CHAPTER 44

At exactly 9:00 on Thursday morning, a bailiff called the court to order and all rose for the entrance of His Honor. When the jury was in place, he said abruptly, "Continue, Mr. Zinc."

David rose and said, "Your Honor, the plaintiff rests."

Judge Seawright was not at all surprised. "Lost some more witnesses, Mr. Zinc?"

"No sir. We've simply run out of them."

"Very well. A motion, Ms. Karros?"

"No, Your Honor, we are ready to proceed."

"I suspected that. Call your first witness."

David suspected it too. He had allowed himself to believe that the trial would end abruptly that morning, but it was obvious Nadine and her client smelled blood. From there on, he would have little to do but listen and watch a real courtroom lawyer.

"The defense calls Dr. Jesse Kindorf." David glanced at the jurors and saw several smiles. They were about to meet a celebrity.

Jesse Kindorf was a former surgeon general of the United States. He held the position for six years and was brilliantly controversial. He castigated tobacco companies on a daily basis. He held large press conferences in which he exposed the fat and caloric content of popular fast foods. He released scathing condemnations against some of the most trusted names in corporate America, consumer product companies that were flat-out guilty of producing and marketing mass quantities of highly processed foods. At various times during his tenure, he was on the warpath fighting butter, cheese, eggs, red meat, sugar, soft drinks, and alcohol, but his most famous brouhaha occurred when he suggested a ban on coffee. He thoroughly enjoyed the spotlight, and with his good looks, athletic build, and quick wit he became the most famous surgeon general in history. The fact that he had crossed the street and was now testifying on behalf of a major corporation was a clear signal to the jurors that he believed in the drug.

And he was a cardiologist, from Chicago. He took the stand and flashed a smile at the jury, his jury. Nadine began the arduous process of going through his credentials in order to have him qualified as an expert. David quickly jumped to his feet and said, "Your Honor, we are happy to stipulate that Dr. Kindorf is an expert in the field of cardiology."

Nadine turned, smiled, and said, "Thank you."

Judge Seawright growled, "Thank you, Mr. Zinc."

The gist of Dr. Kindorf's testimony was that he had prescribed Krayoxx to thousands of his patients over the past few years, with no side effects whatsoever. The drug worked beautifully for about 90 percent of his patients. The drug dramatically lowered cholesterol. His ninety-one-year-old mother was on Krayoxx, or was until it was pulled by the FDA.

The paralegal scribbled a note on her legal pad and handed it to her boss: "Wonder how much they're paying him?"

David scribbled back as if they were discussing a major flaw in the testimony. "A lot."

Nadine Karros and Dr. Kindorf worked their way through a flawless round of batting practice. She served up the fat pitches, he knocked them out of the park. The jury wanted to cheer them on.

When Judge Seawright asked, "Any cross-examination, Mr. Zinc?" David rose and politely said, "No, Your Honor."

To curry favor with the blacks on the jury, Nadine called a Dr. Thurston, a dapper, distinguished black gentleman with a gray beard and finely tailored suit. Dr. Thurston was also from Chicago and was the senior physician in a group of thirty-five cardiologists and cardiovascular surgeons. In his spare time, he taught at the University of Chicago School of Medicine. To move things along, David did not question his credentials. Dr. Thurston and his group had prescribed Krayoxx to tens of thousands of their patients over the past six years, with spectacular results and no side effects. The drug, in his opinion, was perfectly safe; indeed, he and his colleagues viewed it as a miracle drug. Its presence was sorely missed, and, yes, he planned to immediately resume prescribing it when it reappeared on the market. Most dramatically, Dr. Thurston revealed to the jury that he had taken Krayoxx himself for four years.

To get the attention of the Hispanic lady on the jury, the defense called Dr. Roberta Seccero, cardiologist and researcher at Mayo Clinic in Rochester, Minnesota. David gave the green light on credentials, and Dr. Seccero, to no one's surprise, sang like a bird on a spring morning. Her patients were mostly women, and the drug did everything but make them lose weight. There was no statistical evidence that those taking Krayoxx were likelier to suffer heart attacks or strokes than those who didn't take it. She and her colleagues had researched this at length, and there was no doubt. In her twenty-five years as a cardiologist, she had never seen a safer and more effective medication.

The rainbow was completed when Ms. Karros called to the stand a young Korean doctor from San Francisco who, oddly enough, looked remarkably similar to juror Number 19. Dr. Pang enthusiastically endorsed the drug and expressed dismay at its removal from the market. He had given it to hundreds of patients with outstanding results.

David had no questions for Dr. Pang either. He was not about to bicker with any of these renowned doctors. What was he supposed to do—argue medicine with some of the best doctors in the business? No sir. He stayed in his chair and kept one eye on his watch, which was moving rather slowly.

There was no doubt that had there been a juror of Lithuanian descent, Nadine would have pulled another expert from her magic hat, one with a Lithuanian surname and immaculate credentials.

The fifth witness was the chief cardiologist at the Feinberg School of Medicine, Northwestern University. Her name was Dr. Parkin, and her testimony was a little different. She had been hired to do a thorough analysis of Percy Klopeck's medical history. She had reviewed his records from the age of twelve and those of his siblings and parents to the extent they were available, and she also had taken recorded statements from his friends and co-workers, those willing to cooperate. At the time of his death, Percy was taking Prinzide and Levatol for hypertension, insulin for adult-onset diabetes, Bexnin for arthritis, Plavix as a blood thinner, Colestid for atherosclerosis, and Krayoxx for high cholesterol. His happy pill of choice was Xanax, which he either bummed off friends, stole from Iris, or bought online, and he used it daily to battle the stress of life with "that woman," according to one of his co-workers. He occasionally used Fedamin, an over-the-counter appetite suppressant that was supposed to make him eat less but seemed to backfire. He had smoked for twenty years but managed to stop at the age of forty-one with the aid of Nicotrex, a nicotine-laced chewing gum that was known to be highly addictive. He chewed it nonstop, going through at least three packages a day. According to blood work a year before he died, Percy's liver was showing a decreasing level of function. He loved gin and, according to credit card records subpoenaed by Ms. Karros, purchased at least three fifths a week from Bilbo's Spirits on Stanton Avenue, five blocks from his home. He often felt bad in the morning, complained of headaches, and kept at least two large bottles of ibuprofen close by on his cluttered work desk.

When Dr. Parkin finished her lengthy narrative about Percy's habits and health, it seemed patently unfair to blame his death on just one drug. Since there had been no autopsy—Iris had been too upset to even think about it—there was no positive indication that he died of a heart attack. His death could have been caused by the all-encompassing "respiratory failure."

Wally and Oscar had discussed having the body exhumed to get a clearer picture of what killed him, but Iris flew into a rage. Plus, the exhumation, autopsy, and reburial would have cost almost $10,000, and Oscar flatly refused to spend the money.

In Dr. Parkin's opinion, Percy Klopeck had died young because he was genetically predisposed to an early death, one made even more probable because of his lifestyle. She also offered the opinion that it was impossible to predict the cumulative effect of the astonishing barrage of his medications.

Poor Percy, thought David. He lived a short, uneventful life and died peacefully in his sleep, with no clue whatsoever that his habits and ailments would one day be dissected so thoroughly by strangers in open court.

Her testimony was devastating, and there was not a single part of it that David wanted to revisit on cross-examination. At 12:30, Judge Seawright adjourned until 2:00 p.m. David and Helen hustled from the courthouse and enjoyed a nice, long lunch. David ordered a bottle of white wine, and Helen, who rarely drank, enjoyed a glass. They toasted Percy, may he rest in peace.

In David's novice opinion, Nadine and the defense stumbled slightly with the afternoon's first witness. He was Dr. Litchfield, a cardiologist and cardiovascular surgeon from the world-renowned Cleveland Clinic, where he saw patients, taught, and researched. He had the tedious task of walking the jurors through Percy's last echocardiogram, the same video that had knocked them out in the hands of Igor Borzov. Sensing that another viewing of that footage would not be well received, Nadine stepped on the gas and opted for a scaled-down version of the testimony. Bottom line—there was no reduced regurgitation of blood from the mitral valve. The left ventricle was not enlarged. If the patient did indeed die of a heart attack, its cause could not be determined.

Bottom line—Borzov was a fool.

David had a quick vision of Wally, lying peacefully in a comfortable bed, wearing a gown or pajamas or whatever Harbor House distributed, sober now, tranquil due to a sedative, maybe reading or just gazing at Lake Michigan, his thoughts a million miles away from the carnage in Courtroom 2314. Yet it was all his fault. In the months he'd spent racing around Chicago, visiting low-end funeral parlors, passing out brochures in gyms and fast-food joints, he had never, not once, paused to study the physiology and pharmacology of Krayoxx and its alleged damage to heart valves. He had simply and eagerly assumed the drug was bad and, egged on by smart guys like Jerry Alisandros and other tort stars, had joined the parade and begun counting his money. Resting now in rehab, was he even thinking about the trial, about the case getting dumped on David while he and Oscar were laid up licking their wounds? No, David decided, Wally was not worrying about the trial. Wally had bigger issues—sobriety, bankruptcy, a job, his firm.

The next witness was a professor and medical researcher from Harvard who had studied Krayoxx and written a definitive article in the *New England Journal of Medicine*. David managed to get a slight chuckle when he did not question the professor's résumé. He said, "Your Honor, if he went to Harvard, I'm sure his credentials are outstanding. He must be brilliant."

Fortunately, the jurors had not been informed that David was a graduate of the Harvard School of Law; otherwise, the wisecrack could have backfired. Harvard grads who talked about being Harvard grads were not generally well regarded in Chicago.

"Pretty stupid," read the note from the paralegal.

David did not respond. It was almost 4:00 p.m., and he just wanted to leave. The professor droned on about his research methods. Not a single juror was paying attention. Most appeared brain-dead, thoroughly numbed by this futile exercise in civic responsibility. If this is what made a democracy strong, then God help us.

David wondered if they were already discussing the case. Each morning and each afternoon Judge Seawright gave the same lecture about improper contact, the prohibition against reading about the case in the newspapers or online, and the need to refrain from chatting about the case until all evidence had been presented. There were plenty of studies on the behavior of juries, the dynamics of group decision making, and so on, and most found that jurors couldn't wait to begin gossiping about the lawyers, the witnesses, even the judge. They tended to pair off, to buddy up, to separate into cliques and camps and begin their considerations prematurely. Seldom, though, did they do so as an entire group. More often, they hid their little private sessions from each other.

David tuned out his fellow Harvard alum and flipped a few pages of his legal pad. He resumed work on a rough draft of his letter:

> *Dear So-and-So:*
>
> *I represent the family of Thuya Khaing, the five-year-old son of two Burmese immigrants who are in this country legally.*
>
> *From November 20 until May 19 of this year, Thuya was a patient in the Lakeshore Children's Hospital here in Chicago. He had ingested a near-lethal amount of lead, and on several occasions was kept alive by a respirator. According to his doctors, and I have included with this letter a summary of their statements, Thuya now suffers brain damage that is permanent and severe. He is not expected to live but a few more years; however, there is a chance he could survive up to twenty years.*
>
> *The source of the lead swallowed by Thuya is a toy made in China and imported by your division Gunderson Toys. It is a Halloween novelty called Nasty Teeth. According to Dr. Biff Sandroni, a toxicologist you've probably heard of, the fake teeth and fangs are coated with various colors of bright paint and loaded with lead. I have attached a copy of Dr. Sandroni's report for your reading pleasure.*
>
> *I have also enclosed a copy of a lawsuit I will soon file against Sonesta Games, in federal court here in Chicago, in the very near future.*
>
> *If you would like to discuss*

"Cross-examination, Mr. Zinc?" Judge Seawright interrupted.

Again, David stood quickly and said, "No, Your Honor."

"Very well, it is now 5:15. We will adjourn until nine in the morning with the same instructions to the jury."

Wally was in a wheelchair, dressed in a white cotton bathrobe with cheap canvas slippers barely covering his chubby feet. An orderly rolled him into the visiting room, where David was waiting, standing at a large window, staring into the darkness of Lake Michigan. The orderly left and they were alone.

"Why are you in a wheelchair?" David asked as he dropped onto a leather sofa.

"I'm sedated," Wally replied slowly and softly. "They'll give me some pills for a couple of days to, uh, sorta soothe things along. If I try to walk, I might fall, crack my skull, or something."

Twenty-four hours off a three-day binge, and he still looked rough. His eyes were red and puffy, his face sad and defeated. He needed a haircut. "Are you curious about the trial, Wally?"

Hesitation as this was processed, then, "I've thought about it, yes."

"You've thought about it? That's awfully nice of you. We should finish tomorrow, we being me on our side of the room with no one but my lovely wife, who's pretending to be a paralegal and is already tired of watching her husband get his ass kicked, and what seems like an ever-growing mob of dark suits on the other side, all hovering around the lovely Nadine Karros, who, believe me, Wally, is even better than advertised."

"The judge wouldn't continue the case?"

"Why should he, Wally? Continue to when, and why? What, exactly, would we have done with another, say, thirty or sixty days? Go out and hire a real trial lawyer to try the case? Let's hear that conversation: 'That's it, sir, we'll promise you $100,000 and half of our cut to walk into that courtroom with a lousy set of facts, an unsympathetic client, a judge who's even more unsympathetic, against an extremely talented defense team with unlimited cash and talent, representing a large and powerful corporate defendant.' Who would you pitch that to, Wally?"

"You seem angry, David."

"No, Wally, it's not anger; it's just the need to rant, to bitch, to blow off some steam."

"Then go right ahead."

"I asked for a continuance, and I think Seawright would have considered it, but why? No one could say when you might be able to come back. Oscar, probably never. We agreed to go forward and get it over with."

"I'm sorry, David."

"So am I. I feel like such a fool sitting there with no case, no clue, no weapons, nothing to fight with. It's so frustrating."

Wally lowered his chin to his chest as if he might start sobbing. Instead, he began mumbling, "I'm sorry, so sorry."

"Okay, look, Wally, I'm sorry too. I didn't come here to beat you up, okay? I came to check on you. I'm worried about you, so are Rochelle and Oscar. You're sick and we want to help."

When Wally looked up, his eyes were wet, and as he spoke, his lip quivered. "I can't keep doing this, David. I thought I had it whipped, I swear I did. One year, two weeks, two days, then something happened. We were in court Monday morning, I was nervous as hell, terrified really, and I was overcome with this vicious desire for a drink. I remember thinking, you know, a couple of drinks will do the trick. Two quick beers and I'll settle down. Alcohol is such a liar, such a monster. As soon as we broke for lunch, I scooted out of the building and found a little café with a beer sign in the window. I got a table, ordered a sandwich, drank three beers, and, wow, it tasted so good. And felt even better. Back in the courtroom, I remember thinking, you know, I can do this. I can drink and it's no problem. I got it whipped, you know? No problem. Now look at me. Back in rehab and scared shitless."

"Where's your car, Wally?"

He thought about it for a long time and finally gave up. "I have no idea. I blacked out so many times."

"Don't worry about it. I'll find the car."

Wally wiped his cheeks with the back of his hand, then wiped his nose with a sleeve. "I'm sorry, David. I thought we had a chance."

"We never had a chance, Wally. There's nothing wrong with the drug. We joined a stampede that was going nowhere, and we didn't realize it until it was too late."

"But the trial's not over, is it?"

"The trial's over but the lawyers are still at it. The jury gets the final word tomorrow."

Nothing was said for several minutes. Wally's eyes cleared, but he had trouble looking at David. Finally, he said softly, "Thanks for coming, David. Thanks for taking care of me, and Oscar and Rochelle. I hope you won't be leaving us."

"Let's not talk about that now. You get good and detoxed. I'll check you out next week, then we'll have another firm meeting and make some decisions."

"I'd like that. Another firm meeting."

CHAPTER 45

Emma had a rough night, and both parents walked the floor in alternating one-hour shifts. When Helen handed her off at 5:30 and headed back to bed, she announced her career as a paralegal was mercifully over. She had enjoyed the lunches, but little else, and besides, she had a sick baby to deal with. David managed to quiet Emma with a bottle and, as he fed her, went online. Varrick's stock had closed at $40 a share Thursday afternoon. Its steady rise throughout the week was even more evidence that the Klopeck trial was going badly for the plaintiff, though no additional evidence was really needed. Out of his usual morbid curiosity, David checked in with the Hung Juror, who wrote:

In what has to be the most lopsided trial in the history of U.S. jurisprudence, things continue to go from bad to worse for the estate of the late and now much maligned Percy Klopeck. As Varrick Labs' defense team continues to steamroll over the hapless and grossly incompetent lawyer for Klopeck, one almost feels sorry for the underdog. Almost, but not quite. The question that screams to be answered is, how did this dog of a case manage to get into court, stay in court, and stumble its way to the jury? Talk about an obscene waste of time, money, and talent! Talent, that is, for the defense. Talent is sorely lacking on the other side of the courtroom, where the clueless David Zinc has adopted the unique strategy of simply trying to become invisible. He has yet to cross-examine a witness. He has yet to make an objection. He has yet to make a single move to help his case. He just sits there for hours, pretending to take notes, swapping little messages with his new paralegal, a hot thing in a short skirt brought in to show some leg and try to divert attention from the fact that the plaintiff has no case and the lawyer is incompetent. Unknown to the jury, the new paralegal is actually Helen Zinc, wife of the idiot sitting in front of her. This bimbo is not a paralegal and has no training or experience in the courtroom, so she fits in nicely with the clowns from Finley & Figg. Her presence is obviously a clever ploy to catch the eye of the male jurors and counterbalance the overwhelming presence of Nadine Karros, who is perhaps the most effective courtroom advocate this Hung Juror has ever watched.

Let's hope this dog is put to sleep today. And maybe Judge Seawright has the guts to grant sanctions for such a frivolous case.

David flinched so hard he squeezed Emma, who momentarily stopped working the bottle. He closed his laptop and cursed himself for looking at the blog. Never again, he vowed, not for the first time.

With the verdict solidly in hand, Nadine Karros decided to push a bit harder. Her first witness Friday morning was Dr. Mark Ulander, Varrick's senior vice president and director of research. Working from a script, they quickly laid the groundwork. Ulander had three graduate degrees and had spent the past twenty-two years supervising Varrick's vast development of myriad drugs. Krayoxx was his proudest achievement. The company had spent over $4 billion bringing it to market. His team of thirty scientists had labored for eight years to perfect the drug, to make certain it worked to lower cholesterol, to take no chances with its safety, and to gain FDA approval. He detailed the rigid testing procedures used, and not just for Krayoxx but for all Varrick's fine products. The company's reputation was on the line with every drug it developed, and the Varrick reputation for excellence pervaded every aspect of his research. With Nadine's skillful direction, Dr. Ulander painted an impressive picture of a diligent effort to produce the perfect drug, Krayoxx.

With nothing to lose, David decided to roll the dice and join the action. He began his cross-examination with "Dr. Ulander, let's talk about all of those clinical trials you just mentioned." The fact that David was at the podium seemed to catch the jurors off guard. Though it was only 10:15, they were ready to deliberate and go home.

"Where did the clinical trials take place?" David asked.

"For Krayoxx?"

"No, for baby aspirin. Of course for Krayoxx."

"Sorry, of course. Let's see. Well, the clinical trials were extensive, as I said."

"Got that, Dr. Ulander. The question is rather simple. Where were the clinical trials?"

"Yes, well, the initial trials were done with a test group of high-cholesterol subjects in Nicaragua and Mongolia."

"Keep going. Where else?"

"Kenya and Cambodia."

"Did Varrick spend $4 billion developing Krayoxx to reap dividends in Mongolia and Kenya?"

"I can't answer that, Mr. Zinc. I'm not involved in marketing."

"Fair enough. How many clinical trials were conducted here in the United States?"

"None."

"How many Varrick drugs are in clinical trials as of today?"

Nadine Karros rose and said, "Objection, Your Honor, on the grounds of irrelevance. Other drugs are not at issue here."

Judge Seawright paused and scratched his chin. "Overruled. Let's see where this is going."

David wasn't sure where it was going, but he had just won a tiny victory over Ms. Karros. Emboldened, he pressed on. "You may answer the question, Dr. Ulander. How many Varrick drugs are in clinical trials today?"

"Approximately twenty. I could name them all if given a moment or two."

"Twenty sounds good. Let's save some time. How much money will Varrick spend this year on clinical trials for all of its drugs in development?"

"Roughly $2 billion."

"Last year, 2010, what percentage of Varrick's gross sales came from foreign markets?"

Dr. Ulander shrugged and looked perplexed. "Well, I'd have to check the financial statements."

"You're a vice president of the company, aren't you? And you have been for the past sixteen years, right?"

"That's true."

David picked up a thin binder, flipped a page, and said, "This is last year's financial report, and it plainly states that 82 percent of Varrick's gross sales were in the U.S. market. Have you seen this?"

"Of course."

Ms. Karros stood and said, "Objection, Your Honor. My client's financial records are not at issue here."

"Overruled. Your client's financial records are a matter of public record."

Another tiny victory, and for the second time David got a taste of courtroom excitement. "Does 82 percent sound right, Dr. Ulander?"

"If you say so."

"I'm not saying so, sir. It's right here in the published report."

"Okay, so it's 82 percent."

"Thank you. Of the twenty drugs you're testing today, how many of their clinical trials are being conducted in the United States?"

The witness gritted his teeth, clenched his jaw, and said, "None."

"None," David repeated dramatically and looked at the jury. Several of the faces were engaged. He paused a few seconds, then continued: "So Varrick derives 82 percent of its income in this country, yet it tests its drugs in such places as Nicaragua, Cambodia, and Mongolia. Why is that, Dr. Ulander?"

"It's very simple, Mr. Zinc. The regulatory environment in this country stifles the research and development of new drugs, devices, and procedures."

"That's great. So you're blaming the government for your routine practice of testing drugs on people in faraway places?"

Ms. Karros was back on her feet. "Objection, Your Honor. That's mischaracterization of what the witness said."

"Overruled. The jury heard what the witness said. Continue, Mr. Zinc."

"Thank you, Your Honor. You may answer the question, Dr. Ulander."

"I'm sorry, what was the question?"

"Is it your testimony that the reason your company runs its clinical trials in other countries is that there is too much regulation in this country?"

"Yes, that's the reason."

"Isn't it true that Varrick tests its drugs in developing countries because it can avoid the threat of litigation if things go badly?"

"Not at all."

"Isn't it true that Varrick tests its drugs in developing countries because there is virtually no regulation?"

"No, that's not true."

"Isn't it true that Varrick tests its drugs in developing countries because it's much easier to find human guinea pigs who need a few bucks?"

There was a scramble over David's left shoulder as the defense horde reacted. Ms. Karros sprang to her feet and said firmly, "Objection, Your Honor."

Judge Seawright, who was leaning forward on his elbows, calmly said, "State your objection."

For the first time all week Nadine struggled for words. "Well, first, I object to this line of questioning on the grounds of irrelevance. What my client does with other drugs is not relevant to this case."

"I've already overruled that objection, Ms. Karros."

"And so I object to counsel's use of the term 'human guinea pigs.'"

The term was clearly objectionable, but it was also commonly used and seemed to fit the situation. Judge Seawright thought about it for a while as everyone stared at him. David glanced at the jury and saw some amused faces.

"Overruled. Continue, Mr. Zinc."

"Were you supervising all of Varrick's research in 1998?"

Dr. Ulander replied, "Yes, as I've said, that has been my role for the past twenty-two years."

"Thank you. Now, in 1998, did Varrick run clinical trials for a drug called Amoxitrol?"

Ulander shot a look of panic at the defense table, where several of the Varrick lawyers were sporting their own looks of panic. Ms. Karros jumped up again and forcefully announced, "Objection, Your Honor! That drug is not in question here. Its history is totally irrelevant."

"Mr. Zinc?"

"Your Honor, that drug has an ugly history and I don't blame Varrick for trying to keep it quiet."

"Why should we talk about other drugs, Mr. Zinc?"

"Well, Judge, it seems to me as if this witness has placed the company's reputation into issue. He testified for sixty-four minutes and spent most of his time trying to convince the jury that his company places great importance on safe testing procedures. Why can't I explore this? It seems quite relevant to me, and I think the jury would find it interesting."

To which Nadine quickly replied, "Your Honor, this trial is about a drug called Krayoxx, nothing more. Anything else is a fishing expedition."

"But as Mr. Zinc correctly pointed out, you placed the company's reputation into issue, Ms. Karros. You weren't required to do this, but that door is now open. Objection overruled. Continue, Mr. Zinc."

The door was indeed open, and Varrick's history was fair game.

David wasn't certain how it had happened, but he was thrilled none-theless. His self-doubt was gone. The gnawing fear had disappeared. He was on his feet, all alone against the big boys, and he was scoring points. It was showtime.

"I asked about Amoxitrol, Dr. Ulander. Surely you remember it."

"I do."

With a bit of flair, David waved his arm at the jury and said, "Well, tell the jury about that drug. What was it intended to do?"

Ulander sank a few inches in the witness chair and again looked at the defense table for help. Grudgingly, he began talking, but in very short sentences. "Amoxitrol was developed as an abortion pill."

To help him along, David asked, "An abortion pill that could be taken up to one month after conception, sort of an expanded version of the morning-after pill, right, Doctor?"

"Something like that."

"Was that a yes or a no?"

"Yes."

"The pill would basically dissolve the fetus, and its remains would eventually be flushed out with other bodily waste, is that correct, Doctor?"

"In a simplified form, yes, that is what the drug was supposed to do."

With at least seven Catholics on the jury, David didn't have to glance over to see how this was being received.

"Did you conduct clinical trials for Amoxitrol?"

"We did."

"And where did these trials take place?"

"Africa."

"Where in Africa?"

Ulander rolled his eyes and grimaced. "I can't, uh, you know, I would have to check that."

David walked slowly to his table, riffled through some papers, and extracted a binder. He opened it, flipped pages as he walked back to the podium, and asked, as though he were reading from the report, "In what three African countries did Varrick conduct clinical trials for its abortion pill Amoxitrol?"

"Uganda for sure. I just can't—"

"Do Uganda, Botswana, and Somalia sound right?" David asked.

"Yes."

"How many African women were used in the study?"

"Do you have the answer there, Mr. Zinc?"

"Does the number four hundred sound right, Doctor?"

"It does."

"And how much money did Varrick pay to each pregnant African woman to abort her pregnancy with one of your pills?"

"Do you have the answer there, Mr. Zinc?"

"Does $50 per fetus sound right, Dr. Ulander?"

"I guess."

"Don't guess, Doctor. I have the report right here."

David flipped a page, took his time, let the pathetic amount of the bounty rattle around the courtroom. Nadine Karros rose again and said, "Your Honor, I object. The report Mr. Zinc is using is not in evidence. I have not seen it."

David snapped, "Oh, I'm sure she's seen it, Your Honor. I'm sure all the big shots at Varrick have seen it."

"What report are you using there, Mr. Zinc?" the judge asked.

"It's an investigation done by the World Health Organization in 2002. Their scientists tracked the world's largest pharmaceutical companies and the way they use human guinea pigs in poor countries to test drugs they hope to market in rich countries."

The judge held up both hands and said, "That's enough. You can't use the report if it's not in evidence."

"I'm not offering it as evidence, Your Honor. I'm using it to impeach this witness and question the fine reputation of this wonderful company." By now, David felt no restraint in choosing his words. What was there to lose?

Judge Seawright frowned and scratched his chin some more, obviously uncertain. "Ms. Karros," he said.

"He's picking facts from a report that's not in evidence, a report the jury will not see, unless he can somehow get it admitted into evidence," she said, still composed but clearly agitated.

"Here's what we are going to do, Mr. Zinc. You can use the report for impeachment purposes only, but the information must be conveyed in a manner that is exact, straightforward, and not the least bit slanted to suit your purposes. Understand?"

"Sure, Judge. Would you like a copy of the report?"

"That would be helpful."

David walked to his table, picked up two more binders, and as he sort of strutted around the courtroom, he said, "I have an extra copy for Varrick, though I'm sure they've already seen it. Probably buried in a vault."

"That's enough of the extraneous comments, Mr. Zinc," His Honor barked.

David said, "Sorry." He handed a copy to the judge and then tossed one on the table in front of Nadine Karros. Back at the podium, he looked at his notes, then glared at Dr. Ulander. "Now, Doctor, back to Amoxitrol. When Varrick was testing the drug, was your company concerned with the ages of these young pregnant African women?"

For a few seconds, Ulander was unable to speak. He finally mumbled, "I'm sure we were."

"Great. So how young was too young, Dr. Ulander? What were Varrick's guidelines on age?"

"The subjects were required to be at least eighteen years old."

"Have you ever seen this report, Doctor?"

Ulander again looked desperately at Nadine Karros, who, along with the rest of her squad, was cowering and making eye contact with no one. Finally, he uttered an unconvincing "No."

Juror Number 37, a fifty-one-year-old black male, made a hissing sound that was meant to be heard and vaguely sounded like the word "shit."

"Isn't it true, Doctor, that pregnant girls as young as fourteen were given Amoxitrol to abort their fetuses? Page 22, Judge, last paragraph, second column."

Ulander did not respond.

Reuben Massey was sitting next to Judy Beck in the first row, defense side. As a seasoned veteran of the tort wars, he knew it was crucial to maintain a veneer of complete calm and confidence. But his heart pounded with anger, and he wanted to leap forward and grab Nadine Karros by the neck. How was this happening? How had this door been not only cracked but kicked wide open?

Varrick could have easily won on summary judgment, and he would be back at his desk, safely ensconced at corporate HQ relishing the victory and pulling strings to get Krayoxx back on the market. Instead, he was watching his cherished company get thrashed by an absolute novice.

The novice pressed on. "Now, Dr. Ulander, did Amoxitrol ever make it to the market?"

"No."

"Had some problems with it, didn't you?"

"Yes."

"What were some of the side effects?"

"Nausea, dizziness, headaches, fainting, but this is common with most emergency contraceptives."

"You failed to mention abdominal bleeding, didn't you, Dr. Ulander? Just an oversight, I'm sure."

"There was abdominal bleeding. That's why we stopped the testing."

"You stopped it rather quickly, didn't you, Doctor? In fact, the trials were terminated about ninety days after they began, right, Doctor?"

"Yes."

David paused for drama; the next question was the most brutal. The courtroom was silent. "Now, Dr. Ulander, from Varrick's sample of four hundred pregnant women, how many died from abdominal bleeding?"

The witness slowly removed his glasses and placed them in his lap. He rubbed his eyes, glanced at Reuben Massey, then gritted his teeth, looked at the jurors, and said, "We were made aware of eleven deaths."

David hung his head for a moment, then took a load of paperwork to his table and swapped it for another stack of papers. He had no idea how far he could go at this point, but he was not quitting until instructed to do so. He returned to the podium, arranged things, and said, "Now, Doctor, let's talk about some of Varrick's other drugs that did make it into the marketplace."

Ms. Karros stood and said, "Same objection, Your Honor."

"Same ruling, Ms. Karros."

"In that case, Your Honor, could we please have a brief recess?"

It was almost 11:00 a.m., past Judge Seawright's usual break time of 10:30. He looked at David and said, "How much longer, Mr. Zinc?"

David held up his legal pad and said, "Gosh, Judge, I don't know. I have a long list of bad drugs."

"Let's meet in chambers and talk about it. Fifteen-minute recess."

CHAPTER 46

With three blacks on the jury, David made the tactical decision to spend more time in Africa with Dr. Ulander. During the recess, Judge Seawright decided to allow David to explore the backgrounds of only three additional drugs. "I want the jury to get this case this afternoon," he said. Ms. Karros was still objecting, hotly at times, and the judge was still overruling her objections.

The jurors were brought in and took their seats. Dr. Ulander returned to the witness stand. David addressed him, "Now, Dr. Ulander, do you remember a drug called Klervex?"

"I do."

"Was it made and marketed by your company?"

"It was."

"When was it approved by the FDA?"

"Let's see. Early in 2005, I believe."

"Is it now on the market?"

"It is not."

"When was it taken off the market?"

"Two years later, 2007, in June, I believe."

"Did your company voluntarily recall the drug, or was its removal mandated by the FDA?"

"FDA."

"And at the time of its recall, your company was facing several thousand lawsuits because of Klervex, correct?"

"Correct."

"In layman's terms, what kind of drug was this?"

"It was for hypertension, for patients who suffered from elevated blood pressure."

"Were there any unpleasant side effects?"

"According to the mass tort lawyers, there were."

"Well, what about the FDA? It didn't yank the drug because the mass tort lawyers were upset, did it?" David was holding another report, and he waved it slightly as he spoke.

"I guess not."

"I didn't ask you to guess, Doctor. You've seen this FDA report. Klervex caused severe, even blinding migraine headaches in thousands of patients, did it not?"

"According to the FDA, yes."

"Do you dispute the FDA's findings?"

"I do."

"And you supervised the clinical trials of Klervex?"

"My staff and I supervise the testing of all pharmaceuticals made by our company. I thought we had already established that."

"My deepest apologies. How many separate clinical trials were conducted during the testing of Klervex?"

"At least six."

"And where did these take place?"

The beating would not end until the cross-examination was over, so Ulander plunged ahead. "Four in Africa, one in Romania, one in Paraguay."

"In Africa, how many subjects were treated with Klervex?"

"There were roughly one thousand patients in each trial."

"Do you remember what country or countries?"

"Not precisely. Cameroon, Kenya, and perhaps Nigeria. I can't recall the fourth."

"Were these four trials conducted simultaneously?"

"Generally speaking, yes. Over a twelve-month period in 2002 and 2003."

"Isn't it true, Doctor, that you, and I mean you personally, knew almost immediately that there were significant problems with the drug?"

"What do you mean by 'almost immediately'?"

David walked to his pile, picked up a document, and addressed the court: "Your Honor, I would like to admit into evidence this internal memo sent to Dr. Mark Ulander from a certain Varrick technician by the name of Darlene Ainsworth, dated May 4, 2002."

"Let me see it," the judge said.

Nadine stood and said, "Your Honor, we object on the grounds of relevance and lack of a proper predicate being laid."

Judge Seawright scanned the two-page memo. He looked at Dr. Ulander and said, "Did you receive this, Doctor?"

"I did."

David jumped in to help. "Your Honor, this memo was leaked by a Varrick whistle-blower to the plaintiffs' lawyers in the Klervex litigation two years ago. Its authenticity was established at that time. Dr. Ulander knows it well."

"That's enough, Mr. Zinc. It will be admitted."

Mr. Zinc plowed on: "The memo is dated May 4, 2002, correct, Dr. Ulander?"

"Correct."

"So, some two months after Varrick began its clinical trials in Africa, this memo comes across your desk. Look at the second page, last paragraph. Would you please read that to the jury, Dr. Ulander?"

The witness obviously didn't want to read anything, but he adjusted his glasses and began: "Patients have been taking Klervex for six weeks, forty milligrams, twice daily. Seventy-two percent show decreased blood pressure, systolic and diastolic. Side effects are worrisome. Patients complain of dizziness, nausea, vomiting, and many, approximately 20 percent, suffer severe headaches so debilitating it is necessary to stop the drug. After comparing notes with other med techs here in Nairobi, I strongly suggest that all trials be suspended for Klervex."

"Now, Dr. Ulander, were the trials suspended?"

"No, they were not."

"Were there similar reports from the field?"

Ulander sighed and looked at the defense table, helpless.

"I have copies of the other reports, Dr. Ulander, if they might refresh your memory," David offered helpfully.

"Yes, there were other reports," Ulander said.

"And this technician, Darlene Ainsworth, is she still employed by Varrick?"

"I don't think so."

"Is that a yes or a no, Doctor?"

"No, she is not employed."

"Isn't it true, Dr. Ulander, that she was terminated one month after sending you this memo about the horrors of Klervex?"

"She wasn't terminated by me."

"But she was terminated by Varrick, wasn't she?"

"Well, I'm not sure how she left the company. She may have resigned."

David again walked to his table and picked up a thick document. He looked at Judge Seawright and said, "Judge, this is Dr. Ulander's deposition from the Klervex litigation two years ago. May I use it to refresh his memory?"

"Just answer the question," the judge snapped angrily at the witness. "Was this employee terminated by Varrick one month after she sent you that memo?"

Startled by the rebuke from His Honor, Dr. Ulander's memory was instantly refreshed, and he said, "Yes, she was."

"Thank you," the judge said.

David looked at the jury as he spoke. "So, in spite of these warnings from the field, Varrick pushed on and gained FDA approval in 2005, right, Dr. Ulander?"

"The drug was approved in 2005."

"And once it was approved, Varrick aggressively marketed the drug in this country, right, Dr. Ulander?"

"I have nothing to do with marketing."

"But you are on the board, right?"

"Right."

"Then all hell broke loose. Complaining of severe migraines and other side effects, at least eight thousand Varrick consumers filed lawsuits in 2005, right, Doctor?"

"I don't have access to those numbers."

"Well, let's not nitpick here, Doctor. I'll try to wrap this up a bit quicker. Has your company gone to trial anywhere in this country to defend its drug Klervex?"

"Once."

"And Varrick has settled over twenty-five thousand lawsuits for the drug as of last week, right, Doctor?"

Nadine was back. "Objection, Your Honor. Settlements in other cases are not relevant to this one. I think Mr. Zinc has stepped over the line."

"I'll decide that, Ms. Karros. But your objection is sustained. Mr. Zinc, no talk of other settlements."

"Thank you, Your Honor. Now, Dr. Ulander, do you recall a Varrick drug called Ruval?"

Ulander sighed again and began to study his feet. David walked to his table to reshuffle his files and fetch another stack of memos extracted from Varrick's dirty laundry. In short order, he established that (1) Ruval was supposed to alleviate migraine headaches but it also dramatically increased blood pressure; (2) it had been tested on migraine sufferers in Africa and India; (3) Varrick knew of its side effects but tried to bury this information; (4) damaging internal company memos were discovered by trial lawyers in the ensuing litigation; (5) the FDA had eventually recalled the drug; (6) Varrick was still defending various class actions and not a single case had gone to trial.

At 1:00 p.m., David made the decision to quit. He had grilled Dr. Ulander unmercifully for almost three hours, with no counterpunch from Ms. Karros, and he had scored enough points. The jury, at first amused by the dirt on Varrick, now seemed ready to eat lunch, deliberate, and go home.

"A quick lunch," the judge said. "Back here at 2:00 p.m."

David found an empty corner of the café on the second floor of the building and was eating a sandwich and looking over his notes when he felt someone approach from behind. It was Taylor Barkley, a Rogan associate, one of the few David had met and occasionally nodded to across the courtroom. "Got a second?" he said as he slid into a chair.

"Sure."

"Nice cross. Nadine makes few mistakes, but that was a big one."

"Thanks," David said, chewing.

Barkley's eyes darted around as if they were swapping crucial secrets. "Have you come across a blogger who calls himself the Hung Juror?" David nodded, and Barkley continued: "Our tech guys are very good, and they've tracked him down. He's in the courtroom, three rows behind you, navy sweater, white shirt, thirty years old, balding, glasses, pretty nerdy looking. Name's Aaron Deentz, used to work for a mid-range firm downtown but got whacked in the recession. Now he blogs and tries to be important, can't seem to find a job."

"Why are you telling me this?"

"He has the right to blog; the courtroom is open to the public. Most of his stuff is harmless, but he took a shot at your wife. Me, I'd deck him. Just thought you'd want to know. See you around." And with that, Barkley eased away and was gone.

At 2:00 p.m., Nadine Karros stood and announced, "Your Honor, the defense rests." This had been discussed in chambers and was no surprise. Judge Seawright wasted no time and said, "Mr. Zinc, you may address the jury in closing statement."

David had no desire to address the jury and ask for compassion for his client, Iris Klopeck, but it would be extremely awkward for a lawyer who had tried a case from beginning to end to waive final argument. He stood at the podium and began by thanking the jurors for their service. Then he confessed that this was his first trial, and, frankly, he had not planned on doing anything but research. However, events had conspired to thrust him into this arena, and he felt bad for not doing a better job. He held up a document and explained that it was the pretrial order, sort of an outline for the trial that both sides agree on long before the jury is selected. Of interest, on page 35, was a list of the experts for the defense. Twenty-seven! All with the word "Doctor" attached somewhere to their names. Thankfully, the defense did not call all twenty-seven, but they certainly hired and paid them. Why would any defendant need so many well-paid experts? Perhaps the defendant had something to hide. And why would the defendant need so many lawyers, David asked, waving an arm at the Rogan Rothberg team? His client, Iris Klopeck, could not afford such talent. The field was not level. The game was rigged. Only the jury could equalize things.

He spoke less than ten minutes and happily left the podium. As he walked back to the table, he glanced at the spectators and made eye contact with Aaron Deentz, the Hung Juror. David stared at him for a few seconds, then Deentz looked away.

Nadine Karros argued for thirty minutes and managed to shift the attention back to Krayoxx and away from those other unpleasant tests Mr. Zinc had talked about. She vigorously defended Varrick and reminded the jurors of the many well-known and trusted drugs the company had given to the world. Including Krayoxx, a drug that had survived the week nicely since the plaintiff had failed miserably to prove there was anything wrong with it. Yes, she and Varrick may have twenty-seven noted experts in their lineup, but that was beside the point. Much more important was the expert proof offered by the plaintiff, who filed the lawsuit and had the burden of building a case and had thoroughly failed to do so.

David watched her performance with great admiration. She was smooth and skilled, and her trial experience was obvious from the way she moved around, spoke, chose her words effortlessly, looked at the jurors, smiled at them, and trusted them. From their faces, there was little doubt they trusted her too.

David waived his rebuttal argument. Judge Seawright went straight to the reading of the jury instructions, the most tedious segment of any trial. At 3:30, the jury was led from the courtroom to begin its deliberations. David wanted to get away, so he carried a large box of his documents to his SUV in the garage. As he was riding the elevator back up to the twenty-third floor, his cell phone vibrated. The text message said: "The jury is ready." He smiled and whispered, "That didn't take long."

When the courtroom was quiet, a bailiff brought in the jury. The foreman handed the written verdict to the clerk, who gave it to Judge Seawright, who said, "The verdict appears to be in order." It was returned to the foreman, who stood and read, "We, the jury, find for the defendant, Varrick Laboratories."

There was no reaction from anyone in the courtroom. Judge Seawright went through his post-verdict rituals and released the jurors. David had no desire to hang around and suffer through the happy horseshit of "Nice job," "Tough set of facts," "Better luck next time." As soon as the judge tapped his gavel and adjourned court, David lifted his heavy briefcase and dashed from the room. He beat the crowd and was hustling down the hall when he caught a glimpse of a familiar blue sweater entering a restroom. David followed, and once inside he scanned the room and saw no one but Aaron Deentz. David washed his hands, waited, and when Deentz finished at the urinal, he turned and saw David. "You're the Hung Juror, right?" David said, and Deentz froze, unmasked.

"So what?" Deentz said with a sneer.

David cocked his arm and shot a right cross that landed perfectly on the fleshy left jaw of the Hung Juror, who was too stunned to react. He grunted as his jaw popped. David followed with a quick left hook that landed on the nose. "That's for the bimbo, you ass!" David said, as Deentz fell to the floor.

David left the restroom and saw a crowd at the far end of the hall. He found the stairs and sprinted down to the main lobby. He dashed across the street to the garage and was safely locked in his SUV before he took a deep breath and said, "You idiot."

After a circuitous route back to the office, David arrived late on Friday afternoon. To his surprise, Oscar was sitting at the table having a soft drink with Rochelle. He looked thin and pale, but he had a smile and said he was feeling okay. His doctor had cleared him to spend no more than two hours a day at the office, and he claimed he was eager to get back to work.

David gave a highly condensed version of the trial. He mimicked the Russian accent of Dr. Borzov, and this drew laughter. All jokes were on Finley & Figg after all, so why not laugh at themselves. When he described his frantic efforts to find Dr. Threadgill, they laughed some more. They could not believe that Helen had been drafted into service. When he described the faces of the jurors during Iris's video, Rochelle wiped her eyes with a tissue.

"And in spite of my brilliant performance, the jury reached its verdict in only seventeen minutes."

When the humor was gone, they talked about Wally, their fallen comrade. They talked about the bills, the line of credit, their bleak future. Oscar suggested they forget about it until Monday morning. "We'll figure out something," he said.

David and Rochelle were startled at how thoughtful and kind he had become. Perhaps the heart attack and surgery had softened him up and provided a glimpse of his own mortality. The old Oscar would have been cussing Figg and griping about the firm's imminent financial ruin, but the new one seemed oddly optimistic about their situation.

After an hour of the most pleasant conversation David had experienced around the office, he said he needed to go. His paralegal was waiting with dinner and wanted to know about the trial.

CHAPTER 47

Over the weekend David puttered around the house, ran errands for Helen, pushed Emma through the neighborhood in her stroller, washed and shined both vehicles, and kept an eye on the online buzz about the trial and Varrick's great victory. There had been a small story in Saturday's *Sun-Times* and not a word in the *Tribune*. The online publications, though, were busy with the aftershocks. Varrick's public relations machinery was in full swing, and the verdict was being described as a major vindication of Krayoxx. CEO Reuben Massey was quoted everywhere touting the drug, condemning the mass tort bar, promising to crush "those ambulance chasers" in any courtroom they dared to enter, praising the wisdom of the Chicago jurors, and clamoring for more laws to protect innocent corporations from such frivolous lawsuits. Jerry Alisandros was unavailable for comment. Indeed, there were no comments from any of the lawyers suing Varrick Labs. "For the first time in recent history, the entire tort bar has gone silent," observed one reporter.

The call came at 2:00 on Sunday afternoon. Dr. Biff Sandroni had received the samples of Nasty Teeth by FedEx on Friday morning, about the time David was grilling Dr. Ulander on the stand. Dr. Sandroni had promised to test the samples immediately. "They're all the same, David, all coated with the same lead-based paint. Highly toxic. Your lawsuit is a cinch. Open and shut, the best I've ever seen."

"When can you finish the report?"

"I'll e-mail it tomorrow."

"Thanks, Biff."

"Good luck."

An hour later, David and Helen loaded Emma into her car seat and set off for Waukegan. The purpose of the trip was to check on Wally, but there was the added benefit of having the baby finally go to sleep.

After four days of sobriety, Wally looked rested and was eager to leave Harbor House. David recapped the trial and, not wanting to repeat himself and not entirely in the mood for humor, omitted the parts that Oscar and Rochelle had found so funny Friday afternoon. Wally apologized repeatedly until David asked him to stop. "It's over, Wally. We have to move on." They talked about ways to unload their Krayoxx clients and the problems this might create. It really didn't matter how complicated things became—their decision was final. They were finished with Krayoxx and Varrick.

"I don't need to stay here any longer," Wally said. They were alone at the end of the hallway. Helen had stayed behind in the car with the sleeping baby.

"What does your counselor say?"

"I'm getting tired of the guy. Look, David, I fell off the wagon because of the pressure, that's all. I consider myself sober right now. I'm already counting the days. I'll jump back into AA and hope and pray I won't fall off again. Hear me, David. I don't like being a drunk. We got our work cut out for us, and I gotta stay sober."

With his portion of the meter ticking at $500 a day, David wanted Wally out as soon as possible, but he was not convinced a ten-day detox would work. "I'll talk to the counselor—what's his name?"

"Patrick Hale. He's really beating me up this time."

"Maybe that's what you need, Wally."

"Come on, David. Get me outta here. We've dug a hole for ourselves, and it's just you and me this time. I'm not so sure Oscar will be much help."

Left unsaid was the fact that Oscar had been the great skeptic about Krayoxx and mass torts in general. The deep hole in which they now found themselves had been dug by Wallis T. Figg. They talked about Oscar for a while, his divorce, his health, his new girlfriend, who was not really that new, according to Wally, though David did not press for details.

As he left, Wally pleaded again, "Get me outta here, David. We have too much work to do."

David hugged him good-bye and left the visitors' room. The "work" Wally kept referring to was little more than the imposing task of getting rid of four hundred or so dissatisfied clients, mopping up the remains of the Klopeck trial, grappling with a lot of unpaid bills, and laboring away in a building now burdened with a $200,000 mortgage. In the past month, the firm's other clients had been neglected, many to the point of hiring other lawyers, and the daily inquiries from prospective clients had declined dramatically.

David had thought of leaving, of opening his own shop, or looking at other, smaller firms. If he walked away, he would, of course, take the Thuya Khaing case with him. Oscar and Wally would never know about it. If the case eventually paid off, David could write a check to Finley & Figg for his share of the mortgage on the building. But these thoughts were bothersome. He had run away from one firm and never looked back. If he ran away from the second one, he would always have regrets. In reality, David knew he could not leave Finley & Figg with the two partners ailing and a swarm of unhappy clients and creditors pounding on the door.

The phones rang constantly Monday morning. Rochelle answered a few times, then announced, "It's all those Krayoxx people, asking about their cases."

"Unplug it," David said, and the racket stopped. The old Oscar was making a comeback. He was in his office, door tightly closed, shoving paperwork around his desk.

By 9:00 a.m., David had composed a letter to be mailed to the four hundred or so clients who only thought they had a lawsuit. It read:

Dear _____:

Last week our firm tried the first lawsuit against Varrick Labs for its drug Krayoxx. The trial did not go as planned and was not successful. The jury ruled in favor of Varrick. With all the evidence now presented, it is clear that additional litigation against the company would be ill-advised. For that reason, we are withdrawing as your counsel. Feel free to consult with another attorney.

For what it's worth, Varrick presented convincing proof that Krayoxx does not damage the heart valves, or any other part of the body.

Sincerely,

David Zinc

Attorney and Counselor-at-Law

When Rochelle's printer began spitting out the letters, David went upstairs to prepare for another fight in federal court, which, on that Monday morning, was the last place he wanted to go. He had a rough draft of a lawsuit to be filed against Sonesta Games and a rough draft of a letter he planned to send to the company's chief in-house counsel. He polished and tweaked both as he waited on Sandroni's report.

Varrick's stock opened at $42.50 on Monday morning, its highest value in over two years. David scanned the financial sites and blogs, and they were still buzzing with speculation about the future of Krayoxx litigation. Since David had no role in that future, he was losing interest fast.

He searched the near-impenetrable Web site of Cook County—Courts—Criminal—Warrants & Affidavits and found no record of a complaint for assault filed by one Aaron Deentz. On Saturday, the Hung Juror had blogged about the ending of the Klopeck trial but did not mention getting punched out in the men's restroom on the twenty-third floor of the Dirksen Federal Building.

Oscar had a friend who had a friend who worked in Warrants & Affidavits, and this friend was supposedly on the lookout for a filing by Deentz. "You really decked him?" Oscar had asked with genuine admiration.

"Yes, a stupid thing to do."

"Don't worry. It's just simple assault. I got friends."

When Sandroni's report arrived, David read it carefully and almost salivated at its conclusion: "The levels of lead in the paint used in coating the Nasty Teeth toys are of toxic levels. Any child, or person, using this product in the exact manner in which it was designed to be used, to wit, insertion into the mouth, over the real teeth, would face the grave risks of ingesting quantities of lead-based paint."

For good measure, Dr. Sandroni added: "In thirty years of testing products for sources of poisoning, primarily lead poisoning, I have never seen a product so grossly and negligently designed and produced."

David copied the six-page report and placed it in a binder with color photos of the original set of Nasty Teeth used by Thuya and photos of the samples David had purchased the week before. He added a copy of the lawsuit and a medical summary prepared by Thuya's doctors. In a pleasant but straightforward letter to a Mr. Dylan Kott, chief in-house counsel for Sonesta Games, David offered to discuss the matter before filing suit. However, this offer was good for fourteen days only. The family had suffered greatly, continued to suffer, and was entitled to immediate relief.

When he left for lunch, he took the binder and shipped it to Sonesta Games by FedEx, overnight priority. No one else at the firm knew what he was doing. For contact information in the letter, he used his home address and cell phone.

Oscar was leaving as David returned, and his chauffeur was a tiny little woman of dubious ethnicity. At first David thought she was Thai, then she appeared more Hispanic. Regardless, she was pleasant to chat with on the front sidewalk. She was at least twenty years younger than Oscar, and during the brief conversation David got the clear impression that the two had known each other for some time. Oscar, who looked quite frail after an easy morning at the office, slowly folded himself into the passenger's seat of her little Honda, and away they went.

"Who is that?" David asked Rochelle as he closed the front door.

"I just met her myself. Some weird name I didn't get either. She told me she's known Oscar for three years."

"Wally's skirt chasing is well-known. I'm kinda surprised about Oscar. Are you?"

Rochelle smiled and said, "David, when it comes to love and sex, nothing surprises me." She held out a pink phone message slip. "While we're on the subject, you might want to call this guy."

"Who is it?"

"Goodloe Stamm. Paula Finley's divorce lawyer."

"I don't know a thing about divorce law, Rochelle."

Rochelle gave an exaggerated look around the room, around the offices, and said, "They're all gone. I guess you'd better learn fast."

Stamm began with a sappy "Too bad about the verdict, but I really wasn't surprised."

"Nor was I," David said tersely. "What can I do for you?"

"Well, first of all, how's Mr. Finley?"

"Oscar's fine. His heart attack was only two weeks ago today. He actually came to the office this morning for a few hours, and he's making steady progress. I suppose you're calling to ask about the Krayoxx litigation and hoping there might still be a chance of some fees coming our way. The answer, unfortunately for us, for our clients, and for Mrs. Finley as well, is that there is no prospect of making a dime off these cases. We are not going to appeal the Klopeck verdict. We are in the process of notifying all of our Krayoxx clients that we are withdrawing as counsel. We hocked the office to finance the trial, which cost us about $180,000 in cash. The senior partner is recovering from a heart attack and bypass surgery. The junior partner has taken a leave of absence. The firm is now being run by me and one secretary, who by the way knows a lot more about the law than I do. In case you're curious about Mr. Finley's assets, let me assure you that he has never been broker than he is right now. As I understand his offer to your client, he is willing to give her the house, all the furnishings, her car, half the cash in the bank, which was less than $5,000, in return for a simple, uncontested divorce. He just wants out, Mr. Stamm. I suggest you and your client take this offer before he changes his mind."

Stamm digested this and finally said, "Well, I appreciate your candor."

"Good. Here's some more. On behalf of your felonious client Justin Bardall, you've filed a lawsuit against Oscar Finley for that unfortunate shooting incident. As I read the file, your client is headed back to prison for attempted arson. As I mentioned, Mr. Finley is quite broke. His insurance company is refusing coverage because it deems his actions intentional, as opposed to negligent. So, with no insurance coverage and no personal assets, Mr. Finley is judgment-proof. You cannot squeeze a nickel out of him. Your lawsuit is worthless."

"What about the office building?"

"Heavily mortgaged. Look, Mr. Stamm, you cannot get a verdict, because your client is a twice-convicted felon who was caught in the act of trying to commit a crime. Extremely lousy jury appeal. But if you got lucky and got a verdict, Mr. Finley would file for bankruptcy the next day. You can't touch him, you understand?"

"I get the picture."

"We have nothing and we are hiding nothing. Please have a chat with Mrs. Finley and Mr. Bardall and explain this to them. I would love to close these files as soon as possible."

"Okay, okay. I'll see what I can do."

CHAPTER 48

A week passed with no word from Sonesta Games. David watched the calendar and the clock. He fought the urge to dream of a quick settlement, and he dreaded the idea of filing a lawsuit in federal court against a large corporation. That treacherous road had just been traveled. At times he felt like the old Wally—lost in dreams of easy money.

The firm slowly returned to a routine that somewhat resembled the old days. Rochelle arrived at 7:30 each morning and enjoyed her quiet time with AC. David was next, then Wally, whose car had been towed during the drinking spree and was not damaged. Oscar rolled in around ten, delivered to the front door by his girlfriend, a charming lady who managed to impress even Rochelle. At some point each morning, Wally faced each of his colleagues and said, "Day 12 of sobriety." Then Day 13, and so on. He received congratulations and encouragement and was once again proud of himself. He found an AA meeting almost every night somewhere in the city.

The phones were still ringing with calls from disgruntled Krayoxx clients, all of whom Rochelle routed to Wally and David. The ex-clients were generally subdued, even pitiful, as opposed to belligerent. They had been expecting money—what happened? The lawyers were apologetic and tended to blame things on some mysterious "federal jury" that had ruled in favor of the drug. The lawyers were also quick to point out that "it had been proven in court" that Krayoxx was safe.

In other words, your lawsuit is gone but your heart is much healthier than you thought.

Similar conversations were being repeated across the country as dozens of high-flying lawyers backtracked from the drug. A lawyer in Phoenix filed a motion to dismiss four lawsuits involving clients allegedly killed by Krayoxx. His motion met a Rule 11 response straight from the Nadine Karros playbook. Varrick Labs demanded sanctions for the filing of the frivolous cases and provided detailed billing and expense records to prove it had spent over $8 million defending the lawsuits. With the mass tort lawyers in retreat, it soon became apparent that Varrick was in hot pursuit. The wars over Rule 11 sanctions would rage for months.

Ten days after the verdict, the FDA lifted its recall of Krayoxx, and Varrick flooded the market. Reuben Massey would quickly restock his cash reserves, and his first priority was to pound away at the mass tort bar over its mistreatment of his beloved drug.

Eleven days after the verdict, and still no word from Aaron Deentz. The Hung Juror had taken a break from his blog, without an explanation. David had two thoughts about a prosecution for simple assault. First, if Deentz filed charges, he would run the risk of blowing his cover. Like many bloggers, he relished his anonymity and the freedom it allowed to say virtually anything. The fact that David knew who he was, and called him out right before he punched him, had to be unsettling. If Deentz pressed charges, he would be forced to appear in court and admit to being the Hung Juror. If he was really out of work and looking for a job, his blogging might haunt him. In the past two years, he had said terrible things about judges, lawyers, and law firms. On the other hand, he had been on the receiving end of two solid punches. David had not felt bones breaking, but there had to be damage, if only temporary. Since Deentz was a lawyer, he would probably insist on getting his day in court, and his revenge.

David had yet to tell Helen about the assault. He knew she would react with disfavor and she would worry about an arrest and prosecution. His plan was to tell her only if Deentz filed charges. In other words, he would tell her later, maybe. Then he had another idea. There was only one Aaron Deentz in the phone book, and late one afternoon David dialed his number. "Aaron Deentz, please," David said.

"Speaking. Who is this?"

"David Zinc, here, Mr. Deentz, and I'm calling to apologize for my actions after the jury's verdict. I was upset, angry, and I acted rashly."

A pause, then, "You broke my jaw."

At first, there was a flash of macho pride in the fact that he could throw a punch with such ferocity, but all bravado vanished when David thought about a civil lawsuit for personal injuries. "Again, I apologize, and I certainly did not intend to break anything or cause bodily harm."

Deentz's next response was most revealing. He asked, "How did you learn my identity?"

So, he was afraid of being exposed. David fudged a little by saying, "I have a cousin who's a geek. Took him twenty-four hours. You shouldn't post at the same time each day. Sorry about the jaw. I'm willing to cover your medical expenses." He made this offer because he was compelled to, but he flinched at the thought of another outlay of cash.

"Are you trying to offer a deal, Zinc?"

"Sure. I'll cover your medicals, and you agree not to press charges or pursue damages."

"You're worried about an assault charge?"

"Not really. If I have to defend myself for the assault, I'll make sure the judge sees some of your comments, and I doubt he'll be impressed. Judges despise blogs like yours. Judge Seawright followed it daily and was furious, thought it might affect the case if any of the jurors stumbled across it. His clerks were trying to learn the identity of the Hung Juror." David was spinning this wild fiction on the fly, but it had a legitimate ring to it.

"Have you told anyone?" Deentz asked. David couldn't tell if he was timid, scared, or just dealing with a broken jaw.

"Not a soul."

"I lost my insurance when I lost my job. The medicals are $4,600 as of now. The wires are in for a month, after that I don't know."

"I made my offer," David said. "Do we have a deal?"

A long pause, then, "Yes, I guess."

"There's one other thing, Mr. Deentz."

"Okay, what is it?"

"You called my wife a bimbo."

"Yes, I, uh, shouldn't have done that. Your wife is very attractive."

"She is, and she's a very smart lady."

"My apologies."

"And mine."

Wally's first post-trial victory was the successful completion of Oscar's divorce settlement. With little in the way of assets and both parties desperately wanting out, the agreement was actually quite simple, if any legal document could ever be considered simple. When Oscar and Wally signed their names just below Paula Finley and Good-loe Stamm, Oscar stared at the signatures for a long time and did not attempt to suppress a smile. Wally filed the agreement in circuit court, and an appearance date was set for mid-January.

Oscar insisted on a celebratory bottle of champagne, nonalcoholic of course, and the firm met at the table for an unofficial meeting late in the day. Since all four knew the score—Day 15 of sobriety—Wally was toasted along with the newest bachelor on the block, Oscar Finley. It was Thursday, November 10, and though the little boutique firm was facing a mountain of debt with few clients, they seemed determined to enjoy the moment. Wounded and humiliated, they were still standing and showing signs of life.

Just as he drained his glass, David's cell phone vibrated. He excused himself and went upstairs.

Dylan Kott introduced himself as the senior VP and chief counsel for Sonesta Games, a position he had held for many years. He was calling from the company's headquarters in San Jacinto, California. He thanked David for his letter, its tone and reasonableness, and assured him the package had been studied by the company's top brass, and, frankly, there was "deep concern" up there. He, too, was concerned and said, "We'd like to get together, Mr. Zinc, face-to-face."

"And the purpose of the meeting would be to . . . ?" David asked.

"Discuss ways to avoid litigation."

"And to avoid negative publicity?"

"Certainly. We are a toy company, Mr. Zinc. Our image is very important to us."

"When and where?"

"We have a distribution center and office in Des Plaines, your neck of the woods. Could you meet us there Monday morning?"

"Yes, but only if you're serious about a settlement. If you plan to walk in with some lowball scheme, then forget it. I'll take my chances with a jury."

"Please, Mr. Zinc, it's too early to start with the threats. I assure you we recognize the gravity of this situation. Sadly, we've been here before. I can explain it all on Monday."

"Fair enough."

"Has a legal representative been appointed by the court for this child?"

"Yes. His father."

"Would it be possible to have both parents on hand Monday morning?"

"I'm sure they can be there. Why?"

"Carl LaPorte, our CEO, would like to meet them and, on behalf of our company, offer an apology."

CHAPTER 49

The facility was one in a long row of modern warehouses that covered acres and seemed to stretch endlessly west from Des Plaines and the Chicago suburbs. Thanks to his GPS, David found it with no trouble, and at 10:00 Monday morning he escorted Soe and Lwin Khaing through the front door of a redbrick office complex stuck to the side of a massive warehouse. They were immediately led through a hallway and into a conference room where coffee, pastries, and juice were offered. They declined. David's stomach was flipping, and his nerves were on edge. The Khaings were thoroughly overwhelmed.

Three well-dressed corporate types entered the room: Dylan Kott, chief counsel; Carl LaPorte, CEO; and Wyatt Vitelli, chief financial officer. Rapid introductions were made, and then Carl LaPorte asked everyone to have a seat and did his best to reduce the tension. More offers were made of coffee, juice, and pastries. No thanks. When it soon became apparent that the Khaings were too intimidated to converse, LaPorte grew somber and said to the parents, "Well, first things first. I know you have a very sick boy and he is not likely to improve much. I have a four-year-old grandson, my only grandchild, and I cannot imagine what you are going through. On behalf of my company, Sonesta Games, I take full responsibility for what has happened to your son. We did not make the product, this Nasty Teeth toy, but we own the smaller company that did import it from China. Since it's our company, it is our responsibility. Any questions?"

Lwin and Soe shook their heads slowly.

David watched in amazement. In a trial, these comments by Carl LaPorte would be fair game. An apology by the company would be admissible into evidence and carry great weight with the jury. The fact that he was accepting responsibility, and doing it without hesitation, was important for two reasons: first, the company was sincere; and, second, the case was not going to trial. The presence of the CEO, CFO, and top lawyer was a clear sign that they had brought their checkbook.

LaPorte continued: "Nothing I can say will bring back your little boy. All I can do is say I'm sorry and promise you that our company will do all that we can to help you."

"Thank you," Soe said as Lwin wiped her eyes. After a long pause, during which LaPorte watched their faces with great sympathy, he said, "Mr. Zinc, I suggest the parents wait in another room down the hall while we discuss matters."

"Agreed," David said. An assistant suddenly materialized and led the Khaings away. When the door was closed again, LaPorte said, "A couple of suggestions. Let's take off our coats and try to relax. We could be here for some time. Any objection to using first names, Mr. Zinc?"

"Not at all."

"Good. We're a California company, and our culture leans to the informal." All coats were removed and ties loosened. Carl continued, "How would you like to proceed, David?"

"You called the meeting."

"Right, so a little background might be helpful. First, as I'm sure you know, we're the third-largest toy company in America, sales last year of just over $3 billion."

"Behind Mattel and Hasbro," David said politely. "I've read all your annual reports and a ton of other stuff. I know your products, history, financials, key personnel, divisions, and long-term corporate strategy. I know who insures your company, but of course the limits of liability are not disclosed. I'm happy to sit here and chat as long as you guys would like to. I have nothing else planned for the day, and my clients have taken off from work. But to move things along, I suggest we get down to business."

Carl smiled and looked at Dylan Kott and Wyatt Vitelli.

"Sure, we're all busy," Carl said. "You've done your homework, David, so tell us what you have in mind."

David slid across Exhibit 1 and began, "This is a summary of brain damage verdicts over the past ten years, kids only. Number 1 is a $12 million verdict in New Jersey last year for a six-year-old who ingested lead by chewing on a plastic action figure. The case is on appeal. Look at Number 4—a $9 million verdict in Minnesota that was upheld on appeal last year. My father sits on the Minnesota Supreme Court and is fairly conservative when it comes to upholding large verdicts. He voted to affirm that one, as did the rest of the court. Unanimous. It was another lead-poisoning case—a kid and his toy. Number 7 involves a nine-year-old girl who nearly drowned when her foot got caught in the drain of a brand-new swimming pool at a country club in Spring-field, Illinois. Jury deliberated less than an hour and awarded the family $9 million. On page 2, look at Number 13. A ten-year-old boy was hit with a piece of metal flung from a commercial Bush Hog with no chain guards. Severe brain damage. The case was tried in federal court in Chicago, and the jury awarded $5 million in actual damages and $20 million in punitive damages. The punitive award was cut to $5 million on appeal. I don't need to go through every case, and I'm sure you guys are familiar with this territory."

"It should be obvious, David, that we would like to avoid a trial and jury."

"I understand, but my point is that this case has tremendous jury appeal. After the jurors spend three days looking at Thuya Khaing strapped into his high chair, they might bring back a verdict larger than any of these. That potential should be factored into our negotiations."

"Got it. What is your demand?" Carl asked.

"Well, a settlement should include several areas of compensation, some relatively easy to tally, others not so easy. Let's start with the financial burden on the family to care for the child. As of now, they're spending about $600 a month on food, medications, and diapers. Not much money, but a lot more than the family can afford. The boy needs a part-time nurse and a full-time rehab specialist to at least attempt to retrain muscles and reprogram the brain."

"What's his life expectancy?" asked Wyatt Vitelli.

"No one knows. It's a moving target. I didn't put it in my report, because one doctor says a year or two, off the record, and another one says he could live to be an adult. I've talked to all the doctors, and no one thinks it's smart to predict how long he might live. I've spent some time with him during the past six months, and I've noticed a slight improvement in some functions, very slight. I think we should negotiate as if he has twenty years left."

All three men nodded, quick to agree.

"It's obvious that his parents do not earn a lot of money. They live in a small, cheap apartment with two older daughters. The family needs a home, with plenty of space and a bedroom outfitted for Thuya's special needs. Nothing elaborate—these are simple people, but they have dreams." At this point, David slid across three copies of Exhibit 2, which were quickly snatched off the table.

David took a deep breath and plowed forward. "This is our settlement proposal. First, you see the specific damages. Number 1 covers the expenses I mentioned, plus a part-time nurse at $30,000 a year, plus the mother's lost salary of $25,000 a year because she would like to quit work and stay home with the boy. I've also added the cost of a new car so they can take him to and from rehab on a daily basis. I've rounded it off to $100,000 a year, for twenty years, for a total of $2 million. You can buy an annuity at today's rates for $1.4 million. Rehab is a gray area because I'm not sure how long it would continue. As of today, it runs about $50,000 a year. Assuming twenty years, the annuity will cost you $700,000. Next is the issue of a new home, in a nice neighborhood, with good schools—$500,000. The next item deals with the Lakeshore Children's Hospital. Their care saved his life and was free, at least to the family, but I think the expenses should be paid back. The hospital was reluctant to give me an estimate, but there it is—$600,000."

David was at $3.2 million, and none of the three executives had removed a pen from a pocket. There were no frowns, no head shaking; nothing to indicate they thought he'd lost his mind.

"Moving on to the nonspecifics, I've listed the kid's loss of enjoyment of life and the emotional distress of the family. I know these are vague areas, but they are compensable damages under Illinois law. I suggest the sum of $1.8 million."

David folded his hands together and waited on a response. No one seemed surprised.

"A tidy sum of $5 million," Carl LaPorte said.

"What about attorneys' fees?" Dylan Kott asked.

"Gee, almost forgot about those," David said and everyone smiled. "My fee is not taken from what the family gets. It's extra. Thirty percent on top of what you're looking at there, or $1.5 million."

"That's a nice payday," Dylan said.

David almost mentioned the millions each of the three had earned the previous year in salary and stock options, but let it pass. "I would like to think I could keep it all, but that will not be the case."

"Six and a half million dollars," Carl said as he laid down his copy of the report and stretched his arms.

"You guys seem intent on doing what's right," David said. "Plus, you don't want bad publicity, just like you don't want to roll the dice with an unsympathetic jury."

"Our image is very important," Carl said. "We don't pollute rivers or make cheap handguns or deny insurance claims or bilk the government on bad contracts. We make toys for kids. It's just that simple. If we get the reputation for harming children, we're dead."

"Can I ask where you found these products?" Dylan asked.

David told the story of Soe Khaing purchasing the first set of Nasty Teeth a year earlier, and of his search high and low in Greater Chicago for similar packages. Carl described the company's efforts to track them down too and admitted that Sonesta Games had settled two other similar cases within the past eighteen months. They were cautiously hopeful that all lead-painted samples had been removed from the market and destroyed, but not certain. They were at war with several factories in China and had moved most of their production to other countries. The purchase of Gunderson Toys had been a costly blunder. Other stories followed, as if both sides needed a break to think about the settlement proposal on the table.

After an hour, they asked David to step outside so they could huddle in private.

David drank a cup of coffee with his clients, and after fifteen minutes the same assistant asked him to return to the conference room. She closed the door behind him, and David was ready to cut the deal or walk away.

When they were situated and poised, Carl LaPorte said, "We were prepared to write a check for $5 million and put this matter to rest, David, but you're asking for a lot more than that."

"We will not accept $5 million, because the case is worth twice that much. Our number is $6.5 million, take it or leave it. I'll file the lawsuit tomorrow."

"A lawsuit will take years. Can your clients afford to wait?" Dylan asked.

"Some of our federal judges use this Local Rule 83:19, nicknamed the Rocket Docket, and believe me, it works. I can have this case before a jury in a year. The last case was far more complicated, and it went to trial ten months after it was filed. Yes, my clients can survive until the jury brings back the verdict."

"You didn't win that case, did you?" Carl asked with his eyebrows arched, as if he knew everything about the Klopeck trial.

"No, I did not, but I learned a lot. I had a lousy set of facts. This time, I own the facts. By the time the jury hears everything, $6.5 million will seem like a bargain."

"We'll offer $5 million."

David swallowed hard, glared at Carl LaPorte, and said, "You're not hearing me, Carl. It's $6.5 million now, or a lot more a year from now."

"You're turning down $5 million for these poor Burmese immigrants?"

"I just turned it down, and I'm not negotiating. Your company is well insured. The $6.5 million is not coming off your bottom line."

"Maybe, but the insurance premiums are not cheap."

"I'm not haggling, Carl. Deal or no deal?"

Carl took a deep breath and exchanged looks with Dylan Kott and Wyatt Vitelli. Then he shrugged, smiled, surrendered, and offered a hand. "A deal." David grabbed his hand and shook it firmly.

"On the condition that this is extremely confidential," Carl said.

"Of course."

Dylan said, "I'll get our guys in Legal to prepare an agreement."

"Not necessary," David said as he reached into his briefcase. He pulled out a file, removed four copies of a document, and passed them around. "This is a settlement agreement that covers everything. It's pretty straightforward and includes all manner of language about confidentiality. I work for a tiny law firm, but it has some complicated problems. It's in my best interests to keep this quiet."

"You had a settlement agreement prepared at $6.5 million?" Carl asked.

"You got it. Not a penny less. That's what this case is worth."

Dylan said, "This settlement has to be approved by the court, right?"

"Yes. I've already established a guardianship for the kid; his father is his legal representative. The court must approve the settlement, and over the years it will supervise the money. I'm required to prepare an annual accounting and meet with the judge once a year, but the file can be sealed to ensure secrecy."

They reviewed the agreement, then Carl LaPorte signed it on behalf of his company. David signed it, then Soe and Lwin were brought into the room. David explained the terms of the settlement to them, and they signed under his name. Carl apologized again and wished them well. They were shell-shocked, overcome with emotion, and unable to speak.

As they were leaving the building, Dylan Kott asked David if he could have a moment to discuss a matter. The Khaings moved on and waited by David's SUV. Dylan deftly slid a white unmarked envelope into David's hand as he said, "You didn't get this from me, okay?"

David placed it inside his coat pocket. "What is it?"

"A list of other products, mainly toys, with histories of lead poisoning. Most were made in China, but there are some from Mexico, Vietnam, and Pakistan. Made somewhere else, but imported here by U.S. companies."

"I see. And might these companies be your competitors?"

"You got it."

"Thanks."

"Good luck."

CHAPTER 50

Finley & Figg's last firm meeting took place late that afternoon. At David's insistence, they waited until Rochelle was gone. Oscar was exhausted and cranky, a good sign. His girlfriend and driver had been sent away at 3:00 p.m., and David promised to drive his senior partner home after the meeting.

"This must be important," Wally said as David locked the front door.

"Indeed it is," he said, taking a seat at the table. "You guys remember that lead-poisoning case I mentioned back a few months ago?" There were vague recollections, but so much had happened since then. "Well," David said smugly, "there has been an interesting development."

"Do tell," Wally said, already anticipating something pleasant.

David went through a lengthy narrative of his activities on behalf of the Khaings. He placed a set of Nasty Teeth on the table as he slowly spun his story toward its delightful climax. "This morning, I met with the CEO and other top executives from the company, and we reached a settlement."

By this time, Wally and Oscar were hanging on every word and exchanging nervous glances. When David said, "The attorneys' fees are $1.5 million," both closed their eyes and lowered their heads, as if in prayer. David paused as he retrieved copies of a document for each of them.

"This is a proposed partnership agreement for the new law firm of

Finley, Figg & Zinc." Oscar and Wally held the document, but neither looked at its language. They simply gawked at David, both mouths open, both men too stunned to speak.

David continued, "An equal partnership, a three-way split of the bottom line with a monthly draw based on net revenue for each month. You guys keep the building in your names. You may want to look at the third paragraph on the second page." Neither flipped a page.

"Just tell us," Oscar said.

"Okay, there's some pretty clear language about certain activities the new firm will not engage in. It will not pay bribes or referral fees to policemen, tow truck drivers, rescue personnel, or anyone else for case referrals. It will not advertise on bus stop benches, bingo cards, or any other cheap publication. In fact, all advertising must be approved by the Marketing Committee, which, at least for the first year, will consist solely of me. In other words, fellas, the firm will no longer chase ambulances."

"What's the fun of that?" Wally asked.

David smiled politely but kept going. "I've heard talk about advertising on billboards and television; that, too, is prohibited. Before the firm signs up a new client, the three of us must agree to take the case. In summary, the firm will adhere to the highest standards of professional conduct. Any fees in cash will go straight to the books, which will now be kept by a competent CPA. In effect, gentlemen, the new firm will operate like a real law firm. This agreement is good for one year, and if either of you fails to comply with it, then the partnership will dissolve and I'll find work elsewhere."

"Back to the attorneys' fees," Wally said. "I'm not sure you finished that part of the discussion."

"If we can agree on the rules of the new partnership, then I suggest we use the fees from the Khaing settlement to pay off the bank and clean up the Krayoxx mess, including the $15,000 in sanctions levied during the trial. That's about $200,000. Rochelle gets a bonus of $100,000. That leaves $1.2 million for the lawyers, which I think we should divide equally."

Wally closed his eyes. Oscar grunted, then slowly got to his feet and walked to the front door, where he looked through the window. Finally, he said, "You don't have to do this, David."

"I agree," Wally said, though without much conviction. "This is your case. We've done nothing."

"I understand," David said. "But I look at it like this: I would never have found this case had I not been here. It's that simple. A year ago, I was working at a job I hated. By chance I stumbled into this place, met you guys, and then I got lucky and found this case."

"Excellent point," Wally said, and Oscar was quick to agree. Oscar walked back to the table and slowly settled into his chair. He looked at Wally and said, "What about my divorce?"

"No problem. We have a signed settlement agreement. Your wife is not entitled to any fees earned after she signed it. The divorce will be final in January."

"That's the way I see it," Oscar said.

"Me too," added David.

Things were silent for a long time, then AC rose from his pillow and began a low growl. The distant whine of an ambulance siren came into range and grew louder. Wally glanced longingly at the window beside Rochelle's desk.

"Don't even think about it," David said.

"Sorry. Force of habit," Wally replied. Oscar began chuckling, and soon all three were laughing.

EPILOGUE

Bart Shaw closed his files and dropped his malpractice threats against Finley & Figg. He collected almost $80,000 from Varrick for his successful efforts to torment the firm and force it to trial in the Klopeck matter. Adam Grand filed an ethics complaint with the state bar association, but it eventually fizzled. Five other clients, of the "non-death" variety, did the same, with the same results. Nadine Karros made good on her promise not to seek sanctions for the filing of frivolous lawsuits, but Varrick mounted an aggressive, and sometimes successful, campaign in other courts to collect money from plaintiffs' firms. Jerry Alisandros was hit with a huge fine in southern Florida when it became obvious he had no plans to pursue his Krayoxx litigation.

Thuya Khaing suffered a series of violent seizures and died three days after Christmas in Lakeshore Children's Hospital. David and Helen, along with Wally, Oscar, and Rochelle, attended the small burial service. Also in attendance were Carl LaPorte and Dylan Kott, who, with David's help, managed to have a quiet word with Soe and Lwin. Carl offered his heartfelt condolences and again took full responsibility on behalf of his company. Under the terms of David's settlement agreement, all sums were vested and would be paid as promised.

Oscar's divorce became final in late January. By then, he was living with his new girlfriend in a new apartment and had never been happier. Wally remained sober and was even volunteering to help with other lawyers battling addictions.

Justin Bardall was sentenced to one year in prison for attempting to torch the law office. He appeared in court in a wheelchair and was required by the judge to acknowledge the presence of Oscar, Wally, and David. Bardall had cooperated with the prosecutors for a light sentence. The judge, who had spent the first twenty years of his career practicing law on the streets of southwest Chicago and had a low opinion of thugs who conspired to burn law offices, did not show compassion for Justin's bosses. The owner of Cicero Pipe was sentenced to five years in prison, and his construction superintendent got four.

David successfully won a dismissal of Bardall's lawsuit against Oscar and the firm.

Not surprisingly, the new partnership did not survive. After his heart surgery and divorce, Oscar lost steam and spent fewer hours at the office. He had some money in the bank and was drawing a pension from Social Security, and his housemate made a comfortable living as a masseuse. (He had actually met her next door.) After six months under the new agreement, he began dropping hints about retiring. Wally was still smarting from his Krayoxx adventure and had lost his zeal to hustle new cases. He, too, had a new girlfriend, a slightly older woman with a "nice balance sheet," as he described it. Also, it was painfully obvious, at least to David, that neither partner had the desire, nor talent, to put together big cases and take them to trial if necessary. He honestly couldn't imagine walking into another courtroom with those two.

His radar was on high alert, and he saw the warning signs immediately. He began planning his exit.

Eleven months after Emma arrived, Helen gave birth to twin boys. That momentous occasion prompted David to plan a new future. He leased office space not far from their home in Lincoln Park, carefully choosing a fourth-floor suite with a view to the south. He could see the magnificent skyline of downtown, with the Trust Tower squarely in the center of it. The view never failed to motivate him.

When things were in place, he informed Oscar and Wally that he planned to leave when the agreement expired at the end of twelve months. The parting was difficult and sad, but not unexpected. It prompted Oscar to announce his retirement. Wally seemed relieved too. He and Oscar decided on the spot to sell the building and close shop. By the time all three shook hands and wished each other good luck, Wally was planning a getaway to Alaska.

David got the dog, and he also got Rochelle, though the two had been in secret talks for a month. He would never consider hiring her away from the firm, but suddenly she was a free agent. With a higher salary and more benefits, she was given the title of office manager and happily moved into the new digs of David E. Zinc, Attorney-at-Law.

The new firm specialized in product liability law. When David settled two more lead-poisoning cases, it was clear to him and Rochelle and their expanding staff that the practice was about to become quite lucrative.

Most of his work was in federal court, and as business boomed, he found himself downtown more and more. When possible, he stopped by Abner's for a laugh and a quick lunch—a sandwich and a diet soda. On two occasions he had a Pearl Harbor with Miss Spence, who, though pushing ninety-seven, still knocked back three of the syrupy concoctions every day. David could choke down only one, and afterward he took the train back to the office and enjoyed a nap on his new sofa.